THE COLD LIGHT OF DAWN

The King's Greatest Enemy:

In the Shadow of the Storm
Days of Sun and Glory
Under the Approaching Dark
The Cold Light of Dawn

Also by Anna Belfrage

The Graham Saga:
A Rip in the Veil
Like Chaff in the Wind
The Prodigal Son
A Newfound Land
Serpents in the Garden
Revenge and Retribution
Whither Thou Goest
To Catch a Falling Star
There is Always a Tomorrow

Praise for *In the Shadow of the Storm* (first book in The King's Greatest Enemy)

"Overall, this is a story will suck you in from the very first page and refuse to let go. I can't even think of one bad thing to say about it!"
So many books, so little time

"The character cast is plentiful and rich, the historical details – fascinating and illuminating, the tension is ever-present and the fast-paced plot line is sure to leave you breathless. I really loved everything about this book."
Bookish Lifestyle

"A twisted affair of mistaken identities, power struggles, and political strife, In the Shadow of the Storm gives readers a gripping novel that continuously pushes the boundaries of what they think they know and what's really coming."
A Bibliotaph's Reviews

"Belfrage's writing is wonderful, her ability to transport the reader to the setting along with her fully developed and motley characters create an enthralling reading journey."
Unshelfish

Praise for *Days of Sun and Glory*

"Engaging and entertaining, Anna Belfrage has created a masterpiece in Days of Sun and Glory, a book which is impossible to put down, but which you do not – ever – want to end."
Sharon's Book Corner

"The writing itself is a huge success from every angle – great and memorable characters, marvellous descriptions, lively dialogue, a complex and intriguing plot, and large scale conflict."
Readers' Favorite

"This is what historical fiction should be like. Superb."
Historical Novel Society (Indie Editor's Choice)

Praise for *Under the Approaching Dark*

"a not-so-easy-to-put-down novel, the work of a master."
Readers' Favorite

"Anna is a master carver of words and plot in order to bring you a drama rich in history, resistance, tragedy, tension, love, and survival."
Oh, for the Hook of a Book

"a beautifully written story which is firmly ensconced in the early fourteenth century"
Jaffareadstoo

"highly recommended historical fiction"
Historical Novel Society, Editor's Choice

Further to these excellent reviews, all three books have been awarded BRAG Medallions and the Reader's Favorite Five Star Seal.

Praise for The Graham Saga

"An admirably ambitious series"
The Bookseller

"A brilliantly enjoyable read"
HNS Reviews

"This is a series that will take both your heart and your head
to places both light and dark, disheartening and uplifting,
fantastic and frightening, but all utterly unforgettable"
WTF are you reading

"Anna writes deep, emotional historical novels, adding the
fantastical element of the time slip and a "what if?" scenario,
and creates for us a world in which to be lost in on rainy
days and weekend reading fests."
Oh for the Hook of a Book

"It seems Belfrage cannot put a foot wrong. Long may she
continue to give us installments in this truly wonderful series."
Kincavel's Korner

Further to excellent reviews, The Graham Saga has been
awarded multiple B.R.A.G. Medallions, five HNS Editor's
Choice, has been shortlisted for the HNS Indie Book of the
Year in 2014, and the sixth book in the series won the HNS
Indie Book of the Year in 2015.

ANNA BELFRAGE

The Cold Light of Dawn

Matador
9 Priory Business Park,
Wistow Road, Kibworth Beauchamp,
Leicestershire. LE8 0RX
Tel: (+44) 116 279 2299
Email: books@troubador.co.uk
Web: www.troubador.co.uk/matador

ISBN 978 1789010 015 (pb)
ISBN 978 9198405 460 (ebook)

British Library Cataloguing in Publication Data.
A catalogue record for this book is available from the British Library.

Typeset in 11pt Bembo by Troubador Publishing Ltd, Leicester, UK

Matador is an imprint of Troubador Publishing Ltd

This book is dedicated to my very own knight in shining armour.
Jag älskar dig, Johan

England in the early fourteenth century was a complicated place…

A king should not be ruled by favourites, but Edward II was prone to indulging the men whose company he enjoyed. By 1321, the barons of England had had enough of the king's grasping favourite, Hugh Despenser, and rose in rebellion. For a while, it seemed the barons would prevail, but for once in his life, Edward II acted with speed and determination. The uprising was crushed, Despenser became the most powerful man in England bar the king, and the rebellious barons were executed, one by one.

Except one. Edward II committed the mistake of his life when he chose not to execute Roger Mortimer. Instead, he allowed Mortimer to languish in captivity, but in August of 1323, Mortimer escaped the Tower and fled to France.

Edward II further compounded his mistake by alienating his wife, Queen Isabella. After stripping her of her dower lands and exiling her French household, Edward thought her tamed – so much so that Edward sent her to negotiate on his behalf in France. He also sent over his eldest son to do homage for his French lands.

In 1326, Isabella returned to England, accompanied by her son – and by Roger Mortimer, by now the queen's closest companion. Isabella promised to rid the realm of the tyranny imposed by the Despensers, and instead of resistance she encountered support. In November of 1326 Edward II and Hugh Despenser were captured. By early 1327 Despenser was dead and the king deposed. A new young king was crowned, the adolescent Edward III, for the time being very much under the control of his mother and Mortimer.

And then, in September of 1327 came the news that the former king was dead. Fingers were pointed at Mortimer, whispers of murder in the air. But was he really dead? It would seem quite a few of the barons thought not, but the unease caused by the rumours had some of the more powerful barons rebelling, demanding that Mortimer step aside and allow others to counsel the young king.

That rebellion was crushed in January of 1329.

Some months later Queen Isabella and Roger Mortimer remain in control of the kingdom. For now. But Edward III is fast growing into a man, and a confrontation looms between the young king and his regents. It is no longer a matter of *if* the young king will act, only of *when*…

Chapter 1

"France." King Edward, third of that name, tapped at the large map spread out on the table.

"I know where it is, my lord." In fact, Adam de Guirande had been there, so the miniature depiction of Notre Dame that adorned the beautifully written word *Paris* made him smile in recognition.

"It should be mine." The king's hand caressed the outline of England, spanned the Narrow Sea, and slammed down on France. "Mine, Adam."

Adam was saved from the need to comment by the sudden appearance of Queen Philippa. Her veil askew, her cheeks rosy, she looked as if she'd been playing in the woods surrounding Windsor Castle, an impression further reinforced by the smudges on her skirts and hands. Adam could not but smile at her, this very young woman who, he knew from his wife, still retained an inordinate fondness for climbing trees, albeit she restricted such pastimes to when she was adequately out of sight from the court—and especially her mother-in-law.

"Edward?" She danced across the room, those almond-shaped eyes of hers a brilliant brown. "You promised we'd go riding."

"I did." The king drew her close and busied himself with ordering her veil. "Hoyden," he murmured fondly, and she grinned at him. Edward turned to Adam. "We can talk more of this matter later. For now, I must attend to my lady wife."

"My lord." Adam bowed, thinking they were well-matched, those two. Not yet seventeen, King Edward needed someone who now and then encouraged him to be the lad he still was, and his two years younger wife was an ideal companion on such escapades. Besides, Philippa was not only a playmate and a welcoming pair of arms at night, she was

1

also the one person Edward felt he could confide everything to.

"Her and John," he'd said to Adam as recently as last night. "But John is still too much of a child."

Since Prince John was not quite thirteen, that was probably a correct assessment, and Philippa was a keen observer of everything that went on at court. Only a fool would underestimate her, and Adam prided himself on not being a fool. He might be a minor knight, his education was not among the best—he could write and read, but not with sufficient fluidity to enjoy reading—but there was nothing wrong with his brain.

The king and his wife left the room, holding hands. Adam returned to his perusal of the large map. He rubbed his face. Ever since the previous French king's death—more than a year ago, in early 1328—Edward had kept a careful eye on the events in France. King Charles had left a pregnant wife, and when Queen Jeanne was delivered of a girl child, the French had unanimously acclaimed Philippe of Valois as their next king, causing Edward to seethe. After all, he was King Charles' nephew, a grandson of Philippe le Bel, and therefore he had as much a right to the French crown as did Valois. More, even, seeing as Valois was the son of a count, while he, Edward, was the trueborn son of a king.

The French—understandably, in Adam's opinion—did not agree. Unfortunately, the king's mother, Queen Isabella, did, albeit at present she advocated a cautious approach.

"For now, we must keep Cousin Philippe happy," Queen Isabella had said earlier today. "Only once you have the superior forces required should you attack."

God make that very much in the future, Adam thought. He had no desire to ride to war. At present, all he wanted was to ride home to Tresaints, the small manor just north of the Malvern Hills that was his home and where his wife was soon to give birth. As was his wont these days, Adam sent a silent prayer to the Virgin, begging that she keep a protective eye on his beloved Kit.

When Adam exited the king's large chamber, he bumped into his brother-in-law, Richard de Monmouth. As red-haired and blue-eyed as Kit, Richard was in many ways eerily similar to his half-sister, though Kit, thank the Lord, sprouted no beard. And where Richard's hair was a bright shade of red, Kit's was substantially darker, a rich shade the colour of good Bordeaux wine.

"Lord Mortimer wishes a word with you," Richard said, falling in step with Adam as they passed through the gate to the middle ward. Once out of the shadows, Richard stopped and lifted his face to the sun. "Spring, at last."

"Aye." At home, the ewes would be lambing, and knowing Kit, she'd be out in the fields with the shepherds when she should remain at rest. Twins…His throat clogged, and he cast a look at the chapel. A candle—no, three candles: one for Kit and one each for those unformed beings resting in her womb.

Richard elbowed him. "It's not the first time a woman is delivered of twins."

"The first time my woman is." Childbirth was always a risk for women. God had ordained thus, and there was little to do but pray.

Mortimer was pacing back and forth, dictating to one of his clerks. The long skirts of his richly embroidered robe swirled as he walked, revealing hose in bright green and a matching tunic beneath the purple and black of the robe. In silk, Adam would hazard: these days, Lord Roger Mortimer was almost always in silk—or velvet—as befitted one of the richest men in the country. One of the most powerful men as well, the new Earl of March ruling the realm side by side with Queen Isabella on behalf of the young king.

"Ah, Adam!" Lord Roger brightened.

"My lord." Adam reciprocated Mortimer's smile and at his invitation sat down on one of the few chairs. The clerk was dismissed, a page brought wine and goblets, and for some time they discussed everyday matters such as the health of Lord Roger's namesake and grandson, or how the work was progressing with the chapel Lord Roger was presently building at Ludlow.

A comfortable sharing of news between two men who had known each other for twenty years and more, ever since the night Lord Roger found Adam badly beaten and half-naked in the lower ward of Ludlow castle. At the time, Adam had been but a twelve-year-old lad, victim of his father's cruel abuse. Now he was a landowning knight, and all because of Mortimer's patronage.

"Have you heard the news about Lady Eleanor?" Mortimer asked.

"Lady Eleanor?" The land was littered with ladies so named, but Adam suspected Lord Roger was referring to Eleanor de Clare, the unhappy widow of Hugh Despenser, may he rot in hell.

A fine enough lady, in Adam's opinion. She'd paid a heavy price for having been married to Despenser, what with being locked up in the Tower while three of her daughters had been forced to take the veil. This smelled far too much of petty vengeance—the girls were innocent of any crimes, and yet it was them who had now been immured for good behind the walls of various convents.

"Abducted, no less." Mortimer grinned. "By William la Zouche." He laughed. "That must be a right uncomfortable marriage bed. Imagine bedding the man who helped capture your husband."

"They are wed?"

"Oh yes, and our lady queen is livid." Lord Roger cracked a walnut. "Let's hope la Zouche has a true fondness for the lady. If he abducted her to get at her share of the de Clare inheritance, he will be disappointed. For now, I'll not allow her to get her lands back."

Allow? Adam regarded his former lord and master from under a fall of his thick hair. It was the king who should decide on such matters—or at least be involved.

Lord Roger shrugged. "Well, enough of the gossip. What do you think about France?"

"France?"

"Yes, France: the kingdom on the other side of the Narrow Sea now ruled by Philippe, though both my lady love and her son feel it should be him on the throne."

"I think France has little reason to accept an English king," Adam said.

"Just so." Mortimer studied one of his many rings. "We do not see eyes to eye on this, Isabella and I. She says it is Edward's God-given right to claim his Capet inheritance, while I…" He shrugged. "There is enough to do here."

England was a restless realm. Some months back, the Earl of Lancaster's attempted rebellion had been crushed, but just because one grandee was neatly hobbled and leashed did not mean the rest of the English barons were fully amenable.

Mortimer constantly had his back against the wall, defending his position as premier peer and effective ruler of the kingdom. As a consequence, his network of spies had grown larger than ever, Mortimer ensuring every royal appointment was filled by a man more loyal to him than to King Edward. It sat badly with Adam—and he loved Lord Roger. It had King Edward's uncles, the earls of Norfolk and Kent, gnashing their teeth, and as to the rest of the young men who made up the king's inner circle, they considered Mortimer a dangerous rabid dog.

"Edward, however, keeps on harping about his right to France." Mortimer cracked yet another walnut. They sat in silence while he separated the nut from the shell. "Stubborn young fool." Mortimer smiled. "Having said that, if ever an English king has the balls and the ability to conquer France, it is our Edward."

"You truly think so?" Adam asked.

"I do." Lord Roger stretched leisurely. "Takes after his grandsire rather than his sire, thank the Lord."

Adam sipped at his wine. "His father was a disaster as a king, assuredly, but not a bad man."

Mortimer's brows shot up. "Edward of Caernarvon? Weak and with the constancy of an addled hen. Not qualities I associate with a good man." He pursed his lips. "Well, he is safely gone, and I wish him well—as long as he stays well away from here."

"Aye." Adam turned his goblet round and round. "I

wonder where he is." He'd been made responsible for smuggling the officially dead king out of England—a mission that could have ended with his and Kit's deaths. It chafed at him, that to this day he did not know who had authorised the two ambushes that had attempted to kill him, Kit, Edward of Caernarvon, and Adam's man-at-arms, Egard.

No matter how often Adam turned this over in his mind, only three people had the clout and the information required to do so: King Edward, Lord Roger, or Queen Isabella. They were the only people fully acquainted with the planned route, whereby Adam was to take the former king, disguised as a friar, to Canterbury—well, Dover—and there ensure he got passage to France.

"Sometimes, your face is very easy to read," Lord Roger said, and Adam flushed and raised his goblet to his mouth. "You can't let it go, can you?"

"Would you if someone had been instructed to kill not only you but your lady wife as well?" Adam retorted.

"No." Mortimer poured them both some more wine. "It may be a case of overzealousness."

"My lord?"

Lord Roger averted his face. "If I were to tell you that aye, there was an arrangement to kill the former king, what would you say?"

"You ordered it?" Adam asked.

Lord Roger shook his head. "I did not. Neither, I can assure you, did your young lord, our king." He fidgeted on his seat, strong fingers crumbling what remained of the walnut shells.

"The queen." Adam was not surprised. For various reasons, he had already excluded King Edward and Lord Roger from his list of suspects.

"It is not quite as you think," Mortimer said. "She feared the former king would ride directly to Philippe in France, and that would have turned everything upside down. Philippe is no friend of Isabella—or of her half-Capet son—and would have been delighted to place means and men at Edward's disposal." He flashed Adam a crooked smile. "Philippe is a man who upholds a rigid morality—at least when it comes to others. To see his sweet cousin openly take a lover such as me…" He left the rest unsaid.

Adam nodded, no more. Lord Roger Mortimer was a married man, and in Adam's opinion, he was doing Lady Joan a terrible wrong by living so openly in sin with Queen Isabella.

"So she found someone she entrusted with the task of shadowing you and, if Edward showed any indications of wanting to flee, kill him." Lord Roger met Adam's eyes. "She did not think you capable of killing him in cold blood, should it be required."

Adam's instructions had been clear: should the former king attempt to abscond, he was to be killed. It had never been put to the test, and Adam was prone to agree with the queen—he did not have it in him to murder a man.

"I was taking precautions." Queen Isabella glided into the room. She must have been listening for some time.

Adam rose to his feet, bowing slightly in her direction. "Precautions? And did that include killing all of us?"

"Don't be ridiculous! My instructions were clear: should one in the group attempt to escape the others, he was to be killed. I didn't even tell my man who he was to kill; all he knew was that he would probably be disguised as a friar." She licked her lips. "He also knew you would be riding with his potential victim, as would Kit."

"He knows me?" Adam asked.

Isabella inclined her head. "I was not aware of his resentment, though."

"Resentment, my lady?"

Isabella sighed. "The man I chose dislikes you—as was made apparent when we were in Warwick."

At first, Adam did not follow. And then he remembered the heated quarrel. "Robert de Langon."

Queen Isabella nodded.

Adam closed his hand into a fist. De Langon, casually ordering the murder of Adam—and Kit! Next time he clapped eyes on that maggot, he'd throttle him.

"Had you told us about the ambushes when you first returned, he'd have been hanged by now," Lord Roger said with something of an edge to his voice. "I still don't understand how you could think either of us capable of ordering your death." He encircled the queen's waist, pulled her close enough that he could rest his head against her hip, should he want to. These overt displays of affection made Adam uncomfortable. Since Lancaster had knelt in the mud and submitted to the king's justice, the queen and Mortimer had become far less circumspect, and it wasn't only the king sending glowering looks their way.

Isabella studied Adam with a quirk to her beautiful mouth. How a woman could be at the same time so ravishing and forbidding was beyond Adam, but it was an alluring combination, perfect features hiding a core of steel that was rarely visible to those who did not know her. At present, her green eyes were as cold and hard as ice.

"He never suspected you, Roger. It was me he thought capable of such a sinister deed." She laughed softly. "Adam sets a high store by your honour, my love. Mine, on the other hand, he drags through the dirt."

"My lady, I…" Adam's face heated. She held up her hand.

"There's nothing you can say. Besides, how can I blame you? Indirectly, it was my fault, however unintentional." She made a dismissive gesture. "I must talk to Lord Mortimer alone."

Adam bowed and left.

He retired to St Edward's chapel, pushing the heavy red door open. This time of the day, it was empty, and Adam lowered himself to his knees and spent some time in silent prayer. To be precise, he tried to, but he was distracted by what he had just heard. On the one hand, he was relieved to have finally cleared up the matter of who had tried to murder him and his wife. On the other, he was consumed by a fiery rage. Should de Langon ever show his face in court again, Adam would be more than happy to challenge him to a trial by combat, no quarter given.

With an effort, he cleansed his mind of any thoughts of de Langon. He focussed on the fluttering flames of the three little candles he had just lit. He wanted to go home, be there for Kit when she birthed their children. That made him smile. Mabel would no more allow him to enter the birthing chamber than she would have Kit giving birth in the pigsty.

Behind him, the door creaked. Adam turned and lurched to his feet to bow when he recognised Queen Philippa, shadowed by some of her ladies. His damaged foot protested at the sudden movement, and for an instant his leg dipped.

"I did not mean to disturb you," Philippa said, coming to stand beside him. She looked at his candles. "For Lady Kit?"

"Aye." Adam could not quite suppress his sigh.

"Why don't you ride home?"

"There is nothing I would rather do, but…" No point in saying more than that, Adam fixed his gaze on the eastern window, spring sunshine setting the red and yellow glass ablaze.

"Edward says no." Philippa bit her plump lower lip. "I shall talk to him."

"He may not like it, that you intercede for me."

"For you?" She laughed, a soft tinkling sound that had Adam smiling in return. Their queen had a remarkable capacity for imbuing every space with her calming presence. "No, Sir Adam, that will not help: I shall instead remind him of how much he cares for Lady Kit." She gave him a teasing smile. "Surely, by now you've worked out that my Edward has quite the chivalric side to him?"

Adam strangled a laugh. Beyond likening himself to St George, the king rarely spouted anything indicating such chivalric attitudes. His young lord was more into horses and weapons than the ladies, being quite oblivious to females other than his wife.

"You'd best go and pack." Queen Philippa settled herself on her knees, gesturing for her women to do so as well. "You'll be riding for home before vespers." She grinned, and for an instant she looked more like a mischievous urchin than a queen. "Shall we make a wager?"

Adam laughed. "No, my lady." He bowed again. "Your servant, my lady. Always."

Chapter 2

"I know exactly how you feel." Kit stroked the panting ewe's head. "Two babies, kicking at you from the inside in their haste to meet the world."

"You should not be out here," old John said. "A lady like you, so close to her time, and here you are, kneeling among the sheep."

"Every lamb that is born healthy adds to our wealth." Kit sat back on her heels. "Besides, it is at least four weeks before I am due. What would you have me do? Remain in the solar and indulge in baked goods and dried fruit?"

"Better than being here in the mud." But John smiled. "What does Mabel say?"

"You know your sister." Kit set her hands to the ground and heaved herself upright without overbalancing. "She nags."

"Ah. Well, she has always been good at that." John grinned. "God knows she kept the rest of us in good order, despite being only a year or two older than me."

Kit nodded, no more, attempting to catch her breath.

"My lady?" John hovered. Kit waved him away, watching as he dropped back down to help the second of the little lambs into the world.

"Kit!" William came striding over the pasture, all long legs and flapping gown. "What are you doing out here? Adam would have my guts for not keeping a better eye on you." He gestured at the sky, as yet mostly dark, though a faint line of pink tainted the eastern horizon. "You should be sleeping!"

"Tell that to the ewes." Kit rubbed at her back. "They mostly lamb at night."

William took hold of her arm. "To bed, Kit. Mabel says—"

"Mabel says this, Mabel says that." Kit snorted. "Truth be told, Mabel has little experience of either carrying or birthing a child."

"Not necessarily out of choice, my lady," John said. "Her babe died, as did her husband."

Kit spread her hands in an apologetic gesture. "You're right. That was uncalled for."

"Inside," William said. "Bed. Now."

With no further protest, Kit accompanied him. Besides, her toes were freezing, and she needed to relieve herself.

They stopped at the chapel. Kit glanced at William, they shared a smile, and entered. The building was the oldest on the manor—or so Kit's mother, Alaïs, had always maintained—a small whitewashed space in which the painted decorations were kept to a minimum. Not that any of this was visible in the wavering glow of the single candle burning on the altar, but Kit did not need light to know exactly where the statues of the three saints were. They sat just inside the door, St Winifride, St Wulfstan, and St Odo. A Welsh saint, a French saint, and an English one—apt in a manor built by a Norman knight upon returning from the Crusades.

William sank into his own thoughts before the altar. Kit clasped her hands over her swollen belly and wondered what Adam might be doing. She fidgeted, bumping into William. As tall as her husband, William also had the same fair hair and similar build as his brother, but where decades of earning his living with his sword had left Adam a collection of compact muscles, William had ink-splotched fingers and a tendency to squint—this after years of peering at documents and Holy Scripture.

Currently, he was Tresaints' resident priest—and Adam's steward, overseeing an ever-growing combination of pastures, woodlands, and fields. Being in the king's service came with its rewards, and God knew they needed it: with all these children, more land was always welcome.

Beside her, William was praying, and she fell in, adding her voice to the whispered Latin.

"Amen," he finished, and she echoed him before crossing herself. There was enough light in the chapel now for her to make out the Holy Virgin as she stood beside her son on the central panel of the triptych that adorned the altar. Kit whispered yet one more prayer, this one directed to the Virgin, "See me and my babes safe through the coming ordeal." It seemed to her the painted Virgin smiled.

Some hours later, Kit was in the kitchens, discussing food with Mall. There was plenty of salted herring left, and at present two dozen were soaking in cold water prior to being cooked. "Pottage with leeks," Mall said, "and split peas." She smacked her lips. "Will go well with the herring."

In Kit's considered opinion, little went well with herring, but she nodded all the same.

"Mistress?" Tom the Foundling almost fell into the kitchen. "There are people coming down the lane. John said to fetch you."

Kit rose, steadying herself against the table. "People?"

"One of them's a lady, and she has the prettiest palfrey I've ever seen, and—"

"A lady, Mama," Meg interrupted, jumping up and down. "A real lady, and she has—"

Kit waved the children silent. "A lady?" She made for the door, Meg skipping beside her.

"A pretty, pretty lady," Meg warbled, jumping up and down with such enthusiasm her dark braids escaped her coif. "Will they stay?"

"We shall see." In her head, Kit was already considering how to lodge these unknown guests.

"Ah, there you are." William looked anything but happy. "We have visitors."

"So I heard. Who?" She accompanied him over the little bailey towards the gate.

"You'll never guess," he said, just as the first rider came through the gate. Kit's belly cramped, and she took an instinctive step closer to William.

"What's she doing here?" she whispered.

Beside her, Meg gasped in admiration, eyes riveted to the figure clad in green and blue, the hood of her mantle thrown back to reveal a veil in the sheerest of linen.

"I am sure we will find out." William set a hand to her

12

back, sufficient support for Kit to stiffen her spine.

"Sister," Kit offered reluctantly when the neat little mare came to a halt in front of her. Alicia Luytens and she shared a father, but where Alicia had been born in wedlock, Kit was the child of an illicit union, the damage further compounded— at least in Alicia's eyes—by the fact that Kit's mother was a salter's daughter.

Alicia did not reply, narrow face set in an unreadable expression as she gazed at her surroundings. "My father was born here," she said to her male companion as she dismounted. "Imagine that! Such humble beginnings." She landed lightly on her feet, made as if to enter the manor house, but Kit blocked her way.

"I do not recall inviting you," Kit said.

"You didn't. I came anyway—to see." Thinly plucked brows rose in arcs as she took in Kit's rounded state. "Another one? Really, some breed like rabbits, don't they?" She laughed, tugging at her dark green mantle, a beautiful thing edged with squirrel fur. Gloves of a matching green covered her hands, and the silk in her blue skirts rustled when she moved. In comparison, Kit's everyday russet was drab and unflattering, straining over her large belly.

"Why are you here?" William planted himself in front of Kit, arms crossed over his chest.

"Why not? Widow Luytens had a penchant to see her father's birthplace." Her companion threw the reins of his horse to one of his servants and strolled forward. "Small, but with potential," he said, studying the recently refurbished manor house. He was dressed for travel, sensible clothes in good grey worsted and a heavy cloak lined with fleece. His dark hair fell in soft waves to his shoulders, a neat beard covered his cheeks, and eyes as cold and hard as pebbles alighted for an instant on Kit before he reverted to scrutinising the various buildings. The nerve of him! Kit wanted to spit in his face.

"And you are?" William asked.

"That," Kit said, "is Robert de Langon—recently dismissed from the king's service for slandering me." To Kit's satisfaction, this had de Langon paling. "And in view of what you said, you are not welcome here at Tresaints—either of you."

Alicia snickered and made a new attempt to reach the manor house. John surged forward, accompanied by his grandsons.

"Best leave," John said. "My mistress does not want you here."

"Maybe that is not for her to say," Robert de Langon said. "After all, Tresaints was part of Katherine de Monmouth's dowry, not the impostor's."

"And I was cheated by my brother." Alicia swept the neat bailey yet another lingering look. "I should be compensated. I am looking at marrying again." She simpered at Robert.

"Fortunately, my father amended the contracts," Kit said. "Everything is in legal order—as confirmed by the late Earl of Pembroke."

"I have rights!" Alicia hissed. "This is fine land and a good manor. Why should you have it and not me? I shall make claims on my brother, and then we'll see."

"You do that." Something knotted itself in Kit's belly, but she succeeded in sounding unperturbed. "But your quarrel is with him, not with me."

"Knowing Richard, he'll not part with anything of his to compensate me," Alicia said.

"Knowing you, you don't deserve any compensation." Kit looked Alicia up and down. "You look in the best of spirits, despite being so recently bereaved. But then, I suppose you were overjoyed at hearing your husband was dead."

"He abused me!" Alicia hissed.

"Ah. Is that why you had him killed?" Kit said, noting out of the corner of her eye how Robert took a step back from Alicia.

"I did not!" Pale blue eyes glared at Kit.

"So you say." Kit studied her sister. "Have you told Robert about your foiled attempt to poison Queen Isabella and Earl Roger?"

"I…" Alicia spluttered, throwing a look at Robert.

"Is this true?" Robert said.

"She misconstrues." Alicia's face, always an unfortunate

collection of angles and sharp planes, tightened into a grimace. She sniffed and wiped at her long nose. "I was forced to do it. My mother's life hung in the balance."

"Not a great loss to the world," Kit muttered. Lady Cecily inhabited quite a few of Kit's rare nightmares, an apparition dominated by a nose as sharp and long as Alicia's and a mouth set in a permanent snarl.

"She was my mother!" Alicia scowled.

"I can but commiserate," Kit retorted. "And now I must bid you leave."

"What, no hospitality offered to weary travellers?" Robert de Langon asked.

"You are no friend of my husband—or of me. Neither is Alicia, so the answer is no." Kit raised her chin and stared him down.

At long last, he sighed. "We'd best get going," he said to Alicia. "It's quite the ride to Worcester." Once he was astride, he looked down at Kit. "I trust you were not lying about the contracts. Such things are easy to check, and I must of course look out for the interests of my wife-to-be."

"It will not avail you if you do." Kit even managed a cold smile. "Good day to you. I shall be sure to tell my husband of your visit. I dare say he will be less than pleased." She took a step forward. "It would be foolish to anger Adam de Guirande. He has the ear of the king—you do not."

De Langon sneered. "For now."

The moment they were gone, Kit turned to John. "As of now, the gate is kept closed. Always."

"Yes, my lady." John was already halfway to the gate, yelling orders. Meg and Tom scampered after him.

"What was that?" William asked.

"Intimidation." Kit clenched her hand to stop it from shaking. "I must send word to Adam—and Richard."

"Richard?"

"The contracts name Katherine de Monmouth, not me. They will have to be rewritten."

"Or amended." William took hold of her shoulders. "Calm down, Kit."

"My home!" She placed her hands over her heaving stomach. "This is my home, William!"

"And so it will remain." He drew her close enough to kiss her forehead. "It will." Kit rested against him, eyes closed. Long, slow breaths, and the loud thumping of her heart calmed.

"It's all very odd," she said once she'd regained her composure. "Alicia and de Langon—does Richard know?" She scraped at a spot of wax on the sleeve of William's gown.

"She's a wealthy widow. As a widow, she can arrange her affairs as it pleases her—and it seems Robert de Langon does."

"They suit." Kit straightened up. "May they find what they deserve in each other."

"God help them," William muttered. "De Langon is from Gascony, isn't he?"

"He is. A minor lordling who hoped his father's generous gifts to the new king would ensure an exalted position among the king's friends." Kit crouched to wipe her youngest son's face. Harry beamed up at her, pudgy—and dirty—fingers gripping at her skirts. "But as Adam tells it, Edward rarely noticed his presence—or absence."

"Ah. That must be difficult."

"He's not a nice man." Kit took hold of William's offered hand and hauled herself upright. "He doesn't deserve any compassion."

"All men deserve compassion," William admonished. He winked. "Some less than others, to be sure."

Six days later, Kit returned from a difficult lambing just before vespers. Her hands and forearms were covered with blood and other fluids, and all of her ached. She stood for a moment looking to the west, the setting sun colouring the sky that particular shade of pink one only saw during winter and early spring. The nearby shrubs swelled with buds, yellow coltsfoot dotted the ditches, and Easter was not quite a fortnight away.

"You look a right disgrace, m'lady," Mabel said, appearing from the direction of the brewing shed. "Look at you, all bloody and stained. What would your lord husband say if he saw you right now?"

"You smell?" Kit suggested, laughing at Mabel's responding scowl. "But you're right; I look a sight." She unrolled her sleeves. "I need a bath."

"Aye." Mabel's face softened. "And some days in bed, from the look of it." She took Kit's hand. "You need your rest, m'lady. Now if you would only do as I say and—"

"No." Kit gave Mabel an irritated look. "I will not be confined to my solar."

A recurring point of contention between them, with Mabel repeating over and over that well-bred ladies always retired to their chambers prior to a birth, while Kit maintained there was no need, not here at Tresaints, where there was no one to see the lady of the manor going about her business as usual, despite her bulk.

Mabel rolled her eyes and bustled off to arrange a bath.

A rare luxury, to wallow in hot water before the hearth, and Kit sank down with a pleased little exclamation. Other than the fire and the single candle on a nearby table, the room was dark, even though the single shutter had been left open to allow what remained of the daylight to stream in through the newly installed greenish glass, multiple small panels arranged in neat diamonds.

Kit closed her eyes. Ever since Alicia's disconcerting visit, she'd been on edge, and even now that she'd sent off a messenger with letters to Richard and Adam, it nagged at her. Simple malice, William insisted, and he was probably right, but for Alicia to come all the way to Tresaints, she was not making idle threats. It would keep. It had to keep, and Kit had to leave it to her husband to sort it.

The door opened, and an icy draft tickled her bare shoulders. "Leave," she said without turning to face the door. To her relief, the door shut, and she sank deeper into the water. Footsteps, and for an instant her heart was in her mouth, but then she recognised the slightly limping tread, and she sank even lower in the water to hide her smile beneath the surface.

Icy hands slid down her arms and pulled her upwards.

A familiar mouth came down on hers—an odd kiss, his face upside down.

"Sweeting," Adam murmured against her lips, and his hands slid over her breasts to stroke her belly.

"You're here," she said, and that made him smile.

"Aye, so it seems." He nipped her ear. "How are you?" Yet again his hands—no longer cold—slid over her belly. "Mabel tells me you refuse to rest as you should."

"If Mabel had her way, I'd have been bedridden for the last month." She covered his hands with her own, guiding them to where the skin bulged and shifted. "They are restless."

"A miracle." Adam splayed his fingers. "So much life within you." For an instant, his fingers disappeared before returning with some of the soft soap Mabel made. A delicate fragrance of soapwort and rose filled the air as he carefully washed her belly, her breasts, her thighs and arms. And then he had her dip her head and began the process of washing her hair, strong fingers massaging her scalp until she groaned.

No words, just his hands and fingers expressing how much he loved her, worshipped her, even, and by the time he was done, she was tingling all over, her wet hair hanging heavily down her back. He gestured for her to stand and dried her as meticulously as he had just washed her. It was cold, to stand naked while he wiped her down with various linen towels.

"Come here." He opened his arms, and she stepped into the comforting warmth of his body, his well-worn tunic soft under her cheek, his chin digging into her head. "You're big," he said, laughter colouring his voice. "Can't quite get my arms around you."

He swept her up in his arms and deposited her in bed. She was covered in blankets, then he undressed and slipped in to join her, naked skin against naked skin. She luxuriated in his presence, in his familiar scent of leather and horses. He held her close, his mouth at her nape, one hand caressing the contour of her hip. Kit's eyes grew heavy. Her man, keeping her safe with his warmth and strength.

"You must have ridden like the wind," she said through a yawn.

"I always do when I'm on my way back home." He rubbed his unshaven cheek up over her shoulder blades, a scratchy sensation that had her turning towards him—at present a difficult process, what with her belly.

"But still, the message…" Her voice trailed off. The message couldn't have reached him.

"What message?"

Kit struggled up to sit; he followed suit. "Alicia was here. With Robert de Langon."

"What?" He rose off the bed, all six feet and more of him quivering with anger. "That sheep's turd of a man was here? Here?"

"A week ago."

"Damn him! What did he want?"

Kit gave him a summary of the events while he walked back and forth, the reddish light from the fire dancing over his naked body. Golden fuzz covered his legs and arms, grew considerably thicker on his chest and darkened round his groin.

"And you've sent a message to Richard as well?" Adam asked once she was done. He came to sit beside her.

"I have." She rested her head against his shoulder. "William says it was an empty threat."

"It is. I will ensure it is." He pulled her into his lap. "Alicia, with her eyes set on de Langon? This is a right mess." His chest rose on a deep inhalation. "It was de Langon who set out to have us murdered last year." Words spilled out of him at an alarming rate, about Queen Isabella and her little plan. Kit pressed her ear closer to his chest, half of her listening to the reassuring sound of his heartbeat, the rest attempting to make sense of all this.

"Do you believe her?"

"About not aiming to have us murdered? Aye, I do— mostly. But at the same time, I find myself pondering her choice of man to do the job. She maintains she had no idea de Langon disliked me, but only a person blind and deaf would not have noticed."

"You forget Queen Isabella expends little attention on

those beneath her." Kit pressed her lips to his clavicle. "She may have been speaking the truth."

"We must hope so." He sighed. "I wonder if Alicia knows Robert attempted to kill us."

"Not something he'd share with his future bride," Kit said. "On the other hand, she wouldn't have cared—we both know that. No love lost between her and me. What will you do about de Langon?"

"Ensure he understands it is best for him to leave England." He dragged his fingers through her tangled, damp hair. "Preferably with his viper of a chosen bride."

Chapter 3

Tresaints had visitors some days later. A large group of men, headed by the man Adam considered his best friend, for all that Thomas was a royal earl and Adam nothing but a minor knight. All the same, the sight of the Earl of Norfolk trotting down the long lane to Tresaints had Adam pursing his lips: the earl was a long way from home.

"We've been in Gloucester," Thomas told Adam once he was off his horse. "Some matters to sort regarding some land I hold. And I visited with Berkeley."

Adam was spared the need to reply as Kit came forward to greet their guest. Thomas visiting Berkeley was odd. Where Thomas was critical of Roger Mortimer, Lord Berkeley was one of Lord Roger's most trusted allies, married to the eldest of the Mortimer offspring, Margaret. By now, she'd given him four or five sons, and from what Adam had heard, it was a happy enough marriage. Berkeley was also the man Mortimer had put in charge of the imprisoned Edward II, and that in itself ensured there was little love lost between Thomas and him.

"Kit! As round as an apple and as rosy," Thomas said, a hand closing on Kit's elbow when she attempted a reverence. "Don't do that. You may never rise again." He grinned; Kit smiled back before taking a step backwards, thereby bumping into Adam. He slipped a proprietary arm round her shoulders.

"Ale?" he asked.

"Food." Thomas patted his belly. "A full day on horseback has left me starving." He did a slow turn. "Is it my imagination, or has the house grown since I was here last?"

"It has been expanded." Adam swelled with pride. "New kitchens, new rooms, a new gatehouse and new stables." Nothing in comparison with the earl's magnificent Framlingham or Walton, but Adam loved his home.

"You've been quite the builder," Thomas said with a laugh. "Almost as busy as Mortimer." His brow clouded. "That man is constantly improving his many abodes."

"And you do not?" Kit asked.

"Oh, I do." Thomas gave her a brief smile. "But I find I have fewer castles than he does to renovate." He cleared his throat. "Any new horses in those stables of yours, Adam?"

"A few." Adam led the way. "Goliath breeds true."

"God spare us," Thomas muttered. "In temper as well as looks?"

"No." Adam laughed. "His get are more biddable than the sire." He held the door open for the earl, and they stepped into the murky warmth of the stables. Goliath was stabled furthest away from the door, while Adam's Flemish stallion, a surprisingly docile beast named Raven, was half asleep in his stall some yards away.

"And was Berkeley doing well?" Adam asked casually as they stood admiring the new foals.

"We didn't discuss his health." Thomas leaned over to scratch the little colt. "We mostly talked about practical matters." He straightened up. "And my brother." Even in the weak light, Adam could see the scowl on Thomas' face. "He maintains Edward died in 1327."

"What else can he say? He was the one who informed our king of his father's death."

"He's lying! You know, he knows, and I know! And damn him, it's my brother we're talking about here." Thomas inhaled. "You swore to me in January that he was hale but if so, where is he? That fool of a castellan at Corfe told Edmund he'd seen him a year ago, but since then we've heard nothing." He whirled. "So maybe he *is* dead and maybe he wouldn't have been dead had I done something—anything—to help him."

"He's not at Corfe." Adam kept his eyes on the dark bay hide of the foal.

"But he is alive?"

The desperate hope in Thomas' voice had Adam nodding. "As far as I know." He looked at his friend. "I can't tell you more than that. I have sworn an oath not to do so, and I have a wife and children to think of."

"As I have a brother."

"And a nephew," Adam reminded him sharply. "Our young king would not benefit from it being common knowledge his father is alive."

"Our young king would not even be king then," Thomas retorted. "Nor would the Great Seal reside in the hands of Queen Isabella and her lover."

It was Adam's turn to scowl. "Anyone threatens my lord, and I'll—"

Thomas held up his hand. "No one is threatening Ned. And yes, I know as well as you do my brother is not cut out to be king. But from there to remain forever behind walls…" His Adam's apple bobbed up and down. "It's not right."

"As God ordains, Thomas." Adam stood aside to allow Thomas to exit the stables first.

"As Mortimer ordains, you mean. Together with dear Isabella." Thomas shook his head. "I did not think a woman could be so ruthless."

"She's protecting her son."

Thomas' brows rose. "Don't be obtuse, Adam. It may have started out like that, a concerned mother defending her young, but these days it is more about defending herself—and Mortimer—from her son."

Adam didn't reply. Only a fool would disagree with that statement. Time was running out for Queen Isabella and Lord Roger, and God alone knew how it all would end.

When they entered the hall, Kit ushered them to a table set close to the large hearth. Ale, one of Mall's excellent leek pies, and a little platter of dried fruits—not much to offer an earl, but Lent fare was what it was.

Thomas' men were seated some distance away, and from their single-minded concentration on trenchers and platters, they'd not eaten since they broke their fast.

"Did you know Godfrey of Broseley was apprehended in

Gloucester some weeks ago?" Thomas speared a roasted clove of garlic, eyes glancing briefly at Kit.

"Apprehended?" She clasped her hands in front of her.

"Aye. They were set to hang him, but…" Thomas fell silent as he chewed, "he got away."

"What? That man has more lives than an accursed cat!" Adam exploded.

"Maybe. Or someone didn't want him to tell the assizes that he believes the old king is alive." Thomas shrugged. "Whatever the case, one morning he was gone."

"Gloucester?" Kit's voice quavered. "He's in Gloucester?"

"Not anymore." Thomas wiped his hands and sat back. "Last anyone heard, he was making for Bristol."

"Still too close," Adam muttered, throwing Kit a concerned look. She'd gone as still as Lot's wife—after she'd become a pillar of salt.

"Likely, he's in France." Thomas leaned forward and gave Kit a smile. "Nothing left for him here, not with Thomas Wake and Lancaster laid low."

Adam took her hand. "Thomas is right, sweeting. He has no reason to stay."

"Unless he's still looking for the former king," she replied. "He strikes me as a determined man." A shiver coursed through her, and for an instant her composure cracked, eyes wide with fright, fingers tightening like a vice round Adam's digits.

"Shhh." Adam drew her close, glaring at Thomas over her head. "He'll not hurt you again. Ever."

"I'm sorry." Thomas poured Kit some more wine. "I did not mean to disconcert you. I just felt you should know." He cleared his throat. "Broseley would be a fool to come back here. That old man you've got guarding the gate would have him looking like a hedgehog before he made it down the lane."

"Aye, John has his own score to settle with Broseley," Adam said, and Kit's mouth twitched into a weak smile. He lifted her hand to his mouth. "I'll send to Bristol in the morning. Let's see if we can find out where he went—a man as ugly as Godfrey cannot have gone unnoticed."

Scar-faced and about as wide as he was tall, Godfrey of Broseley was difficult to forget, menace leaking from him like wisps of smoke from a hearth. The scar to his face was Adam's handiwork; the scar that supposedly adorned Godfrey's groin was the result of Kit's knife, which was why Godfrey had abducted Kit last summer, threatening to kill her unless Adam told him where the former king was held. Seven days in hell—for Kit, at the mercy of Godfrey, but also for Adam, searching for her.

"I've already set men to do just that," Thomas said. "And should Broseley still be there, I've sent word to the sheriff. Thomas Rodborwe is good at his job."

Thomas went on to change the subject, but Adam wasn't listening, submerged in dark thoughts about Broseley. The bastard should have been dead, and it was Adam's fault that the miscreant was still around to draw breath. He tightened his hold on his eating knife, a series of quick stabbing movements that reduced the dried fig before him to fragments.

Beside him, Kit laughed. There were roses on her cheeks, a sheen to her eyes, her recent discomfiture clearly a thing of the past as she leaned towards Thomas.

"You protest too much," she said. "I think you secretly like romances."

"Like them?" Thomas beckoned for Stephen, Adam's page, to replenish his goblet. "What is not to like? But it's all so predictable. Either it all ends in tragedy or the lovers are happily reunited."

"Two very different outcomes," Kit objected, "not at all predictable."

"Tristan and Iseult? Death. Guinevere and Lancelot? Very tragic."

"Guinevere was married elsewhere," Adam interjected. "They deserved a tragic end."

"Ah, ah." Thomas wagged his finger. "Love, Adam. So powerful it sweeps everything else aside. What can mortal man do against such forces?"

"Fight the urge," Adam said drily.

"Sometimes, that doesn't help." Thomas studied his hands.

Kit's lashes swept down to shield her eyes. Black jealousy twisted like a snake through Adam's innards. Until he caught the look she gave Thomas: compassion, not passion.

"He wed impetuously," Kit said later, walking slowly up the stairs to their solar. Tallow candles in shallow sconces lit their progress, light flickering over the whitewashed walls. "Not always a guarantee for contentment." They'd bid Thomas good night, Adam's squire, Gavin, escorting the earl to the chamber above the kitchens—part of the extensions made last year, and furnished with a new bed and new tapestries.

"No." Adam steadied her up the last few treads. "Not everyone is as fortunate as we are."

Kit reclined against him—an instant of her warm, rounded shape against his chest. "Ours was not the best of beginnings."

"I disagree." He held the door for her. "The beginning was quite spectacular. But afterwards, when I found out you'd duped me—"

"Not me! I was forced, you know that. It was Lady Cecily who—"

"Shush, sweeting." He dropped a quick kiss on her forehead. "I know." Now and then it still rankled, that Lady Cecily should have played him the fool by replacing her true-born daughter with her husband's bastard to safeguard the Monmouth fortunes. Not that he ever regretted his wife: he'd never known Katherine de Monmouth, but rumour had her as grasping and cold-hearted as her mother, hoping for more than marriage with a mere knight such as Adam de Guirande. "In truth, she did me a favour, the witch." He tugged at her veil. "Without her scheming, I would never have met you."

Kit gave him a brief smile. "Or I you." She twisted. "Will you help me with my laces?"

He helped her out of the heavy wool kirtle, lifted her chemise over her head, and dropped to his knees to undo her garters and roll down her hose. His hands closed on her ankles; he slid them upwards, over her thighs, her hips, her flanks, all the way to her bosom, two soft breasts nestling in his grip.

He undid her heavy braid, and hair the colour of a fox

pelt spilled down her back, grazing the upper slope of her buttocks. Her belly protruded like a giant orb, and he couldn't resist the desire to set his hands on it, caressing the taut skin.

"As round as a harvest moon," he said.

"But not quite as yellow," she teased.

"No. You're more of a pearly pink." He backed her towards the bed, had her sit and watch while he undressed.

"We shouldn't," she said, giving him a coy look. She was right: they should abstain during Lent, and besides, it was a sin to lie with your wife other than for procreation, but Adam had long since decided this was a sin so minor so as to not matter. He took great pleasure in his wife, was careful to ensure her pleasure was as great as his, and surely the good Lord would not deny them something so full of joy. Not that he'd ever shared these opinions with a man of God—this despite his own brother being a priest—nor did he intend to.

"Would you rather we didn't?"

"No." The tip of her tongue darted out to lick her lips.

"Good." He pulled a heavy sheep's fleece off the bed and knelt before her. She widened her legs, and he covered her dark curls with his hand. She was moist and warm, eyes glazing as his finger slid back and forth. He leaned forward and kissed her, his tongue following the contour of her lips. They kissed for a long time, a slow dance of tongue and lips, a gentle exploration that left him short of breath and with a thudding cock. Kit shifted closer to the edge of the bed. He entered her. Hot. Tight. There was a sudden rush of air as she exhaled, leaning back to move her belly out of the way and give him better access. Adam slipped his hands under her buttocks, lifted her closer, and drove into her.

They lay close together afterwards, her cheek on his chest.

"Mabel says lovemaking this close to birth may well start things off." She ran a hand over her belly; he followed suit, marvelling at all the life contained within. It bulged and shifted under his touch. His seed: his children.

"Really? Why?"

"Mabel says it's akin to the father knocking at the door

27

of the womb." She giggled, her hand sliding down to fondle him. "Knock, knock."

Adam spread his legs. "Is that an invitation, my lady?"

Her warm lips left a series of moist imprints down his chest. "Always, my dearest lord and husband. Always."

Chapter 4

Whether Mabel was right or not, by the time Good Friday dawned, Kit had been safely delivered of twins—a little daughter and yet another son, both of them with golden fuzz on their heads and lashes so fair they were near on invisible, the line of their brows mere dustings of light downy hair.

"Two." Adam had both infants in his arms. "Two," he cooed. "One lad, one fair maid."

"They're both fair." Kit held out her arms to receive one of them, suppressing a groan when the little mouth latched on to her breast. It was as if with every pull at the teat, the babe was tightening invisible threads round her womb—as it should be, according to Mabel, who insisted Kit should feed both the babes for a month at least.

Adam was leaving on the morrow. With Easter come and gone, his time away from court was up, and he'd be riding off at daybreak with Gavin and four of his men. The other four would remain behind—all of them Tresaints men who'd prefer to stay at home helping with the sheep and the crops.

"Good men," Adam told Kit. "Fully capable of seeing de Langon off should he come calling."

"Do you think he will?"

"No." Adam rubbed his newest son gently over the head. "Likely they're halfway to Bordeaux by now. That's where de Langon has his lands."

"I still don't understand why he wants to wed her."

"Wealth—and land. She has some manors in Gascony, doesn't she?"

"Lady Cecily was a major landowner—through her mother. But most of that remains with Richard."

"Aye." He furrowed his brow. "He was not fair to Alicia when she wed Luytens."

"No." Kit sighed. "But that does not mean she has a right

to compensate herself here." She shifted the babe—Eleanor—to the other breast.

"Alicia will not have as much as a shovelful of Tresaints land." He glanced at her. "I'll have a word with Richard. I'll not be cheated out of what is mine—ours."

They exchanged children, Adam sitting beside her with a contented Eleanor while she fed Peter. He draped his free arm round her shoulders and pulled her close.

"Once you're recovered and churched, I want you to join me at court."

"Of course." She shifted that much closer. "Queen Philippa expects me back as well." Kit stifled a sigh: she was in two minds about returning to court. Yes, her place was with Adam—but with their increasing brood, there were times when she was torn apart between her husband and her children.

"Bring Mabel and the babes with you." He smiled. "They'll need you for some time longer."

The first person Adam met when he rode into Westminster was Thomas of Norfolk. In an old gambeson and muddy boots, dark hair plastered to his head, the earl was far from his normal elegant self—but in an expansive mood, jesting with his squires as he handed them his weapons and equipment.

"Adam!" Thomas waved before disappearing in the heavy folds of the gambeson, re-emerging even more tousled, the thin shirt he was wearing sticking to his skin. A page hurried forward with a tunic, another with an ewer of water and several linen towels. By the time Adam had dismounted, Thomas was clean and adequately attired, his hair hidden under one of those new-fangled Italian hats that mostly looked as if someone had draped a length of fabric haphazardly round his head.

"Want one?" Thomas asked with a grin, setting a hand to his head.

"Never." Adam preferred hoods—with the occasional coif beneath if it was truly cold.

"No sense of fashion," Thomas sniffed. "And have the babes arrived?"

"They have. Big and squalling—one son, one daughter." Adam's chest expanded.

"I suspect we'll never hear the end of this." Thomas slapped Adam so hard on his back he actually stumbled. "I trust Kit is doing well?"

"She is." Adam nodded to Stephen to take Raven. His page gave him a toothy smile and led off the large stallion.

"I'm right glad to see you back," Thomas said. "At last, someone to work the edge off Ned's temper."

"I'm not a quintain," Adam retorted. Bouting with their young king was a wearisome business, and of late it happened far too often that the royal whelp won, something Adam had a hard time accepting.

"No. But you're the only one who still stands a chance of winning against him—well, bar me, of course."

"You?" Adam snorted. "I think not. Besides, he'd have a hard time matching Mortimer." He fell into step with Thomas, crossing the large bailey towards the hall. Lord Roger was meticulous in maintaining his fighting skills, as keen a proponent of jousting as was the king.

"Ned would never invite Mortimer to do mock battle with him. And thank God for that—it would not end well, I fear." Thomas skirted a puddle or two.

"How so?"

Two bright eyes met his, something dark moving in those hazel depths. "Let's just say the Angevin temper might very well take over." Thomas knotted his fist, banged it lightly against his other hand.

"Mortimer could easily hold his own. Experience goes a long way in the face of youthful enthusiasm."

"Aye. But would it make things better between them if Mortimer humiliated Edward in the tiltyard?" Thomas shook his head slowly.

"Are things that bad?"

Thomas nodded, no more.

As always, an assortment of nobles graced the royal court with their presence. Adam was surprised to discover the Earl of Lancaster sitting in one of the window embrasures of the hall.

Impeccably dresses in blue robes over a matching silk tunic and hose, he sported silver on his belt, a heavy gold collar, several rings, and one of those hats Thomas was wearing, the exact same shade as the robe and decorated with a peacock feather.

"What is he doing here?" Adam asked in an undertone. Not so long ago, Lancaster had knelt at Mortimer's and the king's feet, begging for his life after his failed rebellion.

"Ned does not hold grudges—or so he says. And it makes sense to mend the relationship with the most powerful baron of the realm bar Mortimer, don't you think? Besides, Henry of Lancaster is no longer a threat: the poor man can't see much more than his hand before his face."

"He can't?"

"No. His son or one of his squires is always at his side." Thomas crossed himself. "God spare us losing our sight."

"Amen to that." Adam scanned the assembled men. "And your brother, is he not here?" He didn't much like Edmund of Kent, a man so different from his brother it was at times difficult to believe they sprang from the same mother and father. Where Thomas was dark, Edmund was fair, and so radiantly handsome he turned heads wherever he went. He was also something of a weathervane, his allegiances as shifting as tidal sands.

"Edmund?" Thomas laughed. "He has no liking for humble pie—which is what he and I must eat whenever we're in the presence of the mighty Earl of March." He made a face. "It irks him no end to see Mortimer strutting about as the cock of the roost."

"And you?"

"Oh, it irks me, all right. As it does our valiant young king."

"And his companions," Adam added with a sigh.

"Yes." Thomas nodded in the direction of Montagu and Stafford, standing very close together by one of the windows. "It is but a matter of time, I think."

"How a matter of time?" Adam glowered at him. "Mortimer does a good job managing this realm—together with Queen Isabella."

"He does," Thomas conceded. "The man is an administrative genius, and God knows he works day and night. But this is not his—or her—kingdom. It belongs to him." He nodded discreetly in the direction of King Edward, presently engaged in a game of chess with his younger brother.

Prince John had shot up over the winter, all arms and legs but now almost as tall as his brother. King Edward, meanwhile, had filled out, his shoulders wide and strong for one so young. All those hours battering at Adam with a sword and axe were paying off, Adam thought with a little smile.

"My lord." Adam knelt briefly.

Edward sprang to his feet and embraced him. "Adam! My congratulations." Behind him, Will Montagu stood and smiled.

"Congratulations, de Guirande," Montagu said. "Two, eh?"

"Two." Adam beamed, and Ralph Stafford grinned and said something about besotted fathers, provoking the rest of the little group to break out in laughter.

"I aim to be just as besotted," Edward said. "A child is always a gift, is it not?"

"Always, my lord." Adam peered down at the board. "Your brother has you neatly trapped, I see."

"I always win at chess," Prince John drawled, studying him from slanted eyes as green as those of his lady mother. He tugged long, elegant fingers through a head of curls that were somewhat darker than his brother's. "Maman says it's because I have the patience required to wait for Ned to make a mistake."

"You don't always win," Edward protested. "And who cares about chess? Battles are rarely fought on a chequered board."

"And even more rarely with a fighting queen," Thomas said. "Not all women are as brave as your lady mother. Remember how she rode with you to Bedford?"

Queen Isabella had been quite the sight: in armour, easily keeping pace with her son and lover as they rode through the frozen landscape to punish the rebellious Lancaster.

Edward scowled, causing a smile to flicker over Thomas' face. "I'll not have it, that women don armour like that!"

Adam had the distinct impression this was just the reaction Thomas had hoped for. But his friend said nothing more, steering the subject to the king's new Norwegian gyrfalcon instead.

It was not until after vespers that the king suggested he and Adam sit and talk alone. The hall was still full of people, the fire in the large hearth had recently been replenished with more wood, and pages scurried back and forth with wine and ale. The king led the way to his solar.

"Will Kit be joining us soon?" Edward crouched to scratch his large hound, Lancelot, behind the ear.

"As soon as she has recovered, my lord."

"Good. Philippa is anxious to have her back." The king sat down, gestured for Adam to do the same. A pleasing room, the walls hung with tapestries depicting various stages of the hunt, a large bed strewn with pelts and pillows standing against one wall. A garderobe, a little altar, and on the floor a carpet Adam had heard Longshanks had brought with him when he returned from his crusading adventures in the east. Resting against one wall was a new bastard sword, long enough that it was impossible to wield with only one hand.

"For show," Edward said. "A gift from my father-in-law."

"And that?" Adam pointed at a cloak in heavy, embroidered grey silk, edged with wolf's fur.

"A gift from our dear Earl of March."

From the sound of it, not a gift that the king set much value on.

"It's beautiful," Adam said.

"It is." Edward sighed. "But I don't think I will ever wear it."

"Why not?"

"Because it feels like a collar," the king replied. "A gift with a hook, if you will—or a bauble, presented to a child to keep it from fretting."

"Not a bauble," Adam objected. "That must have cost a minor fortune."

"Maybe not—but he treats me like a child, not a king. As does my lady mother."

"To her, you will always be a child."

Edward gave Adam a dark look. "I know that! But I'm not a child, not anymore, and with every day Mortimer grows more powerful, so inflated with pride he swells." He picked at a scab on his hand. "I don't like it."

"No, my lord."

Edward gave him a sly smile. "Seeing as Mortimer and my lady mother are not available for me to vent my spleen on, it will be you who'll bear the brunt of my anger." He laughed when Adam groaned but grew serious almost immediately. "I don't mean to use you so, but…"

"…it helps," Adam finished for him. He smiled at his young lord. "I am glad to serve you however you wish, my lord."

"Long swords tomorrow?" Edward asked eagerly, the sensitive subject of Mortimer and Queen Isabella forgotten for the moment.

"God help me," Adam muttered, "but aye, if that is what you want."

"It is." Edward grinned. "And I have practised—a lot."

Adam was still regaining his breath when Queen Isabella, Lord Roger, and their retinue rode in the next day. Edward had retired to change his dirty clothes—and sulk, seeing as Adam had bested him in four out of five mock-combats. A warm sun had Adam sitting in only his shirt, his sleeve rolled up to inspect the ugly bruise Edward's last attack had caused. Even blunted swords could cause substantial pain, but this time there were no broken bones, the heavy quilted gambeson having absorbed most of the blow.

Richard de Monmouth rode in first, astride a spirited animal that Adam had never seen before. A mare, its dark, dappled coat offsetting the light mane and long, sweeping tail. The men at the smithy stood and gawked, three stable lads came running to take care of the little beauty, and Adam whistled in appreciation.

He was already on his feet when Queen Isabella drew her horse to a halt. He hastened forward to help her dismount.

"Thank you, Adam." She gave him a brief smile and hurried indoors, her two ladies sliding off their horses in their haste to accompany her, cloaks and veils lifting.

"Adam." Lord Roger nodded a greeting. Adam took a step backwards, blinked.

"What?" Lord Roger sounded aggravated.

"Nothing, my lord. Something in my eye, no more." Maybe it was the brightness of the April day, or maybe Lord Roger had gone the last few days without sleep, but whatever the case, Mortimer appeared to have aged markedly since Adam saw him last. A fine network of wrinkles radiated from his eyes, his short hair was liberally sprinkled with grey, and there was an underlying pallor to his skin, further enhanced by the purple shadows beneath his eyes that had Adam's heart going out to him.

"You smell," Lord Roger said, wrinkling his nose.

"Tiltyard," Adam explained.

"Ah. And did you let him win so as to mellow his mood?" Lord Roger adjusted the folds of his dark robe. Black shoes, black hose, black robes—the severity of his dress was broken only by the intricate silver embroidery round the cuffs of his wide sleeves.

"No. To let our king win would merely have enraged him."

Lord Roger's mouth quirked into a little smile. "Touchy, isn't he?"

Before Adam could reply, he was gone, surrounded by clerks and various servants.

"He looks tired," Adam commented to Richard.

"He is tired." Richard frowned. "Never stops working." He made as if to follow Lord Roger. "How is Kit?"

"Recovering." Adam set a hand on Richard's shoulder. "But this matter with Alicia and Robert has her concerned."

"Hmm?" Richard's face acquired a vague look.

"She sent you a message."

Richard pulled his brows together. "She did?"

"About the contracts." Adam was tempted to clout his brother-in-law over the head.

"Ah yes." Richard nodded a couple of times. "Another time." He sped off, the plates in his new gold collar glinting in the sun.

"Oh, definitely," Adam muttered to his back.

Chapter 5

Kit had insisted on riding, relishing the wind, the fresh air in her face. As far as possible, she avoided litters, the steady swaying caused by the plodding gait of the sumpters making her seasick.

"Ladies of good repute prefer litters," Mabel told her.

"Not all of them." Kit smiled down at the old woman. "And you know how much I enjoy riding."

"Like your father," Mabel replied, and her dark eyes teared up as they often did when they talked about Sir Thomas de Monmouth, of late converted into some sort of paragon of knightly values by Mabel, who had nursed him at her breasts back when the world was young.

After seven days in the saddle, Kit was sore—not that she ever intended to admit it, which was why she ensured she looked unconcerned when she slid off her palfrey once they'd entered the courtyard at Woodstock.

This was King Edward's and Queen Philippa's favourite residence, and on a May day such as this it was easy to understand why, a soft breeze soughing through the trees that stood sentinel round the royal palace. Set in the midst of a royal demesne, the surrounding woods offered plenty of opportunity to hunt—and climb trees, although Kit suspected the queen was rarely allowed to do so. Rumour had it that the woods were plagued by the descendants of the wild beasts which had once made up Henry II's menagerie, but according to Adam this was nothing but an old wife's tale. All the same, as they'd ridden along the road that led through the dense forest, Kit had kept a careful eye on the undergrowth beneath the silent trees.

A heavy gate set in an old wall allowed access to the palace itself, the original stone buildings expanded with upper storeys in wood. A hall, a chapel, the king's apartments on one side, stables and mews—the buildings followed the circumference of the walls, creating a large open courtyard bustling with people. Nowhere did Kit see the distinctive shape of her husband—or the king—and one of the old grooms who came to take their horses told her the men were out hunting and were not expected back for some hours yet.

Kit dismissed the de Guirande men-at-arms and sent a servant to find out exactly where she was to stay. Two other servants were already busy unloading her possessions from the packhorses while Mabel barked at Bridget, the new wet nurse, to be careful with her precious charges.

Like peas in a pod, Ellie and Peter lay close together in one basket, neatly swaddled and distinguished from each other only in the pattern of their coifs—and the colour of their swaddling bands, green for Peter and a mild blue for Ellie. Kit gently brushed her little daughter's rosy cheek. Eyes the shade of a grey November sky gazed up at her, and Kit stooped to kiss Ellie's brow.

Mabel gave her a penetrating look. "It would be best if you did not fall with child too soon, m'lady."

Kit agreed but did not say as much, tucking a wisp of fair hair into Ellie's coif.

"It's as God wills it," she said instead.

"God?" Mabel snorted loudly. "It's not Him in your bed, is it?" Her face softened into a smile. "Mind you, had Sir Adam been my husband—"

"Mabel!"

Mabel chortled. "A handsome man—and you have both been blessed with fertility." She nodded discreetly in the direction of a woman on the far end of the courtyard. "Not like her."

"Her?" Kit squinted, making out little beyond a veil and wimple.

"That's Alice de Lacy," Mabel explained.

"It is?" Kit stood on her toes to see better. It was difficult to spend time at court and not have heard of Alice de Lacy, the former wife of Thomas of Lancaster. Not that anyone tittle-tattled about the dead earl—no, the gossip that clung to

Lady Alice was the story of her abduction. Some said she'd gone willingly, happy to be reunited with the man she'd loved since before she married Lancaster. Some said de Warenne, the Earl of Surrey, had arranged her abduction to humiliate Lancaster.

"Poor woman." Mabel sighed. "Childless, and by now almost landless as well." She lifted little Ellie out of her basket, gesturing for Bridget to take Peter. "Herbs, m'lady."

"Herbs?" Kit didn't follow. Mabel shuffled closer. The older she got, the more she expanded in width, impacting her mobility.

"To avoid conception," Mabel mumbled. Kit's cheeks heated, her eyes darting this way and that to ensure no one had heard. Mabel shifted Ellie into the crook of one of her arms, used her free hand to grip Kit's wrist. "Women die in childbirth, m'lady. And in my experience, they do so because there's been no respite between the children." There was concern in her voice. "He need not know."

"He must know." Kit took her daughter. "He must consent."

Mabel shook her head. "What do men know of the suffering of women?" She patted Kit's arm. "For now, they suckle at your breast—that offers some protection."

Any further discussion on this matter had to be postponed as Alice de Lacy was now within earshot. A good head shorter than Kit, Lady Alice was as delicate as a fawn, with eyes as dark as forest tarns in a face harshly framed by a tight wimple. She was unfashionably dressed, a loose surcoat atop a kirtle in an indeterminate shade of grey. No furs, no rich embroideries—nothing to indicate this was a lady of wealth. Kit made a deep reverence.

"Stand up, child," Lady Alice said.

"Child, my lady?" Kit laughed. "No one has called me that for very many years."

"Just as no one has offered me such a courteous greeting." Lady Alice smiled, leading the way to a nearby bench. "In general, they're so busy whispering about me they forget to be polite." She peered at Kit. "And the answer is no."

"No, my lady?"

"I was referring to my abduction." Lady Alice's hands clasped together, a large ring adorning her knobbly fingers. While her face was mostly unlined, her hands were not, and Kit was tempted to offer her some of Mabel's lotion, the one with calendula and goose fat. "I did not go willingly," she clarified.

"Ah."

"Thomas was not the best of husbands," Alice's mouth curled into a little grimace, "but I would never have subjected him—or me—to such humiliation."

"Ah," Kit repeated, not quite knowing what to say to this woman who was once the richest heiress in England, but who since then had lost one earldom, been imprisoned after Lancaster's death as the wife of a traitor, been obliged to sign away substantial amounts of her inheritance to regain her freedom, and who was since some years wed to a former retainer of Thomas of Lancaster. Yet another source of gossip, the more uncharitable saying it was as clear as the day was bright that Lady Alice had taken Eubulus Le Strange to bed while wed to Lancaster.

"You're Adam de Guirande's wife, aren't you?" Lady Alice said.

"I am, my lady."

"A good man—or so Eubulus says. And high in the favour of the king."

"He's captain of the king's guard," Kit said, unable to keep the pride out of her voice.

"More than that, surely. Why else would the king spend so much time with a minor knight?" Lady Alice eyed Kit. "And as I hear it, whatever land he has comes from you."

"Not quite." Tresaints and the three adjoining manors had come with Kit—as had the precious flocks of sheep. The rest Adam had received as gifts from Lord Mortimer or the king, all in all generating an annual income of over three hundred marks.

"Well, whatever you do, make sure your dower rights are adequately confirmed by deeds." Lady Alice laughed harshly.

"I know full well just how quickly a determined man can strip a defenceless woman of her lands."

"But surely there were contracts?" Kit asked.

"There were." Lady Alice twisted one of her rings round. A man's ring, so large she wore it on her thumb. "My father thought he had provided for all eventualities. He did not count on treason—or the avariciousness of Hugh Despenser and his royal master." She threw Kit a look. "But you know all that—everyone knows how I was imprisoned, then plucked clean by that damned Despenser."

Kit nodded, no more.

"And now it is the avariciousness of the Queen Mother," Lady Alice continued. "And of her lover."

"My lady, someone might hear you."

"I am but speaking the truth. Isabella and the Earl of March roll about on sheets of silk paid by incomes they've stolen from me." She shrugged. "Greed is a powerful motivator."

"It is," Kit agreed, thinking of her half-sister. She frowned: she'd heard nothing from Richard regarding the amended contracts, but she supposed the matter had been handled by Adam directly.

A high voice called Kit's name, and she rose hurriedly. "The queen requests my presence."

"Best not keep her waiting." Lady Alice's mouth curved. "Now that is a sweet child, all sun and brightness."

"She is." There was more to Queen Philippa than that, but wisely their young queen had shown little interest in pushing herself to the forefront in matters related to the governance of her husband's kingdom. That did not mean she didn't express her opinions in private to the king. Once enclosed by the embroidered bed hangings, Edward and Philippa could whisper their secrets to each other, safely out of hearing from any of Queen Isabella's many spies in her daughter-in-law's household.

"May and green go together," Queen Philippa said in lieu of greeting, twirling to show off her new green skirts and her matching cotehardie, a shade or two lighter, with embroidered roses along the hem and sleeves. Seed pearls and thread of gold decorated the roses, the veil the young queen was wearing similarly adorned and held in place by an elegant gold circlet studded with pearls and miniscule green stones. "From Edward." Philippa smiled broadly. "He hopes that by dressing me in finery, he'll save himself the shock of finding me up a tree."

"And will he, my lady?" Kit asked, returning the smile. There was a loud snort from Mathilde, Philippa's Flemish nurse, her thin mouth wobbling into a smile before it was rearranged into an expression of prim disapproval.

"That will cost him more than this." Philippa stroked the velvet of her sleeve. She took hold of Kit's arm. "I saw you talking to Lady Alice."

"I was."

"Poor woman—but Edward is endeavouring to compensate her as well as he can. That fat husband of hers has been appointed one of the king's officers, which did not go down well with my dear mother-in-law." She lowered her voice. "She says she should always be consulted on such matters. Always? Does she think Edward still in leading strings?" Dark lashes swept down to hide her light brown eyes.

"A court appointment?" Kit asked, sidestepping the thorny issue of Queen Isabella.

"No." Philippa skipped over a puddle, revealing that even her shoes matched her clothes, tied with green ribbons. "He's too old—and more useful serving the king up north somewhere."

They had reached the queen's apartments, the guard at the door bowing politely as he stepped aside to allow them entrance. Last Kit had been here, these rooms had belonged to Queen Isabella, filled with her retainers and her children. Since then, the rooms had been refurbished, the walls plastered and painted in bright colours, a recurring motif of a lady with a unicorn adorning the border along the ceiling. Embroidered bed hangings depicted flowers and remarkably colourful birds, there was an armload of flowers in a huge earthenware jug set inside the empty hearth—the fine weather required no fire—

and most impressive of all, the windows had been enlarged and glazed, the long window bench beneath strewn with cushions.

"For you," Queen Philippa said, handing Kit a bolt of silk. "A gift in honour of your newborn children."

Kit stroked the beautiful fabric. Dyed a deep violet, it shimmered in the sunlight. "This is too much, my lady."

"But you like it, don't you?" Philippa said.

"Oh, I do!" Like water, the cloth slid through her fingers.

"Make yourself something nice out of it." Philippa turned away. "And now you must tell me everything about your babies." There was a yearning note to her voice, small hands resting for an instant on her flat belly. Kit met Mathilde's eyes, received a little shake of the head in response. As yet, no child.

"My lady." Kit took Philippa's hands. "They will come, my lady."

"Truly?" Philippa's eyes glittered with tears.

"I am sure of it." Kit loaded her voice with conviction. God grant them a fertile queen because should Philippa not conceive, the hitherto so happy union between Edward and his wife would quickly sour. A king needed heirs. Kit resolved to include her queen in her prayers. Surely the Virgin would look upon this sweet young woman and grant her the child she so desired.

Philippa wiped her eyes. "Thank you. And to look at you, I need not fear becoming fatter with each child."

Kit laughed. "That varies, my lady." Where Kit was uncommonly tall and willowy, Philippa was round and buxom.

Philippa shrugged. "I shall eat less." She grinned. "And climb more trees."

"*Mon Dieu*," Mathilde muttered. "Or you stop climbing trees and hope the good Lord takes it as a sign of your genuine wish for a son."

"Would it help?" Philippa asked.

"God works in mysterious ways." Mathilde crossed herself; Kit and Philippa followed suit.

The queen pursed her lips. "Very well. I shall not climb trees ever again."

A commotion outside had the queen darting over to the window. "They're back!" She rushed down the stairs, skirts hiked high. Behind her came her younger ladies, while Kit hung back.

"She worries too much," Mathilde said. "Every month she hopes; every month she is disappointed."

"She is healthy, and her mother has birthed several children."

"As has her older sister." Mathilde sighed. "Marguerite is only three years older than Philippa, and already the mother of four. Ah well; in God's hands."

"May He bless her—and the king—with an heir."

"Amen to that." Mathilde's heavy face settled in a deep frown. "Although the birth of a prince may upset the apple cart. At least for some."

Chapter 6

Adam held in his borrowed courser. The king was already at the gatehouse, his fair hair distinctive among his companions, a loud collection of noble young men, for the day in various shades of muted green and brown. Next came Queen Isabella with Lord Mortimer at her side, and then followed a varied collection of Mortimer retainers, several royal officers and, right at the back, a group of barons, among which rode Thomas of Norfolk and his brother.

Adam sighed. It had been bad enough at Westminster, where the royal palace was large enough to allow the king to steer clear of his mother and Mortimer, but here at Woodstock space was restricted, and accordingly the king and his regents saw far too much of each other. Tensions had exploded into a full-blown quarrel when Queen Isabella had insisted Mortimer be given chambers adjoining to hers, thereby effectively ousting her son from the king's apartments.

"You spend most of your time with little Philippa anyway," Isabella had said dismissively, and Edward had looked at her as if she were a flea-bitten rat, the tendons along his neck stiff with contained rage.

Yesterday, Earl Edmund had ridden in, ostentatiously sitting with his royal nephew while ignoring Lord Roger, who merely raised his brows at this impolite behaviour but chose to say nothing. And today, the hunt had quickly split into two groups: one with the king and his boon companions, attended by the earls of Norfolk, Kent, and Surrey, the other consisting of Queen Isabella and Lord Roger, surrounded by loyal Mortimer men such as Richard de Monmouth.

The thought of his brother-in-law further soured Adam's mood. So far, Richard had evaded every attempt Adam made at discussing the need to amend the wedding contracts. It didn't help that Richard flaunted his wealth. Other than the new mare, there were new clothes, new boots, elegant gloves—all of it courtesy of his wife and her impressive dowry.

Deep in thought, Adam rode his horse through the gate, nodding in greeting to the guards. They straightened up, adjusting hauberks and swords.

"Your wife is here, Sir Adam," one of them said.

"She is?" The day took a turn for the better. He clucked the horse into a trot, emerging into the sunlit bailey. Horses, stable lads, servants running back and forth, and in all this bustle all he saw was Kit, emerging from the queen's apartments. A hand over his heart, a slight bow, and her face broke into a wide smile. His wife, elegant and willowy—albeit her bosom was impressively round—dropped into a reverence.

"My lord?" Stephen's messy thatch of hair appeared by the horse's head. "Shall I take your mount?"

"You do that." Adam dismounted and handed his page the reins. Scullions were already carrying the deer carcasses towards the meat larders, the dogs were being led to the kennels by the huntsmen, and over by the trough Lord Roger was helping Queen Isabella dismount. His hands lingered for far too long on her waist, there was an instant when her fingers tightened on his arms, all of her clinging to him, and Adam looked away.

"My lord husband." Kit's dark voice had him turning.

"My dearest lady wife." He set the back of his fingers against her scarred cheek. "Are you well?" She looked radiant, her milky skin tinged with a pink flush that he knew was due to him and his proximity.

"I am. And you?" She dragged her thumb over the skin under his eyes. "You look tired."

"Aye." He rolled his shoulders. "Long days, short nights. Our young king is presently most demanding."

She cast a look in the direction of Queen Isabella and Lord Roger, walking side by side towards the hall.

"Aye," he said in response to her unspoken question. "Tempers are fraught, and this upcoming visit to France does not make things better."

"France?" Her voice hitched. "Who is going to France?"

"The king." He looked at her from under his lashes. "And me." Among others, he added, explaining the king had no choice but to travel to Paris and do homage for Gascony. Philippe of Valois demanded it, and for all that King Edward seethed, insisting he had a better right to the French crown than his Valois cousin, he had no option but to acquiesce—for now.

"When?" she asked, her hand slipping into his.

"Sometime in June—at the earliest. And the babes?" he asked in an effort to change the subject. "Do they thrive?"

"They do." Her eyebrows rose, indicating she'd seen through his little ruse. "Meg is utterly enchanted by her little sister and was devastated when we left her behind." She laughed. "A determined madam, your eldest daughter, my lord. She tried to smuggle herself into one of the chests."

"Like her mother, then."

"At times." Kit sighed. "Must you go?"

"I must."

"Can I come with you?" Kit leaned her weight against him.

"I don't know, sweeting. It will be an arduous journey. You'd be better off here with Queen Philippa—or at Tresaints."

"I want to be with you. We've spent most of this year apart."

"As do most knights and their ladies." He touched his lips to her brow. "We can discuss this later."

They bumped into Richard in the doorway to the hall.

"Sister!" He sounded surprised rather than pleased.

"Richard," Kit replied. "Have you and Adam sorted the contracts?"

Adam suppressed a guffaw. Richard looked as if someone were holding a torch to his balls.

"Not yet, no." He ducked his head, a curtain of bright red curls falling over his face. "No time, Kit. I have other matters to deal with—important matters."

"This is an important matter—to me," Kit said. "Besides, it will not take you long, will it?"

"Rewriting a contract must be done carefully, and I'm not even sure we have to do it. What claim can Alicia possibly make against you? It is a far graver matter if she demands a larger settlement from me based on our mother's lands in Bordeaux."

"I want my name on those deeds. My name, not that of my dead half-sister." Kit blocked his way. "And as to Alicia, God alone knows what she might be capable of doing. She's as full of spite as an adder is of venom."

"That she is and as cunning as a snake as well." Richard brushed past her. "We will deal with this matter in due course." He departed at a half run, making for the far end of the hall.

"That's how he's been every time I've tried to discuss it with him," Adam told her. "My patience is worn to a thread, and unless dear Richard does as I ask, I am tempted to belt him."

"But why?" Kit's gaze was locked on her brother. "I am not asking him for anything not already mine. I have no right to do so."

"Precisely. One could argue you have no right to any property of Thomas de Monmouth, and if so, what better way for Richard to buy Alicia off than by handing her your dower lands?"

Kit's face hardened. "I won't have him cheat me out of what our father gave me."

"As I said, Alicia will not touch your lands." Adam gave her a reassuring smile. "I'll have Richard see reason, sweeting."

Adam guided his wife into the cool and shadowed interior of the hall. Two large trestles were laden with food for the returning hunters—everything from miniature pies to wedges of cheese and elegantly carved chickens. People stood about in little groups, pages scurried about serving ale or wine, and at one end the king was laughing with Montagu and Stafford while Lord Roger was deep in conversation with the Bishop of Hereford, Richard, and Lord Berkeley. Of Queen Isabella there was no sign—nor of her female companions.

Philippa joined her husband, trailed by a gaggle of laughing young ladies. Adam had to smile at their sheer exuberance—

it was like watching the antics of spring-fevered calves. The more sedate among the queen's women went in search of their husbands, some of them stopping to greet Kit and congratulate her on her two healthy babes.

"Two! I am not sure whether to congratulate or commiserate." Lady Margaret, Countess of Kent, shuddered. "Taking care of one puling baby is quite enough."

Not that Lady Margaret had ever taken care of her babes. Her handsome husband was rich enough to appoint individual nursemaids to each child. So far, Kent had three children, the latest yet another daughter rather than the hoped-for spare.

"As long as they're swaddled, they are little trouble," Kit said. "But once they start walking…"

Margaret laughed. "Let us hope they turn out nice and biddable." She excused herself and made for Earl Edmund, stopping only to give Lord Roger the briefest of greetings.

"Not much warmth there," Kit said.

"No." Adam made a face. "By now, Lord Roger has gotten used to it: icy politeness rather than genuine warmth."

"Not from everyone." Kit nodded in the direction of Adam of Orleton, the Bishop of Hereford.

"True. His friends are as loyal as ever." Lord Roger counted a number of senior churchmen among his friends, and now and then Adam couldn't help but wonder what these bishops and abbots thought of Mortimer's adulterous affair with Queen Isabella.

Adam found a platter and loaded it with food, devouring half a dozen of the small pork pies. Kit shook her head when he offered her the last one, seemingly content to sip at her wine. At the far end, the king was in deep conversation with Eubulus Le Strange, a newcomer to court, for all that he was old and grizzled and as round as his wife was thin.

"What?" King Edward's voice carried through the hall. He turned on his toes, affixing Mortimer with a glacial stare. "What is this I hear about the sheriff of Lincolnshire?" Beside him, Eubulus smirked.

"Simon Kinardsley? Incompetent buffoon. I had him replaced." Mortimer sounded offhand.

"Without consulting me?" Edward strode towards Mortimer.

Lord Roger halted his goblet midway to his mouth. "Would you want to be consulted on such trivial matters?"

"The replacement of a sheriff cannot be considered a trifle." Edward scowled.

"You've shown little interest previously."

"Have I?" Edward asked. "And here was I thinking that you had purposely excluded me from such discussions." He came to a halt just in front of Mortimer.

"Me?" Mortimer let out a bark of laughter. "I would do no such thing." His dark gaze flitted from one man in the room to the other, his shoulders stiffening.

"No? And yet you just did, didn't you?"

"I discussed it with your lady mother—as I discuss everything with her."

"Ah yes, dear Maman." Edward sneered. "In the future, it might behove you to discuss important appointments with me, your king, rather than my mother. The dowager queen should have little say in the ruling of my kingdom, don't you agree?"

"I suggest you discuss that with the lady herself," Mortimer said, bowing in Queen Isabella's direction. Edward whirled, backing away as his mother floated towards him, pink and burgundy silk lifting with the haste of her movements.

"Son," she said sweetly, eyes like shards of green glass. "We must talk."

Edward crossed his arms over his chest. "So talk."

"Not here." She set a light hand on his sleeve. Her son was tall enough that she had to tilt her head back to meet his eyes. In so doing, the thin material of her wimple exposed the elegance of her neck, the exquisite line of her jaw. As beautiful as a heavenly angel—and as lethal.

"Why not?" Edward shuffled on his feet. "I have no secrets I cannot share with my companions."

"No?" Queen Isabella purred. "Oh, I'm sure you do, my dear son. Besides, as any wise king would know, some things are best discussed in private." Her hold on his arm tightened, fingers disappearing into the fine fabric of his tunic. Edward's nostrils widened, his jaw clenched, and Adam would bet his beloved Raven on Queen Isabella using her nails on her son. "Coming?"

In response, Edward followed his mother in sullen silence.

"And that will cost me," Adam muttered to Kit. "Once she is done with him, he'll come charging back here and demand that he and I retire to the tiltyard."

"I can take your place if you want." Thomas' voice had Adam starting. "Kit, how nice to see you returned to normal size." He grinned, eyes lingering for far too long on her bosom. "Almost."

Adam slapped him on his back; the earl coughed in surprise. "My wife," Adam reminded him in an undertone before handing him his goblet. "And he won't want you to take my place."

"No, probably not. It would not look good to have our young king attempt to murder his own uncle."

"Murder?" Kit asked, eyes flying to Adam's.

"Let's just say he's been excessively harsh on Adam lately." Thomas gave Adam a concerned look. "You have to tell him if he's pushing you too hard. He'd never forgive himself if he did you true injury."

"I can handle him." But he shifted his shoulders. Edward in a foul mood was the equivalent of a devil in armour.

The king did not return. He repaired to his wife's chambers, a little page delivering a message to Queen Philippa that the king required her presence.

So instead, Adam and Kit spent the afternoon with Thomas until Kit was called away by Mabel holding a grizzling child.

Much later, Adam made his way to his lodgings. What he'd intended to be no more than an hour with Thomas and Will Montagu had become much longer, the three of them deep in discussion about their king's stubborn insistence the French crown belonged to him.

"Silly pup," Thomas had said as they bid good night. "It is through the sire that the royal blood counts."

"Well, you would say so, wouldn't you?" Adam had teased.

The May evening was laced with the fragrance of violets and lilies of the valley, the leaves of the nearby elms rustling in the breeze. Adam detoured to check on the guards on duty and even found the time to take a firm grip of Gavin's hair and tug him away from the welcoming arms of one of the village slatterns. Not that Gavin was in any way grateful, but Adam was satisfied with his efforts.

He'd been given rooms in the older parts of the palace. Floorboards as thick as his forearms and dark with age creaked underfoot as he made his way along the narrow passage, the ceiling low enough that he had to crouch. He was humming as he entered the little anteroom. He fell silent at the sight that greeted him, his heart expanding to the point he feared it might burst when he saw his two latest children, fast asleep in their basket.

"Sweet, aren't they?" Mabel beamed up at him, adjusting the blankets around the babes.

"So much bigger than when I saw them last." Adam greeted the wet nurse, an older woman with paps the size of a cow's udder. He stroked Ellie over her downy cheek. "Soon enough, they'll be running about."

"Not quite," Mabel said drily. "Plenty of months left for them as suckling babes." She gestured for Adam to sit and handed him one of the sleeping babes. "I need to talk to you, m'lord." She waved her hand at the wet nurse, who rose with a deep sigh and left the room, taking one of the tallow candles with her.

"Me? Not Kit?" He looked about. "And where is she?"

"Asleep." Mabel pointed at the closed inner door. "She didn't get much sleep last night, what with Peter fretting." She cleared her throat and sat down heavily on a stool. Her chest heaved, like a sea swell it rose and fell, rose and fell, causing the dark fabric of her old-fashioned kirtle to strain over her bosom. She wiped at her upper lip, cleared her throat again.

"What?" Adam demanded, amused by her discomfort.

"M'lord, I…" A cough, eyes that darted this way and that. "I…I…Lady Kit…"

Adam raised his brows and waited. He had a good notion of what she wanted to talk about and had no intention of making this easy for her.

"M'lord, you've been wed for nigh on eight years, and over these years your wife has given you seven children. Seven." She crossed herself, as did Adam, thinking of their dead Tom and the babe who'd died hours after her birth. He waited for Mabel to continue, but the old woman had fallen silent.

"Is that it?" he finally asked.

Mabel squirmed. "Lady Kit needs to recover fully before she is brought to bed of yet another child," she blurted, going on to explain that there were ways of ensuring his wife did not conceive, starting with the most obvious: abstinence.

Adam lifted his child closer, inhaling the warm, milky scent of the sleeping infant. Abstinence was impossible. He did not have the fortitude required to share a bed with his wife and not love her. But there were things he could do, and now Mabel was talking about herbal brews, infusions that she'd prepare for her lady—assuming he gave his approval.

Mabel fell silent, fidgeting on her stool. He returned the child to its basket and stood. To do as she suggested was to tamper with God's will. To not do so was potentially risking Kit's life.

"Find what you need," he told her before entering the inner chamber.

There was just a sheet covering Kit, its folds clinging to the dip of her waist, the rounded slope of her hip and thighs. The skin of her bare back was white and unblemished, her heavy hair collected in a dark braid that lay over one of her shoulders. The shutters were unfastened, dusky light smudging the corners with shadows, while tingeing the bedlinen a faint whitish blue. He undressed, listening to the regular sound of her breathing. From outside came the warbling of a blackbird, the distant barking of a dog.

Adam sat on the bed. "My lady," he murmured, kissing

her shoulder blades. He slid his hand in under the sheet, followed the outline of her hip and waist, traced her ribcage and cupped her breast. Smooth skin, as supple to the touch as the finest silk, but deliciously warm.

"Adam." She was hoarse, half-awake, but she turned towards him, hands coming up to encircle his neck and pull his face down to hers. Their noses touched. Her breasts were warm and heavy against his chest, and all of her smelled of lavender and clean linen.

Kit widened her legs in invitation. He needed no further asking, not when all of him was drowning in her presence. But he took his time, his fingers exploring and touching until she was panting his name, her hips jerking, her hands tugging at his buttocks. Adam held his breath as he entered her. She was warm, she was his. It was a long time since he had last bedded her, and his blood roared through his veins, his balls contracting far too soon. He pulled out, spilling his seed on her belly, and flopped over to lie beside her, gasping like a landed fish.

"Adam?" She half sat up, using the sheet to wipe her stomach. "Why…" She broke off. "Mabel," she muttered. "Meddlesome old bat."

"She cares for you." He rolled over on his side and propped himself up on an elbow. "She and I spoke earlier—or rather she talked and I listened." He took her hand. "I don't like it, sweeting, but I think Mabel is right. It would do you no good should you conceive too soon." Each finger, he kissed in turn. "We can do what we just did, or we can abstain for most of the month, or—"

"I don't want to abstain," she whispered.

"Neither do I, nor do I think I can." A soft kiss to her palm and he placed her hand on top of his heart, covering it with his own. "So I have told Mabel to procure what herbs you might need. Even then, she recommends we be careful during certain times of the month."

"It's a sin," she said, but he could hear in her voice how relieved she was.

"It is. But you are too precious to me for me to risk

your health. I am sure God will understand." He looked at her. "After all, it is His fault, isn't it? He gave me a loving, welcoming wife."

She laughed. "Are you blaming Him for your lust?"

"No." He bit her ear. "I thank Him. Every day."

Chapter 7

Like a thunderstorm, the confrontation between the king and his lady mother cleared the air. Whatever wonders Queen Philippa wrought in the privacy of her bed ensured King Edward emerged tousled and grinning round dawn, and no sooner had he broken his fast but he was charging off for yet another day in the woods, accompanied by his men.

Kit spent the morning with Philippa, long hours of sewing and talking. A fine sunny day had them repairing outdoors, and soon enough the embroidery was set aside as instead the queen and her younger ladies practised dancing on the neat paths of the herbal garden. Kit tapped the time with her foot, smiling as she recalled the first time she'd danced with Adam. A ronde at their wedding, and he'd swung her aloft as if she weighed no more than a feather. These days, Adam rarely danced, uncomfortable in an activity that demanded two hale feet.

The men returned well before dinner. Kit exchanged a smile with Adam before he followed his lord indoors. Mabel came with the babes, and Kit excused herself to nurse her children in the privacy of their chambers. It was peaceful to sit in a spot of sun by the window, a child at her breast, Mabel and Bridget talking softly in the background. Kit nodded off into sleep, awoke with a start when Mabel eased Ellie out of her hold and handed her Peter instead.

"As hungry as his sister." Kit stroked her son's uncovered head.

"He needs it more than she does." Mabel peered down at Ellie, all naked limbs as Bridget changed her. "This one grows daily. Beware, or she may take after her father, a veritable giantess."

"Adam is tall, not a giant." But she hoped her daughter would not grow quite as tall. Kit found it enervating to be half a head taller than most women—it made her stick out—and yet she fit under Adam's chin.

"Well, just in case, we'll have the lad feed first for a couple of weeks—both from you and Bridget." Mabel leaned over to croon over Peter. "Have you grow as fat as she is, my little lamb. Fat and rosy, the both of you."

Kit left Mabel and Bridget to take care of the replete babies and returned to the enclosed herbal garden. Of the queen, there was no sight, and Kit supposed she should set out to find her, but instead she sat down on a bench and inhaled, drawing in the scents of all the greenery that grew in neat squares all around. Here and there a rose or an apple tree, but mostly it was herbs—from the thick borders of lavender, already shifting into purple, to stands of yarrow and tansy, rue and vervain. In a corner stood a selection of mints, and the sight of the robustly growing pennyroyal had Kit's belly seizing. An herb to quench an unborn life. A sin. She crossed herself and clasped her hands together in fervent prayer.

"Sweetest Virgin, please forgive me," she murmured. Some months, no more, she vowed. Some time to heal and ensure she remained strong for the children she already had, for her man. Surely, the Virgin understood? As if in response, the petals from a nearby rose drifted down to land on her lap. Seven white petals, tinged with pink. Seven months.

She was still sitting on the bench when King Edward vaulted the low wall and came bounding towards her.

"Lady Kit!" Strong arms round her waist, and she was lifted in a twirl.

"My lord!" Kit clapped a hand to her veil. "This is unseemly."

"My apologies." He released her immediately. "It's just…" He looked at her from under his lashes, a bright blush staining his cheeks. "You're like a sister—very dear to me."

"As you are to me my lord." She finished adjusting her veil. "But you're no longer a lad, you're a full-grown man, and tongues will wag should they see you greeting me so familiarly."

"Full-grown?" He straightened up.

"Beyond any doubt." She took a step back and made a deep reverence. "My king."

"Stop that." He raised her. "Not between friends, Lady Kit." His brows knit together. "What is this I hear about your sister—"

"Half-sister," Kit interrupted.

"—and your dower lands?" he finished.

"Who told you? Adam?"

"Adam? No, he would never bring such matters to me. One of the reasons I like him so much, I think. Stafford overheard parts of your conversation with Monmouth yesterday, Montagu heard something some days ago, and I," he tapped his head, "well, I put two and two together." He sat down on the stone wall. "Tell me."

Kit twisted her hands together. "I—we—want Richard to amend the contracts so as to ensure Alicia can never claim Tresaints and the rest of the dowry my father settled on me." She gave him a crooked smile. "Under the wrong name, unfortunately. Richard says there's no need, but I don't agree. One should never underestimate Alicia."

"No. Or de Langon." He gave her a level look. "Should I see him again, I may well be tempted to run him through myself."

"I think Adam would resent you for taking that joy from him."

"Hmm. Well, for now, let's concentrate on sorting the matter of your dowry. I'll talk to Monmouth today."

He was as good as his word. Come vespers, a surly Richard approached her, carrying a number of deeds.

"Here." He shoved the rolls into her hands, the attached seals dangling this way and that. "Adam needs to affix his seal and return one of the copies to me." He didn't stop for an answer.

"Thank you," she called after him. No reply, not even a responding wave. Kit cradled the deeds to her chest and bumped straight into Mortimer.

"My lord." She made a reverence.

"Lady Kit." He studied the rolls. "It was unnecessary to

raise this minor matter with Edward. You should have come to me."

"I took it to my brother."

"And the king."

"No. He asked, and I told him." Kit tightened her hold on the precious deeds. "And I am very grateful that he listened."

There was a speculative gleam in Mortimer's eyes. "I'm not so sure it is a good thing that you have his ear. He should listen less to bastard-born ladies—no matter their generous attributes—and more to the men who rule his realm." He threw a meaningful look at her bosom, at present uncommonly round with milk.

"That was uncalled for, my lord," she said stiffly.

Mortimer dragged a hand over his face. Dark eyes in purple hollows met hers. "You're right. My apologies. I can only put it down to lack of sleep." He grimaced. "Too much work, too little gratitude." He sounded bitter. Nor did his mood improve when Earl Thomas joined them.

"Roger," Thomas said. "You look worn. The dreamless sleep of innocence eluding you?"

"It is decades since I was an innocent. I dare say the same thing goes for you." Mortimer gave Kit a curt nod and left.

"There goes an increasingly cornered man," Thomas mused. "At times, one can almost feel sorry for him."

"Do you?"

"Me?" Thomas pursed his mouth. "Rarely. The man is like a magpie. Anything that glitters, he covets."

"That's not fair," Kit protested.

"No, probably not. But he doesn't help himself by pushing one daughter after another into an advantageous marriage."

"Your son?" Kit guessed, carefully tucking the rolls under her arm.

"To Beatrice Mortimer." Thomas looked glum. "This summer, and the bride's proud father is planning a major jousting event at Wigmore to celebrate."

"I am sure you'll find Beatrice a nice girl. Lady Joan raises her daughters to be good and loyal wives," Kit said.

"Like she is. Joan de Geneville is a true lady. How

unfortunate—for all of us—that her husband prefers the bed of another to hers." He fell silent as one of Queen Isabella's many pages hurried by, his tabard a size or two too big. "They don't even try to hide it anymore. Mortimer even has rooms adjoining hers at Westminster. A queen, to act like a harlot!" He scowled. "And to cap it all, she spends hours on her knees in the chapel."

"She is conflicted."

"She is damned—and she knows it."

Kit stooped and broke off a daisy. It seemed harsh, to be forever damned for loving someone. Surely, love could never be a sin? Pride and greed, yes—and the Lord knew both Queen Isabella and Mortimer were guilty on that count—but love?

Thomas snatched the daisy out of her hold. "She loves me, she loves me not," he said, dismembering the flower while looking at her from under his dark lashes. "Not," he sighed at the end, clutching at his heart.

Kit laughed. "Fortunately, seeing as I am married elsewhere, my lord."

"As am I. As is Mortimer, as is the queen. Sometimes, love cannot be denied." There was an odd tone to his voice.

"But sometimes it must be denied."

Earl Thomas sneered. "Tell Queen Isabella that—and Mortimer. My lady," he added formally before slouching off.

A week after Kit arrived at Woodstock, the court was on the move, this time headed for Westminster. Normally, travelling with Kit was no imposition, but what with Mabel and Bridget, the babes, and all that went with them, Adam was obliged to organise room on one of the carts.

The king rode first, shadowed by Montagu, Stafford, Ufford, and the de Bohun twins. Of late, they formed a constant presence round the king, as bright as nosegays, the lot of them. Embroidered tabards and cotehardies, silks in daring colours—these men flaunted their wealth, with the exception of Stafford, who had none and therefore was restricted to two or three sets of robes.

In the king's train rode chaplains and clerks, a couple of London merchants, the king's old tutor Richard Bury, his brother Prince John, and at least a score of eager noble offspring, here to curry favour with their young and handsome king. Further to this were the men-at-arms under Adam's command, their tabards sporting the royal arms of England— as did Adam's.

The ladies mostly travelled in litters, but Kit was not the only woman preferring to ride, which led to a knot of horsed ladies with Lady Margaret at their head, riding just behind the royal party but well before Mortimer and Queen Isabella, who chose to travel at a more sedate pace.

"Interminable," Adam commented to Gavin, standing in his stirrups in a futile attempt to give himself an overview of the entire progress. Way ahead fluttered the royal banner, right at the back came the baggage carts—one of them carrying the two youngest de Guirande children.

"Aye." Gavin scratched at his ragged beard. He nodded at the straggly line of men-at-arms riding escort on either side. "Spread thin."

"Mortimer has his own men." But Adam glanced over his shoulder to the encroaching woods. "Have our men ride closer to the king and queen." He urged Raven into a trot and rode down the line to check on the baggage train before wheeling the horse around and returning the way he'd come.

Afterwards, he would not be able to say what it was that had him turning Raven off the broad grass verge and into the forest. A flash of colour? A sudden movement? In he went, riding through glades of dappled sunlight. The road was on his left, visible through the undergrowth. The Mortimer banner fluttered by, or and azure, and beneath it rode Lord Roger and Queen Isabella, side by side. A rustling further in, and there, almost invisible in the shadows, stood a bowman. Adam held in his horse, a hand on Raven's neck to keep him still.

The archer had his back to him. As all bowmen, he had one arm and shoulder larger than the other, but other than that Adam could make out little beyond the hood and the impressive longbow. The man drew the bowstring back.

Adam did not stop to think. With a loud yell, he pulled his sword and charged. The archer turned, staggered backwards, and released the arrow. Thank the Lord, it flew high. Eyes widened, his mouth fell open, and then he was dead, his head near on hacked off by Adam's sword.

From the road came shouts, Adam heard Lord Roger yell out a series of commands, and moments later he was surrounded by men sporting Mortimer colours.

"It's me, de Guirande," Adam said, wiping at the blood that had sprayed his face.

"Adam?" Lord Roger shouldered through. "What in God's name…" He fell silent, eyes on the corpse.

"What is going on?" King Edward rode up, accompanied by his two uncles.

"An assassin." Lord Roger pointed at the dead man and crossed himself.

"Really?" The king dropped off his horse. "Are you unharmed?" he asked Adam, who nodded, no more. The king prodded at the body with his toe. "A pity," he added in an undertone. "Had you come upon him some instances later, it would have made all the difference."

"My lord!" Adam said but broke off when Earl Edmund joined them, Thomas at his heels.

"An outlaw?" Edmund asked.

"A man on a mission," Adam replied. "He had his arrow notched and aimed at his target."

"Lord Mortimer," Thomas put in, casting a look at Lord Roger, who looked drawn.

"Or Queen Isabella." Adam lowered his voice. "She was riding closest."

"My mother? I think not." Edward's mouth thinned. "Well, we will never know, will we? Dead men rarely speak."

"No," Thomas agreed, his gaze boring holes in the back of his younger brother's head.

"Sometimes, they do." Lord Roger knelt by the body and patted it down. "Aha!" He produced a purse and shook it. It jangled heavy with coin. "A surprisingly rich archer."

"Very," Thomas murmured, elbowing Edmund.

"Which tells us nothing we did not already suspect," Edward pointed out.

"You are of course right, my lord." Lord Roger got to his feet. "But there may be more than coin in the purse." He lobbed the purse over to Richard, Edmund's eyes following it. "I shall have my men investigate this matter thoroughly."

There was nothing to find beyond the three gold florins in the archer's purse. Few men had access to foreign coins, and this, coupled with the odd looks Adam had seen pass between Thomas and his brother, left him with an unsettled sensation in his gut.

Queen Isabella insisted she required more protection, and no matter how often King Edward repeated that he was convinced she was not the intended victim, she remained adamant—and enraged, her voice dropping to glacial temperatures when she reminded her son that even if the arrow had been intended for Lord Mortimer, that was the equivalent of an attack on her.

"Killing him is disembowelling me," she stated, and Edward went the colour of a strawberry at this admission. His lady mother had cornered him on his way to mass, demanding an audience here and now.

"If that was the plan, it failed," Edward reminded his mother and made as if to move on but was blocked by the queen.

"And what is to stop them from trying again?" Isabella set a hand on the king's arm. "I need more men, son."

Edward shook himself free, backing away until he accidentally trod on Adam's foot. "You have the means to pay for them on your own," he retorted. "As does Mortimer."

"They should be your men! A signal to the realm that you will not have it that someone attempts to murder us."

"I cannot afford it." Edward snapped. A scarlet cotehardie in velvet and embroidered with pearls and silver thread gave lie to the statement. Their king needed only to snip off a dozen of those pearls and he'd have as many men to ride with his lady mother.

64

"Of course you can!" Queen Isabella said.

"But so can you, Maman. After all, aren't you the richest person in England bar myself? And I have to pay the royal officers out of my income, while you…" Edward's jaw set. "I will not change my mind."

Isabella laughed—a brittle sound that jarred on Adam's ears. "On your head be it if I end up shot dead."

With that parting shot, she left, leaving a faint fragrance of violets in her wake.

"Mothers," Edward sighed, resuming his walk to the chapel.

"I wouldn't know, my lord." Adam had few memories of his mother, a hazy outline dominated by blue eyes and fair hair that she braided and rolled up on either side of her face. A mild woman with a soft voice and soft hands—a far cry from Isabella Capet, who was about as mild as a peregrine falcon.

"She died young?"

"Aye." Adam had no desire to discuss his childhood with his lord. Inevitably, it would lead to explaining just how big a part Lord Roger had played in saving Adam from misery, not something King Edward wanted to hear.

"In childbirth?" the king asked.

"Aye." The babe had died, his mother had bled to death, and his father had never recovered.

"Terrible." Edward shook his head. "I pray daily that I never lose Philippa like that. How to love a child who caused its mother's death?"

"It isn't the child's fault."

"No. It is in the hands of God." Edward crossed himself. "Always in the hands of God."

Chapter 8

At Westminster, King Edward spent most of his days in the Painted Chamber, planning his upcoming visit to France.

"He doesn't want to go," Queen Philippa explained to Kit. "I can't say I blame him. Uncle Philippe can be terribly superior." She wrinkled her nose, and Kit was hard put not to laugh. King Philippe was old enough to be their queen's father, and she supposed that the few times he'd met his little niece he'd at most patted her on the head.

"But go he must," Philippa continued with a little grimace. "No choice, not unless he wants to lose Gascony."

"No, so I heard." Kit bit off the thread and held out her effort at arm's length. The embroidered pomegranate tree looked very nice, an adequate decoration on Adam's new cotehardie.

"A ruse," Philippa explained. "First, Edward aims to teach the Scots a lesson. Then he'll turn his eye on France and claim what is rightfully his."

"Not so rightful," Kit objected. "His claims come through his mother."

Philippa laughed. "Well, I don't intend telling my mother-in-law her claims are less than valid." She stabbed her needle through the heavy velvet. "And in this, my husband and his mother are in total agreement: he has Capet blood, and so his claim is the stronger."

"Hmm." Kit threw the queen a look. "But you are of Valois blood."

"I am. But I have no designs on the throne of France beyond that of queen consort." She grinned. "Edward wants a large family, many, many sons. We will need plenty of land to distribute among them."

"Maybe the French don't want an English king."

"Maybe. But Edward will teach them otherwise." She

sounded so convinced Kit swallowed down on any further comments. Instead, she shared a look with Lady Margaret—a mistake, as Margaret's wildly rolling eyes had Kit strangling a guffaw.

"They're so young," Margaret said once Philippa had left them. "The realities of life have as yet not crushed their dreams."

"Have they crushed yours?" Kit asked.

"No. But then I never dreamt of being queen consort of England and France." Margaret grinned. "I am quite happy being a countess, and my Edmund would make a very bad king."

Kit silently agreed.

"He should, however, be given a larger say in how the kingdom is ruled." Margaret had her eyes on the fabric on her lap. "It should not all be left to Mortimer."

"Your cousin," Kit reminded her.

"Tell that to my brother," Margaret said bitterly. "Fined and bound over by our dear cousin."

"He's still alive." Kit folded together her work. Thomas Wake had ridden with Lancaster in the failed rebellion. "He could have been found guilty of treason."

"He followed his father-in-law!"

"Against the regents." Kit stood. "Sooner or later, the king will do his own ruling. But until then, his lady mother and the Earl of March rule in his name. Best keep that in mind." She placed a light hand on Margaret's shoulder. "A few more years, no more."

Margaret covered her hand with her own. "You're right. This land of ours has seen enough strife. A few more years, and then the king comes into his own."

Kit emerged in the large courtyard and made her way slowly in the direction of her lodgings, two dank rooms close to the river. As always, the palace of Westminster was thronged with people, everything from tradesmen to clerics and nobles riding in, hoping for some precious moments with the king or Queen Isabella.

Other than the Privy Palace—at present housing Queen

Isabella and Mortimer—and the huge hall, Westminster consisted of various subsets of rooms, the grander reserved for the use of the royals. There was a smithy, a bakery, a huge buttery with an adjoining brewery; there were larders and wine cellars, endless passages, and a veritable warren of small rooms. For those requiring spiritual solace, St Stephen's chapel was wedged in at a right angle with the hall, but it was usually as full of people as the rest of the palace—unless one had access to the private upper level.

Stables, mews, and kennels—there were grooms and kennel lads, a score or more of bargemen, who were responsible for guiding the royal barges up and down the Thames as needed, and everywhere were clerks, men in dark robes who hurried about with rolls, delivered messages, and strutted along pompously behind Mortimer and the king. Add to this all the male butterflies that fluttered in constant attendance, and it was at times overwhelming.

Kit brightened when she recognised Adam's distinctive shape come towards her, shone up even more when she saw William come striding beside him.

"William!"

Her brother-in-law grinned in greeting. He was looking suspiciously neat, newly tonsured and shaved, his dark robes new and well-cut.

"A new appointment?" she guessed, trying to sound happy. William was an important part of Tresaints, but she'd known for some time he fretted, longing to be part of the larger world.

"With Mortimer himself." William stretched with pride. They were very alike, the de Guirande brothers, sharing the same messy thatch of hair, the same general features. But where Adam had eyes the colour of pewter, William had been gifted with eyes as blue as harebells, at present all a-glitter with excitement.

"He's to act as one of Lord Roger's personal clerks." Adam patted his brother on the back. "An honour, well-deserved after your service to him some years back."

William's face flushed. "I didn't do much. I merely acted the messenger."

"And risked your life," Kit said. "Repeatedly."

William made a dismissive gesture. "No more than did hundreds of other." Someone called his name, and he waved in response. "I must go. My new master requires my presence."

"Did you know?" Kit asked Adam as William rushed off.

"Not until I saw him this morning. It puts me in a difficult position—no steward, no priest." He frowned. "Richard could have told us."

"Richard?"

"Aye. His suggestion, apparently." He gave Kit a crooked smile. "One could almost think it was his way of getting back at us."

"It probably is." Kit had at most exchanged a dozen words with her brother since the new deeds had been signed and sealed, mostly along the lines of a polite greeting, no more. "So what do we do?"

"I'll be sending Gavin back with Mabel and the babes. He can act the steward for now—together with John."

Kit had stopped listening after 'Mabel and the babes'. "And me?"

"You are accompanying me to France." He tugged at her veil. "Queen Isabella wants someone to carry a personal message and gift to Dowager Queen Jeanne, and I suggested you."

"You cannot go to France on your own, m'lady." Mabel set her hands on her hips and frowned. "How would that look? You and all those men!"

"One of whom is my husband," Kit tried.

Mabel sucked in her lip and shook her head. "No, m'lady, absolutely not. I shall come with you."

"You?" Kit blinked. "But what about Ellie and Peter, our other children at Tresaints?"

"Bridget can manage the twins—they do little but eat, sleep, and shit—and as to the others, Rhosyn has them firmly in hand. No," Mabel continued, "this time, you need me the most."

"I do?"

Mabel grinned. "I've never been to Paris, m'lady. About time, don't you think?"

And so it was that in the second week of June, Kit stood beside Adam, watching a flushed Gavin ride off at the head of a small party consisting of the litter carrying Bridget and the babes and six men-at-arms.

"A month, at most, before you see them again," Adam said, his fingers closing for an instant round Kit's. "God's blood! Now what!" he said in an entirely different tone, and moments later Kit was hurrying to keep up with him as he strode across the bailey.

Kit had never seen her brother fight. The snarling man circling Stafford was only recognisable by his bright red curls.

"Take it back!" Richard spat. "Do it now, or I'll geld you here and now." The point of his sword hovered close to Stafford's genitals. Ralph Stafford was breathing hard, his back against a wall, his unhanded sword lying some feet away. They were both dirty and scratched, and Richard's left sleeve was stiff with blood.

"Never," Stafford said, relaxing somewhat when he saw Adam. "How can I take back the truth?"

"The truth?" Richard jabbed him in the leg, Stafford yelped. "Calumnies, damn you!"

"Enough!" Adam stepped between them.

"Get out of the way," Richard warned. "I aim to impale this lying bastard on my sword, and if you're in the way, I'll stick you too."

"I think not." Adam took a step towards Richard. "Put away the sword. Now." He didn't flinch when Richard's blade pressed against his thigh. Eyes dark with anger bored into Richard. "You dare to disturb the king's peace? Here, in his palace?"

"He spoke ill of the queen! And Mortimer." But Richard lowered his sword.

"Did you?" Adam wheeled, and Stafford pressed himself against the wall.

"I said nothing that isn't the truth."

"Such as?" Adam's voice was like a whiplash. Stafford licked his lips.

"I…"

"He called Queen Isabella a whore!" Richard yelled. Adam slapped him.

"Fool! You want the world to hear?"

"The world already knows," Ralph Stafford put in.

Adam turned on his toes and grabbed him by the scruff of his neck. "And will you repeat this to our king?"

Stafford blanched.

"No, I thought not." Adam released him, shoving him so hard he fell to his knees. "King Edward will not have his mother disparaged."

Richard snickered; Adam rounded on him. "And if you ever pull a blade on one of the king's favoured companions again, I'll have you in stocks."

"Who do you think you are, to order me around?" Richard demanded.

"He is Adam de Guirande, captain of the king's guard— in case you don't recognise your brother-in-law." Where Mortimer had come from, Kit had no idea, having had all her attention focussed on the ongoing brawl.

"My l-l-lord," Richard stuttered.

"I'll not have my closest men lowering themselves to fighting like rabid dogs," Mortimer said. "You'd best apologise to Lord Stafford here."

"But he—"

"I don't care. Apologise."

Richard did, bright blue eyes spitting venom.

"Your turn," Mortimer continued, turning to Stafford. "But in your case, I think the apology should be directed to Queen Isabella—and me." He smiled coldly, revealing strong teeth. "I can't wait to hear you explain to her why you called her a whore, sharing her bed with a maggot-eaten traitor."

Stafford looked about to faint. He licked his lips, opened his mouth, but said nothing.

"What? Cat got your tongue?" Mortimer circled Stafford, all of him lithe menace. For a man more than forty, he moved with impressive grace, the width of his shoulders a clear indication of his strength. He stopped, his nose almost touching Stafford's. "You do best to remember you're in the presence of a belted earl," he said mildly, and Stafford nearly fell to his knees. "I'll take it from here, Adam," Mortimer continued without taking his eyes off Stafford. "Disperse the crowd, will you?"

"Yes, my lord."

The crowd was already dispersing—as fast as it could. Mortimer stepped back, invited Stafford to regain his feet, and set off in the direction of the entrance to the Privy Palace, a cringing Stafford at his heels.

"You shouldn't have interfered," Richard told Adam.

"No? And if you'd injured Ralph Stafford, then what?" Adam shook his head. "You'd have hanged, that's what. The king is very fond of his inner circle of friends. Best keep that in mind."

Richard sniffed and set about ordering his dress. "You expect me to be grateful?"

Adam exhaled. "I don't really care one way or the other."

"Good." Without as much as a look at Kit, Richard left.

"He'll never forgive me for the king ordering him to draw up new deeds regarding Tresaints," Kit said.

"No." Adam rubbed a hand over his thigh. "But there is nothing you can do about it. Besides, you were in the right."

Chapter 9

In the week prior to the king's departure to France, the court accompanied him to Dover, and for some days the old castle spilled over with courtiers, servants, and men-at-arms. Even so, the castle was large enough to have some spaces that offered seclusion, such as the long wall-walk.

Adam had been down to check on the guards at the gatehouse, had sent off a detail to inspect the posterns, and only climbed up to the wall to take in the sunset. The sea lay becalmed, a feathery fringe of clouds tinted a soft pink by the setting sun. Gulls called and wheeled overhead, and had it not been because Kit was in attendance on Queen Philippa, Adam would have fetched her, wanting her to stand beside him as the sea shifted from blue to burning orange, the sun beginning to dip beneath the horizon.

He found an adequate spot and made himself comfortable, his head buzzing with the upcoming journey to France. Some days at sea, and then there'd be several days of hard riding to reach Paris. Once there, it was in the hands of God how long things would take, but King Edward had made it clear he had no intention of staying away more than what was absolutely necessary.

"Very wise," Queen Isabella had said. "No reason to give Philippe opportunity to gloat."

"He will gloat," Lord Roger had remarked. "Philippe of Valois is incapable of not doing so." He'd bowed to King Edward. "The important thing is not to take it to heart, my lord. Let Valois bleat and crow—soon enough the most valiant and skilled of kings will have him eating his words."

Arse-licking at the highest level, but most efficient, King Edward having graced Lord Roger with a genuine smile before returning to the matter of planning his French journey.

Adam rubbed at his cheek. He needed a shave and a

haircut, his hair long enough that his fringe was distracting, forever flopping forward. It would not do to arrive in Paris looking like a bumpkin—the French were ever making the point that the English had little style—which was why King Edward had agreed to shave off his unimpressive effort at a beard, despite grumbling it made him look too young. Adam did not agree: King Edward had from his mother regular features and a beautiful mouth, from his father a strong chin and eyes like sapphires—attributes enhanced by his new clean-shaven look.

Adam wasn't the only one on the wall-walk. From somewhere to his left, he heard the sound of laughter. The soft sound of leather soles on stone, the rustling of silk and velvet, and a low melodious voice he recognised had him straightening up. Queen Isabella was standing a stone's throw away, and beside her, as always, was Lord Roger. She in sunset colours, he in black, and as Adam watched, she leaned back against Lord Roger, his hands slipping round her waist to hold her safe.

Lord Roger rested his chin on the queen's shoulder and whispered something in her ear. Her hand drifted up to cup his cheek, long fingers tugging at his dark hair. They moved closer to the wall. She set her hands on the parapet, his fingers closed round her wrists and she was pinned in place, her head thrown back as Lord Roger nuzzled her throat. Adam chose to leave, taking the long way round.

"I'm not fond of boats," Mabel said next morning, giving the moored cog a suspicious look.

"Ship," Adam corrected. "And unless you plan on walking on water, there is no way to France but by ship."

Mabel huffed. "I know that, m'lord. But I'm telling you, if God had intended for us to traverse the seas, he'd have given us fins."

"Some of us know how to swim," Kit said. "Like a fish, in fact."

"Hmph!" Mabel gave Kit a disapproving look. "I hope you don't intend to show us, m'lady."

"She won't." Adam had a firm grip on Kit's elbow. "No need to, seeing as we're travelling by ship."

It would be a short crossing, tides and winds so favourable the captain assured them they'd be in Wissant come nightfall the next day.

"Do you recall the last time we went to France?" King Edward leaned his elbows on the railing and studied the sea beneath.

"I do, my lord." A nightmare. Hugh Despenser had taken their children by force just as they were about to sail as a surety for Adam's good behaviour. Kit had been struck mute, despair in her eyes, in her posture. He exhaled softly. They'd never seen Tom again; he had died while in Despenser's care, and to this day Kit had not forgiven herself for having allowed Hugh to take their eldest, no matter that there was nothing she could have done.

"I was but a child," Edward said, interrupting Adam's dark musings. "A boy, longing for his wronged mother. A lad, wanting to do his father proud." He hung his head. "I never did him proud, did I? Instead, I became the sharpened weapon that caused his downfall."

"Your father has himself—"

"Had, Adam, had. Beware of using the wrong tense."

"My apologies." Adam cleared his throat. "Your father had himself to blame for his downfall. Had he been a wiser and a better king, none of what transpired would have happened."

"You mean had he not been enthralled by the Despensers." Edward spat over the side of the ship. "God curse them!"

"Aye." Adam looked towards the aft. Kit was standing alone, her mantle lifting in the wind. "The secret to being a good king is to manage your barons."

"Ah. Like I manage Lord Mortimer?"

Kit crossed her arms over her chest, and even at this distance Adam could see she was weeping, likely afflicted by the memories of their son, screaming for her as Despenser's men carried him off.

"Hmm? Oh, I think you handle him better than you give yourself credit for." Adam turned his back on the distracting vision of his wife and attempted to concentrate on what the king was saying. "You are young, my lord. Time enough, you'll grow into your kingship. Until then, Lord Mortimer and your lady mother rule England wisely in your name."

"Surely, you're not that much of a fool." Edward's lower lip jutted. "They enrich themselves, and every important position in the kingdom is held by one of their supporters. Lancaster says—" He broke off.

"Henry of Lancaster has his own axe to grind when it comes to Mortimer."

"He does. And yes, I am fully aware that not so long ago he threatened me and my crown. But all the same…And it's not only Lancaster. It is my uncles as well; it is de Warenne and Audley. They chafe under Mortimer's yoke and so do I." He gave Adam a wary look. "And now that I've told you, will you go running to Lord Mortimer?"

"Never." Adam made a reverence, his knee brushing the deck for an instant. "I am your man, my lord. While I care for Lord Mortimer, I will never betray you or your confidences."

Edward gripped his arm and helped him stand. "I know. But it is cruel of me to burden you with this." He smiled sadly. "As cruel as it was to have a lad of twelve choose between his mother and his father." He shook himself. "Well, that is all in the past now. I must think of the future."

"Aye, my lord."

Over by the railing, Kit wiped her face.

"Starting with how to grovel convincingly at Cousin Philippe's feet." Edward scowled. "It's not right that the son of a king be obliged to do homage to the son of a mere count."

"Charles de Valois was more than a mere count, my lord." Son of a king, brother of a king, and now a father of a king. Charles de Valois must be smiling in heaven.

"True. Best French general of his generation." Edward patted Adam on his shoulder. "Go to Kit. She is weeping." Adam needed no second bidding.

"It's just…" Kit hiccupped.

"I know, sweeting." He drew her close and leaned his cheek against the top of her head. "I miss him too."

76

"Our Tom," she said. "Thomas de Guirande." She braided her fingers with his. "We never speak of him."

"Do you want us to?"

"I do. If we remember him, he still exists, somehow."

"He does exist." He tilted her head upwards and pointed at the summer sky. "Our Tom is there somewhere. One little angel among thousands of others."

"But I don't want to think of him as an angel. I want to think of him as my son—a robust lad who wanted to be like his father when he grew up, who chased the kittens in the stable and bawled when he skinned his knee." She wiped at her eyes. "The boy who stole the entire sugar loaf from Mall's spicery, the little lad with sticky fingers who fell asleep in my arms." She inhaled. "Losing a child happens to very many. But the fact that I never saw him dead, it makes the loss that much harder to bear."

"Aye." He tightened his hold on her. "We will talk more of him. I thought it would hurt you to do so." She didn't reply, she just turned in his arms and rested her head against his chest.

"Am I interrupting?" Thomas of Norfolk sidestepped a couple of barrels and joined them. "Your maid is looking very green."

"Mabel?" Kit disengaged herself from Adam's hold. "I told her she was too old for adventure."

"Too drunk, more likely," Thomas commented as Kit disappeared down the ladder that led to the main deck.

"Drunk?"

"One of the sailors told her the one thing that truly helped was ale—plenty of it." Thomas leaned against the railing. "Looking forward to the French adventure?"

"About as much as the king is."

Thomas laughed. "Ah yes, Ned is none too pleased at having to bend knee to Valois." He nodded at Henry Burghersh, the Bishop of Lincoln, now standing beside the king. "In actual fact, no one is pleased, but what to do when Philippe so clearly demonstrated to what lengths he was willing to go?"

Some months ago, Philippe had confiscated the income from Gascony, saying that unless his vassal did homage, the lands would return to the French crown. An elegant move, forcing Isabella and Edward to accept the unavoidable. A dangerous move, making of the young king of England a determined enemy. Like his lady mother, King Edward had the capacity of waiting and planning for his revenge.

"Someday, there will be war," Thomas stated. "And my gold is on our Ned."

"Well, with you as his earl marshal, success is guaranteed," Adam teased.

"Yes, it is, isn't it?" Thomas grinned. "How lucky he is, my young nephew."

They rode for Paris, Mabel riding pillion behind Kit. To his credit, the Bishop of Lincoln did not complain, no matter long hours in the saddle, short nights in one tavern or other. During the day, King Edward mostly rode with Montagu, Ufford, and some of Montagu's retainers. The bishop preferred the company of John Maltravers and a couple of other Mortimer men. Truth be told, so did Adam, having far more in common with Maltravers than with the king's boon companions. He'd campaigned with Maltravers, ridden to battle with him, bled with him. Experiences that, at some level, left you bonded for life. But he was not fool enough to show his preferences, choosing instead to ride at a distance from both parties.

"You're the middle ground," Thomas said as he rode beside Adam. "The bridge between the Mortimer faction and the king. Not a position I'd much relish to have."

"Not one I hold," Adam said calmly. "I am but a captain of the king's guard."

"Such modesty." Thomas rolled his eyes. "Well, an earl can't very well pass the time with a mere captain, so I fear I must leave you to consort with those closer to my lofty station."

"Piss off," Adam replied, which made Thomas laugh.

"It saves me from taking sides," Adam explained to Kit

once Thomas rode off. "I am responsible for the king's safety, no more, no less. Politics and such, I leave to others."

"As long as you can," Kit said.

"Aye." He looked away. "As long as I can."

After a week of hard riding, Paris lay before them, the air hazy with smoke from countless cooking fires. The old city walls encircled a city that was bursting at the seams, buildings standing cheek to jowl in every street, on every bridge across the Seine.

Adam had his men ride closer to the king, with one of Montagu's men holding the royal banner aloft. The closer they got to the gate, the more people on the road, but with Adam's men clearing the way, with Montagu yelling that they make way for the King of England, grandson of Philippe le Bel, they made reasonable progress, entering the city in tight formation.

It was even worse on the other side. Narrow streets made riding at anything faster than a sedate trot impossible. Houses up to four stories high rose above them, closing off the sky and the sun, leaving the cobbled streets dark and damp, reeking of offal and grime. Adam rode closer to the king, a hand on the hilt of his sword.

"We have lodgings in Saint Germain," Montagu said. "Close enough to the palace without being in the palace."

"Good." King Edward grinned. "Now that I'm in Paris, I plan to enjoy myself."

Adam swore to himself. If the king chose to go out, Adam would have to go with him, and going anywhere in Paris after curfew was difficult business.

They rode down Rue St Denis, and the crowds became better dressed the closer they got to the river, the houses somewhat more spacious and elegant, many of them with gardens enclosed by high walls. The streets, however, remained littered with rubbish and waste.

"It smells like a shithouse," Mabel commented—loudly. Fortunately, she was speaking English rather than her usual French. "Much worse than London."

"It's ten times larger," Adam told her.

"And full of Frenchies," Mabel sniffed.

"Quite a few of us have French blood," Thomas said.

"Oh, aye, but look at you, m'lord, and then look at them. You are clearly an English lord, all hale and handsome." Mabel gave Thomas a winning smile.

Montagu led the way to their lodgings: an entire house at their disposal, and there was even a minute courtyard and stabling for the horses.

"Aim you to pay your respects immediately, my lord?" Adam asked.

"Oh, he must," the bishop said. "To not do so would be a personal affront to Philippe."

"Lovely." Edward frowned at Adam. "Best clean yourself up. We'll leave within the hour—on foot."

"Aye, my lord."

"A farce," Edward spat as they walked back to their lodgings. He'd belted up his robes to stop them from dragging in the filth and had tucked the golden circlet he'd worn in Philippe's presence into some fold or other. "My dearest cousin," he mimicked. "At last, my young English kinsman. A pleasure to welcome you to the grandest court in Europe." King Edward kicked at a stone. "Pah!"

Adam shared a quick look with Thomas. Philippe of Valois had been at his most resplendent, a mountain of silk and precious furs seated in his magnificent chair. Bejewelled hands had gripped the armrests, the lanky frame had half risen from the throne in some sort of greeting, and then he'd sat back down, forcing King Edward to cross the entire length of the chamber to exchange the traditional kiss. A subtle signal, telling the upstart young English king to remember his place—at the bottom of the pecking order.

"Dignity comes from within," Bishop Henry said. "You carried yourself as a warrior prince, my lord."

He most certainly had. Their liege might be young, but he was taller than average, with the width of shoulders and chest that came from many hours in the tiltyard. A comely man, he'd turned every female head present as he'd walked slowly up the length of the room, each step seeming to echo in the silent room.

"What do you think?" Edward asked, looking at Montagu.

"I think English lions beat French lilies any day," Montagu drawled. "You, my lord, are a lion. Philippe, on the other hand, is not even a lily, more of a pansy."

Adam raised his brows. Lily or not, Philippe of Valois was no mean warrior—he'd learnt the art of warfare from his father and had proved his skills a year or so ago when he'd intervened in Flanders.

They turned in to their lodgings, two of Adam's men standing guard at the gate.

"As bloated with pride as a toad," Edward muttered. "A Valois, sitting on the throne of France when there is an heir of Capet blood."

"Yes, yes," the bishop said. "And now you and I must go over just how to phrase that oath of fealty you have to swear." He smirked. "Lord Mortimer and your lady mother have been quite creative."

"Have they?" Edward scowled. "Now why does that not surprise me?"

"A ruse, my lord. All of this is to keep Philippe happy—for a while." Bishop Henry cleared his throat. "The tricky part is to ensure you don't promise something that you then break. Remember how things went for Harold when he broke his oath to your illustrious ancestor, William the Bastard."

"Doesn't sound all that illustrious when you name him thus," Edward replied, but he was smiling. "So no perjuring."

"Precisely." Bishop Henry grinned. "Once you land in France to claim the throne of your grandfather, you don't want anyone saying you broke your vow to Philippe of Valois."

"Do you think he will?" Adam asked Montagu and Thomas once the king and the bishop had retired. "Claim the French throne?"

"Does the sun rise in the east?" Montagu laughed. "Of course he will. And for those that ride with him, it will be glory and riches."

"Assuming he wins," Adam said.

"Win?" Thomas clapped him on the shoulder. "What other outcome is there?"

Adam retired to his room—a tiny space under the eaves that contained nothing but a bed. Fortunately, they did not have to share it with Mabel, who was incapable of negotiating the narrow and rickety stairs. So Mabel slept off the kitchen with Stephen, and Adam had his wife all to himself for the first time in over a week.

She'd washed her hair, the fine-toothed lice comb lying on one of their chests. He had to smile: Kit remained of the opinion that France was more infested with lice and bedbugs than England—a consequence of her first visit to the country.

"None today either?" he teased, blowing out the taper he'd use to light his way. Their little room was lit by candles, a soft light that cast the corners in shadows and illuminated the bed.

"None." She was in her chemise, no more, the shutters open to the night beyond. A large pitcher of water was waiting for him, tepid rather than warm, but on a night as balmy as this, Adam didn't mind, stripping down to his braies before he started washing.

"Let me." Kit's hand closed over his, arresting the rag he used as a washcloth. He relinquished it, savouring her touch, the damp cloth that slid up his arms, down his chest, over his shoulders and along his back. His face, his neck, a rivulet of water running down his front to slide into his braies. Hands on the drawstring, the linen sliding over his hips, and there were her fingers, cupping and fondling.

Her chemise came off, joining his clothes on the floor. Between kisses and caresses, he backed her towards the bed—a matter of a couple of strides, no more. The straw mattress rustled; the bedlinen was coarser than he liked, but smelled of lavender. And she, his wife, she smelled of salty arousal, of crushed rose petals and fragrant mint. Her nipples stood like dark raspberries against the milky whiteness of her skin.

He gripped her wrists in one hand and raised them over

her head. "My wife. My love." A hand under her buttocks and he rolled them over, she on top. "Kiss me."

Kit complied, her breasts pressing against his chest. Adam followed the contour of her body, fingers splayed wide. His cock was already hard, and it hardened even further when she rubbed her sex over it, moaning his name. He sat up, arms wrapped round her. Some fumbling, a lot of loud breathing, and then he was inside her, her legs round his waist. He set the pace, hands on her hips giving him the leverage he needed to plunge into her, withdraw, plunge back in. He loved it when she threw her head back, when she breathed his name in time with his thrusts.

"Oh God!" Her hand flew out, clutching at the dusty bed hangings. "Adam, I…" She climaxed, a hoarse sound accompanying the rip as she tore the bed hangings down.

"Look at me." He had her on her back now, smoothed the thick fall of her hair off her face. "Look at me, sweeting. Look at me, look at me, look at me," he said through clenched teeth. His thighs were cramping, his hips grinding his cock deeper and deeper into her. Her eyes, locked in his. Her arms, round his neck. Her body, so warm, so close. He should pull out. No, no, he couldn't, not now, not when all of him was burning from within. He should. She made it impossible, legs hooking round his as he drove himself to his finish.

There was a sheen of sweat on her skin; her lips were swollen and bruised. Kit propped herself up on an elbow and brushed a finger over his mouth. "All that washing," she said, laughter colouring her voice. "And look at us now, sweaty and sticky all over."

"I like you sticky." He grabbed her hand and planted a kiss on her palm. "I love you sweaty." He swept a strand of her hair behind her ear. "I couldn't help myself."

"And I did not want it otherwise." There was an unreadable look in her eyes. "If it happens, it happens."

"But you—"

"Shhh." She set a finger to his mouth. "I take precautions. Mabel has me drinking the most obnoxious infusions on a daily basis. If that is not enough…" She shrugged. "So be it."

Chapter 10

King Edward spent the following morning at the palace. So did Kit, having been invited to present herself to the Dowager Queen Jeanne, at present residing within the household of the new queen, Joan the Lame.

"As if I want to!" Queen Jeanne wrapped her arms around herself. "That Joan thinks she's something now that she is queen—and it doesn't help that she has a male son to parade before her, albeit little Jean is sickly and frail."

Kit had met the boy when looking for Queen Jeanne. He seemed a polite and gentle child, not so much frail as slight. "The queen recently lost a child, did she not?"

"She did." Queen Jeanne crossed herself. "Terrible—it always is. So how is Isabella?"

Kit handed over the letter she'd been charged with, as well as a heavy pouch. "She wished you to have this but thought it better the pouch be delivered straight into your hands."

"In case of theft?" Queen Jeanne laughed. "Dear Joan is always helping herself to my possessions, and rarely do I get them back." She shook out the contents of the pouch. A heavy crucifix studded with amethysts and rubies fell out, followed by the massive gold chain from which it hung.

"Oh!" Queen Jeanne lifted the cross and peered at the depiction of Christ our Lord, wrought in gold and with the crown of thorns made of silver.

"Queen Isabella said it came from her mother—as devout as you yourself are. She felt you should have it, to help you remember you are a Capet queen."

"A Capet queen incapable of presenting her husband with a son," Queen Jeanne said in a bitter voice. "What good is such a queen? What good is such a bloodline? The Valois are a vigorous race in comparison." She hung the crucifix round her neck and tucked it out of sight.

"Not that vigorous," Kit objected. "King Philippe and his queen have been wed for sixteen years, and all they have to show for it is a boy of ten and a little daughter."

"What are you gossiping about?" Queen Joan joined them, moving with surprising speed despite her lame leg.

"The inexplicable workings of God," Jeanne replied with a sweet smile that was in no way reflected in her eyes.

Queen Joan waved Kit up from her reverence. "Waste of time. It is better to consider how to control the minds and works of mortal men."

"In my experience, men rarely appreciate such meddling," Queen Jeanne replied.

"Of course they don't. But strong women don't sit back and allow fate to throw them this way and that—they take control over their destiny, which usually means controlling their husbands. Or killing them," Joan added with a barbed look in the direction of Kit. "Like Isabella did."

"My lady!" Kit half rose. "How can you say such? Edward of Caernarvon is—"

"Dead. Like a rock." Joan smirked, an avid look in her eyes. "Murdered, they say."

"He died of natural causes," Kit said.

"Ah." Queen Joan chuckled. "If that is how Isabella wants to call it. I have it on the word of an English witness that the poor king was held down and a red-hot poker inserted up his rear."

Jeanne made a gagging sound, but Queen Joan ignored her. "An apt end to a man who had the temerity of preferring male company to the fair Isabella. I must say I find it highly amusing that Isabella, sanctimonious prig that she used to be, should be the one living openly in sin." She sniffed. "Without Isabella, no Tour de Nesle scandal."

"It wasn't dear Isabella who was faithless," Jeanne interjected. "How can she be blamed for Marguerite's and Blanche's infidelities? Or for telling her father?"

The story of Queen Isabella's sisters-in-law was sad indeed—the lovers had been cruelly executed, the princesses imprisoned in Chateau Gaillard. One had died under suspicious circumstances; the other had spent endless years in the underground dungeons before being consigned to a nunnery, where she promptly expired.

"Who told you the lies regarding Sir Edward's death?" Kit asked.

Joan frowned. "Sir Edward, is it? Once crowned, always crowned in my opinion."

"He abdicated in favour of his son." Kit gave the queen an irritated look.

"Ah yes, the strapping young man who seems to think he has a claim on our throne." Joan pursed her lips. "He was there, he says. A Godfrey of Broseley, since some months captain of my guard."

"Godfrey?" Kit gripped the sides of the stool she was sitting on. "Here?"

"You know this man?"

Kit could only nod. Her hand fluttered up to the ugly scar she tried mostly to forget but which now throbbed red-hot high up on her cheek.

"Clearly, not a kindly acquaintance." Queen Joan moved Kit's hand aside. "His work?" She traced the awry cross. "He marked you like a heretic?"

"Him and Lord Despenser." Kit's voice shook. "Is he here?"

"He was this morning. Why?"

"Because if he knows Adam is here…" Kit was on her feet. "Adam!" She rushed for the door, remembered herself at the last moment, and turned, offering the gape-mouthed queens a deep reverence. "I must go, my ladies."

"We've already gathered that." Queen Joan waved her hand. "Go, then. But I expect you to return and explain."

"Yes, my lady." With her heart in her mouth, Kit ran off to find her husband.

The royal palace in the Ile de la Cité was a confusing combination of buildings expanded successively over the centuries, but fortunately Kit knew her way around after an extended stay some years ago. So it did not take her long to ascertain that her husband, the large English captain, was not within the castle walls, but had instead last been seen on his way to Notre-Dame.

"Lady Kit?" King Edward came out from the royal apartments, accompanied by King Philippe. "Why are you looking for Adam?"

"Godfrey," she said. "He's here."

"Here?" Edward surveyed the enclosed courtyard as if expecting Broseley to pop up from behind one of the several water butts.

"He serves as the captain of Queen Joan's guard, and we both know he has a debt or two to settle with Adam." And with her.

"Who is this Godfrey of Broseley?" Philippe asked.

"A blackguard," Edward replied. "An abductor of innocent women, a man who murders for money."

"Ah. A useful man." Philippe held up his hand to stop Edward from interrupting. "Not necessarily a man I'd like to retain. Now, do we know where he is?"

"Gone, my liege," one of the guards said. "Had the day off, he said."

"Well, we must look for Adam," Edward said. "Uncle Thomas, will you take Lady Kit back to our lodgings? Adam may be there. Montagu, Maltravers and I will take a little walk round the nearby streets."

They hurried through the streets, Thomas with a steadying hand at her elbow. She was out of breath long before she spied the gate, but she pushed along, hoping against hope that Adam would be sitting in the little courtyard, supervising Stephen as he honed Adam's sword.

No Adam. Kit wrung her hands, not knowing what to do.

"Stay here. He may be back any moment." Thomas gave her a reassuring smile. "We will scour the city for him."

A city the size of Paris was impossible to scour—Thomas knew that, Kit knew that.

"Stay here," Thomas repeated. "You're safe here." He left. Kit sank down on a bench and prayed.

Adam had no fondness for crowded cities. London was bad enough; Paris was three times worse, the old walls enclosing an area far too small to accommodate the ever-growing number of inhabitants. Urchins, beggars—the normal complement of harlots and louts, of dogs and pigs, of vendors peddling everything from sausages to miniature carvings of the Notre Dame. No, Adam did not like all these people, the way he had to walk with one hand on his purse, the other on the hilt of his dagger. He'd have preferred wearing his sword, but foreigners were not encouraged to carry arms, and King Edward had insisted that when in Rome they do as the Romans do, which sounded like horse dung to Adam, seeing as this wasn't Rome.

It was, however, impossible not to be impressed by the city, all the way from the central island that housed the palace and the huge cathedral to the bridges that spanned the Seine, lined with buildings. There were churches everywhere, their bells ringing out the hours more or less in harmony, and like so many others, Adam gravitated towards Notre Dame and the open space in front.

Should he ever want a relic, this was the place to buy one, with offers of everything from splinters of the True Cross to one of St John the Baptist's knuckles. The moment one of the many priests serving in the cathedral appeared, the relic-sellers miraculously melted away, only to reappear the moment the priest turned his back. Adam was not interested in false relics. Truth be told, he had little faith in any relics, Lord Roger once having told him that should one add together all bones purportedly belonging to St John the Baptist, one would end up with a three-headed monster.

As he moved along the various stands that clogged the approach to the cathedral, he had the repeated sensation that someone was following him. Whenever he turned, he saw no one, but he tightened his hold on his dagger—just in case.

He ambled across one of the bridges, winked at the pretty girls who offered him their wares, and once on the right shore, he asked his way to the Rue des Lombards, where he'd heard the best goldsmiths in Paris were to be found. He had still not rid himself of the sensation he was being followed, and at one point he ducked into a doorway, pulled his hood over his hair, and studied the passersby. No one seemed remotely interested in anything but their own business.

It took him some time to find something for Kit. At long last, he settled for a small medallion depicting the Virgin and Child and a thin chain on which to carry it. The goldsmith wrapped it up in a wisp of cloth, and Adam carefully tucked it into the depth of his pouch.

He moved off, stood for some time attempting to get his bearings before turning into a street that meandered in a southwesterly direction. A man bumped into him, apologised, and hastened on. Adam sidestepped a begging woman and her sore-encrusted child, shooed away the lads that held out their hands and asked for a coin. He took a right, and the number of people was markedly reduced.

The crooked street was dark, the sunlight blocked out by the upper storeys of the narrow houses that lined it. The gutter smelled of piss and shit, the cobblestones covered with a thin layer of slimy mud, green mould growing on the timbered corner posts. A woman stood in her door holding a grizzling child. In a tavern, several men were yelling and drinking, dice flying across the table. Adam hesitated as he reached an alley. A set of steps led downwards, the walls close enough he'd brush both sides with his shoulders. But it was in the right direction, and at the further end he could see the glitter of sunlight on the waters of the Seine.

The moment he went down the uneven stairs, he regretted it. The walls above him were blind, the ground so soft he sank up to his ankles, whatever cobbles had once existed having been stolen long ago. Sweat broke out along his spine, and all of him trembled and shivered. He did not do well in enclosed spaces, and for all that there was nothing above him, he felt as if the walls were closing in on him, threatening to strangle him. His blood pounded in his veins, his mouth dried up, and all he could hear was the harsh sound of his breathing. And the sound of a blade slicing through the air.

Adam took a leap forward, turned at the same time as he pulled his dagger.

"De Guirande." Godfrey of Broseley sneered, his sword held high. "At last."

"You!" Adam tightened his hold on his dagger.

"Didn't expect to encounter me here, did you?" Godfrey chuckled. "How unfortunate. For you." Yet again, the blade came down. Adam jumped out of range, but in the narrow passage, his size was a drawback, and his dagger was of little use against a sword.

Broseley came after, his sword like a lance before him. Adam retreated, eyes never leaving the honed point advancing on him. He slipped, went down on a knee, and only his instinctive ducking saved his neck, Broseley cursing as his sword hit the nearby wall.

A window of opportunity, and Adam threw himself forward, aiming for Broseley's belly. A squeal, Broseley overbalanced, and Adam snarled, the sharp tip of his dagger at Broseley's navel. And then he was blinded with pain, his head ringing with the force of the blow to his head. Adam staggered backwards, trying to blink his eyes clear of the spots that rose and surged before them.

He fell against the wall, incapable of doing more than watch as Broseley slowly regained his feet, one hand to his abdomen, the other gripping his sword. At least he'd wounded him, Broseley's fingers coming away smudged with blood. Dark eyes met his. Ostentatiously, Broseley wiped his fingers, one by one, on his tunic. Adam took the opportunity to regain his feet but couldn't quite stand up straight, his head a deadweight of pounding pain.

"I'm going to enjoy this." Godfrey lunged. Adam stumbled backwards, raised his arm in defence, giving thanks to the Lord for the foresight of wearing his gambeson beneath his tunic. The blade snagged; Broseley cursed as he yanked it free. "No matter. I'll soon have you bleeding out of so many wounds you'll beg for death."

"I think not." Blood ran into his eyes, but he'd regained his wits and wrapped his cloak round his left hand, a makeshift shield of sorts. He'd sell himself dear, and if he was meant to die here, then so would bloody Godfrey of Broseley—

although at present Adam didn't quite know how. The sword came slicing down. He slipped in the foul slime in his haste to retreat. Godfrey laughed and came after. Up went the sword. Down it came, and this time Adam blocked it with his wrapped hand, the tip cutting through the cloth to slice at the base of his thumb.

Again, and Adam retreated, caught his heel on something hard and went down on his rump.

"Oh dear." Godfrey grinned, that warped, scarred face of his resembling one of the gargoyles on the Notre Dame. Adam kicked, his foot connecting with Godfrey's shin. Not hard enough to send him flying, but enough to give him time to stand.

Broseley edged closer, as hampered by the narrow walls as Adam was, which restricted his options to overhead swipes. Unfortunately, the sword gave him a longer reach, and no matter he was a bastard of the first order, Broseley knew how to handle his sword, a series of fast swipes having Adam scuttling backwards like a crab. To turn and run was no option: his damaged foot would have Broseley snapping at his heels in an instant, and so they played out a deadly dance, every avoided swipe bringing Adam that much closer to the safety of the distant street.

Damn! Adam hissed as the blade glanced off his arm, the blow hard enough to send him reeling for a pace or two. This time, the gambeson did not hold, for all that it mitigated the damage. Blood flowed down his arm.

There was a shadow behind Godfrey, a dark hooded shape approaching at speed. A Broseley henchman? Adam didn't think so, but his moment of distraction ended with a muffled yelp, Godfrey's blade striking him over his unprotected thigh. God's blood! The blade sank deep, blood spurted, and Adam's leg buckled. He fell, smashing his face against the damp wall. Godfrey laughed, using the flat of his sword to deal Adam a vicious blow over his shoulders.

"Die!" Godfrey hissed, raising his sword. Adam threw himself flat in the slime. The blade struck the wall, Godfrey cursed, and somehow Adam got hold of Godfrey's ankle and yanked. The man went down like an uprooted tree. Now! Kill him now! They rolled in the mud, and Adam's leg was on fire. Godfrey tried to lift his sword. Fool. Adam grinned and stabbed him with his dagger.

Kill him. He was going numb, a thick fog taking over his brain. Kill him! Now, before you bleed out. Kill. Adam got his hands round Godfrey's throat and squeezed. Nails dug into his face, Godfrey bucked and squirmed, and still Adam held on. Squeeze. Harder. Must not leave him alive. Kill. Godfrey tugged at his hands. His ugly face turned a deep red; his mouth fell open. Kill!

"You can let go now. He's dead." With an effort, Adam turned his face towards the voice, seeing little but a dark cloak and hood. He tried to stand, but his vision clouded, and he was aware of a creeping cold sneaking up his body.

"You're bleeding like a stuck pig!" The unknown man knelt beside him, his hood falling back to reveal a familiar face.

"My liege," Adam croaked. No, not his liege, not anymore.

Sir Edward of Caernarvon snorted. "Spare me the niceties, Adam."

Adam closed his eyes.

"Adam?" Sir Edward shook him—hard. "Don't you go fainting on me, man."

Adam tried to say something but instead cried out when Sir Edward whipped off Adam's belt and looped it round Adam's thigh, pulling it tight. He gasped as he was hoisted upwards, couldn't quite suppress a curse when he was lifted to hang like a sack of grain over Sir Edward's shoulders. Each step Sir Edward took jarred him, and there was blood dripping from his mouth, from his nose.

"Down by Saint Germain," he croaked.

"I know." Sir Edward adjusted his weight. "God's blood, de Guirande, you weigh like an ox!"

"If you keep this up, m'lady, you'll wear a groove in the floor," Mabel said.

"What else can I do?" Kit was frantic. Thomas had come

and gone, saying they were still looking, but so far they'd seen neither hide nor hair of Adam. And as to Broseley, he had gone up in smoke, not to be found in his normal haunts.

"The master can take care of himself," Mabel said—as she'd done countless times since the bells rang for terce.

"He's unarmed. Broseley is not—he can carry arms openly." She kept seeing Godfrey of Broseley howling in triumph as he stood over the bleeding corpse that was her Adam. Nonsense, she tried, but her heart hammered at her ribs, and she had to gulp down air, bracing herself against her legs, as if she'd just run a long distance.

"My lady!" One of the sentries came rushing through the door. "A man—"

Kit shoved by him, picked up her skirts, and ran to the gate. She recognised the hair first. That thick thatch of fair hair swung from side to side, in time with the movements of the hooded man carrying her husband. There was an instant of fear, but the tall stranger shook his head.

"He's alive."

Kit was already beside him, hands reaching out to touch her husband.

"Not here. I can't be standing like this in open view," the voice continued. Kit peered into the hood and strangled an exclamation.

"This way." She hurried across the outer wards. "Mabel! I need boiled water and rags."

"No need to yell, m'lady. I've done this before. I'll send one of the lads up with it."

"Good." Kit had a hand to Adam's back, relief rushing through her when she felt his ribs expand with his breathing.

At long last, they had Adam in their little room. Without a word, Sir Edward stripped him, using his dagger when necessary.

"The thigh," he said.

Kit was already inspecting the deep gash. "Did you?" she asked, pointing at Adam's belt.

"Yes—else he'd have bled to death."

"Not quite as bad as all that," Kit replied, using her fingers to press the lips of the wound closed. It would be difficult to stitch, but first it had to be washed. Kit left the belt in place while examining the rest of him. A long gash to his arm, an ugly contusion to his head, bloodied in places, some damage to his mouth and nose—all of it superficial.

"I can't stay." Sir Edward twitched his cloak around him. "Should anyone recognise me"

"I know." She clasped his hand and pressed a kiss to his palm. "Thank you, my lord. You saved him for me."

"I owed him." Sir Edward brushed Adam's hair off his face. "Let us hope he lives."

"Oh, he will." Dearest Virgin, please hold your hands over my man and help him heal. Kit's hands shook. "He will."

Sir Edward was already at the door.

"Wait!" She grabbed hold of his cloak. "What can we do in return?"

He laughed—a hollow sound that had little to do with mirth or pleasure. "I had hoped to ask Adam to arrange for me to see my son." He exhaled. "I'd been following him around for hours, hoping for the opportunity to talk to him."

The door opened, and one of Adam's men barged in, Stephen tagging at his heels. They came to an abrupt halt at the sight of the stranger, the man-at-arm's hand dropping to the hilt of his sword.

"No." Kit frowned. "This Good Samaritan saved your master. He deserves gratitude, not steel." She ushered Sir Edward towards the door. "Meet me at Notre Dame tomorrow after the bells ring vesper," she said in an undertone, and then he was gone.

Kit took a deep breath and returned to her unconscious husband.

Adam came to just as Kit was setting the last of the stitches. It was an effort to open his eyes, but from under his lashes he made out her face, tight and pale. He raised his hand, wanting to touch her. All he achieved was his fingers scrabbling at her skirts.

"Adam?" Her eyes were very close, her exhalations warm

94

on his face. He nodded. She cupped his face and kissed his eyes. "You're safe."

Adam licked his lips and attempted to form words. His tongue was thick, his mouth and cheek hurt, but he had to tell her. "Godfrey."

"I know."

"Dead," he managed to say. His eyes closed. Damned lids were simply too heavy to keep open.

He woke in the middle of the night. Water. He licked his parched lips, tried to sit up but fell back against the pillow. She woke immediately, and moments later she was holding a mug of water to his lips, one arm round his shoulders to support him as he drank.

"Sir Edward saved me," he croaked. "This cut to my thigh—" He broke off, having to move his leg to reassure himself it was still there. Infernal infidels, but that hurt! He pressed his lips together and breathed through his nose.

"He's dead, sweeting. I strangled him to death. May he rot in hell," he added viciously.

Chapter 11

"My father? Here?" King Edward's voice was not much more than a whisper.

"Aye, my lord." Adam shifted in bed. His thigh thudded in time with his heartbeat, flares of pain rushing up and down his leg. "Saved my life."

"And he wants to see me?"

"He does." Kit sat down on the other side of the bed, her voice as low as the king's. "I am to meet him at vespers to tell him if you are willing." She handed Adam a wooden cup.

"Willing?" Edward's mouth wobbled. "Willing? But what can I possibly say to him?"

"Leave it up to him," Kit suggested. "It is he who wants to see you."

Edward reclined against one of the bedposts. "And you do not suspect a ruse?"

Adam swallowed the last of the bitter dregs. "What sort of ruse?"

"Him the bait, Philippe the intended gaoler, and my father returns to England while I rot in Chateau Gaillard."

"No." Kit adjusted Adam's sheet. "He is as much at risk as you are."

"Not really." Edward set his shoulders. "He is the wronged king; I am his usurping son. The law will support him over me."

"The barons of England will not."

The voice startled all three of them. Edward leaped to his feet.

"What are you doing here?" he demanded of his uncle. "I said I wished to be left alone with Adam."

"And so you are—bar me. And I am mostly here to inquire about Adam's health. I just happened to overhear your conversation." Thomas sauntered over to sit down on the single stool, close enough that he could clasp Adam's hand. "You had us scared, de Guirande. When Kit found out Godfrey was in town…" Thomas mimed a slashed throat.

"Aye." Adam tightened his hold on his friend's hand. "And it almost came to that. I'd have bled to death if your brother hadn't saved me."

"Adam!" Edward scowled. "I'll not have you talking about this to all and sundry."

"Oh, I won't, my lord. But your uncle has a right to know."

"That is for me to decide, not you." Edward ran a hand through his hair. "What should I do?"

Adam disengaged his hand from Thomas' and sat up. "See him, my lord. For his sake, but mostly for yours. We will take precautions," Adam continued. "Lord Thomas could accompany you."

"Try stopping me," Thomas growled. Edward threw him an angry look. "Ned, please. Just some moments to verify with my own eyes he is still alive."

"Instead of being skewered by a red-hot poker?" Edward said.

"Whoever put that about deserves to die by those self-same means," Thomas muttered.

"Too late. He's dead." Kit crossed herself. "I hope he burns forever in hell."

"Amen to that," Edward said. "Very well, I will see him. With Thomas—and you, Adam."

"Me?" Adam gestured at his leg.

"He'll have to come here," Edward said. "He can play the part of a Dominican friar, a trained healer. But I will not see him on other ground than mine."

"And if he wants to bring someone with him?"

"One man." Edward said. "One—also dressed as a friar. Tell him to come just after prime tomorrow. We're going carousing tonight, so with any luck all but the guards will be fast asleep anyway." He punched his uncle on the shoulder. "And now we had best hasten over to the royal palace. My dear cousin Philippe will be most put out if I do not dance attendance on him." He adjusted his heavy gold collar. "One day, I'll have him eating all his disparaging remarks about his young inexperienced English cousin."

"But not today." Thomas rose, fiddled with his elaborately embroidered sleeves, and grinned at his nephew. "Look at us, as gaudy as peacocks."

"I prefer my hunting green," Edward mumbled.

Thomas broke out in loud laughter. "Liar. You love preening, Ned. And so, I must admit, do I."

They bantered their way down the stairs, their voices fading. Kit curled up beside Adam, her head on his shoulder.

"You didn't sleep much last night," he chided, tugging at her heavy braid.

"No." She yawned. "Too upset, I think."

"I'll live, sweeting."

"But you could have died." Her fingers tightened on his shirt. "And then what, Adam? How would I live without you?"

She did not like leaving him. He was running a fever, his shirt sticking to his sweaty skin, and for all that Mabel had dragged herself all the way up to their little room, Kit would have preferred to remain with Adam rather than set off for the distant cathedral.

"Why all the way there?" Will Montagu complained. He gave Kit an irritated look, muttered yet again that he had better things to do than act her watchdog.

"I pray to the Virgin, and if you don't want to come, I'll go by myself." Much better, in Kit's opinion, but the king had insisted, as had Adam, that she not walk about unaccompanied, and so here she was, escorted by a surly Montagu and two men-at-arms.

"He'll recover," Montagu said, surprising her by offering her his arm. "De Guirande is as stout as good English oak."

Kit gnawed her lip. The wound had been thoroughly cleaned—she'd doused it in hot salt water and a meadowsweet infusion so strong the distinctive almond scent still clung to her garments and hands—and a fever was, as Mabel told her, not unexpected. But she didn't like it and had ordered Mabel to ensure he drank all of the willow-bark infusion.

They arrived just as the bells began tolling for vespers. As always, people were milling about, some pilgrims come to visit the mighty two-towered church, others out for a stroll, enjoying the gardens beyond. The vast majority were hawkers, the air pungent with the smell of the greasy fritters and skewers of roasted chicken the food vendors offered in loud voices.

In all this humanity, it was easy to be invisible, something Kit was grateful for as she and Montagu manoeuvred their way through the crowds. Unfortunately, Montagu was in bright green, a matching hat decorated with a pheasant's feather bobbing above the heads of the people around them.

"Montagu! Wait up!"

Will Montagu turned, his hand resting on the hilt of his dagger. Through the crowds came a man, and Kit groaned inside.

"Imagine seeing you here," Robert de Langon said, so far not having as much as glanced at Kit. "What are you doing here?"

"I could ask you the same," Will Montagu said frostily. His gaze slid over Robert's shoulder. "And why are you travelling with Widow Luytens?"

Kit shrank into her hood and cloak. She had no desire to meet Alicia.

"No longer a widow." Robert de Langon grinned. "My wife. Another thousand pounds in annual income, Montagu. Not bad, eh?"

If Alicia resented being talked about in such a derogatory manner, she did not show it. She smiled politely at Montagu but said nothing.

"So what brings you to Paris?" Montagu asked, looking Robert up and down. The man dripped wealth, all the way from his long tunic in blue silk to the fur-trimmed surcoat in contrasting green, embroidered with red and gold roses. In comparison, Alicia looked dowdy, yellow silk doing little for her complexion.

"King Philippe holds me in high regard," de Langon replied. "Finds me invaluable."

"Really?" Montagu drawled. "In difference to King Edward, then. In fact, our Ned would be very displeased should he see you here." He moved closer. "Even more so should he hear you are held in such high esteem by King Philippe. After all, one can't help but wonder why the French king would consort with a minor Gascon lord like you." Montagu shook his head. "Tut, tut, Robert. Best keep in mind you owe your Gascon lands to Edward of England, not Philippe of France."

"I have land elsewhere as well," Robert said stiffly.

"Ah. A foot in both camps." Montagu shook his head. "Now that Edward will not like. At all."

Kit muffled a laugh. De Langon looked in pressing need of a privy. Alicia frowned, took a step closer, the frown converting to a scowl.

"You!"

"Me." Kit managed to sound unruffled. Alicia looked her up and down, all the way from Kit's worn shoes, at present stuck in pattens, to her heavy green kirtle, for the day enhanced by a simple cotehardie in russet. No rich embroideries, no gold, every garment serviceable rather than flattering.

"You'd do better to stay in the country," Alicia said, a malicious twinkle in her eyes. "You stick out like a sore thumb among the elegant ladies of Paris."

"Lady Kit always sticks out," Montagu said. "Beautiful women don't need to swathe themselves in silk."

"Beautiful?" Alicia spluttered. "Her?"

"Assuredly. And now you must excuse us." Montagu took hold of Kit's arm and forged ahead.

"Thank you," Kit said, smiling up at him.

"For what? Speaking the truth?" Montagu cast a look over his shoulder to where Robert and Alicia were still standing. "They leave a sour taste in the mouth, those two."

Montagu promised to wait for her outside, and Kit hurried up the stairs to the massive doors. Inside, the space was sunk in dusk; from somewhere came the sound of a choir, the plaintive song echoing between the pillars. Kit came to a halt, allowing her vision to adapt to the darkness within after the sunlight without. There were people everywhere, most of them standing in little groups, but here and there standing alone. She threw back her hood and moved as silently as she could to stand in the multicoloured light that fell in from the huge stained-glass window, hoping Sir Edward would see her and make himself known.

From behind one of the pillars stepped a distinctive lanky shape, shrouded in black. The hood fell back, a tumble of gold and silvered locks visible for an instant before the hood was tugged into place.

"How is he?" was the first thing Sir Edward said.

"Alive," Kit replied. Some yards away stood another man, and it took but one look for Kit to recognise this massive man. "Egard!" She pitched her voice low, but it carried all the same, and the large man took a step towards her and bowed.

"My constant companion," Sir Edward remarked drily. He smiled at Egard. "My faithful friend."

Egard shuffled on his feet. "I am but doing my duty, my lord."

"Ah yes. Your duty. To me, right?"

"To you." Egard's face broke into a smile. "Ever since those events in Avignon, I'm your man, my lord."

"What events?" Kit asked.

"Never mind." Sir Edward grinned. "Let's just say the pope was a tad surprised."

They huddled together in the shadow of a pillar, Kit relaying the instructions for the meeting.

"I don't like it," Sir Edward said. "Should he want to imprison me, I am helpless."

"If he wanted you imprisoned, he'd not have let you leave England, my lord," Kit pointed out. "And he let you go because he couldn't bear the thought that someone might decide it was best to kill you."

"Hmm." Sir Edward stroked his beard. "As a friar, you

say? And here I was, at last back to looking normal." He pursed his lips. "Tell him I'll come."

Just like that, he was gone, moving swiftly towards the doors. Egard followed, and Kit blew out her cheeks. She was not made for secret assignations, she reflected as she stopped to light a candle for her children and her ailing man. For some moments she remained deep in prayer, her eyes on the statue of the Virgin that adorned this particular chapel.

Kit rose from her knees, crossed herself, and hastened towards the exit, her pattens clip-clopping over the floor. From behind one of the various screens stepped Alicia, blocking her way.

"Who was that?" she asked.

"Who was who?" Kit stepped aside.

"The man—men—you were talking to." Alicia moved with her.

"What man?"

"I saw you! Standing by that pillar and whispering. What would Adam say? His wife, meeting men unchaperoned." Alicia snickered. "Oh, I am so looking forward to telling him."

Kit was tempted to slap her. On the other hand, having her believe Kit was meeting men on the sly was better than the alternative. She held her tongue.

"I am right, aren't I? A lover."

Kit pushed her aside, but Alicia grabbed hold of her. "Or maybe not. Who would you know here in Paris?"

She was quick, Kit thought. Too quick.

"If not a lover, then who?"

Kit made as if to yank free.

Alicia tightened her hold. She had her mother's fingers, long and strong. "Who?"

"Let me go," Kit said.

"Tall, hiding under hood and cloak," Alicia mused out loud. Kit pulled free, half running for the door with Alicia at her heels. "Might it have something to do with the friar you smuggled out of England last year?" Alicia asked just as they stepped outside.

Kit whirled. "How do you—" She swallowed back on the rest.

"Robert told me." Alicia eyed her speculatively. "A friar, travelling in haste. A hooded man, meeting you in Paris. Could it be—"

"Don't," Kit interrupted. "Leave this alone. For your own sake."

"As if you care about me." Alicia sneered. "If that man is who I think it is, who will pay me the most? King Edward for my silence or King Philippe for the information?"

Kit swallowed audibly.

Alicia laughed. "It is, isn't it? Edward, the second of that name, is alive, not dead."

"Nonsense," Kit said briskly. "You were there when we buried him."

"When we buried someone," Alicia corrected.

"Kit?" Montagu stood some steps further down. "Is she bothering you?"

"Oh, you have no notion, Sir William." Alicia snickered before disappearing into the crowd.

"What was that all about?" Montagu asked.

"Alicia at her most endearing," Kit replied while her stomach churned. This was bad—very bad.

Chapter 12

When she returned from her excursion to Notre Dame, it was to a tossing Adam, and such was Kit's concern for her husband that she forgot about Alicia—or rather, she shoved the thought of her sly sister to the back of her mind.

"Cold water to wash him with, more willow bark to drink, and I'll need more yarrow and meadowsweet," she ordered. Stephen scampered off to do as bid while Mabel joined Kit by the bed.

"Infection," the old woman said, pressing a finger into the red area just above Adam's thigh wound. Even unconscious, he jerked. "You're going to have to open it again, m'lady."

"I know." Kit's hand shook. "Fetch some men to hold him still—and I'll need hot water and salt." Mabel shuffled off, already calling for help.

"Adam?" She shook him; he grunted. "I have to cut the wound open." His tongue darted out to wet his dry lips, a sliver of grey eyes visible beneath his lids. She took his hand. "It will hurt." Yet another grunt. His fingers tightened round hers.

Thomas was the first man to come rushing up the stairs, accompanied by Montagu. To Kit's surprise, next came Bishop Henry, and soon enough there were four men in their small room.

Stephen came with salt and herbs; Mabel huffed and puffed as she brought clean rags, a scullion bringing up the rear with a heavy pot filled with steaming water.

Kit had Mabel throw in the salt and stir. She heated her knife in the flame of a candle, nodded to the men to hold on, and cut. Pus spurted, Adam's voice rose in a hoarse scream, and the poor bishop was thrown to the floor but bounded back immediately, throwing himself over Adam's left arm to keep it still.

Thomas had Adam's leg in a vice, Stephen was sitting on his calf, and Kit went on with her cutting. Two abscesses, and she lanced and pressed until the pus was gone, replaced by blood. Adam was no longer moving, but he was breathing, his pulse thrumming under the finger she held to his groin. Salted water, and Adam's limbs jerked. She poured the hot water repeatedly over the wound, finished by washing it with vinegar before stitching it together. More herbs, yarrow, and meadowsweet in layers, a tight bandage, and Kit sank to her knees, trying to stop her hands from shaking.

Stephen and the scullion cleaned up as best as they could, clean linen was brought, and soon enough Adam was lying in dry sheets. Bishop Henry excused himself, promising he'd pray for Adam's recovery. Montagu went with him.

"Do you need more help?" Thomas asked. Kit shook her head. All she wanted was to be alone with her man. Once they were all gone, she opened the window wide. In the bed, Adam stirred, and she managed to get him to drink some of the willow bark. He drifted off into feverish sleep, and she curled up beside him, clinging to his hand as she prayed that the Virgin heal him.

She woke to the sound of the bells of prime. Beside her, Adam was still sleeping, but he was no longer hot as a furnace, and at some point during the night he had drunk what was left in the mug. Heavy steps on the stairs, and Kit flew to her feet, brushed at her crumpled skirts, found her veil.

The door creaked open. The scullion again, holding a lantern. "A Brother Edward to see you, mistress. Says he's a healer."

"Let him in."

No sooner had Sir Edward and Egard entered but there were more footsteps. In the doorway stood the king, in only his shirt and hose. With his hair rumpled, his skin still rosy with sleep, he looked touchingly young. Sir Edward made a strangled sound and opened his arms. The king took a step towards him before coming to a halt. The arms remained open. Father and son looked at each other for a long time.

"Come here, son." Sir Edward's voice shook. Kit had to look away as they embraced.

She retreated to the further side of the bed. Adam had woken, and she slipped her hand into his. He pressed gently, enough for her to meet his clear eyes, see the soft curve to his mouth. The door opened again. Thomas was as undressed as the king but had covered himself with a cloak. He stood on the threshold, and all of him wilted under the weight of Sir Edward's eyes.

"Brother," Sir Edward said with sufficient chill to freeze the Seine.

"Sire." Thomas knelt.

"Not anymore," Sir Edward told him. "These days I am nothing but Edward of Caernarvon. No, wait, I'm not even that: Edward of Caernarvon is dead and buried since some years back."

King Edward winced. "I didn't know—"

"That I would be deposed? Killed, even?"

King Edward shook his head. "I just—"

"Did as your faithless whore of a mother told you," Sir Edward filled in bitterly.

"Father, I—"

Sir Edward waved him silent. "You were a child. Thomas here was not."

"I was not. Which was why I had to act before you and Despenser brought ruin to us all."

"Me?" Sir Edward slammed his fist into the rickety table. "I am the king! I do as I please!"

"Begging your pardon, but that is precisely why you no longer are the king," Thomas replied.

"How dare you?" Sir Edward demanded, taking a step forward. Egard set a hand to his arm, no more, and Sir Edward inhaled, held his breath, and let it out loudly. "Just go. I have no words to say to you."

Thomas bowed slightly. "As you wish. I just…" He licked his lips. "I wanted to see with my own eyes that you were still alive—not murdered, as some say."

"King Edward was murdered. Sir Edward remains alive,"

was the curt reply, and it struck Kit that maybe it wasn't Godfrey who had started the rumour about Edward II's death. An elegant revenge, to spread this lurid legend that would forever besmirch the reputation of Queen Isabella and Mortimer.

Thomas left, looking so bereft Kit's heart went out to him.

"Kit, we should leave." Adam bit his lip as he swung his leg over the side of the bed. "Egard, come and give me a helping hand."

"You mustn't move," Kit protested.

"Too late, sweeting." But he collapsed back down, breathing heavily.

"You stay," King Edward said. "My fath—Brother Edward and I will repair to the passage."

They did not stay away for long, both of them looking as if they'd wept when they returned.

"We have to go," Sir Edward said.

"Do you…" Edward cleared his throat. "Do you need funds?"

"No." Sir Edward shared a look with Egard. "We have been most gainfully employed these last few months, haven't we?" He patted his son on the shoulder. "You were more than generous last summer—well, generous may be the wrong word, seeing as it is ultimately my kingdom, but still."

Edward flushed.

Sir Edward cuffed him lightly. "What is done is done, Ned. As I said, I don't hold you responsible." He pulled his son into a rough embrace, and they clung to each other like limpets.

"Where will you go?" Edward's voice was thick with tears.

"Wherever my fancy takes me." Sir Edward wiped his eyes. "Italy, I think. Or Spain."

"Maybe…" Edward sounded wistful.

"No," Sir Edward said. "We will likely not meet again. Too much of a risk for you, son." He nodded at Egard. "My man and I will leave Paris today, and you will go back to England and become the king you're destined to be." He smiled down at Adam. "According to de Guirande, you will be a great king, more like your grandfather than your failure of a father."

"Don't, Father."

"The truth, Ned. Only a failed king ends up an exile in disguise." Sir Edward shrugged. "And just so you know, a great king does not allow others to rule in his stead."

"I already know that." Edward raised his chin, blue eyes meeting his father's.

"Good. I can't wait to hear the French she-wolf has been adequately collared—she and that accursed Mortimer." Sir Edward clasped his son's shoulder. "God be with you always." He nodded a farewell to Adam and Kit before disappearing through the door, Egard hastening after him. King Edward sank down on the single stool and hid his face in his hands. Kit fidgeted, not quite sure what to do. In the end, she opted for offering him some wine.

"Thank you." The king raised wet eyes her way. "He looked well, didn't he?"

"He did." She smiled at him. "You did the right thing, letting him go. A man such as him to rot behind walls…" She shook her head. "Like caging a hawk in the darkness."

"Aye." After finishing his wine, the king left, closing the door behind him.

"Will we ever see him again?" Kit asked Adam once they were alone.

"I hope not." Adam gave her a dark look. "I didn't like it, how he urged King Edward to punish them."

"What did you expect? That he forgive them?" Kit had him lie down as she inspected his leg, still swollen and bruised, but no longer red with infection.

"No." Adam covered his face with his arm. "But he brought it on himself—something he seems to forget."

"Does this hurt?" she asked, prodding none too gently at his leg.

"Aye. But that's because you're using more force than you normally would." He lowered his arm. "How long must I remain in bed?"

"Some more days."

"The ceremony is the day after tomorrow."

"And you will not attend." She kissed his brow. "The king will be adequately accompanied—a bishop on one side, an earl on the other."

They were both there two days later, Kit so angry she refused to speak to Adam. He ignored her and concentrated on the events unfolding before them. The large hall of the royal palace was filled with the scions of the French nobility, standing as tightly packed as salted herrings in a barrel in their eagerness to watch the young English king bend knee to Philippe Valois. The air was heavy with the scents of roses and lavender, of wormwood and mint—some of the ladies present were wearing finery normally consigned to the depths of their storage chests, carefully packed away with herbs to deter moths.

King Philippe, magnificent in a fleurs-de-lis mantel, sat on his throne while King Edward approached—just as magnificent, the scarlet of his embroidered samite robes contrasting with his fair hair—kneeling once upon entering, a second time halfway down the room, a third time at Philippe's feet. Every time he knelt, Edward's jaw tightened. Once at Philippe's feet, he stared straight ahead as he spoke the words of his vow, his hands clasped firmly between Philippe's.

King Edward's oath was short—and conspicuously lacked a promise to serve Philippe during war. A hushed whisper flew through the room; Queen Joan's hands tightened on the shoulders of her young son, Prince Jean. King Philippe was not pleased. His mouth turned down; his bushy brows lowered threateningly over his deep-set eyes. One heartbeat, two, and Adam moved that much closer to his king, eyes on the French men-at-arms who stood on each side of the dais.

Philippe cleared his throat and pasted a benign smile on his face. King Edward kissed his hand, and Philippe rose, as did King Edward, turning to face the assembled people. When they stood side by side, it was like seeing an English sun beside a French moon.

Adam was given the honour of attending on King Edward during the following feast. If anything, this had Kit throwing black looks not only at Adam but also at the king.

"You must rest," she hissed. "Not stand about for hours while dancing attendance on your precious king."

"*Our* precious king," Adam corrected. "And if it gets too bad, I'll have someone take over."

Kit snorted, clearly not convinced. "Let me check on it."

"Here?" He looked about the huge hall.

"Of course not here." She led the way down one of the side aisles to a narrow staircase.

There was sufficient room beside the stairs for her to kneel down and undo his hose, a light finger ensuring the bandage sat as it should. It didn't hurt much—it mostly itched—and Adam had been injured often enough to know the itching was a good thing, a sign of healing. Another good sign was the other effect her touch had, those fingers so close to his groin causing his member to harden somewhat.

"Adam!" But her eyes glittered, her hands more intrusive than strictly necessary as she helped him adjust his clothing.

Adam kept Edward's goblet supplied with wine while his young lord feasted on capons with grapes and pigeon breasts boiled in wine. Warm bread, smoked tongue, pork with prunes, roasted lamb—Adam's mouth watered.

The two kings shared a trencher, conversing lightly about horses and dogs, the merits of Norwegian birds of prey, and the future of the papacy. Philippe was of the opinion the pope should remain in Avignon forever, while Edward made the point that it was in Rome, not Avignon, where St Peter had died a martyr's death.

"I heard some interesting news today," Philippe said casually, spearing a piece of cheese with his eating knife. "Very interesting." He glanced at Edward. "Does you credit, I suppose. After all, deception is better than patricide."

"I do not know what you are referring to," Edward said stiffly. "Yes, my father is dead—but I can assure you not by my hand."

"Is he?" Philippe drummed his fingers on the table. "And

here I have an informant telling me your father lives."

"The informant is wrong—or a liar."

"Well, someone is lying, that's for sure." Philippe belched discreetly. "Imagine what havoc it would cause if your father should reappear, risen from the dead." He chuckled. "What would dear Isabella do then? Come to think of it, what would you do? He'd be entitled to have you hanged, drawn, and quartered for treason."

"We will never know, dear cousin," Edward replied calmly. "As I said: lies. Someone is trying to sell you a falsehood. I hope you didn't pay too much for it."

Philippe clouded. "De Langon swore it was true."

"De Langon? Robert de Langon?" Edward's knuckles stood stark against the skin of his hand.

"The same." Philippe smirked. "A useful man."

"My subject," Edward reminded him coldly.

"And mine." Philippe stared him down. "He holds his Gascon lands from you, but you hold them from me."

All the way to their lodgings, King Edward strode in icy silence. Only once they were inside the gate did he speak, whirling to glare at them all.

"How?" he demanded. "What has de Langon found out that has him putting two and two together? Aye, he must have suspected that friar he was to kill was someone important, but from there to tell that accursed Philippe he is certain my father is alive…"

Kit paled. "Dear God, I forgot!"

"Forgot what?" Edward asked.

"The day I went to meet Sir Edward in Notre Dame, we met Alicia and de Langon." Words spilled out of her, a garbled description of events that had Adam closing his eyes.

"Why haven't you told us this before?" the king demanded.

"It was Adam." Kit twisted her hands together. "He was so ill when I came back." She lifted her shoulders. "I'm sorry."

"Sorry!" Edward exclaimed. "You silly goose of a woman! How could you forget something that important?"

"I—" Kit began.

"Silence!" Edward pointed at the door. "Out."

"My lord," Adam said, stepping forward.

"I said out!" The king made as if to shove Kit, who beat a hasty retreat. Adam went to follow. "You stay. I haven't given you leave to go."

Adam turned slowly. The king was marching up and down the little room, for all the world like a caged bear. Thomas was leaning against one of the walls, arms crossed over his chest. Other than the three of them, the room was empty.

Edward stopped in front of Adam. "Find them. Do what you have to do to silence them."

"My lord?"

"You heard!" Edward hissed viciously. "You've been wanting to gut de Langon since you found out he's the one who ambushed you. Now I'm telling you to do so. And as to that wife of his—" He broke off, slammed a fist against a wall. "Well, I know exactly what to do with her."

"How am I to find them here?" Adam asked.

"I'll help." Thomas pushed himself off the wall.

"Make sure you're back before dawn. We ride for the coast at daybreak." He scowled at Adam. "And if you fail, I'll have your wife whipped."

Adam's fists knotted. Let him try, and he'd belt the young fool, king or no king.

"Come." Thomas had Adam by the arm. "Best get started."

"I have to rest." Adam's bandaged leg throbbed after hours of walking, and even with a stick he was hobbling. He jerked his thumb in the direction of a small tavern. "Wine?"

"Why not?" Thomas found them a table, ordered wine and something to eat, and slouched over the table. "God's blood, but he was angry."

Adam grunted, no more. Unfairly so in his opinion. Aye, Kit should have told them about her conversation with Alicia, but was it so strange she'd been distracted when she came home to find her husband burning with fever?

"He'd never as much as break a hair on her head," Thomas

112

continued. "He is too fond of Kit to do so."

"Is he? That's not how it sounded to me just now."

"He was angry. You know us Angevins—we suffer greatly from the capital sin of ire. Once he has calmed down, he'll come to his senses." Thomas chuckled. "An angry Angevin is best ignored. Chances are if you do as they demand while they're enraged, you end up killing a future saint. Look at Henry, second of that name, and St Thomas."

"So what does that mean exactly?"

"It means we find de Langon and his wife, but you abstain from slitting his throat." Thomas shoved a bowl of hot stew in Adam's direction. "Eat. Next we go to the other side of the river."

Robert de Langon was an ostentatious man—which was how they finally found him and his wife, seated at an early supper in the private residence they'd rented from an affluent Paris merchant. Thomas marched into the dark-timbered hall, smiled wolfishly, and demanded that they both accompany him—or die on the spot.

De Langon protested and called for his men—futile, as Adam and Thomas had knocked all six of them unconscious before tying them up. Alicia rushed for the inner door but never made it, Thomas grabbing her by the back of her kirtle. The fabric tore along one of the seams.

"A litter," Thomas suggested, leaving Adam to guard the pair while he went out to find one. De Langon made one more attempt to flee, Adam clobbered him over the head, and when Thomas returned, Alicia was screaming invectives at Adam while cradling her husband's bleeding head in her lap.

"They're still alive," Adam commented laconically. He was in a hurry to get back to his lodgings and Kit.

"For now," Thomas replied, and Alicia's screaming took on a hysterical edge. Thomas slapped her, told her she would most certainly die of a slit throat unless she shut up, and some while later they were all in the litter.

They returned to a household in uproar. If he'd been in a foul mood previously, now the king was incandescent, and his men fell

113

over themselves in their efforts to contain his rage. Packed chests were being loaded onto a cart, the horses were already saddled, and the first thing the king said was that they were leaving. Now.

"They close the gates at sundown. We must be on our way before that."

"And what do we do with de Langon and his wife?" Thomas asked.

"Take them with us. I'll deal with them later."

"Why the hurry?" Thomas asked.

"Why?" Edward thrust a piece of parchment at Thomas. "Here's why! No sooner do I turn my back but yet another meddlesome earl decides to act." He glanced at Adam. "Can you ride?" he asked gruffly.

"Do I have a choice?"

"Not really." The king moved closer. "And I didn't mean what I said about Lady Kit."

"No need to tell me that, my lord." Adam dipped his head in the direction of Kit, presently closing the straps on one of their bulging saddlebags.

"Hmm," the king said and went back to his shouting.

In the meantime, Thomas had gone quite still, blinking down at the message in his hand.

"What?" Adam asked.

"My fool of a brother is riding to Avignon," Thomas groaned. "Apparently, he aims to tell the pope our former king languishes in a dungeon at Corfe and must be freed."

"Much good it will do him."

"Other than marking him as a potential traitor, none at all," Thomas replied. "This is from Mortimer, which means he must have spies in Edmund's household."

"Not exactly surprising, is it? Kent likely has spies among Mortimer's men."

"He does?" Thomas crumpled the parchment together. "Not quite as easy as you seem to think, dear Adam. For whatever reason, Mortimer inspires a lot of loyalty."

Which just went to prove Thomas had tried to place spies with Lord Roger. But at present, Adam wasn't all that interested. He needed to talk to his wife.

Chapter 13

Four days later, they were back on the coast, England lying just beyond the hazy horizon.

"At last!" King Edward said before calling for a halt. No sooner was he off his horse but he disappeared behind a stand of trees. When he returned, the entire party had dismounted and were either sitting or reclining in the grass.

"Will you tell us why you've had us riding as if all the hounds of hell were at our heels?" John Maltravers asked, sharing a look with Bishop Henry Burghersh.

"Cousin Philippe expressed a certain dissatisfaction with the wording of my vows," Edward replied, thereby breaking what had been a sullen silence interspersed only with short orders.

"So we've been fleeing the French king?" Maltravers' brows rose.

"No. But by absenting ourselves, we've made sure he didn't succumb to the temptation of having us restrained."

"A good liar," Kit commented in a low voice to Adam. She'd kept her distance from the king the last few days and had every intention of continuing to do so. "Although I don't understand why this business with Edmund requires him to return home so hastily."

"Me neither. Maybe there's some truth in what he said about Philippe." Adam stretched out in the grass, massaging his thigh. The cut had closed neatly, but all this riding about had not done him any favours—yet another sin Kit held the king responsible for.

"And them?" Maltravers asked, gesturing at de Langon and Alicia. "What is their part in all this?"

"None. My business with them is of a more personal nature," the king said, giving de Langon and his wife a wolfish smile. Fettered and gagged, Alicia was still in the purple

Byzantine brocade she'd been wearing when she was carried off, Robert's sleeves were dirty round the edges, and neither of them looked as if they'd slept much, the impression further reinforced by the bandage that decorated Robert's head.

"I hit him with the pommel," Adam had told Kit some days ago. "Not much of a blow, really, but the corner tore his scalp. Head wounds always bleed a lot."

"He might need someone to see to it."

"Not you," Adam said. "You're not going anywhere near either Robert or Alicia, and neither is Mabel."

Kit protested, more for form's sake than any genuine desire to spend time with her sister or brother-in-law. Adam's eyes had hardened as he repeated his order, making it very clear he would not tolerate any disobedience in this matter.

Soon enough, the king was back in the saddle, and with a lot of groaning his companions sat up. In the distance, the waves pounded the shore; before them stretched what looked like a sea of grass—an easy ride to the distant village of Wissant. Except it wasn't, the entire afternoon spent crossing one dyke after the other.

"A pox on these damned marshes," Adam muttered. "I'm wet through after all this up and down in water."

"Aye," Mabel commented from where she was sitting behind Kit. "Why not build nice bridges instead?"

"It floods," Kit explained. "Anything you build may very well be swept away."

"Oh." Mabel had been uncharacteristically quiet for most of their journey, even if now and then Kit had caught her throwing Alicia the odd, anguished look. Now, however, she tightened her hold on Kit's waist and whispered, "Why?"

"Hmm?" Kit guided the palfrey down one slope and sent it splashing through the shallow water before urging it up the next slope.

"Lady Alicia," Mabel clarified. "Why is she here? What has she done to displease the king so?"

"Why do you think she's displeased him?"

"It may have something to do with the fact that she rides

with her hands tied to the man on the same horse," Mabel retorted sharply. "Like a criminal. So what has she done, poor misguided lamb, to deserve being treated so?"

Kit wasn't quite sure what to tell her. The truth was out of the question. Adam came to her rescue, riding his big stallion as close as he could.

"Her husband has been spying on the king," he confided in a low tone. "And King Edward believes she may have helped him."

He met Kit's eyes and gave her a wry smile. As a lie, it served.

"Spies?" Mabel clutched at Kit. "Mother of God, poor Sir Thomas would revolve in his grave to hear such." She sighed. "Well, if he had one, that is."

"They were all buried at some point." So, at least, Kit hoped. Sir Thomas had been hanged in Shrewsbury in 1322, his head set to decorate a pike above the main gate, his body left to rot on a gibbet.

"Aye, when there was nothing left of them but bones picked clean by carrion." Mabel mumbled a prayer under her breath. She cleared her throat. "So what happens to spies, m'lady?"

"I don't know." Kit glanced in the direction of Alicia. "I trust the king will find it in him to be merciful."

At long last, they reached a stretch of passable road bordering the sandy shores. Montagu was despatched to find them a ship, while Ufford and some of the others galloped off to arrange lodgings.

"Come tomorrow, we'll be safely on our way to England," King Edward said to Kit. It was the first time he'd spoken to her since his heated words in Paris.

"Yes, my lord," she replied politely.

"I imagine you must be longing for your little ones," he persisted.

"Yes, my lord."

"Look, Lady Kit." He cleared his throat. "My apologies." With that he was off, sending his horse into a wild gallop along the water's edge.

"Apologies for what?" Mabel asked.

"Nothing," Kit replied.

"Nothing, m'lady?" Mabel snorted. "Of late, you've been ignoring the poor lad, and him looking as abject as a whipped dog whenever you've been near." She cackled. "Men. They're all very much the same, no matter if they be kings, knights, or simple peasants. Give them a strong woman and they go all weak-kneed."

"Am I a strong woman?" Kit asked.

"You?" Mabel burst out in laughter. She was still chuckling when they reached the inn.

Adam had been wondering how much longer the king intended to keep Alicia and Robert waiting before he dealt with them. On this their last evening on the Continent, the king apparently found the time ripe and ordered Adam and Thomas to join him in his chambers—together with Alicia and de Langon.

The king's room was bright with the light of the setting sun pouring in through a series of small glazed windows in the wall facing the west. A large bed showed the indent of the king's body, he'd tracked mud over the fine carpet the innkeep had produced upon hearing his guest was the king of England, and when Adam entered with Alicia and de Langon, the king was seated at the little table, quill in hand.

He didn't look up or in any way acknowledge their presence. Instead, he kept on writing, and Adam was put in mind of Lord Roger, who excelled at intimidating people by the simple act of pretending they were invisible and continuing with what he was doing.

Finally, the king wiped his quill, stoppered the ink pot, and set the document aside to dry. And then there was silence. Yet another of Lord Roger's techniques, to allow the silence to grow into an oppressive burden that squashed the air out of the lungs of the poor unfortunate standing trembling before him. In this case, there were two unfortunates.

"I think we deserve an explanation, my lord," de Langon began.

"An explanation?" Edward rubbed at an ink spot on his hand. "How so?"

"My lord, we were dragged away by your men!" Two red spots appeared on Alicia's cheeks. "No by your leave, no opportunity to pack—we were taken by force."

"Ah." The king rubbed some more at the spot. "And you have no idea why?" He lifted his head, the light from the windows setting the bristles on his cheeks on fire and turning his blue eyes into pools of liquid gold.

De Langon swallowed audibly. "No, my lord. I would never do anything to inspire your ire."

"Oh, but you have." Edward plucked a cluster of raisins from the large platter on the table and popped one into his mouth. "The moment your wife suspected she'd seen my father alive—which, I might add, was a preposterous mistake—you did not come to me, did you? No, you went straight to Philippe."

"He's my king, my lord."

"I am your king!" The goblets on the table jumped with the force of King Edward's blow. "Me!" He stood. "And more importantly, it was my father your simpleminded wife thought she'd seen—not Philippe's, unless she's now saying it was Charles Valois she saw in Notre Dame?"

"Simpleminded?" Alicia squeaked. "Me?"

"Charles Valois is dead, my lord," Robert de Langon said, frowning at his wife.

"So is Edward of Caernarvon."

"But…" Robert de Langon slid a look at his wife.

"Precisely." King Edward's lip curled. "But. You've done a good job of sowing that doubt, haven't you? Or rather your idiot of a wife has done so."

"What doubt? I saw him!" Alicia shrieked, and Adam wanted to take her by the shoulders and shake her silent. Fool!

"Hold your tongue!" Robert de Langon yelled.

"Why should I?" Alicia straightened up. "I am no fool, my lord. I know what I saw."

"You do? When was the last time you saw my father?"

"I…" Alicia stuttered. "I…"

"You've never met him, have you?" Edward asked, his voice a soft caress.

"I…"

"Answer me," the king said, just as softly.

"No, my lord."

"So you just jumped at conclusions, didn't you? Feebleminded women often do."

"I'm not feebleminded!"

"No?" The king smiled, and for an instant he reminded Adam of a cat playing with a mouse.

"Item one: no one ever saw your father's corpse. Item two: who was the man you had Adam de Guirande escort in secret last summer? The man who under no circumstances was to be allowed to escape alive while in England?" Alicia raised her chin, a superior twist to her mouth. "Robert told me, you see. He told me the queen had charged him with the responsibility of ensuring the prisoner was killed should he attempt to flee." She gave Adam a scornful look. "The queen knew de Guirande didn't have the balls required to do his duty."

Adam shared a quick look with Thomas. Stupid woman, she was damning herself with every word.

"And then we have Kit de Guirande meeting a stranger in Notre Dame—and she was even willing to let me think he might be her lover rather than tell me who he was." Alicia laughed. "Who's the fool now, my lord?"

"You," Robert de Langon said with a deep sigh. He threw himself to his knees, pulling Alicia down with him. "Forgive us, my liege. We were wrong."

"Hmm." Edward steepled his hands and regarded them in silence. "No," he finally said. "I can't trust you—especially not your viper of a wife." He sat forward, elbows on his thighs. "As I see it, there are a couple of choices." He raised his voice, calling for one of his squires. The lad entered carrying two objects, a hammer and some sort of tongs. Robert's eyes widened; Alicia looked bemused.

The king waited until the squire left. "You see, I must make sure you never talk of this again. Ever." He lifted the tongs. "The Moors have methods to ensure people never talk. You grab hold of the tongue," he demonstrated by closing the tongs round his forefinger, "pull it out, and slice it off."

Alicia emitted a series of high-pitched sounds as she scrambled away from the king, eyes on the tongs.

"Do you know how to write, Lady Alicia?" the king continued, lifting the hammer. "If you do…" He mimed crushing his hand. Alicia shook her head back and forth, cradling her hands to her chest.

Enough. Adam took a step forward but was arrested by the king's raised hand. The little room was silent but for the sound of Robert's heavy breathing and Alicia's muffled sobs.

"There is, however, an alternative," the king said after a while. Two sets of eyes flew to him; two mouths wobbled with hope. "You could enter religious orders—very far from here." King Edward lifted the tongs again. "Benedictine or Cistercian, I think. "

Robert de Langon swallowed. "I have no inclination to religious life, my lord."

"No?" King Edward shook his head. "A pity, de Langon." The tongs closed on his finger. "Would you prefer walking the world mute and mutilated?"

"I haven't done anything to merit such," Robert tried.

"Oh, but you have. What did Philippe pay you for your news about my father being alive? Come to think of it, how long has Philippe been paying you?"

"N-n-no." Robert's eyes darted from the king to Adam to Thomas, back to the king. "I swear, I haven't—"

"Spied on me?" King Edward released the tongs to clatter on the floor. "I don't believe you." He stood. "You have a choice. I will give you some time to think about it, but I want your answers before compline."

"I have a daughter." Alicia's voice was hoarse with tears.

"I have no quarrel with her." Edward was at the door. "We will leave you to think things over, shall we?"

The moment they were outside, Adam braced himself against a wall. Thomas was staring at his nephew as if he'd never seen him before, and Adam couldn't quite stop himself from running his tongue over his teeth, clenching and unclenching his hands.

"You look as if you think me capable of doing such," Edward said in a light tone, looking from one to the other.

Adam did not for a moment doubt he was—not after witnessing the recent performance. No king could make such threats unless he was willing to carry them out, and it was with a shiver of fear he studied his king from under his lashes.

"You were most convincing," Thomas said.

"Yes, I was, wasn't I?" Edward sounded pleased. "I dare say they'll go for the somewhat less harrowing life in a monastery or a convent."

"Aye," Adam croaked. "Seems a much better option, all in all."

"That will not necessarily silence them," Thomas warned.

"Oh, it will." Edward's face set. "And I will take precautions."

Hostages, was what Adam would have called it, he reflected later. In Alicia's case, her daughter's well-being would depend on her mother's silence. In de Langon's case, his family would be thrown off their lands if he did not hold his tongue.

They stood holding hands as the king informed them of their future destinations. Not a word, not as much as a sound of protest.

"I will give you one last night to spend as man and wife," the king finished. "Come the morrow, your ways will part, so make the most of it."

Adam was horrified by his callousness. From the look on Thomas' face, so was he, but at the king's orders they escorted their stunned prisoners to the little room the king had procured for them. No windows through which to escape, and the door could be barred from the outside, but at least there was a bed and a fire, a pitcher of wine, and some food.

"What will you tell Kit?" Thomas asked in a hushed voice as they made their way back to the main room of the inn.

"Nothing." Adam's bowels cramped. "Do you think he would've—"

"Oh yes. As would my father." Thomas gave him a crooked smile. "A cornered lion is a terrible beast."

"Indeed." Adam crossed himself, hoping he would never be on the receiving end of King Edward's vindictive anger. Never.

Come morning, the guards opened the little room only to find Alicia and Robert dead, both of them hanging from the rafters.

"That, of course, was their third alternative," the king commented coolly. He looked the bodies up and down. "Not one I would have chosen myself."

Chapter 14

Ever since Alicia and Robert had been discovered dead, Adam had walked about in stunned silence. When Kit had asked what he thought might have driven them to such extremes, he'd given her an odd look, those beautiful eyes of his glazed as if he'd drunk too much ale, and said he assumed they'd found dangling at the end of ripped bedsheets the better alternative.

Better alternative to what? Kit did not push for a reply but couldn't help notice that Adam was doing his utmost to avoid being alone with the king. Most of the time on the ship to Dover he spent with Thomas, the two of them standing very close together by the railing. Come evening, Kit had had enough. For all that it was June, the nights were chilly, and she wanted the company—and warmth—of her husband as she attempted to sleep on the open deck.

"You'll tell me eventually," she said as they sat down together, she snuggling up close beneath his heavy cloak. He looked down his nose at her.

"Aye."

No smile, no more than this one word answer, a haunted look on his face.

"I love you," she said, having no notion what else to tell him to alleviate whatever it was that was hurting him so. This time, he did smile. He raised her hand to his mouth and kissed her fingers, one by one.

As the evening progressed, the stars came out, faint pinpricks against a sky that refused to darken much beyond a greenish blue. Now and then a crewmember padded by, but otherwise it was mostly quiet beyond the occasional burst of laughter from the captain's cabin—the king had requisitioned it for the journey.

Beside them, Mabel twisted and turned, sighed and wept, before abruptly falling asleep. She'd been in a state all day, alternating between praying for poor Alicia's soul and berating the foolish child for ending her life thus.

"I'd never have thought Alicia was capable of taking her own life," Kit ventured, crossing herself. Hastily shrouded, hastily buried, Bishop Henry being prevailed upon by the king to say some words over the newly dug graves just outside the graveyard.

"No."

More silence, and Kit was drifting off to sleep despite Adam's constant fidgeting.

"He made them choose." Adam's voice shook. Kit rested her cheek against his chest, straining to hear as he told her of tongs and hammers, of exile in distant convents. Kit cast a look in the direction of the cabin, from which still came the sound of voices. Yesterday, their king had threatened two people with mutilation. Today, he was carousing.

"They chose the easiest alternative," Adam finished with a sigh. He tightened his hold on her. "They preferred to die together."

Or with someone they knew. She held her breath and listened to his heartbeat, reassuringly strong and steady beneath her ear.

"It changed something," Adam said after a while. "I find him a lesser man."

Kit sat up. "He is a king, Adam. Your king. He is young and confused, this matter with his father has him twisting with guilt, and then Philippe rubs further salt in that wound. What was he to do but attempt to silence Alicia and her husband?"

"That's not it." Adam looked away. "He enjoyed it."

Kit shook her head. "He knew they would never choose mutilation."

Adam laughed hoarsely. "Who would?" He braided his fingers with hers. "But he liked it, that their future was in his hand."

There was a messenger waiting for the king in Dover. The court was at Canterbury, and Queen Isabella bid him come as fast as he could.

"As fast as I can," Edward grumbled. "Seems to me all I've been doing lately is travelling at speed from one place to the other." He scowled. "And why Canterbury? The castle is not fit for a king."

"I dare say your lady mother rather enjoys emptying the archbishop's cellars," Thomas said. "He's supposed to have some excellent wines." He was already mounted, surrounded by four or five men. "God's speed to you, Nephew."

"And to you." The king clasped his uncle's hand. "Ride safely."

"I wish we were going home as well," Kit commented to Adam, raising her hand to wave at Thomas.

"Aye." He gave her a wry smile. "It helps if you're an earl."

A day later, they were in Canterbury, where they found the court installed in the Benedictine priory. King Edward was less than pleased, finding the accommodations far too cramped. He brightened upon seeing his young wife, greeted Lord Roger cordially, and bowed to Archbishop Mepeham but refrained from kissing his ring, thereby signalling the archbishop remained unforgiven for his participation in Lancaster's recent rebellion.

The king was whisked off to be pampered by his wife and mother, John Maltravers and Bishop Henry gravitated to Mortimer, and the rest of the royal party disbanded to find their respective lodgings.

"Adam!" William waved as he came towards them. "Kit!" He beamed, embraced them both, and offered to show them the way to their chamber while directing Mabel to the room that housed the female servants. A long trudge, as it turned out, but in Adam's present mood, being far from the king was not a bad thing.

"Why are you limping?" William asked.

"I always limp." In difference to Alicia and Robert, he'd not been given a choice. It was mutilation or mutilation.

William rolled his eyes. "Why are you limping more than usual?"

"A close encounter with Godfrey of Broseley," Adam said. "He ended up dead."

William's brows knit into a frown. "And you?"

"Healing." He gave his brother a reassuring smile. "Truly. And you? How are things with you and Lord Roger?"

William launched into an enthusiastic description of long days at work, even longer days on horseback. Lord Roger was a man with an eye for details, William explained, and it was men like William who compiled the details.

"Ah." Adam followed him up a set of narrow stairs. "I take it you don't miss Tresaints."

William half turned, shaking his head. "Not much." He looked beyond Adam to Kit. "I love Tresaints, you know I do, but this…" He inhaled. "I feel alive, a part of things."

"A spy," Adam said to Kit once they were alone. "Not that he fully understands it yet, but that is what he is. All that compiling, all those details—Lord Roger is ensuring he knows more about everything than any other man in the kingdom."

"Is it dangerous?"

"That would depend on what he is compiling," Adam replied. "If he's counting horses and men-at-arms, aye, it can be. If he is assessing the overall wool harvest, not so much."

He sat down on the bed and bounced a couple of times. A good bed—his brother had ensured a feather mattress and clean linen. He held out his hand to her. He needed her. Had needed her since that terrible night in Wissant, but there'd been no opportunity. Until now.

She came to stand between his legs, him resting his head against her belly. Strong fingers tugged at his hair, and he buried his nose in the fabric of her skirts. She stroked his hair, his bristled cheeks. He took hold of her and tipped her over into the bed.

No words. He had no need for those. He wanted her proximity, her heat, the softness of her skin, the warmth of her mouth. He slipped a hand under her veil, slid his fingers into her hair to hold her still as he moulded his lips to hers, his tongue demanding entry. As always, she was just as voracious, her breath coming in hot gusts between their heated kisses.

Adam lifted himself sufficiently to undo his braies and shove her skirts out of the way, and then he was inside her, a slow sinking into her that had her widening her legs to accommodate him. As it should be, his woman welcoming him inside, moving in time with him. Blue eyes never left his—not even when he rubbed the tip of his nose against hers. It made them both cross-eyed, she laughed, he raised his head—but their eyes never broke contact.

He moved slowly. It was immersion, not completion, that he craved, this sensation of being welded to her, physically joined—if only briefly—with her. And she understood, her body undulating in time with his. No haste, no words. But he braided his fingers with hers, and her chest rose on a held breath when he kissed her just beneath her ear.

Inevitably, his blood came to a boil. It bubbled through his veins, thudded in his head and in his loins. Her name echoed in his brain, her eyes were so close, so very close, and in their depths he saw himself, he saw her. He kissed her just as he climaxed.

They lay close together afterwards, her hair tickling his face. Remarkable how well they fitted together, he thought drowsily, it was as if she'd been made for him, the curve of her buttocks fitting so snugly against his groin. She *had* been made for him, he amended, smiling through a jaw-cracking yawn. His woman. Only his.

They'd lost track of time. Kit started awake at the loud banging on their door, was busy ordering her clothes when Mabel spilled into the room.

"The queen is asking for you, m'lady." Mabel sniffed and grinned. "Good thing I didn't send Stephen instead."

"The queen?" Kit looked about for some water.

"Queen Isabella." Mabel set down a pitcher brimming with water and politely turned her back. "She is expecting news from France."

Kit twisted her hair into a messy braid and stuck her feet into her shoes.

"Here, m'lady." Mabel held out her veil. "And don't

forget this." She handed Kit the twisted piece of cloth that held Queen Jeanne's gift to Isabella.

Kit flew out of the door, barged into a monk, who gave her a black look before moving aside, and walked as fast as she could towards the cloisters.

"There you are." Queen Isabella motioned for Kit to enter.

"My lady." A deep reverence, some moments of looking at the floor, and then she was standing in front of the queen.

"Sit," Queen Isabella ordered. "And do something about your hair, Lady Kit." Mortified heat flew up Kit's cheeks. With as much speed as she could muster, she untangled her hair and rebraided it before covering it yet again with the sheer veil.

"How was my dear sister-in-law?"

"She was well, my lady. Happy to be retiring to her own lands soon."

"I can imagine. Day in and day out with Lame Joan would drive any normal person insane." Queen Isabella sniffed. "She was not meant to be queen of France."

"But now she is, my lady."

"Hmph! Well, we shall see for how long. And if God is just, that weakling of a son will die before he reaches manhood, and then there will be but one heir: my Edward."

"Prince Jean seems a fine lad, my lady."

"The son of the Valois usurper." Queen Isabella looked away. "How could it all end like this? Not yet twenty years ago, the Capet dynasty was strong and vibrant. And now…" She sighed. "Only me left. Me and my sons." She cleared her throat. "Well, what else did Lame Joan have to say?"

"Not much, my lady. I spent more time with Queen Jeanne."

"Did she like the gift?"

"Very much. And she gave me something to give to you." Kit produced the little scrap of cloth. "She said she'd taken this from Charles upon his death and that it rightly belonged to you—or your son—not the Valois king."

Queen Isabella unfolded the cloth. A long, elegant finger

caressed the large ring lying nestled within, the intricate design of blue and red jewels dulled by dust.

"My father's." There were tears in her green eyes when she looked at Kit. "Philippe le Bel—and what a handsome man he was. My mother always said it was as if someone had sprinkled angel dust on him when he was a babe." She laughed softly. "A great king, and my lady mother was ever a good queen to him." A shadow flitted over her face. "A dutiful wife, not like me."

"A different royal husband, my lady," Kit said.

"Yes." Isabella reached across to cover Kit's hand with her own. "Thank you for saying that."

A page boy entered with honeyed wafers and cool wine, and Queen Isabella moved the discussion to other matters, first and foremost a detailed description of King Edward's homage.

"And what's this about Godfrey of Broseley?" she asked.

"My lady?"

"My son tells me everything." Isabella gave Kit a complacent smile. "Adam found him in an alley, did he not?"

"Er…yes, my lady. Although it was Godfrey finding Adam."

"Doesn't really matter, does it? The important thing is that Adam killed him."

There was a flurry of colour at the door, and Queen Philippa came dancing towards them.

"My lady." Kit made yet another reverence.

"Kit!" Philippa beamed. "Is it true what Edward says, that the French ladies have taken to exposing all of their bosoms?" She mimed a neckline that would leave both her breasts in full view.

Kit laughed. "No, my lady. But they do wear their necklines lower than ours."

"They do?" Isabella sat forward. "What else did you see?"

The rest of the afternoon was whiled away discussing fashion, from the narrow sleeves that the French ladies buttoned tightly round their forearms—"Buttons!" Queen Isabella exclaimed. "How innovative."—to the increasing use of expensive Byzantine brocade. Soon enough, it was twenty ladies discussing the merits of adopting French fashions, and right in their midst Isabella sat with her daughter-in-law, looking as excited as Philippa at the thought of embroidered unicorns and daring necklines.

After an afternoon spent on fripperies, Queen Isabella insisted they all attend service together. They bumped into Lord Mortimer and his entourage just outside the queen's apartments, and soon enough it was Isabella and Mortimer walking side by side together, leaving the rest of them to follow as they wished.

"It's as if there are invisible threads between them," Philippa commented in a low voice to Kit. And it was. If Mortimer turned to face the queen, she reciprocated. If he gestured with his left hand, hers would shadow his movement. Unconsciously, Kit suspected, just as they were both entirely unaware of how fluidly they moved together, her skirts flaring in time with his strides.

Mortimer bent his head to hers. The queen laughed; for an instant, her hand fluttered up as if to caress his face. He took it, kissed her wrist, and bowed deeply before releasing her.

Philippa sighed. "If it weren't so wrong, it would be so beautiful. As it is…" She crossed herself. "They will burn in hell, those two."

"Or God will find it in His heart to forgive them," Kit replied. "One should not burn in hell for loving."

Some hours later, Kit returned alone to their little room. She'd seen Adam enter the hall with his brother, and when she left he mouthed that he'd come soon, before returning to whatever their intense conversation was about.

The summer dusk was purple, the sky to the east still streaked with light. Kit detoured through the herbal garden, strolled slowly along the neat borders while inhaling the scents of the various plants. Her mother had always said that herbs should be picked just after sunset—or just before sunrise—as that was when they were at their most fragrant. Kit stooped, broke off a sprig of pennyroyal, and crumpled it. Such a sweet smell, such a dangerous herb.

In their room, she found her daily infusion, the scent of ginger mixing with the far more delicate fragrance of crushed raspberry leaves. She drank it hastily, guilt rising through her.

"Forgive me, Blessed Virgin Mary," she whispered. "Five more months, no more."

Chapter 15

When Kit had hurried off to wait on Queen Isabella, Adam presented himself to the king in case his services were required.

"Your services?" Montagu laughed. "I think not, de Guirande. The king is more interested in his wife's services at present." He nodded in the direction of the inner door. "They've been in there since the queen mother left, and from the sound of things, they're enjoying themselves."

"As it should be." Adam sat down and accepted a goblet of wine.

"I can see that," Montagu retorted drily. "You really should order your hair after bedding your wife. Besides, you could do with a haircut and a shave—unless you are planning on finally emulating us real men and growing a beard."

Adam smiled into his goblet. "No. I find it itches." He extended his leg and rubbed absentmindedly over his recent wound.

Montagu poured them some more wine. "Nice to be home, isn't it?"

"Home?" Adam chuckled. "Here? I didn't take you for a monk, Will."

"You know what I mean." Montagu shifted on his seat. "Seems to me we've spent the better part of a month on horseback. And he was in a damned hurry to get back."

Adam sipped his wine.

"Did he truly feel threatened by Philippe?" Montagu asked.

"Ask him, not me." Adam bit into a wafer.

"And what was this with de Langon? I admit I never liked the man, but to find him hanging by his neck like that…" Montagu crossed himself.

"Not by order of the king," Adam said.

"No. But he must have said something to them—and you

133

were there." There was an edge to Montagu's voice. "You're always there, aren't you?"

"Not by choice, I can assure you."

"Hmm. So why? Why drag de Langon and that broomstick of his wife along?"

"Robert de Langon and his wife were selling information to the French king," Adam replied after some thought. "The king was most incensed."

"Yes, we all noticed," Montagu said. "Like travelling with an aggravated bear. He must have threatened them with severe punishment for them to take their lives."

"Take their lives?" William echoed from the doorway.

Montagu scowled. "How long have you been eavesdropping?"

"Apologies, my lord," William said smoothly. "I was hoping for a word with my brother."

"With me?" Adam rose. "About what?"

"Does it have to be about anything?" William smiled, eyes darting to Montagu.

"No, of course not." Adam bowed to Montagu. "Should the king have need of me, I'll be with my brother."

"I'll be sure to let him know." Montagu belched discreetly. "On the other hand, you've both been avoiding each other lately, haven't you?"

"Have you?" William asked once he and Adam were outside. He nodded in the directions of the cloisters.

"Have what?"

"Been avoiding each other."

Adam shrugged. "I am at my master's service—always."

"Ah." They walked side by side down the north side of the cloisters. "But something has happened."

Adam gave his brother a long look. "What makes you say that?"

"You seem tense. When you rode in earlier, it was not you hastening over to stand by the king as he dismounted— nor was it you riding the closest to him."

"Making mountains out of molehills, William?" Adam teased.

"I don't think so. Am I?" There was such genuine concern in William's voice that Adam sighed.

"No," he grudgingly admitted. "It was an elucidating journey."

"Tell me." William sat down in one the large arches, inviting Adam to do the same. "You can start by telling me how Godfrey of Broseley died."

"I strangled him."

"You did? And yet I assume it was him who caused your injury."

"It was." Adam licked his lips and looked this way and that. Other than a group of brethren walking purposefully towards the southern entrance to the cathedral, they were alone. "I'd have bled to death had it not been for Sir Edward."

William went quite still. "Sir who?"

"You heard." Adam shuffled closer. To anyone watching, this could be a priest taking confession. "Edward of Caernarvon saved my life."

"Why?"

"He was following me, saw me and Godfrey fight, and came to my aid."

"Why would he be following you?" William's light blue eyes bored into him. Adam stroked his chin, tugging at the bristles.

"He wanted me to arrange a meeting with his son," he finally said.

"Dearest Lord! Why? Does he mean him harm? I swear it would have been best for everyone had he truly died." William was up, his sandals clacking as he walked back and forth.

"So now you condone murder?"

"Murder? No, no. But as long as he's alive…Sweetest Jesus, imagine the turmoil for our poor king had they met."

"They did," Adam told him.

William sank down beside him. "What?"

"You heard. A good meeting, I believe. Unfortunately, there were those who saw enough to put two and two together."

"Alicia." William closed his eyes, offering up a mumbled prayer in Latin. "*Requiescat in pace*," he finished, and Adam mumbled an "Amen". "I heard she was dead—men-at-arms are not good at keeping secrets—but I did not believe it when they said she'd hanged herself."

"She and Robert both." Adam glanced at his brother. "They were driven to the ultimate sin of despair by the king."

"No!" William moved closer.

Hesitantly, Adam told him all about that evening in Wissant. It felt good to share this with his brother—in much more detail than he'd burdened Kit with. Once he was done, he sat back, reclining against one of the arches.

"Ruthless," William said after a while. "Not necessarily a bad quality in a king."

"No. As long as it is tempered with mercy."

"And you don't think him capable of mercy?"

Adam studied his hands. "I do—once he is old enough to understand the concept."

"He offered them a choice. He didn't have to." William patted him on the leg. "I'd say he has all the makings of a good king."

Adam found that most comforting. When William suggested they repair to the guest hall and find themselves some food, he happily went along, spending the rest of the evening in the company of his brother and some other Mortimer men—old friends from when Adam was Lord Roger's most favoured captain.

Kit had been asleep when he returned to their room. She'd been just as sunk in sleep when he woke to the sound of the cock crowing, but that matter was easily remedied, and by the time he left her, she was most certainly awake—and sated, her naked body rosy all over.

Adam hummed as he walked. A pleasant start to the day, made even better by the sunlit peace of the cathedral close.

He reached the cloisters just as Lord Roger exited the cathedral, accompanied not only by Bishop Henry but also by his younger son, Geoffrey. Since the untimely death of two Mortimer lads last year, Lord Roger only had two sons left to him, and while Edmund preferred to stay well away from the court—and his father, finding it unbearable to see Lord Roger with Queen Isabella—Geoffrey was a far more frequent visitor.

"Adam!" Geoffrey shone up and broke into a trot.

"My lord," Adam bowed at this his favourite Mortimer offspring. He had his father's looks, was as skilled a jouster as Lord Roger, and coupled his physical attributes with a honed intellect Lord Roger always generously insisted came from his mother.

"Are you well? I heard you were recently injured."

"I am. And you?"

"Oh, most hale. Just back from France—as are you, I hear."

"I am. And your lady mother?"

Geoffrey's face fell. "In the best of health but bitter." He shuffled his feet. "Even more so now that I've accepted my father's offer to work more closely with him."

Betrayed by her husband and now by her son—or so Adam supposed Lady Joan must feel, having to suffer the humiliation of seeing her husband living in open sin with Queen Isabella.

"He needs me." Geoffrey straightened up. "It is not an easy task, to rule a kingdom."

"Some would argue it is not him who should rule," Adam replied, keeping his voice down.

Geoffrey rolled his eyes. "Aye. And he does not make things better by flaunting his power as much as he does."

"Does he?" To Adam, Lord Roger was never ostentatious—beyond his fondness for rich and colourful garments. Neither did he put himself forward unnecessarily.

"There's not a man in England who doesn't know with whom true power resides." Geoffrey sounded proud, but there was a concerned pucker to his forehead. "Appointments, wardships, proposed laws—they all go to the Earl of March for decision." He threw a quick look at his father, still engrossed in his conversation with the Bishop of Lincoln. "A lot of work, Adam. That's why he needs me."

137

Adam desisted from pointing out that Lord Roger already had the ablest of men helping him, men like Henry Burghersh of Lincoln and Adam Orleton, Bishop of Hereford. What a stripling like Geoffrey Mortimer could bring to the table was doubtful, but Adam supposed it heartened Lord Roger to have at least one son beside him. Which was why he smiled and told Geoffrey he was looking forward to seeing more of him—not an untruth, given that he liked the young man.

"Adam." Lord Roger's dark eyes surveyed Adam from top to toe. "Recovered from your little scrape with that rat Broseley?"

"I am, my lord."

"Good, good." Lord Roger took Adam by the arm. "A word? In private?" It was said in the softest of voices, and yet Adam shivered. Lord Roger was upset, further demonstrated by his punishing hold on Adam's arm.

"I can walk unaided, my lord," Adam said. Lord Roger released him immediately and led the way to his lodgings in absolute silence, his gold-embroidered green mantel billowing around him.

"So," Lord Roger said once they were inside. "Alicia de Monmouth." He sat down but did not offer Adam to sit.

"Dead, my lord."

"I know that. By her own hand, no less." His lip curled. "A fitting end to that warped young woman. I even know why she died. What I don't know…" He leapt to his feet. "Is it true?" Lord Roger crowded Adam back against the wall. "Did you set up a meeting between our king and his cocksucker of a father?"

Damn William to hell and back! "Indirectly."

"With what right? You do not decide who Edward sees or doesn't see." Lord Roger slammed his hand against the wall. "You do as you're told, damn it!"

"The king has a will of his own," Adam countered. "And I am the king's man, not yours."

"The king's man?" Lord Roger hissed. "My, my, how high the gutter-rat has clambered. You owe everything you are to me, de Guirande. Best not forget it."

Adam gritted his teeth. "I am the king's man, my lord," he repeated.

While his brother, William, was Lord Roger's, and Adam would never allow himself to forget that again. Ever.

"Aren't we all," Lord Roger replied. "But as holder of the Great Seal and regent of this kingdom, I would have you know that it is I, not you—or our young king—who has the final say on everything. And I did not authorise a meeting between our Edward and his sorry excuse of a father."

"Neither did you forbid it, and as I said, the king wished it so." Adam pushed free of the wall, using his larger frame to force Lord Roger to take a step backwards. He had never used his size to intimidate his former lord before, and he saw shock in Lord Roger's face. "Nothing happened," Adam continued. "They met, they embraced, they parted."

"God's blood, Adam." Lord Roger retook his seat. "He could have killed him. Or denounced him to Philippe Valois."

"His own son?" Adam shook his head. "But it is unfortunate Philippe now suspects Sir Edward is alive."

"Unfortunate? A bloody understatement. He'll turn France upside down looking for him, anything to spite Isabella and me—and your precious king."

"He won't find him." Adam replied, praying this would prove true. "Sir Edward does not intend to remain in France."

"No?" Lord Roger sloshed some ale into a cup. "Privy to his plans, are you?"

"No." At Lord Roger's invitation, Adam sat down. "But he knows he's been given an opportunity to make a new life for himself, and he is not about to risk ending up Philippe's puppet." Adam made a face. "Who would?"

Lord Roger burst out laughing. "You don't like him?"

"Not much, my lord. Too pompous by far."

"Too insecure, that's why. When your bloodlines are weak, you compensate with glitter and pomp." He ordered the documents on his table. "Have you heard about Robert Bruce?"

"My lord?"

"Dead. And so Scotland is now in the hands of a puling

child, or rather his guardian. Moray is a good man. He'll keep both his young king and his equally young queen safe. Until our own king decides to ride north to claim the Scottish throne, that is."

"War, my lord?"

"Inevitably, I'd say. Edward will not rest until he's taught the Scots a lesson—but for now that matter will have to wait. First he must handle his dear uncle—and I'm assuming you've heard about Kent's sudden desire to visit the pope."

"Aye."

"Fool! I am almost tempted to have His Holiness send us some legate or other and invite them to tour every castle in the kingdom." Lord Roger grinned. "Very many castles, no king in any of them—thanks to you, a most useful and loyal man." That was as much of an apology as Adam would get. Mortimer sat back. "You weren't much taken by the tongs and hammers, I hear."

"No, my lord."

"I found it cleverly done." Lord Roger found a quill, brushing his clean-shaven cheeks with the feather. "And he achieved his purpose, didn't he? Permanently silenced."

Adam blinked. "He didn't expect them to hang themselves."

"No? Locked into a small room with suitable rafters and plenty of sheets?" Lord Roger smiled. "Maybe not. Maybe yes. We will never know, will we?"

Adam was in a foul mood when he left Lord Roger. It did not help that the first person he clapped eyes on was William, hovering like a huge black fly just beyond the door.

"You told him."

"So what if I did? Lord Roger was concerned for you, so I told him what I knew."

"Except that wasn't the way it happened, is it?" Adam wheeled and pushed his face into his brother's. "Mortimer told you to find out what had happened in France."

William backed away. "He was concerned."

"Or curious. And whatever the case, I told you in confidence." He cleared his throat of the raw burning sensation his brother's betrayal caused. "I thought I could trust you, but apparently I was wrong."

"You can trust me." William held out his hands. "I love you—and so does Lord Roger."

"He does? Fine way to show it, to have my brother spy on me."

"I wasn't spying!"

"Of course you were. Not so surprising, really, not now that you're one of Mortimer's men."

"I am not a spy!" William drew himself up tall. "But aye, I am Lord Roger's man—and proud of it. I owe him for everything I am—and so do you, Adam. Best not forget it."

"In between the two of you, neither Lord Roger nor you will let me. But I am the king's man now, not Lord Roger's. Best keep that in mind." He scowled. "He won't be pleased about all this."

"Who?"

"The king. Lord Roger will tell his queen, and she will no doubt have a long and heated discussion with her son about the idiocy of seeing his father. And I will be the tell-tale." He laughed mirthlessly. "And so he will trust me less."

"I…" William licked his lips.

"And I will never trust you again." He liked it, how William's face fell. "I would prefer it if you stay away from me and Kit."

"Please, Adam." William made a grab for him.

"Leave me alone." Adam marched off. He wanted food—and a barber. And then he had to find his wife and tell her she was not to talk to William. That would not go down well.

There was no opportunity to talk to Kit—according to Mabel, she was with Queen Philippa. So Adam retired to the stables, where he spent an hour or so seeing to Raven while listening with half an ear to Stephen's chatter.

"There you are." Richard sent Stephen on his way and came to stand in the spot Stephen had vacated. "I do think you could have done me the courtesy of telling me about Alicia's death."

"I would have—had I seen you." Adam bent down to inspect one of Raven's hooves. "My condolences on your great loss. I can only imagine how devastated you must be."

"No need for that," Richard muttered. "Aye, I did not much care for her, but she was my sister. I gather she had herself to blame?"

"Aye. Too sharp for her own good." Adam straightened up. "And her daughter?"

"With me—or rather with Maud." Richard looked pleased. "A rich little niece, and better off without that harpy of a mother. Maud will see her well cared for."

Adam nodded. He'd met Maud a handful of times and found her sweet, plump, and innocent, despite being the mother of two, soon to be three.

"A little girl would be nice this time," Richard confided.

Adam slapped Raven on the rump and eased out of his stall. "I need to work the stiffness out of my leg. Care to help?"

"Help?" Richard grinned. "Does that mean I can hope to see you flat on your arse?"

"You can always hope," Adam replied. "Not about to happen, though."

They used wooden staves, circling each other as they worked their way through set combinations of blows at first. Soon enough, they'd collected an audience, and the staves whirled, the blows became harder.

"Does it hurt?" Richard panted, blowing his fringe out of his eyes.

"Not much." His thigh strained and ached, but it was bearable.

"Good." Richard attacked.

They were both sweating, both hurting, when Richard suddenly dropped his stave and made a reverence. Adam turned and followed suit.

"I want to talk to you, Sir Adam," the king said testily. With that he was off, striding at speed towards the low wall that enclosed the fish ponds. Adam exchanged a look with

Richard before hurrying after Edward as best as he could.

"You told them." The king sat on the wall, feet dangling.

"I did not." Adam remained standing. "I told my brother, fool that I am."

Edward eyed him from under his hair. "I don't think he meant you any harm. Little brothers just have a tendency to talk too much." He smiled. "John did that all the time, telling Maman things I did not necessarily want her to find out."

"Did, my lord?"

"I no longer tell him everything," came the short reply. Edward fiddled with his belt. "I suppose you won't be telling William everything either."

"No. But there's a difference: William is no half-grown lad speaking out of turn."

The king patted the wall beside him. "He didn't do it out of ill will."

Adam sat down. "He had me confiding in him, my lord. And then he turned right round and told Mortimer everything."

Edward set a hand on his shoulder, no more. "Maman was furious," he said after a while.

"As was Mortimer."

They shared a smile.

"I am glad I met him," Edward said. "Glad to have embraced him once more." His face set. "I am less than happy with the other matter."

"Aye." Adam wiped at his sweaty neck. "It ended badly."

"That it did." The king nibbled at a nail. "Ah well, no major loss, is it?"

Adam held his tongue, his gaze on the dark water of the pond.

Beside him, the king sighed. "Why don't you go home for some weeks? Take Kit and spend time ordering your affairs. I'd be sleepless if I had Gavin as my steward."

"Truly, my lord?"

"Truly." The king slid off the wall. "I'll expect you at Windsor before Lammas Day."

"Yes, my lord."

They passed an arch; the king broke off a sprig of the woodbine that decorated it. "I would never have done it."

"My lord?"

The king handed him the woodbine. "You know what I refer to. And this is for Lady Kit." He grinned. "Tell her I don't think geese like flowers."

With that he was gone, loping towards the little group of people assembled by the chapter house.

Chapter 16

Tresaints on a summer evening was a sight for sore eyes—or so Kit thought, incapable of keeping the smile off her face as they rode down the long lane towards their home. On either side, barley and wheat rustled, the fallow strips in between offering pasture to their few cows.

"Good crop," Adam commented, riding close enough to inspect the peas that grew closest to the lane. They were no longer green and tender, but drying slowly, a safeguard against hunger during the winter months.

Kit nodded, no more, her gaze riveted on the approaching gatehouse and more specifically on the little shape she could see balancing atop the parapet.

"Meg!" she breathed.

"Mama!" Meg's high voice came floating towards them. "Mama, Mama!" She leaned out, waving wildly, and there was a sickening instant when Kit feared she would fall, but then she saw Tom the Foundling standing behind her, holding on to her skirts.

By the time they reached the bailey, the household was there to welcome them home, with Meg being the first to throw herself at Kit. And then came Ned and Harry, one running, the other toddling, and Kit crouched, arms full of her children, not minding in the least that her sons' hands were muddy or that Meg nearly strangled her when she wound her arms round Kit's neck.

"No welcome for me?" Adam asked, crouching down beside Kit. With a little squeal, Meg transferred her arms to Adam, squealing all the louder when he rose and threw her straight up a couple of times.

"Me, me!" Ned had hold of Adam's hose.

"Me, me," Harry echoed, and Kit was abandoned, her three eldest dancing round their Papa. Tom stood to the side, fair hair hiding most of his face. But he smiled shyly at Kit, his ears going bright red when she gave him a quick hug.

"My lady." Old John bowed deeply. "It is a pleasure to have you back."

"Thank you." She scanned the people surrounding them, grinned at Gavin, who grinned back before making a determined effort to rid Adam of children.

"Best he not take hold of little Meg," John said, watching the uneven fight with obvious amusement. "Anyone as much as touches her and that protective beast of a cat flies at them."

Kit laughed. Flea was a most unusual cat in that he acted the guard dog when it came to Meg. The little kitten William had given their daughter had grown into a large, bad-tempered tom who spent his days in the proximity of Meg, his nights doing God knew what.

Adam disentangled himself, shooed the children in the direction of Mabel, and came over, Gavin trotting beside him. A hasty greeting, and the men set off to inspect byres and stables, Gavin one step behind Adam and John.

Much later, Adam came to find Kit in the orchard. "God's blood! Our Gavin is not made out to be a steward—the lad wants adventure and glory, fool that he is." He dragged a hand through his hair. "I must find someone immediately."

Kit pursed her lips. "John could act your steward."

Adam brightened. "He could—if he knew how to read and write. So maybe what I need is a clerk." He scowled in the direction of the chapel. "And a new priest."

Five days later, after ensuring the babes were fast asleep in the shade of the apple trees, supervised by Bridget and Mabel, Kit stole away for some hours on her own. The July day was agreeably warm, and in some of the fields the harvest was already ongoing, men in shirts and braies wielding sickles or scythes while the women came after with rakes. Last came the lads responsible for tying the sheaves, a scratchy business that left you itching all over.

Kit shaded her eyes. She could just about make out Adam, standing on the very far end of the narrow field. Not that she could properly see him at this distance, but she knew for a fact he was wearing one of his old linen tunics, his bare legs stuck into old shoes, a battered hat on his head.

"What else to wear for harvest work?" he'd teased as he left her after a long, wet kiss. Not that the lord of the manor would do much harvesting, but he'd gladly join in the ale drinking afterwards.

She ducked under the large alder that leaned out over the little stream, shadow and sun rustling through the foliage to dapple the surface of the dark water. The tree was old, and bits and pieces had dropped off over the last few winters, a dead branch trailing in the water. On the other side of the tree was a small clearing bordered by brambles and briars. Kit's special place, a little corner of the world that belonged only to her and Adam.

Here, the stream widened into a pool—shallow enough that she could wade back and forth without the water ever reaching higher than her waist. There was a large flat rock on which to sit, and from the shrubs came the constant chirping of wrens and sparrows, the odd wagtail walking saucily up and down along the water's edge.

She'd brought work with her, and soon enough she was sitting cross-legged, engrossed in her sewing. Meg was shooting up like a leek in dung, and Kit was working on a new gown for her, adorning the blue fustian with an embroidered band she'd bought in France.

A twig snapped, and Kit raised her head, hand groping for her dagger. On the opposite side, the outline of a deer was momentarily visible before it darted off, and Kit relaxed. It irked her that despite knowing Godfrey of Broseley was dead, she could not entirely rid herself of the fear he'd installed in her, not even here, where she knew she was safe, John and his crossbow only a stone's throw away.

Not that John really had the time to loiter in the shade while his mistress sat by the water—not now that Adam had announced John was the new steward of the de Guirande lands—but he'd waved away her objections, saying some habits were hard to break. Kit smiled. Things were falling neatly into place, and soon enough there'd be a new priest. Adam had been more than pleased at Kit's suggestion that he ask Lady Joan to help in this matter, and Gavin had set off three days ago for Ludlow with a message for the lady.

Kit set aside her work and undressed down to her chemise. With the fabric lifted high, she waded into the pool, shivering at the chill of the water. She'd only intended to wet her legs, but soon enough she was floating in the water, staring up at the cloud-dotted sky above. William always said each and every cloud represented one of God's sheep, some of them as white as driven snow, some of them somewhat more grey around the edges—but all of them loved. William. Kit bit her lip. No matter her attempts at making him forgive his brother, Adam remained obdurate: William had betrayed him, and he would not discuss the matter.

"He's your only brother," Kit had tried as late as last night.

"Not anymore." Adam had jerked off his tunic and thrown it to the side before giving her an irritated look. "Must we talk about this again?"

What he did not seem to grasp was that it was not only him losing a brother, it was her as well. Since she first became Adam's wife, William had been her pillar of strength, a constant support during the months when Adam was imprisoned, a shoulder to lean on when events took a turn for the worse.

Kit paddled back to the shore and stretched out on the warm rock. The fine linen of her chemise moulded itself to her body like a layer of onion skin, so transparent she could as well have been naked. She wrung the water out of her hair and shook it out, her nose to the sun. She'd talk to William next she met him, she decided, no matter what Adam might have to say about it.

The linen had dried by the time Adam came to find her—as she's known he would. Kit regarded him from under her half-closed eyes, pretending to be drowsier than she was as he undressed and waded in to wash off the dust and chaff. And then he was leaning over her, his hair dripping water onto her face, his mouth covering hers.

"I want you naked," he said, already lifting her chemise. Kit shivered, a reaction to the combined sensation of being chilled and the heat his calloused fingers ignited when they grazed her nipples. The rock was rough and warm, he was hard and cold, and she was trapped in between, her buttocks pressing against the unyielding texture of the stone, her breasts squished against his hairy chest.

He came inside of her, most of his weight on his knees and elbows. She hooked her legs round his waist and lifted her shoulders off the stone so as to kiss him. A devouring kiss, one in which she explored him, tasted him. Adam smiled beneath her lips, a pleased rumble emanating through his trapped mouth.

"My lady," he said hoarsely when she released him. He rose above her, bracing himself on his arms, and drove into her.

It didn't matter that the stone scraped her skin. All that mattered was the sensation of his groin against hers, the way he thrust himself deeper and deeper, leaving her devoid of words, of any thoughts but those of him. Him—the man whose head was backlit by the afternoon sun, whose mouth contorted in a silent *Kit* when he climaxed, his hips jerking repeatedly. An instant of holding him in her arms, of feeling his heart beat against hers, and then he moved to the side, his fingers tracing patterns over her skin.

Adam stretched and nipped off a briar rose. He brushed her nose with the flower and then tucked it gently into her hair. In the distance, the bell rang out vespers, and with a little sigh Adam stood. They dressed in silence. Hand in hand, they walked back home, the setting sun throwing their elongated shadows before them.

The coming weeks were a collection of long days with no opportunity for further visits to the quiet pool. While their peasant tenants harvested, supervised by John and Adam, it fell to Kit to organise the food, and together with Mall she packed baskets of pasties and bread—food easy to eat while standing in the fields.

The children ran wild, playing among the sheaves, leaping over rakes. Leading them all was Meg, Ned doing his best to keep up with his sister. Not so Harry, who'd discovered early on that stubble was hard on the knees if you fell on it, and so preferred to stay close to his Mama and the food. A placid child, their Harry, fair hair falling in soft curls to his shoulders.

"They do everything together." Mabel handed Harry a crust of bread, hairless brows pulled into a little frown. "It's not right, m'lady."

"They're children." Kit smiled at her daughter and her constant companion, Tom the Foundling. As fair as her dead son, this Tom had dark eyes and a narrow face in which an overgenerous mouth battled with a large nose. He'd grow into his features, but at present he reminded Kit of a fledgling, all beak and nothing else.

"She is the daughter of the lord of the manor, m'lady. He's the son of a whore. It does not do to mix the two."

"He knows his place," Adam put in. "And if he doesn't, I'll make sure he does." He accepted a jug of ale from Kit with a little bow, his gaze on his eldest daughter. "If needs must, we'll send him away to serve elsewhere."

"Meg would be heartbroken," Kit objected. "Like peas in a pod, those two."

"Aye. And for now, I have no objection." Adam crouched to kiss Harry on his cheek. "What happened to your coif?" he asked, deftly adjusting it atop his son's head.

"For now?" Kit asked.

"In some years, we'll be looking for a husband for our Meg. Best she is weaned of the companionship of future stable lads before that."

"A stable lad?" Kit looked at Tom.

"What else can he be?" Adam dug about in a basket. "No pasties left?"

"Over here, m'lord." Mabel handed him two.

"He could be a clerk or a reeve," Kit said, still stuck in the contemplation of Tom's future. "We could ensure he learnt to read and write."

"And upset the order of things?" Adam bit into his pasty.

150

"He's a nice lad, but he should not be given notions above his station."

"William was teaching him to read. He—"

"What William did or didn't do is neither here nor there." Adam stood. "And no matter how much I like Tom, I'll not have him tutored alongside my own children."

"And where would you be had someone not given you an opportunity to rise above your destiny?" Kit got to her feet as well.

Adam swallowed down the last of his food. "That was different. My father was a wastrel but of good Norman descent, and my mother was no whore."

"But…"

"No." He shook his head. "We've given the lad a home, food in his belly, and clothes on his back. When the time comes, he may rise to be head groom or help with the sheep. Best make sure he is content with that—for his sake." His eyes narrowed as he studied Meg, presently gambolling about like a spring-fevered calf. Dirty shins were clearly visible, and her coif was nowhere in sight, her dark braids bouncing in time with her movements. "And our Meg could do with learning some decorum."

"She's only four!" But he was right, she acknowledged. Their daughter was wayward and loud, happier with the sheep and the horses than the spindle and her needle.

"For now," he rejoined before striding away to help with one of the carts.

"He's right," Mabel said quietly. "Lady Cecily—or Lady Joan—would never have allowed their daughters to run about like that." She moved closer. "She has to learn; a woman's place is always a step behind her husband, a meek and dutiful companion. At least outwardly," she added with a little smile.

Kit sighed. "Meg," she called. "Come here!" Out of the corner of her eye, she saw Adam look at her and smile.

Chapter 17

Four days before Lammas Day, they rode out from Tresaints, accompanied by Gavin and Stephen. No maid for Kit, as Mabel had been left at home, charged with taking Meg in hand—an anything but pleasant task as their daughter protested loudly at her new curtailed life.

"I don't want a husband," she'd wailed when Adam had explained that little girls grew up to be young wives. "I only want Tom." That had not gone down well, either with Adam or Kit, and so Meg was to be taught Scripture and reading by the new chaplain for two hours a day, after which she was to sit with Mabel and practise her stitching.

"If you do as you're told, you can spend some of the afternoon outside," Adam had promised her. "And I've told John it is high time you learn to ride."

"On Goliath?" Meg had snivelled hopefully.

Adam had laughed. "No. But if you're good and obedient, I'll let you ride him next I'm home."

A somewhat mollified Meg had kissed them both farewell, with Tom standing some distance away. It ached in Kit to see the lad's longing looks at Meg. If Meg's life had been severely disrupted, so had Tom's, now set to work under the head shepherd.

"It has to be done," Adam said. "And Tom is old enough to earn his keep."

Kit nodded, no more. The world was as it was, and Tom was luckier than most. She rode her palfrey closer. "Looking forward to returning to court?"

"No." Adam raised his hand to his newly shaved face. He was in a new tunic, the royal coat of arms emblazoned on his tabard. "I'd prefer to remain here."

Kit laughed. "Liar." Over the last week or so, she'd watched him grow restless, bored by the practicalities of sheep and harvesting.

He gave her a rueful smile. "Aye. But whenever I'm there, I long for here."

"A donkey, my lord?" she teased. "Ever yearning for the greener grass on the other side of the hedge?"

"And you?" he asked. "Where do you prefer to be?"

"With you," she replied and was rewarded by one of those soft smiles that Adam reserved for her.

They rode into Windsor with a squall at their backs. Adam had insisted on wrapping Kit in his thick cloak, and as a consequence he was wet through while his wife was at most damp. The men on duty at the main gate straightened up when they recognised Adam, and he greeted each of them by name.

"Any news?" he asked the sergeant-at-arms, a dour Hainaulter called Nicholas.

"None. It's been a right boring summer." Nicholas bowed in greeting to Kit and scratched at his chest. "A nice little rebellion would do me and the lads just fine."

"We've had enough of those." Adam dismounted and threw the reins to one of the stable lads and went over to help Kit.

"You think?" Nicholas sniffed. "There's more coming."

"Oh?"

Nicholas shifted from foot to foot. "Kent," he muttered. "Everyone is on about how he is sick and tired of being lorded over by an upstart earl and a wayward queen."

"But it isn't the Earl of March who lords over Kent," Adam replied. "It is his king—and nephew."

"Not so you'd notice." Nicholas nodded in the direction of a group of men standing a fair distance away. "Mortimer men. Everywhere."

"Aye." Adam had already seen the distinctive badges that adorned the men's cloaks. "But in the service of the king."

"So one hopes." Nicholas glanced at Kit and bit his lip.

"My wife does not tell tales," Adam said.

"No, of course not. But it behoves a man to be careful these days." He threw yet another look at the Mortimer men.

153

"What happens the day the king no longer wants Mortimer by his side?"

"Then Lord Mortimer will hand over the seal and retire," Adam replied.

Nicholas brayed with laughter. "When pigs fly, Sir Adam."

Aye, probably. Adam quelled Nicholas with a look, ordered Gavin to ensure their belongings ended up in their lodgings, and with his wife by his side made for the gate leading to the middle ward. The skies had cleared, the sun warm enough to make their cloaks redundant. Adam unpinned his cloak from round Kit's shoulders and handed it to Stephen, instructing the lad to ensure it was properly dry before he folded it together.

They sidestepped a little group of chaplains emerging from St Edward's chapel, passed through yet another gatehouse, and emerged in the inner ward. The sun had brought out all those who'd been sheltering inside, a loud company consisting mostly of the king's friends and retainers. Adam found a page and was informed that both the king and his queen were to be found in the privy apartments, while Queen Isabella had installed herself in the queen's apartments. Mortimer, it seemed, had been offered accommodation in one of the gatehouses.

"De Guirande!" Montagu came loping over to greet them. "You look horribly healthy," he commented. "A summer doing nothing has agreed with you."

"Not so sure I'd call it doing nothing," Adam replied, nodding at Eubulus Le Strange, who'd joined them. "And how are things in the north?"

"Fair enough," Eubulus replied. "Lancaster is ever the loyal subject of the king, and where Lancaster leads, his retainers follow. He's here, come with Grosmont to pay his respects."

"Grosmont unhorsed Edward the other day." Montagu grinned. "Did not please our king, and poor Grosmont has been falling over his feet to make amends since. Last I heard, he'd offered the king his new destrier as some sort of salve to that bruised pride."

"Beautiful animal," Eubulus said. "And about as vicious as a cornered wolf."

"Not the best of gifts, then," Adam commented. "How fares Lancaster?"

"Badly. He rarely ventures outside his rooms on his own. The king is much affected by his blindness." Montague made a discreet gesture to the other side of the open ward, where Lancaster was standing as tall as ever beside the young king. "And being blind, Lancaster no longer aspires to power. Like a lion with his teeth pulled, impressive but docile."

Adam steered his wife towards the king, bent knee before him, and was graciously invited to rise.

"Adam. Lady Kit." The king smiled at Kit. "I fear that you'll have to step beyond the walls to find Philippa." He tugged at the ears of Lancelot, his huge wolfhound.

"Among the trees, my lord?" Kit asked.

The king laughed. "Where else?" He leaned closer to Kit, his voice dropping. "She prefers my oaks to my courtiers. At least to some of them." He turned to Adam. "I have a new horse to show you."

Beside him, Lancaster's mouth twisted, the sour expression hastily smoothed away.

"My Lord Lancaster," Adam said politely, bowing deeply.

"De Guirande, isn't it?" Lancaster held out his hand as if wanting to touch Adam's face.

"Aye, my lord."

"My horse." King Edward tugged at Adam's sleeve. "You're going to go green with envy."

Adam was dragged away, and Kit was left alone with Lancaster. She couldn't very well leave him standing in the midst of all these people, so she took a step towards him.

"Would you want me to…"

"Lead me somewhere?" Lancaster laughed harshly. "How useless and pitiful a man becomes without his eyesight."

"You look anything but pitiful, my lord."

Whoever had helped Lancaster to dress was familiar with the great baron's love of fine clothes. Purple hose contrasted with a saffron mantel worn over a deep red tunic embroidered with purple flowers along its hem. A beautifully tooled belt,

a heavy gold collar, and a hat the same purple as the hose—
Lancaster would have been at home in the French court.

"I feel pitiful," Lancaster mumbled. "And angry." But he
set a hand on her shoulder and followed her towards a nearby
stone bench. "Is Mortimer here?" he asked abruptly. Kit came
to a halt, standing on her toes to look about.

"No, my lord."

"Good, good. I can't stand it, to have him sit beside me
and commiserate when all I can hear in his voice is how
delighted he is that I am thus laid low."

"That is unfair."

"Is it?" Lancaster cackled. "I can assure you he sleeps much
better now that I am incapacitated." He sat down carefully,
and Kit helped him arrange the folds of his garment.

"Thank you, my lady." His bony fingers circled her wrist.
"Do you see my son?"

"Yes, my lord."

Henry of Grosmont was making way towards them. As
tall as his father, he was broader of shoulder and walked with
the light step of a man accustomed to much exercise. Some
years older than the king, he shared the king's fascination
for all things military and was, according to Adam, as good
a contender in the lists as the king himself. In difference to
his father, he was simply dressed, dark hose and a matching
dark tunic of excellent cut enhancing his physical strength.
No beard, and his hair was cut unfashionably short, not quite
reaching his ears.

"Father," he said when he was a yard or so away. "Taking
the sun with a pretty lady?"

Kit blushed.

"A kind lady, at any rate." Lancaster turned his face
towards Kit. "I can't make out more than your shape."

"That is not a major loss, my lord." Kit stood and made a
reverence. "I must go."

"Ah yes. To find our fair queen lady among the oaks."
Lancaster's thin lips pulled into a smile.

Grosmont graciously offered to accompany her to the
postern, but Kit assured him she was familiar enough with

the castle to find her way on her own. After a quick nod to the slouching guard, she was outside, negotiating the grassy incline that flowed into woodlands.

Queen Philippa was sitting under the trees, accompanied by her ladies. Mathilde looked up at Kit's approach and nodded, but the other ladies did not pay her much heed—not until Philippa saw her and clapped her hands together.

"Kit!"

"My lady." Yet again she kneeled. "You look well."

"I am." But the reply was curt, and Kit dared a look at the queen's waist, as trim and narrow as ever.

Philippa dismissed her ladies and insisted she and Kit walk further in among the trees, trailed by two of her Hainault guards and Mathilde.

"Why?" Philippa twisted her girdle. "Why is it that I do not conceive? I pray to the Virgin every day, I kneel for hours in the chapel, and still God denies me this."

"You're young, my lady."

"I am fifteen! Old enough to carry a child." Philippa wiped at her eyes. "And what if I am barren?" She gnawed her lips. "He'll have to request an annulment," she said in a choked voice. "And I will be shamed as the useless wife, with no future but that of a nun somewhere." She turned anguished eyes on Kit. "I do not want to be a nun! And I—" She broke off.

"Love him, my lady?"

"Yes." A whisper, no more. "My mother always said a marriage was not about love. It's a partnership in which a woman provides the heirs and the husband provides everything else. Love, she said, was for fools. And here I am, incapable of supplying the heirs, but in love."

"The king is very fond of you."

"I know. But he is anxious for a son, and if I do not give him one…" Philippa lifted her shoulders. "Why else has he delayed my coronation?" She sat down in a patch of sunlight.

"That may be due to others," Kit said.

"Oh, I know my mother-in-law goes the colour of green bile at the thought of there being two crowned queens in

157

England, but had Edward truly pushed the issue, she'd acquiesce, if nothing else to keep him from meddling too much in how his kingdom is ruled." A brief smile, revealing her somewhat crooked incisor. "But he hasn't pushed, Lady Kit." She tugged at the grass. "He says that once I am with child, he will give me the most magnificent coronation a queen has had." She met Kit's eyes. "Once I am with child."

Kit sat down beside her. "Sometimes, wanting too much can stop the seed from growing."

"How can I stop wanting?" Philippa's voice was thick with tears. "All I want is to give my lord husband a child."

It was a fish day, and so dinner consisted of one fish dish after the other, with Adam picking at the elaborately presented pike, lampreys, and fish pie. On his one side, Eubulus was keeping up a monologue about the sad state of affairs in Northern England, the Scots an ever-present burr up the arse of the northern lords. Adam wasn't really listening but managed to produce the odd 'ah' at regular intervals.

"Did you like the horse?" Montagu asked from his other side.

"Magnificent beast." A dark dappled grey with a mane and tail as white as spun silver, the king's new horse was eye-catching, but with a vicious streak that had Adam staying well away. A horse like that could just as easily turn on its rider. What Grosmont was doing with it to begin with was a mystery, and Adam was in two minds about the wisdom in giving it to their king.

"Edward says he can handle him," Montagu said.

"What else can he say?" Adam grinned. "To refuse the gift would be to admit Grosmont is the better horseman." He grew serious. "But I don't like the beast. Should he unhorse our king, he may very well trample him—out of spite."

"That's what you get when you use violence to break a horse," Eubulus put in.

"Oh?" Montagu winked at Adam. "And have you done much horse-breaking, dear Eubulus? Maybe while you were in Thomas of Lancaster's employ?"

Eubulus wiped his fingers on his napkin. "Maybe so."

"I've always found that breaking a horse to the saddle is much the same as teaching a woman how to please you in bed," Montagu continued, a wicked gleam in his eyes.

"Really?" Eubulus sounded mildly bored. "If so, allow me to express my deepest sympathies for your wife."

Adam choked back a gust of laughter. Montagu glared at him. "Katherine has no complaints," he said.

"Ah. I am glad to hear it." Eubulus dabbed at his mouth. "Neither does mine, and just to make things absolutely clear, I did not touch her—not like that—until we were married."

Adam found that doubtful, what with all the whispering that surrounded Alice de Lacy, but he saw no reason to say so. Instead, he returned to the subject of the horse. "Horses like that are best let out to pasture among the mares—before they break their rider's neck."

"Say that to the king and he'll be even more determined to prove you wrong." Will Montague used a thumbnail to dislodge something from between his teeth, mumbling an apology for doing so.

"Aye." Adam sat back. "Unfortunately."

Chapter 18

Two days later, Adam was nearly sent sprawling by the hard slap to his back.

"Ha!" Thomas grabbed for his arm. "Nearly got you there."

"Nice to see you too," Adam replied, easing his shoulders. "That hurt."

"You're going soft, old man." Thomas hung an arm round Adam's neck.

"Old?" Adam shoved at him. "I'm only five years older than you."

"Decrepit, nearly," Thomas said, his laugh converting into a groan when Adam punched his arm. "Wine?"

Kit was with the queen—the ladies were busy with a new counterpane for the royal bed—so Adam followed Thomas to his lodgings, a set of small rooms in one of the gatehouses. Adam had to grin. "The earls get gatehouses this season," he commented. "Although Mortimer's rooms are in the next gatehouse."

"Of course. Saves him having to walk too far after his nightly visits to Isabella." Thomas called for wine, and a thin little boy appeared, balancing a large pitcher. "My son," Thomas introduced, ruffling the boy's hair. Large hazel eyes fringed with dark lashes regarded Adam cautiously.

"Master Edward." Adam bowed, and the laddie squirmed, fleeing when his father dismissed him. "Handsome lad," Adam offered.

"Mmm." Thomas sniffed at the wine. "Somewhat cautious. Has it from his mother. So what news of the king?"

The evening disappeared in Thomas' company, a sharing of news, of concerns. By the time the wine was gone, it was dark, and after bidding Thomas good night, Adam made his way carefully down the stairwell and strolled off towards his own lodgings in the lower ward.

As he passed the stables, he heard a commotion inside. A muffled squeal, and Adam cursed. The king's new horse—now named Boreas—was proving a handful. Compact, with powerful hindquarters and a deep chest, Boreas was everything one could wish for in a warhorse—strong enough to carry a man in armour, fleet and nimble. But he was fretful and mean, not above crowding the stable lads into a corner and then stamping all over them.

The stable was sunk in gloom. In his stall, Boreas was fighting his halter, hooves skidding this way and that. A lad was nursing his arm, an overturned bucket of oats at his feet.

"He bit you?"

"Aye, sir."

"Get it seen to." Adam swept up the oats. "And let's give this one hay only for a while."

The lad darted off. Adam approached the stallion warily, crooning softly. The ears tipped forward, the neck arched. When the horse lunged, teeth bared, Adam grabbed it by the halter and tugged—hard.

"Behave."

Some stalls down, Raven had his head up, and after ensuring Boreas was adequately tethered, Adam went over to give his stallion an affectionate pat. He entered the stall and stroked Raven over his massive back, laughing softly at how the horse whickered in response.

There was a clatter by the door. Two men, talking in hushed tones, and Adam slipped behind Raven, standing silent in the shadows.

"So this is our king's new horse, is it?" Lord Roger stopped by Boreas' stall. "Must have cost Grosmont a fortune."

"Spanish," Richard said. "But they say he's vicious."

"Is he now?" Lord Roger made as if to stroke the horse's nose, retracted his hand with a curse when the horse's head snaked out. "Brute."

"I warned you, my lord. But he's handsome, isn't he?"

"Oh yes." Lord Roger beckoned for Richard to raise the

lantern he was carrying. "Well worth the little walk just to see him. And Kent is going to Spain, you say?"

Kent? Adam crouched, a hand on Raven's withers.

"With his lady—so dear John informs us." Richard lowered his voice. "He's been to Avignon, that we know. But we have no idea what transpired between Kent and His Holiness."

"Treason," Lord Roger replied with a bite to his voice. "What else?" To judge from the sound of his footsteps he moved further into the stables, and Adam remained where he was, his cheek pressed to Raven's side. Should he make himself known? He was just about to straighten up when Lord Roger spoke again.

"It's a perilous road to Santiago de Compostela, is it not?"

"Very, my lord," Richard replied. "People die all the time, what with the bandits that live in those mountains."

"Yes, they do, don't they? Wouldn't it be terrible if our handsome peacock of an earl were to meet with a fatal accident?"

No. Adam closed his eyes. He must have misheard.

Richard snickered. "Terrible, my lord. Devastating. And imagine if Lady Margaret were to die as well?"

"Three little orphans." Lord Roger sighed. "Sad. It would be very, very sad. But convenient."

"Yes, my lord."

Lord Roger and Richard came to a halt just beyond Raven's stall, two dark shapes, no more. Adam lowered himself further, glad of Raven's bulk. He tugged his hood up and sank into the darkest corner, wincing as the straw rustled.

"What was that?" Lord Roger's voice was sharp. Adam held his breath. One of the other horses snorted, a hoof scraped against the cobbles, and Richard laughed.

"Nothing, my lord."

"My Lord Mortimer?" someone called out from the door.

"Yes?" Lord Roger replied.

"A messenger, my lord."

"Yes, yes, I'll be right there." Lord Roger was already on the move, Richard in his wake. Adam sat down in the straw, hooked his arms around his legs, and did his best to stop trembling.

The first thing he did once he'd regained some control was find his wife. The only person whose advice he truly wanted was Kit's—or Thomas', but going to his friend to discuss a potential assassination of Thomas' brother could lead to some nasty repercussions, like a sword through Mortimer's bowels.

"I might have misunderstood," he said to Kit some time later. "Maybe he was expressing genuine concern."

Kit just looked at him. She'd been asleep when he entered their room, but now she was wide awake, the blanket over her shoulders.

"I know," Adam groaned. "But to think Lord Roger capable of…" He threw her a pleading look. "You once said Mortimer was too honourable to lower himself to murder."

"I did. But since then the stakes have gone up, and Kent is walking a thin line. If he truly went to Avignon to discuss the former king, then one could argue he's betraying his nephew. Mortimer will do anything to keep the king safe." She smiled crookedly. "For his own sake, mostly."

"Aye." He sank down on their bed.

"You have to tell the king."

"And in so doing, betray Lord Roger?" His throat clogged.

"All you need to say is that you suspect there may be a plot afoot, and that Earl Edmund should be warned."

Adam pinched the bridge of his nose. "Edward is no fool, sweeting."

"No. But you don't need to name anyone." She moved closer. "If you want, I can tell Philippa. Say I overheard something." She smiled. "Not in the stables, obviously, but maybe in the chapel?"

His wife spent a lot of time in St Edward's chapel, having confided to Adam it was one of those spaces—just like the chapel at Tresaints—where she felt God's presence keenly.

"No, it must be me." He took her hand. "But I'd like you with me."

"Now?" She was already on her feet, retrieving her kirtle from the clothes pole.

Adam drew in a long breath. "Now."

The guard at the entrance to the king's rooms was surprised but did not question their right to enter, despite the late hour. In the antechamber, one of the king's squires was snoring on a pallet, two sleepy page boys sitting by the door. In response to Adam's low voice, they pulled the door open, and Adam stood aside to allow Kit to enter first.

Propitiously, they found the king and queen out of bed, bent over a chessboard. Edward was scowling, his wife was smirking, and from the look of the board it was but a matter of moves before the king lost.

"Check," the queen said sweetly, moving her rook. "I have you neatly cornered, Ned." In the privacy of her bedchamber, she'd undone her hair, hanging like a dark curtain down her back. She had also removed her outer garments, sitting with her legs pulled up in only her chemise.

"Again," Edward demanded. He was equally undressed, the hem of his shirt having ridden up to expose most of his bare legs. His fair hair shone in the candlelight, sweeping down in soft waves to just below his ears. At his side, Lancelot raised his head, looking directly at Adam and Kit.

"Of course." She grinned. "Not that you'll win this time either." She saw Kit and Adam and rose. "Are you any good at chess, Adam?" She found a robe and draped herself in it.

"Aye, my lady." Adam bowed, as did Kit. "My wife never wins."

Beside him, Kit huffed.

"Never?" Philippa asked.

"No, my lady." Kit shrugged. "I've not played much."

Adam hid a smile. She'd played much more than him and hated how easily he'd bested her.

"Why are you here?" the king asked bluntly. "It is late for a courtesy visit."

"I overheard something," Adam began. He came to a halt, had to wet his lips. Kit slipped her hand into his.

"That bad, is it?" The king sat down. "Is it my mother?"

"No, my lord." Adam swallowed. "It's your uncle."

"Thomas?" The king flew to his feet. "Is he ailing?"

Adam shook his head. "I…" Why did it have to be him who'd overheard this? Kit squeezed his hand in silent support. "I fear there is a plan afoot to arrange the death of Edmund of Kent."

"What?" The king took a step back. "No! Why would… Damn it, what has he done now?"

"Who, my lord?"

"Edmund, of course! Off he goes to tell tales to His Holiness, so what is he up to now? Is he planning a rebellion?"

"He's thinking of going on a pilgrimage, my lord. To Santiago de Compostela."

"A pilgrimage?" The king blinked. "Edmund? Then why…" He gritted his teeth. "Mortimer, ridding himself of competition."

"Or of a potential traitor," Philippa put in, and Adam would gladly have fallen to his knees and kissed her feet for that comment.

"Edmund would never betray me!"

"No? And yet he rode all the way to Avignon without informing you beforehand." Philippa poured her husband some wine. "Edmund loves you—but he walks confused. Very confused. And so he could very well betray you."

Edward drank deeply before responding. "Maybe." He frowned. "I have to do something. I can't let him ride off into the Spanish wilderness only to be killed." He strode to the door. "Gerald! Fetch Earl Thomas—but do it quietly, you hear?"

It did not take long for Thomas to appear at the door in only his shirt and a robe. His shoes were unlaced, and he smothered a yawn as he entered, his eyes going from drowsy to wide awake the moment he saw Adam. His gaze never left Adam as the king explained why he'd been dragged out of bed, and in his eyes Adam saw compassion—and love.

"We must send Edmund a messenger," Edward finished. "Tell him to abort his planned pilgrimage." He took a turn around the room. "Do you know someone your brother would trust implicitly?"

Thomas nodded in the direction of Adam. Blood scalded Adam's cheeks, at once honoured and embarrassed.

"Not him!" Edward scowled. "I send Adam to France, and Mortimer will know why." He threw himself into an armchair and waved a hand to indicate they could sit as well. "Who else?"

"One of my men will do." Thomas scrubbed at his face. "And to think my son is to wed one of his daughters."

"I prefer it that his daughters wed the sons of men I trust," Edward said. "And as I hear it, the Mortimer girls are all a credit to their mother." He looked from one to the other. "Not a word—to anyone. And now if you will excuse me, I wish to retire."

Adam stumbled to his feet, numb all over. It had happened, the one thing he'd always hoped he'd never have to do. He'd betrayed the man he loved above all others—God's teeth, how it hurt to admit that to himself!—and how was he to live with it? How was he to look Lord Roger in the eyes and pretend nothing had changed?

Thomas squeezed his shoulder as they parted company. "Thank you. I know what it cost you."

Adam shrugged off his hand. "No you don't."

"Adam, I—"

"Not now, Thomas," Kit interrupted. She stood close enough that Adam could inhale the scent of her, feel her warmth. He draped an arm round her shoulders and made his way to their distant room, glad of her silent support, of the strength with which she held on to his waist.

"It is really no great matter. One could argue Lord Mortimer was acting out of concern for the safety of the realm," Philippa commented in a low voice the next morning. She and Kit were sitting on their own in one of the window seats, working on the gold border that was to surround the English lions. The gold thread was difficult to handle, requiring great precision in the needlework. "And, as I told Ned, he would never do anything without discussing it with Isabella first."

"Probably not, my lady." Queen Isabella had little time for the younger of her brothers-in-law, alternating between calling him fickle and difficult.

"But it was the right thing to do—for Adam," Philippa continued. "Difficult, I imagine." She gave Kit a quick look.

"Yes, my lady." It had taken hours before he had finally fallen asleep, as shocked by the fact that Mortimer would contemplate assassination as he was by what he saw as his own betrayal.

"What are you whispering about?" Queen Isabella had entered on soundless feet, causing both Kit and Philippa to start.

"My lady." Kit rose automatically and made a reverence. Isabella slipped into her vacated seat and bent over to peer at their handiwork.

"Very nice." She smiled at her daughter-in-law. "Edward will be very pleased."

"Edward will not notice," Philippa replied. "When do men ever notice anything but their hounds and horses, their new tunics and weapons?" She stroked the plush, dark red velvet. "This is for me, more than for him."

Isabella laughed, a light tinkling sound. "Wise beyond your years, my dear." Long, elegant fingers brushed ever so lightly over Philippa's sleeve. "But surely by now you know what to do to catch his attention, don't you?"

"My lady?" Philippa sat erect.

"Seeing as there's no heir…" Isabella left the rest hanging. She patted Philippa on the cheek. "Ah well, still plenty of time for that. Not an infinite amount of time, mind you." She reclined against the stone wall and gave Philippa a little smile. "Fortunately, I have a younger son as well. Just in case."

Philippa raised her chin. "There will be a son, my lady."

"Good." Isabella stood, a collection of silks in various shades of blue. "It would be such a pity to have to send you back to your mother branded a barren wife."

Kit was tempted to sink her embroidery needle into Queen Isabella's arm. Instead, she made yet another reverence, her eyes on the floor as the queen mother departed in a swirl of skirts.

Philippa was sitting as still as a statue. A single tear slid down her cheek.

"Do you think we should have tassels?" she finally asked, her voice thick with tears.

"My lady, you shouldn't take what she says to heart. She's—"

"A queen. Mother four times over." Philippa cleared her throat. "So, tassels?"

Chapter 19

"Does it feel like coming home?" Kit held in her palfrey some distance away from the imposing gates of Wigmore Castle. They'd come up from Gloucester with the king's retinue, and after an hour or so riding in a fine drizzle, Kit looked bedraggled and cold.

"Home?" Adam squinted at the distant inner gatehouse above which flapped the Mortimer banner. "Not anymore."

He mentally calculated how many years it was since he'd been here last: almost eight years, his last visit being in January of 1321, mere weeks before Lord Roger was obliged to submit to the king. Lord Roger... Adam sighed.

His sore conscience had eased over the last few weeks. As Kit had pointed out repeatedly, it could be argued he'd saved Mortimer from indirectly committing a most grievous sin. But he kept his distance from his former lord, and especially from Richard de Monmouth, not quite being able to forget how his redheaded brother-in-law had snickered at the thought of Earl Edmund—and Lady Margaret, whom both Adam and Kit liked—dead.

They crossed the first drawbridge, rode through the large outer bailey, rode over the inner protective ditch, under the gatehouse, and emerged in the lower bailey. For an instant, Adam imagined himself ten years back in time: Lord Roger returning victorious from Ireland, his men as dirty and tired as him, and out from the hall came Lady Joan, neat and serene as she welcomed them home.

This time, there was no Lady Joan—and more was the pity, with Adam's innards tightening at the sight of Queen Isabella where Lady Joan should rightfully be, at Lord Roger's side. Lord Roger had ridden ahead to prepare his grand castle for his guests, and he was presently greeting the king with a customary reverence, his velvet robes a most becoming green.

"And does it bring back fond memories?" Kit shivered, her hands tightening for an instant on the mane of her palfrey.

"Some. Not for you, I can see."

"Not many." Her eyes acquired a faraway look. "The first time I came here, you weren't speaking to me."

"No." He dismounted. It had been too raw at the time, with him recently having found out his wife was not the woman he thought her to be, Katherine de Monmouth, but instead was Kit Courcy and illegitimate to boot.

"And then you rode off to war, and I spent as much time as I could on the battlements, hoping to see you come riding home. But you never did, and soon enough we heard that you'd been imprisoned by the king." She gave him a little smile before sliding into his receiving arms. "Awful weeks, in truth."

"Aye. But all that is in the past." He pressed his lips to her forehead.

"Adam!" A red-cheeked King Edward came leaping down the stairs to the hall. "Did you see? I rode him all the way, and not once did he attempt to throw me."

"I did, my lord." Not, in Adam's opinion, due to Boreas becoming docile. The horse had been tired after four days on the road. For all its mettle, the stallion was sadly out of shape.

The king tore back up the stairs to where his wife was waiting for him. Of late, Queen Philippa looked out of sorts, her plump mouth pressed together into a thin line whenever the king had his attention elsewhere. Not to wonder, given what Queen Isabella had said to her.

"Unnecessarily cruel," Kit had told him, and Adam could but agree. Philippa did not deserve to be treated with anything but kindness.

Adam spent the following hour reacquainting himself with the castle he had once considered his home. Men to be greeted, some of them laughing at Adam's rusty Welsh, others so pleased to see him they enfolded him in hugs.

He was in deep conversation with old Will, one of the

fletchers who had his workshop in the outer bailey, when someone called his name.

"Adam!" A woman came trotting towards him, arms wide open. "As handsome as ever!"

"Emma." He bowed, neatly avoiding her hug.

She laughed. "What, not good enough for you now?" Her magnificent raven-coloured hair was neatly covered by a veil, little ringlets sprouting along her hairline. Eyes as green as the Welsh hills studied him from under dark lashes, her mouth curving into a little smile.

"I am a married man." And Emma belonged to his past, to a long-gone summer when she gladly went with him into the woods, as eager to explore him as he was to explore her.

"As I am a married woman—well, a widow." Emma did not sound unduly grieved. "Poor Patrick died some years ago."

"Patrick? The master mason?"

"The same." She looked him up and down. "I like big men." She made as if to take his arm; he took a step backwards and collided with Kit.

"Kit!" He heard himself how flustered he sounded.

"That's me." His wife turned her attention to Emma. "And you are?"

"Emma. Adam and I have known each other for years." She emphasised the word *known*, and Kit's eyebrows shot up. Emma made her excuses and left, walking away with a provocative sway to her hips. Kit watched her out of sight before turning to Adam.

"We've been given a room down by the forge." She gestured to a cluster of buildings just this side of the inner drawbridge. "Gavin has brought up our belongings in case you want to change before supper." She brushed at his tunic. "Did you love her?"

"Emma? I was a lad; she was a pretty wench. No more, no less." But he couldn't help casting a look in the direction she had disappeared. The pretty wench had become quite the attractive woman.

Kit went off to attend on the queen, and Adam continued

171

with his disrupted exploration, climbing up to walk the wall, right up to the furthest end, where the oldest part of the Mortimer seat still stood—the ancient keep housing the lord's apartments, surrounded by its own bailey and an assortment of buildings.

Adam ended up at the highest point on the curtain wall, out of breath after the steep climb. From here, the wall sloped all the way to the main gate, and should he lean over too far, chances were he'd end up spattered all over the stones far below. To the west, the sun was disappearing beyond the undulating line of the Welsh hills. A kite soared upwards, the wind caught at his cloak, and for all that it was only early September, there was an edge to it, reminding Adam of winter days spent cold and muddy as he followed Lord Roger on one campaign or the other.

"Reminiscing?" A hand on his shoulder, and Adam turned to find Mortimer smiling at him.

"Aye, my lord." Adam didn't quite know where to fix his gaze.

Lord Roger leaned his elbows on the parapet. "Is it only me, or was life not simpler back then?"

"You never aspired to a simple life, my lord."

Lord Roger dislodged a little pebble from the mortar and sent it flying. "No, I never did. More fool me." He looked at Adam, and the shadows in his eyes had Adam's heart going out to him. "The beauty of a simple life is never apparent until it is no longer achievable. Remember that, Adam."

"Aye, my lord." He edged closer. "Is there something I can do?"

"Do? As one makes one's bed, one must lie in it." Mortimer's teeth showed in yet another smile. "And I can't complain about my bedmate, can I?"

"No, my lord." Adam shifted on his feet. "Lady Joan isn't coming, is she?"

"No." It came out very softly. "She chose not to and who can blame her?" With his eyes on the distant hills he added, almost inaudibly; "I miss her. I wish she knew that."

Emma quickly became a nuisance, appearing seemingly out of

nowhere to smile and simper at Adam, always when Kit was close enough to notice.

"She's very comely," Kit commented on one such occasion, her voice frigid.

"Is she? I really don't notice."

"You're a bad liar." If anything, her tone was even colder.

Adam sighed. "Aye, she is comely, and aye, I have eyes in my head, but it is not me who looks for her, it is her who sets herself in my way whenever she can. All I can do is ignore her and hope she'll find someone else to pester."

"Hmm." Kit tugged her new mantel tight, some of the yellow silk lining visible. "I don't like it."

"Neither do I, sweeting." Out of the corner of his eye, he saw Emma lounging some yards away. He pulled Kit close and kissed her deeply. "But we need not care about her, do we?" he murmured when he released her. He smiled at her responding blush. The early morning had been most gratifying—to them both.

Kit went her way, and after throwing Emma yet another black look—something that only made the damned woman toss her head and grin—Adam stepped into the shadowy interior of the stables.

"Devil of a horse!" someone yelled, and one of the horses screeched in response. Boreas, of course, dancing about like a fiend on fire in his stall. The stable lad took a swipe at him with his broom, his movement arrested by Adam's hand.

"That's the king's horse," Adam warned.

"And these are my toes," the stable lad replied, lifting up his foot covered in a bloody leather shoe. "There's something wrong with him; it's as if he's possessed."

"A horse?" Adam laughed. "Not likely." He beckoned two other grooms over, and together they led out the stallion, tethering him to two stout posts. Some more rope, and the horse was immobilised, eyes rolling as Adam inspected him.

"Best be careful." John Maltravers emerged from one of the stalls and nodded a greeting to Adam. "That horse will be the death of someone."

"Of himself, likely." Adam stood, wiping his hands on a

173

rag. There was a long gash along the inner side of the horse's rear right fetlock where he'd stepped on himself.

"Not what I hear." Maltravers took a turn round the horse. "I hear he's killed two riders already. That's why Grosmont got him so cheap."

"Really?" Adam stroked the horse's sweaty neck.

"Only a fool would ride him," Maltravers continued. "Mortimer has repeatedly tried to get the king to see that."

Adam smiled into Boreas' mane. Lord Roger's concern would only make the king more determined to tame the stallion. "That won't deter him."

"Knowing him, you're probably right. Fortunately, there's a spare, just in case."

"What exactly are you saying?"

"Nothing. I was merely pointing out that the kingdom has other male heirs—one of them much younger and more malleable." Maltravers shook his head. "Personally, I prefer the king we have, which is why I'd recommend feeding this one to the dogs."

"A waste," Adam said. "Is Berkeley here as well?" In general, where John Maltravers was, there was Thomas Berkeley. Joined at the hip, those two, and even more since they'd been charged with the care of Edward of Caernarvon back in 1327.

"With his wife." Maltravers grinned. "A happy family event, these weddings. And then there's the joust—who'd want to miss all the excitement?"

Adam, for one. Mortimer was hosting quite the spectacle, the fields below the escarpment on which Wigmore stood dotted with tents and pavilions. Every knight worth his name seemed to be here, and Lord Roger was paying for it all, a magnificent display of wealth.

"Round Table and all that crap," Maltravers said. "God knows how many will show up pretending to be Lancelot."

"Or King Arthur."

"That part is already taken." Maltravers made an elaborate bow. "Mortimer has named himself king of Camelot, with the fair Queen Isabella as his Guinevere."

"And the king?"

"Lancelot—or maybe not, now that he knows his mother is to play Arthur's faithless wife." Maltravers chuckled. "Fitting, isn't it?"

Adam made a face. "He can't take the part of Arthur!"

"He already has." Maltravers grew serious. "For a man so intelligent, at times he makes the most blatant mistakes."

"Does the king know?"

Maltravers shook his head from side to side. "I think the honour of telling him belongs to you."

"Shit!" Adam slammed his hand against one of the nearby posts. "Why me?"

"Because you have the biggest balls?" Maltravers suggested, escaping outside with a loud gurgle of laughter when Adam threatened him with a pitchfork.

Adam spent the short walk from the stables to the magnificent guest rooms presently housing the king cursing under his breath. His footsteps echoed over the heavy floorboards of the hall, empty of all but a couple of the king's household knights. Up yet another flight of stairs, and the sentry straightened up, a hand on his sword.

Adam greeted the king's squires brusquely, irritated by the suppressed grins. They knew, the little bastards, and they were more than delighted at having someone other than them inform the king. He waited as he was announced and entered a room brimming with sunlight, the shutters thrown wide open.

Adam had not been in this room since 1321. He gawped at the glazed windows, at the recently plastered walls decorated with a recurring motif of dragons and lions. Two Turkish carpets on the floor, one of them presently housing the snoring canine Lancelot, armchairs, embroidered cushions, and in pride of place the large bed, painted in green and gold. The sheets were rumpled, the hangings half-drawn, and by the empty hearth the king was leaning on the mantel, attempting to look as if he had not just leapt out of bed.

"Good morning, Adam." Philippa finished adjusting her clothes.

"My lady. My lord."

"What brings you here?" Edward's flushed face and swollen lips had Adam supressing a smile. And without too much thought, he took a big breath and told his king what he had come to say.

The king was livid. "Him, Arthur? Me, one of his knights? I don't think so!" A mail chausse went flying through the air. "No, if he wants to be Arthur, then I will be Mordred." Yet another chausse, causing Adam to duck. "And Mordred killed Arthur."

"If you go as Mordred, you're telling everyone you see him as your enemy." Philippa came to stand behind her husband, resting her cheek against his broad back.

"He is my enemy!" The chessboard was upended.

"He is one of your regents," Philippa replied calmly, bending down to retrieve some of the chess pieces. "As yet, you have to live with him—and your mother."

"And she as Guinevere! It's tasteless, given that everyone knows she was Mortimer's lover long before my father…" He cleared his throat.

"Died," Philippa supplied. "Officially, at least. We can be Tristan and Iseult instead."

"I should be Arthur," Edward insisted.

"But I could never be Guinevere." Philippa went down on her knees before him. "I would never play a faithless woman. I will never be a faithless woman." Adam gave her an admiring look. Their little queen knew just how to play her husband. The king was staring down at her.

"Philippa." He gripped his wife and lifted her up. "My Philippa." He buried his face in her hair.

Adam decided to leave them alone.

"First the weddings, then this." Thomas scowled, surveying the huge ground set aside for the coming melee. It clearly rankled that his young son had just been wed to one of Mortimer's daughters, no matter that little Beatrice had been generously dowered. "My Edward wed to a Mortimer daughter. I don't like it, no matter how biddable and comely the girl is."

"Surely, you had a say in the matter," Kit said, standing on her toes in an effort to catch sight of her husband.

"Let's just say it was made very clear to me it would benefit me and my son to go along with this wedding." He shrugged. "Well, we shall have the raising of her, and at least they are of an age." He beckoned, and a boy came running.

In colouring, little Edward of Norfolk was his father's son, but his heart-shaped face, the delicate set to his mouth must have come from his mother.

"Will you be cheering for me?" Thomas asked. The lad nodded. "Good. Stay with Lady Kit; she will see you safe."

Kit held out her hand to the boy. "Be careful, my lord. And tell Adam he best be careful too." She had little liking for tournaments.

"Careful? What would be the fun in that?" For all that he was in full armour, Thomas vaulted over the railing.

"Men," Kit muttered.

"My lady?" Little Edward tugged at her hand. "May Beatrice come with us?"

"Beatrice? Is she here?" Kit shaded her eyes, looking for Mortimer's daughter.

"Aye." The boy waved at someone, and a little girl came scampering towards them. "My wife," the boy introduced. All of nine, and already married. Such was the way of the rich and mighty, children wedding children.

"Shall we find somewhere to sit?" Kit ushered her young charges towards the stands. The central section was adorned by a huge canopy, a border of green dragons on white silk. It made Kit frown: first Mortimer styled himself King Arthur, then all these references to Merlin's old prophecy about a future king coming from Wales. One could almost believe Mortimer was planning to usurp the crown—except that Queen Isabella would never let him.

Isabella was dressed in white, swathed in numerous transparent veils held in place by a thick gold circlet. Golden bands decorated her arms, the girdle was in gold and white, and beside her Philippa looked childish rather than young, her choice of bright red and green garish.

177

The children squealed in delight when Mortimer rode up to demand a favour from his queen. In silver and white, he was as elegant as Queen Isabella, his new armour polished so it glittered in the sun. Once Isabella handed him a strip of silk, he rode back to his team, above which unfurled a banner with a roaring dragon.

On the other side of the field sat the king, for the day on his reliable bay stallion. His armour caught the sun, the lion that adorned his helmet bared its fangs, and over his head flew the red cross of St George. Kit swallowed. George, the dragon slayer, facing off against the dragon from the west.

"Look! Look! My father!" Edward hung over the railings, pointing at Thomas, who had taken his place among the king's knights. Kit counted off the familiar arms: Montagu and Stafford, Ufford and de Warenne, Norfolk and Grosmont.

"And there's mine!" Beatrice leapt up and down, clapping her hands. "My father is the greatest knight in the world. He's King Arthur."

In Kit's biased opinion, the greatest knight in the world was presently sitting his coal-black horse some paces behind his king. Kit raised her arm in the futile hope that he'd see her among all these people. And then the horns blew, and the two teams charged towards each other. Kit cheered when Adam unhorsed his opponent.

"As skilled as ever," a soft voice commented from behind her. Kit turned. "My lady." Emma offered her a halfhearted reverence. "Had I known he'd rise to such a position, I'd have insisted he marry me all those years ago."

"Really? As he tells it, you were no innocent."

"Neither was he." Emma smiled. "Handsome and tall, but poor as a church mouse. I wanted more."

"And now he's mine. For good," Kit said.

Emma's green eyes narrowed. "Maybe you're underestimating me."

"You?" Kit fiddled with her veil. "I think not. He finds you crude and brazen."

Emma leaned closer. "At least I'm not a scar-faced bastard.

A pity, such a handsome man wedded to a woman marked like that."

"Lady Kit is a pretty lady," Edward of Norfolk piped up. He glared at Emma. "My father says she's the prettiest woman at court—and the kindest."

"Oh dear; an admirer, Lady Kit? And is it only the son, or is it the father as well?" Emma laughed, tweaked Edward's cheek, and moved off.

Chapter 20

"A good day." Adam winced when Kit placed a poultice of lady's mantle and meadowsweet over a shallow gash on his face. He was covered in bruises and scratches, but the fact that the king had carried the day—a wise move from Lord Roger—had him in a mellow mood, as did the promising smells of roasting meat drifting from the kitchens.

"Hungry?" she teased when his stomach growled.

"Like a starving wolf." He kissed her and pulled her to her feet. "Coming?"

They entered the hall together. On the further side was the dais, and instead of the normal high table, Mortimer had brought in a massive round thing draped in white tablecloths, yet again embroidered with green dragons. The table was decorated with roses—blood red petals that matched the tapestries that hung on the walls, depicting unicorns and dragons, leopards and wolves in gold thread and silver against a scarlet background.

"Ah." Kit stood on her toes. "The Round Table itself." Mortimer was already in his seat—the high seat—with Queen Isabella at his side, still arraigned as the fair Guinevere. When the king entered, all those assembled stood. Except for Lord Roger and Queen Isabella.

"Damn." Adam tightened his hold on Kit's hand. The king walked slowly down the hall, his wife by his side. People bowed, hats came off, and Edward nodded in return, a stately progress towards the high table. Once there, the king halted at Mortimer's chair, as if waiting.

"At last, our young lion himself." Lord Roger patted the chair beside him. "Don't loiter, or the food may spoil."

Without a word, the king sat down.

"He's taking this too far," Adam said to Kit once the meal was concluded. "Who does he think he is?"

"King Arthur?" Kit suggested.

"He's the Earl of March, the king's subject, not his equal."

"I'm sure he knows that," Kit replied. "He's just playing the part."

"Or taking the opportunity offered by the part to send a subtle message." He gestured at the recurring dragons, at the Mortimer men who lined the walls, at the magnificence of the hall itself, the walls hung with Arras tapestries that each cost more than what Adam earned in a year. "These are the trappings of a king in the making."

Throughout the evening's festivities, Mortimer acted the king, treating King Edward with no more courtesy than anyone else. He was served first, he sat while the king stood, he waved the king silent when he had something he wished to say. And with every insult, King Edward grew paler and silent, until he suddenly left, trailed by his wife and his closest companions.

"I have to go." Adam was half out of his seat.

"So must I. The queen will have need of her ladies."

"Rather her than him," Adam muttered. If he knew his lord well, this would end up being a long night.

The waxing moon was brushing the distant horizon when Adam was at last allowed to seek his bed. His head thudded: too much wine, too much anger, and God alone knew how they would all fare in tomorrow's—today's—events. At present, just the thought of donning a helmet had Adam wincing, and as to straddling a horse…

He was almost at the forge when two hands slipped round his waist. "Hello," Emma purred. "I've been waiting and waiting for you."

"Let me go." His tongue was furred and uncooperative, but he managed to disengage himself.

"What harm would it do? Your scarred wife is surely asleep, and as I recall you like to swive when you're drunk."

"If I want to swive, I'll do it with Kit." He lurched, steadied himself against a wall. "And I'd have to very desperate to do it with someone gagging for it."

The blow to his shoulder had him reeling. "Bastard! You liked it well enough, back then."

"Aye." Adam belched. "But I grew out of rutting like beasts."

Only silence greeted this remark. He supposed the shadowed shape he saw pressed into the corner was Emma, and a suppressed snivel had him taking a step towards her.

"That came out harsher than I intended," he said.

"Go to hell," Emma snarled, shoving past him. Adam shrugged. Hopefully, this would stop her chasing after him like a bitch in heat.

Kit had to shake him awake at dawn. A couple of pitchers of cold water later, and he was clearheaded enough to dress and prepare for the coming tournament, with Kit helping him with hose points and drawstrings.

The king's team assembled in the stables, all of them the worse for wear. The king looked as if he'd slept on the floor, Montagu smelled of vinegar and vomit, and even Thomas groaned at the thought of taking the field, this despite being the only one bar Adam to arrive fully armoured.

"He's going to have us eating dust," Thomas mumbled to Adam as they took their positions. On the opposite side of the field, the glorious King Arthur was rallying his troops, their loud responding yells causing Adam to wince.

"Let's make sure it costs them." Adam hefted his blunted lance. No sharp points allowed, thank the Lord, as otherwise today would have seen the ground littered with dead and seriously wounded.

Mortimer raised his hand, and his men set themselves in motion, a steady canter that sent tremors through the ground. With a hoarse yell, King Edward spurred his horse forward, and with him went his men, yelling their defiance as they charged towards the other side. They clashed together, and horses jostled, men grappled. The heralds were everywhere, quick to intervene with their heavy staffs when things got too rough.

By noon, Mortimer's side had been declared the victor, and King Edward rode off the field with murder in his eyes.

"Tomorrow, I'll ride Boreas," Edward told Adam as he dismounted. He smiled, eyes as cold as ice. "If I'm fortunate, the horse will show itself at its most murderous and trample Mortimer underfoot."

An unknown groom snickered, grabbing the king's reins. "Like unleashing the pale rider of the Apocalypse."

"Who asked you?" Edward barked, and the groom apologised, bowing repeatedly before leading away the king's sweaty stallion. The well-educated groom looked vaguely familiar, but try as he might, Adam could put no name to him. Well, no matter. Adam handed over Raven to Stephen and ruffled his page's hair.

"Walk him dry."

"Yes, my lord." Stephen led off the black stallion, and Adam wiped his face, surprised to discover his hand came back streaked with blood.

"Your brow." The king stood on his toes to peer at it. "Nothing to worry about."

"I don't, my lord. And you?"

"Whole and unscathed." Edward called for his squires, snapping impatiently at them while they unbuckled his various pieces of armour. "I think Mortimer—pardon me, King Arthur—has issued an order that I may not be hurt."

"Wise of him," Adam said.

"I can take care of myself!" Edward yanked a robe out of his youngest squire's hands and draped it over his shoulders. "And now for yet another dazzling display of Mortimer's wealth and the skill of his cooks." He spat to the side. "I'd rather eat horseshit." He strode off, calling for wine.

Adam saw Kit in the distance, one among a flock of ladies accompanying Queen Philippa to the hall. He fell in step with Thomas, brushing his hastily donned tunic into some semblance of order. Halfway to the hall he spied Emma, sharing an embrace with the unknown groom. Clearly, he had not left her inconsolable, he thought to himself, although a groom was a substantial step down from a mason—or a belted knight.

Yet again, the king entered only to find Mortimer already there—and seated. In a repeat of yesterday, everyone but

Mortimer and his lady rose when King Edward walked down the long room, his spurs loud on the stone floor.

"What is he playing at?" Thomas hissed when Lord Roger flaunted all rules of courtly etiquette by serving himself first before graciously inviting the king to partake of the suckling pig. The tables groaned under the weight of the dishes: roasted ribs, stuffed pigeons, lamb shanks boiled in oil and herbs, venison with wine and mushrooms, boar sausages that reeked of garlic, ham studded with cloves, pies and baskets of bread, rounds of cheese, platters of fruit, and subtleties made of almond paste, shaped as knights on horseback.

"He is the victorious King Arthur," Adam replied sarcastically. "Has he gone mad?" he continued in an undertone, reaching for the dish containing dried fruits and nuts.

"Or he knows there's nothing Ned can do." Thomas nodded at the Mortimer men, so openly displayed. "Here, the king of the castle is Roger Mortimer, the dragon from the west who effectively is the king of England." Thomas' breath tickled Adam's ear. "Behold the usurper, Adam."

Adam waited until after compline, shrugging off Kit's objections that this was something he should not meddle in. Adam climbed the steep path towards the inner bailey and Lord Roger's rooms—old rooms, but as elegant as the new solar. The guards recognised him and let him in, one of them saying Lord Roger already had a visitor, his son.

"You're goading him!" Geoffrey's voice carried through the half-open door.

"I am merely acting the part of King Arthur. And it does him good to grovel a bit."

"Grovel?" Geoffrey sounded astounded. "He's your king, Father. *The* king. And this…" He kicked at something, sending it rattling across the floor. "Those are the trappings of the King of Folly."

Adam did not have time to step aside. Geoffrey barged into him, sending them both crashing into the opposite wall.

"Adam." Geoffrey wiped his mouth. "Here to talk some

sense into him? Good luck." He took off, and in the door stood Lord Roger, eyebrows raised.

"More visitors? Come in, by all means."

Adam entered a room ablaze with candlelight. In a corner lay the helmet Geoffrey had kicked; on the table were an assortment of rolls and quills, Mortimer's seal lying thrown to the side.

"What can I do for you, Adam?" Lord Roger crossed his arms. "Well?" he demanded when Adam remained silent, taking in the opulence of the room. New tapestries depicting various hunting scenes flanked an impressive hearth, a huge silverware plate held pride of place on one of the tables, with a collection of silver goblets standing to the side. The large bed was covered in a counterpane embroidered with flowers and butterflies, the sheets of shimmering silk. Everywhere, the trappings of a rich man—a very rich man.

Adam cleared his throat. "You're becoming just like him."

"Who?"

"Despenser."

Lord Roger stilled. "Despenser?" He flexed his hands a couple of times, casually picked up his dagger, and locked eyes with Adam.

"Aye." Adam stood his ground.

"Ah. So you have appointed yourself my conscience, have you?" Lord Roger was suddenly close enough that Adam could feel his exhalations. "Have you?" he demanded, his voice rising. "With what right, eh? How dare you compare me to Despenser?" The shove sent Adam crashing against the wall. "Despenser was a sodomite, a miscreant, accursed from the day he exited his mother's womb. A man without honour. Are you saying I have no honour?"

Adam straightened up, wiping spittle from his cheek. "You amass wealth on a daily basis, as greedy as he was for riches and power."

"I am not like him!" Mortimer's face had gone the colour of ash. "Everything I do, I do for the king."

Adam laughed. "Don't lie, at least not to yourself. What is this spectacle of a tournament but you shouting to the world that the true power in England lies with you, not our rightful king? Soon enough, you'll stoop to killing those who stand in your way—and where's the honour in being a murderer?"

He could have heard a mouse fart in the ensuing silence. Lord Roger set a hand to the wall as if to support himself, all of him sagging. "You have no idea," he finally said, turning his back on Adam. His voice shook. "No idea at all."

"My lord," Adam took a step towards him, wanting somehow to lift the burden that had Lord Roger stooping, arms braced against the wall.

"Go." Mortimer kept his back to him. "And be grateful you're no longer in my service, or I'd have you flogged."

"For what, my lord? For telling the truth?"

Mortimer whirled and pushed Adam so hard he went staggering backwards. He slammed into the table, overturning the goblets.

"Get out!" Mortimer yelled. "And don't forget it was I who lifted you out of obscurity. Beware that I don't throw you back into the cesspit whence you came."

"The lord I loved, the man I would gladly have died for, would never have lowered himself to making such threats." Adam bowed slightly. "And I only came because I care." He banged the door closed as he left.

He was too upset to return to his lodgings. Instead, he took a turn on the walls, stopping to exchange a word or two with the guards posted at regular intervals. Far below, the town of tents that housed the majority of the participants at Mortimer's extravagant event was illuminated by cooking fires and the odd torch moving through the dark.

There were people in the armoury, and he whiled away some time talking to Lord Roger's master-at-arms, presently supervising the repair of Lord Roger's hauberk.

"Has to be as good as new on the morrow," Master Heinrich said in that oddly accented French of his. "Lord Mortimer wants everything to be perfect."

"I am sure he does," Adam muttered.

Master Heinrich chuckled. "Sore about losing today?" He

elbowed Adam. "Our king must learn to control that temper of his."

"He will." Adam scratched at his scabbed brow. "He has all the makings of a great general."

Master Heinrich grunted. "Let us hope he also makes a great king."

"Mmm." Adam stifled a yawn. "God willing."

After the warmth of the armoury, it was cold outside. Adam shivered and increased his pace, passing through the inner gate to find his bed when someone called his name.

"Emma?"

She was weeping, the skirts of her red kirtle muddied and torn. "He…he…" She hiccupped. "He attacked me."

"Who?" Adam took hold of her arm.

"I thought…" She began crying in earnest, and one of the guards hurried over.

"Is she all right? She came running over the outer bailey as if she had the hounds of hell snapping at her heels."

"I'm not sure." Adam gave her a little shake. "Emma? Are you hurt?"

She dragged the back of her hand under her nose. "Not as such." She gave Adam a glimmer of a smile. "You know me: I can kick like a mule if I have to."

"And did you?"

"Yes." She dabbed at her eyes. "But I dropped my pouch, and I didn't dare to stay behind and look for it." She gave Adam a beseeching look. "Would you—no, never mind."

"Of course I will. Is it far?" He was already leading the way to the main gate.

"No. Just beyond the stand of junipers by the church." Her face darkened. "Bastard. He waited until we were safely out of sight from either the village or the castle."

"Would you recognise him?" Adam took the proffered lantern, nodding his thanks.

"Not as such. It was dark. But I scratched his cheek, I think."

"Well, him we can look for tomorrow. Now let's see if we can find your pouch."

"I hope so. It had my entire month's earnings in it." Her

187

mouth wobbled. "And Patrick's ring."

They walked quickly over the bridge and down the slope beyond, the narrow path bordered by stands of broom. Just before the church, the path widened. "Here." Emma pointed at a patch of scuffed grass. "That's where he…" She gulped.

"So this is where you dropped the pouch." Not that Adam held out much hope in finding it. Whoever had attacked her had probably taken it. But he made a show of looking at the ground, with Emma holding the lantern.

"Now!" Emma said.

"Now?" Adam twisted to look at her. Something hit him hard over the head, and he fell to his knees. "Emma?" He tried to stand. Hands gripped his arms, twisting them behind him. He gasped. She spat him in the face. "That's for denying me, you stuck-up bastard." She lobbed a fat pouch in the air. "A full year's earnings, Adam. That's what you're worth to me."

Adam struggled, was clapped yet again over the head. He was dragged to his feet. Something was moving under the junipers. A child?

"Help," Adam groaned.

"Shut up!" Something pricked his neck.

"Help, find my wife, find the king!" Adam yelled in Welsh. Someone threw a cloak over his head. He dug his heels in, threw himself to this side and that. One more blow, and he crumpled to the ground.

Chapter 21

It was well past midnight, and Kit couldn't sleep. Had Mortimer thrown Adam into a dungeon, enraged by what he'd come to say? No, she comforted herself, he wouldn't. Or maybe he would. After what seemed like hours tossing this way and that, she gave up, dressed hastily, and sneaked outside.

Wigmore Castle was sunk in sleep. She met no one on her way to Mortimer's chambers and was very embarrassed when she pushed the door open, thereby awakening one of his squires—and William.

"William? When did you get here?"

"Last night." He rubbed at his eyes. "What are you doing here?"

"Looking for Adam."

"Not here, my lady. He left Lord Mortimer hours ago." The squire lowered his voice. "Whatever he said left our lord in a foul temper."

"Ah. But he left?"

"Aye." The squire rolled over on his side and pulled up his blanket.

William offered to come with her, but Kit wasn't convinced that would be a good idea. "Adam might not—"

"Like it," William filled in with a deep sigh. Kit gave him an encouraging smile and left.

She had no notion where to start looking, but after some thought she made for the main gate. Here, the guards were wide awake, four men sitting round a glowing brazier and sharing a jug of ale.

"De Guirande?" The oldest of the sentries shared a look with his companions. "Well…"

"Well what?"

"We saw him some hours ago," another of the sentries

said. He poked at the embers, releasing a shower of sparks. "With Emma."

"Emma?" Kit's throat itched. "Where?"

"Here." The oldest sentry spat into the fire. "She was right upset and dragged him with her. Haven't seen either of them since."

"Dragged him where?"

The youngest sentry—a beardless lad, no more—pointed to the barred gate. "He offered to help her find her pouch."

One of the other men snickered. "I bet he can find that particular pouch in the dark."

"Shut up, Ian." The older sentry swatted him over the head.

"And they never came back?"

All four shook their heads.

"I have to go and look for him."

"Now?" The oldest sentry blinked. "In the middle of the night?"

"Something must have happened to him." She made for the gate.

"You'll have to use a postern, my lady," the youngest sentry told her. "And if you want, I can come with you."

"Would you?" She gave him a wide smile. "Thank you!"

Despite the moonlight, it was a challenge to negotiate the steep path from the postern. Twice, Kit stumbled; twice, the young guard, whose name was Hugh, grabbed hold of her. They crossed the ditch, negotiated the slight incline beyond, and came to a halt by the old church.

"I heard her say the junipers." Hugh did a slow turn, the lantern aloft. The ground was badly trampled, and thrown to the side was a heavy branch. Kit crouched. It was sticky with something, and stuck in it were a number of hairs. Hugh lowered the lantern. Fair hair. Kit stumbled to her feet.

"A ruse. Dear God, someone has taken my husband."

Hugh stared at the branch she was holding. "And Emma?"

"I don't know!" Her instincts were telling her Emma was somehow involved in this. She walked back and forth, trying to read something from the ground. Hugh went with her.

"Here," he said. "He was dragged from here."

"To where?"

"We'll find him, my lady." Hugh pointed at the collection of huddled buildings that made up Wigmore. "Not much to search."

"Assuming he's there." By now, he could have been loaded on a horse and carried God knew where.

"I'll fetch some men, my lady." Hugh led her to an outcrop of rock. "Wait here."

No sooner had Hugh disappeared into the dark, the lantern bobbing along, but something emerged from the junipers. Kit tightened her hold on her dagger.

"Who's there?"

A child, ragged and dirty. It was difficult to make out if it was a lad or a girl, but from the cropped hair Kit ventured it was a boy.

The child spoke in Welsh. Kit moaned.

"I don't speak Welsh," she interrupted. The child blinked, verily like an owl. Then it mimed someone hitting, a man collapsing.

"Yes, yes." Kit knelt before the child. "And then?"

The child pointed north, away from the village and the jousting field, took Kit's hand, and tugged.

"Maybe we should wait," Kit said.

The child tilted its head, tugged again, unintelligible words pouring out of it. One more tug, and Kit got to her feet, affected by the urgency in the child's voice.

They made their way down the hill, took a left, and followed the road due north for a furlong or so. By now, the moon had set, leaving them in relative darkness, and at times Kit could see nothing of the ground beneath her feet. Then they turned onto a narrow path and walked straight into the wilds. A little ditch to Kit's left, and to her right the morning star was visible in the eastern sky. Dawn was not far off.

The child drew them both to a halt and pointed. A dilapidated cottar's cottage, some sheds, and standing to the side, two horses. Reddish light spilled through the cracks of the door, and from somewhere came a muted howl. The child darted off, and Kit was alone.

It took her an eternity to cross the overgrown yard. Stands of nettles stung her hands as she moved carefully along the side of the little building. Two rooms, she concluded. The sounds were coming from the back room, and after crawling on her hands and knees, she was crouched just beneath an un-shuttered window. She rose. Some sort of sacking covered the aperture, and beyond she could see the shadowy outlines of three people, one of whom was slumped on the ground. Was it Adam? As if in reply to her question, she heard him scream.

"That hurts, does it?" an unknown voice said. "Well, that's just the beginning, de Guirande."

Kit stuffed her hand in her mouth.

Adam was not aware of much before he was thrown into a dark room with an earthen floor, landing painfully on his tightly bound hands. He'd then been beaten savagely by a man who kept on yelling invectives at him, and so Adam had found it wise to slump and pretend a deep faint. He was left lying there, drifting in and out of consciousness, while on the other side of the door male voices talked and laughed. The door opened. Someone pulled him upright, water in his face, and Adam gasped, jerking wide awake.

"Ah. Welcome back." A face peered at him. Adam blinked. The unknown groom. "Recognise me, do you? Well, no matter, not now."

"Who are you?"

"All in good time," the man responded. "Chain him to the wall," he ordered the huge man standing beside him. When the man went to do as ordered, Adam kicked him in the head, sending him reeling back. The man howled, cradling his broken nose.

"Like that, is it?" The unknown man stood, looked about, and produced a large mallet. "Let's see how this feels on your damaged foot, shall we?"

Adam screamed as the mallet came down, over and over again.

"That hurts, does it? Well, that's just the beginning, de Guirande." The man threw the mallet to the side and nodded for his companion to approach with the irons. This time, Adam didn't even try to protest when his foot was chained to the wall.

"Why?" he mumbled. "What have I ever done to you?" He sucked in a breath when the huge lout tightened the chain, thereby dragging Adam's damaged foot across the floor.

"To me?" A sudden blow burst Adam's lip. "Nothing. And there are various reasons." Yet another blow, and Adam's head connected painfully with the wall behind him.

"First of all, I aim to rid this world of that good-for-nothing king of yours." The unknown man hunkered down, gripped Adam by the hair, and raised his face. "Oh yes. If all goes according to plan, that precious royal whelp will be dead in some hours."

Adam licked his lip. "How?"

"How?" The groom laughed. "Well, God has handed me the weapon, hasn't he? That accursed hell-spawn of a horse will do it for me. All I have to do is to cut through most of the girth and place a couple of thorns beneath the saddle. Cleverly placed, it will take some time for them to work their way through the caparison, but once they do…" The man laughed. "Well, Boreas will go quite insane, won't he? Even more so as I aim to anoint the beast with a stinging potion. Heats the skin to the point of unbearable pain."

"Just because Boreas throws him does not mean the king will die—or even be injured."

"Clever, aren't you?" The man bumped Adam's head against the wall. "That's where Jacques here, comes in." The groom turned to smile at his companion. Jacques might be huge, but he seemed simple, a vacant look to his eyes. "Jacques has a big, big axe," the man continued, and Jacques nodded repeatedly and grinned. "So there is your king, unhorsed, and Jacques will simply smite him over the head with his axe, and—"

"Hang," Adam croaked.

"Shut up!" This time, his head was slammed with such

force into the wall that Adam saw stars. "Besides, if he does, he'll do so alongside you."

"Me?"

"I need a scapegoat, don't I? No one's going to believe dear Jacques set out to assassinate the king all on his own."

"They'll never believe I had anything to do with it." Adam closed his eyes.

"No? Not even when they find you with a pouch of Judas coins and a jar of that potion?" A heavy pouch landed with a jangle by Adam's knees. "Oh, I think they will. With the king gone, you'll find you have few true friends."

Adam shook his head. "Never." Of this he was certain.

"We shall see." The unknown man rose. "For now, I'll keep you alive in case I do need that scapegoat. And if not…" He looked down at Adam. "Then I'll kill you myself."

"For what?" It cost him to speak. Black spots rose and swirled before his eyes, and his hearing came and went.

"Revenge for my brother, Robert de Langon."

No wonder he'd thought the groom familiar. The likeness was there, in everything from the fine dark eyes to the dimpled chin. Adam coughed, and his mouth filled with blood he tried to spit out. Instead, it dribbled down his chin.

"You abducted him. And now my brother is dead. Dead!"

"By his own hand," Adam said.

"Liar!" More blows to his face; repeated kicks to Adam's side had him trying to curl together. "He died because of your king! And it is only fair that the two of you should die in retribution." He kicked again. "And even if the king escapes with his life, you won't. Either you die at the hands of the executioner or at mine."

"And if they capture you?" Adam croaked. "There are more men than me charged with the king's security."

"If so, my men have instructions to kill you before they leave." De Langon nudged at the heavy chain that fettered Adam to the wall. "Should someone attempt to free you, their instructions are the same: slit your throat. You'll never make it out."

From the little window came a whimper. A glimpse of

Kit's familiar profile, and Adam's heart raced—with hope, with fear.

"What was that?" De Langon whirled. Adam made whimpering sounds of his own but was ignored. "Go and investigate," De Langon ordered Jacques. "And then we must leave." The giant lumbered off. Adam prayed, hoping that his wife would have the sense to hide.

Kit slid into the ditch and hid behind a stand of water hemlock. Her eyes were stinging with tears, her hands aching after having been fisted so tight in her efforts not to cry out that she'd feared her knuckles would burst. De Langon's brother! And dear God, his plan to rid the world of King Edward and Adam might very well work. She cast a look to the east, where the skies were already lightening, the rising sun colouring the few clouds a soft pink.

The large man came crashing through the undergrowth, whined loudly when he came in contact with the nettles, and stood for some time, looking this way and that. He stuck a finger up his nose, transferred it to his mouth, and stared straight ahead. With a shrug, he lumbered off, and Kit relaxed. But she waited until de Langon and Jacques had ridden off until she returned to the window.

"Adam?" she whispered. There was a soft responding grunt.

"Adam?" She pulled at the sacking, reared back at the sight of his bruised and bloodied face.

"The king," Adam said in between shallow pants. "You must get word to the king."

"I have to get you out!"

"You can't," he said shortly. "You must go for help and save the king. I'll not die of this."

She drew in an unsteady breath and blinked her eyes clear of tears. "I can't leave you here unprotected."

Adam somehow made it to the window. If she stretched as far as she could, her fingertips touched his hair, encountering the stickiness of blood seeping from his scalp.

"Dearest God, what did they do to you?"

"No matter, not now. Your dagger, give it to me, and anyone coming in through that door will have quite the nasty surprise." He craned his head back and treated her to a smile, blood rimming his teeth and lips. "Hurry!" he hissed. "The king—"

Always the king—or Mortimer! What about her and their children? But she swallowed back on her recriminations and dropped her dagger into his tied hands. "It's sharp."

"Aye, I know. I'm the one who whets it. Now go, sweeting. Go!"

She flew. No. She stumbled and ran, had to walk with a stitch up her side, ran some more, and all the time she kept an eye on the eastern sky, where the sun was now high enough to have the bells ringing for prime. She had no need of directions, the outline of Wigmore Castle clearly visible in the distance. So far away! She'd no recollection of having walked quite that far with the silent child.

Once on the road, she picked up her pace, and just as she was entering Wigmore village, someone called her name.

"Lady de Guirande!" Hugh came slipping down a steep path. "Where did you get to?"

"Not now. I must see the king." But she was glad of his hand on her elbow, helping her up the last stretch. One drawbridge, through the gates, one more drawbridge, and Kit pressed a hand to the stitch in her side as she entered the lower bailey. She broke into a run, hood pulled forward so as to hide her face.

The king leapt to his feet when Kit fell into his rooms. Already in his gambeson, he was at her side in an instant, and when she began to talk and cry, talk and weep some more, he guided her to a chair, sat her down, took her hands, and calmly told her to be quiet.

"Breathe," he continued. "Deeply."

Kit nodded and complied, but it did little to stop her heart from hammering. "Adam!" she blurted.

"Yes, I've gathered as much." The king rubbed her hands. "You're cold and wet. Where have you been?"

"In a ditch." She giggled. She wept. The king slapped her. It jolted her back to her senses, however much it stung, and when the queen silently handed her a cup of warmed wine, she drank it all.

"Now," the king said. "Let's try again." This time, she managed to tell him the entire tale.

Midway through, they were joined by Thomas, and no sooner was she done but he was on his feet.

"Where are you going?" Edward demanded.

"Adam, of course." Thomas smiled at his nephew. "You're fully capable of dealing with this de Langon character on your own."

"Assuredly."

"Adam." Kit was on her feet. "I must ride with you."

"No." Edward took a firm hold of her arm. "Go, Thomas. Make haste." In the look they shared, Kit saw her own fears reflected.

"Adam," she whispered, staring down at her fingertips, still smudged with his blood.

The king finished dressing, and once he'd found his gauntlets he escorted his queen and Kit to the bailey, having first stopped to whisper instructions to Montagu.

Men were standing about breaking their fast with ale and bread, most of them already in full armour. From the chapel came Mortimer, accompanied by Queen Isabella.

"Ready for one last bout?" Mortimer asked, bowing ever so slightly to the king.

"I am. But there is another matter that must be handled first."

"Oh?" Mortimer asked.

"A word, Lord Mortimer—in private." The king turned on his heel, and Mortimer joined him, their two heads nearly knocking together as they spoke. At one point, Mortimer cast a look at Kit, and then the king was done; Mortimer nodded and went to join his men.

The horses were led out, caparisoned and prancing. Among the first came Boreas, already on his toes, eyes rolling. Kit backed away, studying the groom holding him.

"Is it him?" the king asked.

"I don't know. I never saw him, only heard him." She caught sight of the other man, the huge oaf, and nodded in his direction. "That is Jacques."

"Ah." Edward beckoned for Philippa and Kit to accompany him. "Has he been watered?" he asked the groom once he was standing by the horse.

"Yes, my liege."

"And have you checked his girth?" As Edward fiddled with one of the stirrups, Boreas half reared. "Hmm." Edward frowned. "Have you had him eating oats again?"

"No, my liege," the groom replied. "It's just his fighting spirit shining through. And yes, I've tightened the girth."

"Indeed." The king glanced at Kit. She nodded. Yes, this was de Langon. Edward moved closer to the groom. "What will happen if I have you sit the horse instead? Will Jacques smite you with his axe? " he enquired, and a tremor flew through de Langon's body. The king's gauntleted hand snaked out and grasped de Langon by the wrist. The king twisted, de Langon paled, mouth open in a soundless scream. "More importantly, what will I do should I find Adam de Guirande in any way harmed?"

"Mercy," de Langon gasped, falling to his knees. "Please, my liege, this is all a misunderstanding."

"Is it?" the king growled. "I don't think so." He stood. "Throw him in a dungeon somewhere—him and that huge simpleton. And have Mortimer show you where to build the gallows."

"No!" De Langon wailed, clinging to the king's surcoat. "No, my liege, please, I—"

"—will hang." King Edward tore free. "Take him out of my sight."

Chapter 22

It took Adam much longer than he'd expected to rid himself of the ropes round his wrists. Once he was done, his hands were so slick with blood he had to tear strips off his shirt to bandage the various cuts. A sharp blade indeed.

He dragged himself over to sit beside the door, arranging the broken stool he'd found as a stumbling block. The blade in his hand offered comfort, a certainty that should someone come through the door with the intent of killing him, he'd be able to put up a fight. He tightened his hold on the hilt and rested his head against the wall, trying to close out the discomfort every breath caused him, the throbbing to his broken face and head, the way his right foot was on fire.

He dozed. Kit, in a ditch, her throat slit, her beautiful blue eyes sightless. No. He struggled back to wakefulness, his heart racing.

"God keep her safe," he whispered and slumped against the wall, concentrating instead on the way each inhalation had his ribs groaning in protest. Pain kept the dreams away, but soon enough he slid back into restless sleep, and it was Kit, it was the king, his broken body trampled by a hundred horses, it was Kit, it was blood, and Adam moaned and banged his sore head against the wall, thereby waking up.

He made a careful inspection of his face. Mostly, it was bruises and aching bones, but his mouth was badly swollen, his throat so parched it hurt to swallow.

He dozed, waking with a start to the sound of clatter.

"Shit!" someone said on the other side of the door. "I see horses. Many horses."

"What do we do?" another voice asked.

"Do?" The first man laughed. "We gamble on them being more interested in finding our prisoner than in catching us."

"How?"

"Fire." There was the sound of something being overturned. "More, man—we need more! Bring in wood and hay, and hurry." Heavy feet, rushing off, returning. "That's better. Come on! This way!"

"Hey!" Adam banged at the door. "You can't just leave me here!"

No response. But he could hear the crackling of fire, his nostrils wrinkling at the sour stench of burning straw. A whooshing sound, and on the other side of the door the conflagration roared into a blaze.

"Help!" He was going to burn to death in here. Already, the heat was making him sweat, and the door was hot to the touch, the wood beginning to smoulder. Smoke curled in through the cracks, and Adam had to cough, despite the jarring pain. The window. Too small, too far away, the chain so short he could not get close enough to stand and put his head through the little opening.

Flames licked the lower ends of the door boards, spread to the doorframe. Thick black smoke made it difficult to see, to breathe. God's blood! He batted frantically at his burning sleeve, at his hose, dragging himself as far away from the door as he could. The walls were on fire, segments collapsing inwards when the wattle went from wood to ashes. Fragments of red-hot daub landed on his face and hands, and Adam screamed for help.

Adam took hold of the chain and pulled. It gave—a little—the wooden uprights groaning in protest. Again, and it didn't budge. The thatch overhead was beginning to glow. He heard voices and horses.

"Here!" he yelled, but he was hoarse and the room was full of smoke. "Here!"

The air burned his lungs. The window. He gripped the chain and threw all his strength, all his weight backwards. With a loud crack, the frame gave. Above him, so did the roof, sending a shower of burning embers to the floor as the crossbeams came plunging down on him.

Agony. He was trapped under the burning thatch, and he had the sensation of a myriad of creatures crawling over him, frantic to escape the heat. He couldn't move, the beams pinning him to the floor, and all around him the thatch glowed and smoked. He sucked in air, inhaled thick smoke that burned his lungs and had him coughing until he retched, a puddle of sour vomit round his face. Kit. He had to try…He had to…His fingers scrabbled at the earthen floor. He…Kit.

The first thing he registered when he came to was the grass, cool and wet beneath his cheek. Then came the reek of burnt straw, and he curled together, which caused the skin on his upper arm and left shoulder to shriek in protest.

"Damn it, I don't know where to touch you." Thomas sounded as if he was about to weep.

"Am I alive?" He had to ask because all he could remember was the roof collapsing. He coughed, and his mouth filled with ash and blood. He gulped air, which proved a mistake, his sore ribs sending waves of discomfort through his side. Dead men didn't feel, so reasonably all this pain meant he had survived. The flames, the smoke…He groped for Thomas' hand, was comforted by how tightly his friend's fingers clasped his.

"You are. Here." Thomas held a wet rag to Adam's mouth. He squeezed a trickle of water out of the rag, and Adam swallowed greedily.

"Thank you." Belatedly, he noticed Thomas was covered in soot, one hand looking raw and red. "You saved me."

"Well, I couldn't leave you to roast, could I?"

Adam shuddered and tried to sit up. His tunic was badly singed, the thick fustian probably one of the reasons why he was still alive. His hose were torn beyond repair, his right boot would have to be cut off, and…His vision blurred.

"Adam?" Thomas voice came from a distance. Adam fell into his friend's arms.

They brought him back on a makeshift stretcher, and Kit's heart thronged her throat at the look on Thomas' face.

"Alive," he told her. "In difference to the two bastards who tried to burn him to death."

"Burn him?" No wonder he stank of smoke. A lock of fair

hair was plastered to his grimy forehead, and there seemed to be bruises and blood everywhere.

"They set the cottage on fire." Thomas coughed. "Damned smoke was everywhere—that's what you get when damp thatch burns."

They carried Adam to the small infirmary. Queen Isabella offered the services of her physician, as did the king. Kit preferred the king's Italian doctor, a man with laughing eyes and gentle hands who seemed remarkably unperturbed as he inspected a sedated, naked Adam.

The ribs were set and bandaged, the various burns were to be kept damp and left uncovered. After ensuring Adam still had all his teeth, Pancio the physician dismissed his facial damage as being of no consequence—except for the lip that had to be sewn. Together, Pancio and Kit washed and stitched the few gashes that so merited. And then they came to Adam's poor mangled foot, and there was a long, long silence.

"How…" Pancio cleared his throat.

"The original damage was done almost eight years ago." Kit cradled Adam's swollen foot in her hands. "A red-hot stake."

"*Barbari,*" Pancio muttered. Deft fingers moved this way and that, aligning what bones he could find. "And this time?"

"I don't know. I just heard him scream."

"Hmm." There followed what Kit supposed to be a string of Italian expletives. "This is bad," Pancio finished. "But let's put the foot to soak in hot water, and then we'll see what I can do."

After having softened the tissue in hot water, Pancio sliced Adam's foot open, breaking some of the badly healed bones and then resetting them. He used an unknown liquid, which he said the Arabs called alcohol, to wash the resulting incisions before stitching it all together, and poor Adam gasped awake, screaming that his foot was on fire before slumping back into unconsciousness.

"All done." Pancio sat back, wiping his trembling hands on his bloody apron. "And we'll keep him sedated. I find sleep is a marvellous healer."

Adam didn't want the poppy wine. But Kit wheedled and cajoled, and when she began to cry he sighed and drank it down, holding her hand as he drifted away.

"I dream," he explained a couple of days later. "Bad dreams." He was sitting up in bed, spooning hot broth into his mouth at remarkable speed. He was still a collection of faded bruises, but he was healing rapidly, days of enforced sleep having helped. "What happened to de Langon?" he asked, tearing off a piece of bread and using it to mop up the last in the bowl.

"Hanged. All three of them."

His hand stopped halfway to his mouth. "Three?"

She couldn't quite meet his eyes. "Emma as well."

"Emma?" He set down his bowl on the floor.

She threw him an angry look. "She helped them abduct you! But it was de Langon who gave her up, not me." She'd been called to testify, as had the sentries. An unpleasant experience, to stand before Lord Mortimer in his capacity as the king's representative.

"She did it for money."

"And that is an excuse?"

Their eyes met, a silent staring contest. "No," he finally said. "But to condemn her to hang…"

"She conspired to kill the king."

"As if they'd told her! Emma was many things, but she wasn't a traitor."

"No? And here was I thinking that she definitely betrayed you." Kit retrieved his bowl from the floor and stalked to the door. "She told the judges you'd gone with her to swive her," she said over her shoulder. "How do you think that made me feel?"

"It was a lie!"

"So you say." She shoved the door open with her hip. "But it hurt all the same."

Too little sleep, too many days at Adam's bedside—Kit could think of no other excuse for her sudden burst of temper.

"Kit," he called, his voice muffled by the thick door, but she had no intention of returning to their room—not yet.

203

How could he leap to Emma's defence like that? Now, of course, the poor woman was dead, and Kit felt a flare of remorse at not being able to dredge up as much as an ounce of compassion. Uncharitable, she chided herself, handing over the empty bowl to one of the pages who were constantly at hand.

"I'll be at my prayers," she informed the lad. Anything to get away, to have some moments of precious solitude.

Kit encountered William in the doorway to the chapel. Her brother-in-law shone up, his pleasure so contagious she had to smile.

"Come to pray for him?" William followed her into the dim interior. "I recall you spending very many hours here back in 1322, begging the Good Lord to see your husband safe."

"And He did," Kit said.

"With quite some help from you," William replied drily. "What you did…"

"Yes, yes." Kit blushed. A foolhardy plan that had nearly cost her and an unknown laddie their lives, something William was prone to drag up every time the subject was broached. "But it worked, didn't it?"

"It did." He fell silent. "I wonder if he understands how grateful he should be for you."

"Oh, he does." Kit genuflected before the large cross that adorned the simple altar. In massive silver, it represented a minor fortune, but no one would be so foolish as to attempt to steal from Lord Mortimer. "And when he forgets, I remind him."

She busied herself with her own prayers, most of them words of gratitude. Her man was safe, the king remained alive, and what could have ended in tragedy had instead ended as well as it could. It was difficult to concentrate on her devotions with William beside her, fidgeting and shuffling.

"Will he ever forgive me?" William blurted.

"He already has, it's just that he hasn't realised it yet." Kit gave William's hand a reassuring squeeze.

When she returned to Adam's room, Pancio was there, nose hovering a scant hair's breadth from Adam's naked skin as he sniffed and prodded at the healing sores and bruises.

"Best thing for burns is air," he said as Kit entered, making Gavin sniff in disbelief. "The Arab physicians don't hold with unguents and the like on blistered skin."

"Seems to me the Arabs hold with all the wrong things," Gavin replied. "Starting with them all being infidels."

Pancio smiled. "They don't see it like that. And they have the best physicians in the world."

"They do?" Gavin added yet another dirty washrag to the basin he was holding. "Begging your pardon, but I find that hard to believe. Why would God favour the infidels?"

"Maybe because he's their God too?" Pancio said, causing Gavin to give him a horrified look.

"Their God too? They pray to that Allan fellow."

"Allah," Adam interrupted. "Their word for God."

"Aye, I knew that, my lord!" Gavin swept off, promising to return with hot water and more cloths.

"No infection." Pancio inclined his head to Kit. "Your lady wife excels at cleanliness and herbal infusions."

"And my foot?" Adam asked brusquely.

"Ah." Pancio's lower lip shot out, a gesture Kit had seen frequently over the last few days. "You will find it painful to walk on it."

"It has been painful for years," Adam muttered, covering his face with his arm. "But I will be able to walk, won't I?"

"With a limp." Pancio patted Adam on his thigh. "As you've been doing for as long as I have known you." He hesitated. "A very bad limp—you won't be able to fight on foot. That mallet-wielding bastard pulverised many of the smaller bones, and they are impossible to reset."

"Not fight?" He didn't as much as twitch, his voice steady and low. But Kit saw the glimmer of a tear in his eye.

"No." Pancio busied himself with his various instruments. "All in all, a small thing."

"Aye." Adam turned to face the wall. "A small thing."

Pancio left just as Gavin returned with pitchers of hot

water. Adam remained mute, presenting them with his back, even when Kit rested her hand on it. Gavin excused himself, no doubt eager to escape the sickroom for the company of young, healthy men and horses. Kit waited. At long last, Adam cleared his throat.

"I only went with her to help her find her pouch. Amends, if you like, for being brutally honest with her the night before." He picked at the coverlet. "I wanted to help and ended up more crippled than before."

"You're not crippled." She took hold of his shoulder. "You limp—not the same thing." Kit increased the pressure, and he fell over to face her. "And you're alive."

He lifted his hand to her face. "Because of you." She leaned into his touch, saying nothing at all. His fingers pulled at a tendril of her hair, teasing it free of her braid and veil. He wound it round his finger, released it, and did it all again. Eyes the colour of lead met hers. His hand slid round her nape, pulling her face down to his. A soft, gentle kiss—a wonderful kiss that had her slipping into bed beside him, her mouth never leaving his.

"Too much cloth between us," he murmured, divesting her of her veil.

"Should you…"

Fingers as light as butterflies worked their way up her thigh. "There's nothing wrong with my cock, sweeting. Nothing you can't help me with, at any rate."

She lifted her kirtle; he shoved her chemise out of the way and gripped her hips, steadying her as she straddled him.

Slow, rocking movements, the muscles in his thighs bunching and relaxing in time with hers. His eyes never left hers as she increased the pace, needing him that much closer, so much deeper. A building sensation in her womb, a tightening in her loins, and she could hear her own breathing, feel every beat of her heart. So many sensations, from the bead of sweat on her upper lip to how he strained upwards, his urgency matching hers.

She gasped his name and fell forward, glad of his arms round her back as everything inside of her fragmented.

She washed him afterwards, which he found entirely unnecessary—he could do so himself—until he gathered just how seductive a damp washcloth could be, even on a weakened, ailing man.

"Weak?" She laughed into his neck, fingers tracing the contours of his shoulders and spine. "Twice in less than an hour would indicate you're anything but."

He rolled off, dropped a kiss on her cheek, and pillowed his head on her chest. "Who won the last joust?" All this lovemaking had left him in a state of drowsy contentment, dispelling what aches he still had.

"The king, thank the Lord." Kit combed her fingers through his short hair, recently cut so as to treat his wounds. "Lord Mortimer was a most gracious loser—even went down on a bent knee to hold the basin for the king to wash his hands in."

"Mmm." He yawned, all of a sudden exhausted. She kept on talking, her voice a comforting drone that lulled him to sleep.

When next he woke, Kit was gone, and instead Thomas was sitting beside his bed, dressed for travel.

"You're leaving?"

"I have to." Thomas poured them both some wine, and to Adam's surprise, Thomas' hand was shaking so much he spilled wine on his leather surcoat.

"Thomas?"

"My wife." He inhaled. "She's ailing." He gulped down the wine. "They say she will die. My poor Alice; ten years married to a man who regretted his rash decision to wed her three days into the marriage." He scrubbed at his face. "It wasn't her fault. She never pretended to be something other than who she was—a somewhat simple if pretty burgher's daughter. I thought I could transform her, and when the butterfly never materialised…" He threw the cup to crash against the wall and hid his face in his hands. "And the worst of it is that she has never asked for more than I can give. She has been content with the crumbs from my table, pathetically grateful for those few hours when I made her the centre of my existence."

Adam reached out to clasp his shoulder. "Go to her. Ride like the wind, Thomas, and be there for her."

Thomas nodded repeatedly. "What do I say to her?" His hazel eyes stared at Adam. "I stopped talking to her years ago."

"I think it may be enough just to hold her hand," Adam said.

"Hold her hand." Thomas' voice broke. "I think I can manage that."

The king came by some hours later, shifting from one foot to the other as he stood by Adam's bed.

"We're leaving," he explained. "The court moves to Hereford, there to handle yet another bevy of tedious administrative matters." He wandered over to the hearth. "I've arranged for Edward of Norfolk and his little bride to be escorted back home—his father left in haste. Poor Thomas, I've never seen him so distraught."

"No, my lord. He took the news badly."

The king did some more pacing. "It always seemed to me he didn't love his wife."

"He didn't. But he wed her for love."

"Ah." The king nodded, brows furrowed. "I don't understand."

"I'm not so sure I do either, my lord. But I think it is guilt, not despair, that has Thomas riding like a fiend to Walton."

"Guilt, eh?" The king came closer. "Are you truly on the mend?"

"I am." Adam wiggled the toes of his tightly bandaged foot. "Not so sure how much use I will be to you in the future, though."

"As much use as always." The king clapped his hands, and a page appeared, carrying a bulky package wrapped in sacking. "For you. Pancio thinks they may help."

Boots of the best Italian leather spilled onto the bed. They'd been exquisitely worked, and with them came a strange contraption of leather and thin layers of wood, the rough shape of a foot with a soft cushion where the arch would normally be. Adam turned it over, not knowing quite what use it might be.

"To support your foot. You stuff it into whatever boot you're using on your right foot, and Pancio says it will help you walk." The king tapped his nose. "Arab invention, he says. That Pancio, one could almost think him an infidel himself what with how he lauds their medicine."

"Thank you, my lord." Adam stroked the black leather. He'd never had boots as soft or well-made before.

"The least I could do." The king cleared his throat. "Heal up, man. We—I—need you."

"Yes, my lord. I shall do my best."

Adam was trying out his new boots when Lord Roger entered.

"My lord, I—" Adam put too much weight on his foot and stumbled. He would have fallen flat on his face if Lord Roger hadn't caught him.

"God's blood! What do they feed you? Welsh rock?" Lord Roger helped him back to bed. "How are you?"

"Other than the accursed foot, I am healing." Adam felt oddly shy, naked except for the boots and his shirt.

"I just came to bid you a speedy recovery." Lord Roger leaned forward and ruffled Adam's hair. "And to tell you I know you care," he added gruffly. "We're riding with the king, so we leave within the hour." He pulled on his gloves. "And before that, there's someone I insist you must see."

"Insist, my lord?"

"Insist." Lord Roger's eyes crinkled as he smiled. "He's no bloody use to me at present—hasn't been since Canterbury."

"Ah." Adam looked to the door and found William hovering. "Best come in, then."

Chapter 23

Wigmore without its lord was a silent, deserted place. Until its lady rode in, propitiously the day before Adam and Kit's departure. To judge from Lady Joan's reaction upon seeing them, she'd not known they were there, but any displeasure at finding herself lumbered with unwanted guests was hidden behind a bland face, her plucked eyebrows rising to the edge of her severe wimple when Adam explained the cause of his injuries.

"Are you sufficiently recovered to travel?" Lady Joan asked, eyes drifting to Adam's foot, still wrapped in multiple bandages.

"As long as I don't walk, my lady."

Lady Joan chuckled. "Still riding that devil of a horse, Adam?"

"Goliath?" Adam shook his head. "Too old, my lady."

Lady Joan looked away, her hand resting on her covered throat. "Age happens to all of us eventually."

Sooner for some, Adam thought. Lady Joan had paid a high price for her husband's rebellion, and even now, three years after being released from her captivity, there was a frailty to her, all those years of deprivation having resulted in a shrunken frame and premature wrinkling to her face and hands.

"Assuming we live long enough," Lady Joan continued, eyes on a kestrel. She swept her plain mantle closer, and after insisting Adam and Kit join her for dinner, she excused herself, walking off surrounded by her clerks, her steward, and her chaplains.

"She manages the Mortimer lands," Adam explained to Kit. "It was the least he could do for her, I reckon."

"And is she happy doing that?"

"Happy?" Adam took a careful step forward, waving away

her offer of support. "Lady Joan has never aspired to happiness. But I do think she hoped for contentment, for some years spent side by side with her husband. She deserved as much."

They took the meal in the new solar. All traces of the king's recent residence had been stripped away, including the magnificent carpets on the floor. Instead, the room was decorated with fabrics in soft green and pale yellow, a background which served to soften Lady Joan's stark dress. It came to Adam that she probably took a perverse pleasure in dressing like a nun—a most wealthy nun, as the wool of her unembroidered brown kirtle was of the finest weave, the surcoat lined with silk, albeit in a muted mustard colour.

The table was as frugal as the lady's dress: a large platter of apples, parsnips, and beets, all of it sliced very thinly and decorated with nuts and drizzled honey, a smaller plate of boiled eggs, neatly halved, and to the side a dish of smoked venison. A far cry from the generous table offered by Lord Roger, and with far too little meat.

"You must excuse my simple offering," Lady Joan said. "I take little pleasure in food these days." She grimaced. "I live the life of a nun—in all aspects."

Despite the food, Lady Joan was a gracious hostess, and the hours flew by. Pages crept in to light the candles, Lady Joan called for wine and cheese wafers, and still they talked, at first mostly about Tresaints' new chaplain, whom Lady Joan held in high regard but whom neither Adam nor Kit had yet met.

"He's Welsh, bless his heart, but for all that, Owain is a good subject of the English king. His family has served the Mortimers for generations." Lady Joan broke her wafer into slivers and proceeded to eat them one by one. "Magnificent singing voice, a strict and learned spiritual man. Uncompromising when it comes to sin—as he should be."

"Ah." Adam was not so sure this was what he wanted in his priest.

Lady Joan laughed. "He's a compassionate man, Adam. Knows himself to be as weak as his fellow man."

She insisted on a detailed account of the recent wedding

and festivities, rolling her eyes when Adam described how Lord Roger had claimed the part of King Arthur.

"Aping his grandfather," she said. "For a man so intelligent, at times he is nothing but a fool. No wonder Geoffrey was so upset."

"Aye, my lady."

"It ended well," Kit offered. "The king won."

Lady Joan picked up her silver goblet and ran a finger round its rim. "It hasn't ended yet, dear Kit. And everyone who was here has seen how the upstart Mortimer outshone his liege-lord and king." She sighed. "God keep him."

Kit was dispatched to fetch Lady Joan's book of hours—so transparent a ruse Kit winked at Adam behind Lady Joan's back.

"How is he?" Lady Joan asked once they were alone.

Adam considered his reply. "He's like a man who has reached the top of the mountain only to realise the view was not all it was made up to be," he finally said. "It takes its toll, my lady. On his health but also on his temper. His hours are long, he sees potential enemies everywhere—"

"A correct assumption, I fear," Lady Joan interrupted.

"Aye." Adam scraped at a smear of butter on the tablecloth. "He is not loved by any but his own men."

"And the dowager queen."

"And her." Adam met Lady Joan's eyes. "She does love him, my lady."

"As he loves her." Lady Joan pursed her mouth. "Much more than he ever loved me." She laughed bitterly. "Listen to me, as if love was ever part of the equation when it came to our marriage. A young bride, an even younger groom, and our alliance made our families more powerful and us both that much greater, that much richer." For an instant, her lower lip wobbled. "All those years, all those children…Surely, it was more than a mere dynastic union?"

"Lady Joan, I—"

"—cannot answer that." She patted his hand. "My apologies for burdening you with my pain."

"I wish I could carry it for you, my lady."

"But you can't." Lady Joan sat back, retreating behind a bland face. "She'll be the death of him."

"My lady?"

"Mark my words: Isabella of France will cling to her newfound power until it is ripped from her. She spent far too many years displaced by those glamorous male favourites our former king so loved to ever want to risk being so treated by her son." She met Adam's eyes. "And when she falls, so does Roger."

"The king would never harm his mother."

"You underestimate him. Even worse, so does his mother."

They left just after prime, Kit having spent the last hour or so with Lady Joan in the chapel. They rode over the drawbridge, slowing their mounts when they reached the spot beside the large junipers where Adam had been abducted.

"She's found Geoffrey a bride," Kit said, her eyes darting from one stand of junipers to the other. He glanced at her: Kit had been here every day, wanting to thank the child who'd guided her through the night. He studied the trampled ground, angry with himself for falling for such a transparent ruse. With an effort, he returned to the subject of Geoffrey's wife.

"A bride?" Adam set his heels to Raven. "An English heiress?" he asked over his shoulder.

"No. A French one. She says only a fool lays all their eggs in one basket, and so Geoffrey is being set up for a rich life as a French baron rather than an English one."

"Ah. And has she discussed this with Lord Roger?"

Kit urged her horse into a trot to catch up with him. "I think not. But Geoffrey knows and approves."

"And Edmund?"

"He approves of anything that does not come from his father, it would seem." Kit patted the neck of her palfrey. "Sad, to see a son so distant from his father."

"He was there for the tournament."

"He was. At Lady Joan's command. And you may have noticed he was rarely closer than twenty feet to his father."

213

"Mmm. He can't forgive him for the dishonour caused to his lady mother."

"Understandably so." Kit rode even closer. "I shall raise my sons to be just as protective of me."

"Our sons?" Adam chuckled. "I would be more worried about Meg—and that cat of hers." He took her gloved hand. "Besides, I have no intention of straying from the marital bed."

"Ever?"

Adam tightened his hold. "Men are weak, sweeting. Months away on campaign, leagues from home…" She tugged at her hand, a futile exercise which just caused him to grin. "Even if I should bed another, it would be a matter of the flesh, no more. My heart remains with you."

"As mine is with you when I succumb to the cravings of my body and you are far away," she bit back.

"You do that and I'll belt you," he growled. "I'll not have a faithless wife."

"Nor me a faithless husband." She clapped her heels to her horse, and it responded willingly, carrying her off in a burst of speed that had her veil whipping behind her. He caught up with her, leaning over to grab hold of her reins and bring them both to a jarring halt.

"What's the matter with you?" he asked with a little smile.

"The matter?" She inhaled. "I don't want just your heart! I want all of you, Adam de Guirande. I don't want to end up like Lady Joan, so bitter it leaks out in her voice, in her eyes, whenever she speaks of her husband."

That wiped away his smile. "I will never give you cause to become bitter, that I promise you." This time, he not only took her gloved hand, he pulled off her glove before kissing the palm of her hand. "And you do have me—all of me. Surely, you know that, my dearest lady?"

She gave him a watery smile.

They arrived at Tresaints four days later, tired and sore after long days in the saddle.

"I wish we could stay," Kit sighed as they dismounted. A

week at most, and then they'd be on their way again, hopefully catching up with the king at Gloucester.

"Aye." Adam sounded distracted, already the lord of the manor returned to inspect his lands and home. Kit smiled at his broad back: he loved Tresaints as much as she did, proud of every improvement they'd made. She turned to find herself face-to-face with their new priest, Owain.

He was shorter than she was, but twice as broad, his robe straining over an impressive girth. Small bright eyes under bushy brows, a messy ring of curly red hair bordering his tonsure. He grinned.

"Another redhead, I see." He bowed. "My lady."

Kit tucked the escaped strand of hair out of sight. "Father." Any further words with the priest were interrupted by her children, Meg flying towards her with Harry and Ned in tow. There was straw in Meg's hair, mud on her gown, and from the state of her hands her daughter had not been working on her letters or her needlework, but rather capering about in the orchard. Kit threw a quick look at Adam, still immersed in his discussion with John.

"Mama!" Meg barged into her, followed by her brothers, and Kit nearly landed on her bottom in the mud. Fortunately, Father Owain was there to offer some support and to wag a finger at the de Guirande brood, telling them to give their mother some room.

"And before you ask, she is a diligent student," he said to Kit. "But I find small children learn best when taught without too much coercion."

Meg tugged at Kit's girdle. "I can write my name," she said proudly. "All of it. And I can write Tom's name too, and Goliath's."

"Well done," Kit caressed her daughter's downy cheek. "Your father will be very proud."

"Me too, me too," Ned said, back to clinging at Kit's skirts. "Can write." Eyes the exact shade of his father's stared up at her.

Meg sniffed. "You? You're a baby."

"Not a baby!"

A heated discussion followed, during which Kit took the opportunity to lift Harry up and kiss him, using a rag to wipe his nose clean. Her fair son gave her a placid smile, wound his arms round her neck, and said "Mama", and then demanded to be set down because by now Meg and Ned had seen their father—and so had Harry.

"Comely children, my lady," Father Owain said.

"Thank you." She grinned at the sight of her beleaguered husband, surrounded not only by his clamouring children but his various dogs, big things with brindled coats and huge paws. She lifted her skirts as she walked across the muddy bailey with the priest at her side. "How are you settling in?"

"Well enough. How could I not in a household where a Welsh saint holds pride of place?"

"St Winefride was my mother's favourite," Kit replied.

"To judge from his unworn statue, poor St Odo does not seem to have been anyone's favourite," Father Owain said, making Kit laugh.

"I dare say we are too far away from Normandy to properly appreciate a Norman saint."

At this point, they were joined by Adam, and once introductions had been made, Kit excused herself. She wanted to see her babies.

"Twice as big as last time," Adam commented when he joined her in the nursery—one of the additions he was so proud of. He had his arms full with Peter while Kit was replacing Ellie's coif after having thoroughly inspected her.

"And healthy," Bridget put in. "Eat like horses, they do." She patted her ample bosom. "Fortunately, I am up to it."

"Up to it?" Mabel snorted. "With all the buttered ale you consume, you'd be able to raise an entire litter."

They left the nursery, and the rest of the afternoon Adam spent with John and Father Owain, going over the accounts. Their new priest had offered to help as clerk and accountant, and from the occasional bursts of laughter that came from behind the closed door, Kit gathered the priest was a welcome addition to Tresaints.

"Aye, he seems a good man," Adam agreed much later.

They'd supped in the hall with the whole household, and it was with some relief they'd retired to their solar and the waiting bath Mabel had arranged.

The bath was still warm enough to make Kit reluctant to get out, soap suds and sprinkled herbs floating in the fragrant water. She had Adam's foot in her lap, fingers wandering up and down the newly healed cuts. It was still swollen, and he grimaced when she prodded and kneaded. The bones would take a long time to knit and heal.

"I didn't see Tom at supper," Kit commented.

"Mmm? No, he's out in the pastures somewhere." Adam yawned. "He'll be out there for most of the winter with Henry and Rob—they're staying with the flocks."

"In the old shepherd's cottage?" The little house was a day's walk from the manor.

"Aye. Do the lad good to spend the winter adequately occupied. By the time they bring the sheep down for lambing, he'll have grown accustomed to his new role."

Kit finished with his foot and clambered out of the large tub to grab one of the linen towelling cloths. She stood as close as she could to the hearth as she dried herself briskly, more than aware of Adam's eyes on her naked body.

"Meg must miss him," she said.

"Aye, probably. But it is for the best." He stood, water sluicing off his body, and carefully got out, inhaling when he put too much weight on his damaged foot. "Bed?" he asked once he was dry.

"Bed." She waited until he'd limped across before she snuffed out the two candles, the dull glow from the hearth painting the whitewashed walls in reddish shadows.

"Leave them," he said when she made as if to close the shutters. She set a hand to the precious panes of glass, leaving a handprint in the condensation. "Come here, sweeting."

"Coming." She added an *A* and a *K* to her handprint and padded over the bare floorboards to join her husband in their bed.

Chapter 24

They rejoined the court in Gloucester, riding side by side towards the castle's gatehouse. Through the arch, over the drawbridges that spanned the double moats, and through yet another gatehouse and they were in the outer bailey, the large square keep rising before them.

Once he'd seen Kit installed in their room, Adam went in search of his lord.

"About time," Ralph Stafford said upon seeing Adam. "Our king needs diversion of some sort."

"Diversion?" Adam moved his tightly bandaged foot up and down. He could no longer offer the king an opportunity to work off his anger in the tiltyard.

"He's as fretful as a breeding mare," Stafford continued. "It's not having Will around, I think."

"Will?" Adam followed Stafford up the broad stairs to the king's apartments, one careful step at the time. "Where is he?"

"In France." Stafford gave Adam a cheeky smile. "Entrusted with a secret mission, I believe. A first, isn't it, that he sends someone other than you."

"A mission?"

Stafford sighed. "Either he'll tell you, or he won't. I can't tell you anything, seeing as I don't know."

King Edward was sprawled in a chair with Lancelot at his feet. Sitting beside him was Richard Bury—Master Bury—his old tutor, and from their tones the matters they were discussing were grave.

"Adam." Edward waved Adam up from his reverence. "Recovered?"

"As well as I ever will be, my lord." He rose carefully, trying not to limp too much on his way across the room, but to judge from the way the king's eyes narrowed, he did not succeed too well.

218

"Damn the man," Edward said. "To lame my best knight."

"I limped before as well."

"But not like that."

No, not like this. Pancio held little hope Adam would ever regain his previous mobility and had even advocated using a cane. When hell froze over…

Edward invited him to sit. "A lot has happened since Wigmore." A shadow crossed over his face. "We had words, the self-styled King Arthur and I, in Hereford, and as a consequence I've made some changes. Behold the keeper of the privy seal," he said, pointing at Richard. "Not something Maman or her Welsh dragon liked. In fact, she was most upset."

"But it is your seal, my lord," Adam said.

"Precisely." Edward drummed his fingers against the table. "It is time."

"My lord?" Adam asked.

"Time to act, de Guirande," Master Bury said. "The king must begin to reclaim his powers—little by little."

"Is that why Montagu is in France?" Adam asked, and Edward rolled his eyes.

"Secrets are difficult to keep." He studied Adam in silence for a while. "Will Montagu has been charged with approaching His Holiness on my behalf," Edward explained. His jaws gritted. "Somehow, Mortimer found out. His damned spies are everywhere, aren't they?"

"And what did Mortimer do then?" Adam asked.

"He decided Will needed a companion." Master Bury shook his head. "And so Sir Bartholomew rides with him."

Sir Bartholomew Burghersh was the brother of Mortimer's close friend, the Bishop of Lincoln.

"I imagine Will was delighted," Adam commented drily. The constable of Dover Castle was several years older than Montagu and of a serious disposition.

"If so, he hid it well." Edward extended his legs before him and studied his shoes intently. "He'll manage. Will knows what has to be done, and Bartholomew is not necessarily welded to Mortimer's cause, no matter that his cousin is wed to Edmund Mortimer. Do you know him?" he asked Adam.

"Sir Bartholomew? Not much. We've met on various campaigns, that's all." In Adam's opinion, Baron Burghersh was a man more interested in fulfilling his duties than in partaking of political intrigue. "I deem him a man of integrity."

"So do I," Edward said. "Not Mortimer's best choice as a companion to Will." He stood. "The queen and I are going hawking. I have a new peregrine to try out."

Master Bury and Adam rose, the king's former tutor adapting his pace to Adam's slow limp as they followed their king out into the September sunshine and through the wards to where the hunting party was assembling by the western gate, a noisy collection of horses and courtiers. Queen Philippa was already astride, several of her ladies beside her, among which Adam could make out his Kit.

"Will you not be joining them?" Master Bury asked.

"Me?" Adam shook his head. "I have work to do. A fortnight and more without their captain, and chances are I'll find rusting hauberks and badly honed blades among the king's guard."

Master Bury laughed. "Not unless they're very foolish."

Adam gave him a grim smile, no more.

He'd put the fear of God into those among his men whose equipment he'd found less than impeccable, had subjected all the men to several hours of strenuous training, and had finished by going from gate to gate to inspect the guards on duty. Nicholas the Hainaulter tagged him like an eager dog, promising to make sure every hauberk, every breastplate, was as good as new come morning—not through Nicholas' hard work, but through the frantic work of the men themselves.

"Good." Adam wet his finger and rubbed at what looked like mould on Nicholas' cloak. "How many men on the wall?"

"Other than on the gatehouses? A score or so." He watched Adam approach the ladder that led up to the walk. "Should you really?"

"Aye." Adam was already halfway up the ladder, not about to show his sergeant as much as a glimmer of weakness.

The Gloucester curtain wall was extensive, the walk damnably narrow, causing Adam quite some discomfort as he made his circuit, ensuring his men were alert despite the security offered by the impressive fortress. He'd purposely planned it so that he ended up on the walls overlooking the Severn and the west, the meadows closer to the town giving way to moors and distant woods. To his far right, he could make out the impressive bridge that spanned the Severn, somewhat closer was yet another bridge, crossing the narrower eastern arm of the great river. Cattle and sheep were being herded up from the meadows towards this inner bridge, and to judge from the scent of blood that occasionally wafted his way, the shambles were located conveniently close to the western gate. No reason to herd the beasts further than necessary.

He stood on one leg, relieved to ease up on his bad foot, and rested most of his weight on his arms, braced against the wide parapet. Already, autumn was upon them, made evident by the golden colour of the grasses. The alders that bordered the river were shedding leaves that swirled away or caught in the stands of reeds that grew along the water's edge, and the copses of oaks that stood some distance away presented foliage already tinged with yellow.

"Only a fool would attempt to breach this side of the castle," a voice said.

"And yet they have—with some success, as you well know, my lord. But I'm not standing here considering the defences, but rather to enjoy the view." Adam moved to the side to allow Mortimer to join him, making a token bow.

"Ah, not only a soldier but a man of sensibilities," Lord Roger teased.

"Only a blind man would not see the beauty in this."

Lord Roger rested his elbows on the parapet and looked to the west. "True. It's as if the entire kingdom lies before us, the horizons shrouded in mist."

"Likely rain," Adam said drily, making Lord Roger laugh. They stood in companionable silence, Adam lost in thoughts about Tresaints and his growing flocks of sheep, his eyes on a particularly fluffy cloud.

Beside him, Lord Roger cleared his throat. "I'm to be a father."

"What?" Adam stared at him.

"You heard." Lord Roger looked bemused rather than happy, wide shoulders bowed. Adam was tempted to tell him he already was a father, twelve times over, but the expression on the baron's face invited compassion rather than condemnation.

"With Queen Isabella?"

"What do you think? Of course with Isabella!"

Unfortunately. How would their young king react to the news—especially since his own wife was as yet not breeding?

Lord Roger gave him a crooked smile. "Don't gawk, Adam. And yes, my sentiments precisely: What will the world say?" He dislodged a piece of mortar from between the stones and crumbled it to dust, face set in a pensive frown. "I am overjoyed—and terrified," he said at long last.

"And the queen?"

"The queen?" Lord Roger's mouth softened into a smile. "My lady is, as always, fearless." He dusted off his hands. "But I dare say she'd have preferred for this not to happen." There was a bitter edge to his tone. "I should not have told you, but I've gone about all day with this bubbling inside of me, and it was either tell my confessor or you—and I trust you more."

"I'll not tell." The king would likely brain whoever brought him this news.

"Good man." Lord Roger clasped his hand for a moment. "Any idea why Montagu is in France?"

"In France?" Adam shook his head. "No, my lord."

"Hmm. Well, I'll find out soon enough. I always do." One last pat to Adam's shoulder and Mortimer was gone.

"No!" Kit pulled up her knees and wrapped her arms round her legs. "How—"

"Terrible?" Adam filled in.

"I was going to say complicated." She chewed her lip. "But you're right: terrible is what it is. A queen giving birth to an illegitimate child…"

"Aye. King Edward will go green with bile." Adam pulled off his boots and joined her in bed. "Can't say I envy the one who has to tell him."

"Only one person can."

"Aye. Poor Queen Isabella."

"As one sows, one reaps," Kit said primly.

"Oh, aye?" He tugged at her hair. "Not always, sweeting, else you'd already be rounding with child again."

She went a deep pink. "I don't like doing it, but—"

"Aye, I know. And it was my decision, not yours." He wound her hair round his hand and pulled her close enough to kiss her nose. "I felt sorry for him." Until he'd asked about Montagu, that is.

"God isn't always kind, is he?" Kit pillowed her head on his shoulder. "Or maybe this is divine retribution."

"A child is always a gift."

"Not if you're an unwed mother."

"He can't wed her—he's already married."

"As is she." Kit sat up. "What will Lady Joan say?" Her hands slid up his leg, fingers making short work of the hose points.

"What can she say?" Adam reclined against the pillows, watching her as she tugged off his hose and undid the bandage, head bent over his swollen, ugly foot.

"You've been walking too much," she chided, slipping off the bed to return with a little pot containing that aromatic salve that left his skin throbbing with heat.

"I have duties to fulfil. I intend to do so." He gritted his teeth at the discomfort her fingers caused as she massaged his damned foot. "Edward will make her birth it in secret," he said, reverting to the original subject.

"How? Retire to a convent for some months of contemplation?"

"Why not? And then the child could be spirited away somewhere." More likely, it would be placed behind the walls of a distant convent or monastery, far enough from England that Edward need never fear his half-sibling making an appearance at his court.

"She'd never allow him to do that—nor would Mortimer."

"They will have no say in this."

She sat up, looking astounded. "They're the regents."

"Not for much longer—not if there's a child." At her evident lack of understanding, he went on, "To bed the queen can be construed as high treason. A child would be irrefutable proof, and for high treason you die—or end up locked away behind walls, depending on your gender."

Kit covered her mouth with her hand. "Dear God!"

"Aye, dear God indeed."

"Do you think Edward would?"

"Hang Lord Roger? Incarcerate his mother?" Adam considered this in silence, his stomach roiling at the thought. "As things are…" He nodded. "Maybe."

There was a look to Philippa next morning that had Kit smiling. At times, it was difficult to remember their little queen with her intricate braided hairstyles and exquisitely embroidered clothes was not much more than a child herself, but on a day like this, when she looked about to burst with whatever secret it was that had her hopping from one foot to the other, Queen Philippa looked her age, a mere fifteen.

The moment she saw Kit, she grabbed her by the hands and tugged her in the direction of the large hearth, in front of which was Mathilde, her lap full of sewing.

"What is it, my lady?" Kit asked when the queen's face broke open into a brilliant smile.

"A secret," the queen said, taking a few dancing steps.

Kit looked at Mathilde, who did no more than purse her lips into a narrow funnel, shaking her head at the queen. Kit hid a little smile: this particular secret was not difficult to guess.

"Mathilde says…" Philippa began, casting a wary look at her other ladies, presently sitting by the windows but with all their attention trained on their mistress.

"My lady, a secret is only a secret if you don't tell anyone," Mathilde interrupted in a low voice, wagging a finger. "Besides, one does not count the chicks before they're hatched."

Philippa's face fell, dark eyes widening. "You don't think…"

"I don't think anything." Mathilde looked meaningfully at Philippa's hands, spread over a flat belly. "But unless Lady Kit is a complete fool, she's probably worked out your little secret by now." The old nurse tsked, but she couldn't quite contain the smile tugging at her mouth. "Am I right, Lady Kit?"

Kit looked at the queen. "How many days?"

"Five. And before you say anything, yes, I know this may be nothing, but I am praying that it isn't."

"We will all pray," Kit assured her, making a deep reverence. "For you, my lady, and for the life within."

"A baby," Queen Philippa whispered. "My baby." She turned to Mathilde. "When can I tell N—the king?"

"Not yet," came the dry reply.

"Give it a month," Kit suggested.

"A month!" Queen Philippa's voice rose into a squeak. "I'll never be able to keep quiet that long."

"You could try," Mathilde said. "In these matters, it is best to be sure."

Kit agreed—and said so. To raise the king's hopes and then crush them would not be a good thing. Philippa sucked in her lower lip, two parallel furrows between her plucked brows.

"Very well," she sighed. "I shall try."

"We cannot ask for more than that, *ma petite*," Mathilde said with a warm smile.

There'd been a council meeting during the morning, from which King Edward emerged looking sullen, with Mortimer walking side by side with him, as unruffled as always. Adam frowned; unless explicitly invited, one did not walk side by side with the king. When Mortimer casually draped an arm round the king's shoulders, Adam took a step forward.

The king said something in a vicious tone; Mortimer retracted his arm and came to a halt, dark eyes narrowed into slivers of glittering jet. The king marched on, scowling at nothing in particular.

"Maybe one should hack off one of his hands in warning," a voice said from behind Adam. "So how's the king's lame knight?"

"The what?" If he whirled on his good foot, Adam was still fast, and there was nothing wrong with his hand, which was why Will de Bohun backed away in such a haste he crashed into his twin brother, Ed.

"No offense intended." Will de Bohun held up his hands, eyes on Adam's dagger. "He means it kindly."

"He?"

"Cousin Ned." Ed de Bohun clarified.

"I'm not lame." He'd spent the early morning in an isolated glade in the forest, working his way through his normal sword routines, and at present his foot was killing him. Pancio was right: Adam would never fight on foot again—not if he wanted to survive.

"No, no, as agile as a cat," Will de Bohun replied with a teasing glint in his eyes. They were much alike, the de Bohun twins, and could easily be taken for the king's brothers, sharing with their royal cousin fair hair parted in the middle to fall in soft waves down to their jawline, bright blue eyes, and tall and robust frames.

"You shouldn't mock your elders." Stafford swatted Will over the head. "The queen wants you, by the way."

"Me?" Will asked, looking hopeful.

"No idea which one—best you trot off together like good boys." Stafford made a shooing motion with his hands. "You'll have to get used to it," he said casually once the de Bohun lads were out of earshot. "The nickname is too good not to stick." There was a malicious tone to his voice, but then Stafford and Adam had never seen entirely eye to eye, the noble if impoverished Baron Stafford resenting Adam's position in the royal household.

"Whoever uses it best be prepared to pay," Adam told him, an eye on the king and Mortimer, who were now involved in some sort of heated exchange with Bishop Henry, for the day fulfilling his role as lord chancellor rather than that of a bishop.

"Oooo," Stafford flapped his hands. "See how I quake in fear." He grinned, thereby taking the edge of things.

"Idiot."

"Me?" Ralph's eyes gleamed. "Oh no; the true fool is your precious Mortimer. Did you see him just now? Embracing the king like that?"

"Not my Mortimer," Adam corrected by rote. "And aye, I saw. The affectionate gesture of a man towards his almost stepson."

"His what?" Stafford choked out. "Just because the king's mother is like a bitch in heat in Mortimer's presence, it does not follow the king holds him in similar affection."

"No, that would be odd," Adam agreed, and Stafford went a bright red.

"I didn't mean it like that."

"I know you didn't." Adam's attention was distracted by the man entering the upper ward at a trot. Fair hair stood every which way, the tonsured spot was not as visible as it should be, and William could do with a shave, his cheeks covered in fair bristles.

"Ah. Your dear brother, one of Mortimer's more faithful hounds." Stafford snickered. "I wonder where he's been? In France, to spy on Montagu?"

Adam chose not to answer, making instead for the little group of men towards which his brother was heading.

"William—back so soon?" Mortimer asked, an upraised hand stopping William from going down on his knee.

"Good horse, my lord." William saw the king and bowed deeply. "And a speedy crossing over the Narrow Sea, God help my poor stomach."

Even the king laughed at that. Henry Burghersh merely smiled.

"What news?" Lord Roger asked, and William's eyelids fluttered nervously.

"Here, my lord?"

"Why not? I dare say our king already knows where Montagu is heading." A sly glance at the king accompanied this statement. Edward crossed his arms, his gaze wandering

227

from William to Adam and back again. It made Adam itch: for all that his brother was in priestly garb and he himself sported the colours of the king, they were very alike, tall and fair with light eyes and similar features. Two brothers whose lives had been shaped by the generosity of Mortimer, two brothers who owed everything they had to a man the king had, at best, an ambivalent relationship with.

"Go on, man," the king said, "don't keep our Lord Mortimer waiting."

William cleared his throat. "Sir Bartholomew sends his greetings and wishes you to know he has had satisfactory meetings with the French regarding the recent skirmishes along the borders of Aquitaine. And…"

"That can keep." Mortimer waved his hand. "Such matters we can discuss later, just the two of us—and the lord chancellor. What of Montagu?"

"He's heading to Avignon, my lord," William said.

"Avignon? Ah, he rides to see the pope—like dear Edmund did so recently." Mortimer scratched his brow. "What, one wonders, does Will have to talk to the pope about?"

"Between him and His Holiness," Edward said coolly. "Maybe he has grievous sins to confess."

"Oh, I am sure I'll find out just what they discuss." Mortimer smiled. "Even the papal palace has ears, my lord."

King Edward smiled back, all teeth, no warmth. "As does every palace here in England, Mortimer." He shook out his robes. "And not all of them are yours."

Chapter 25

When Queen Isabella appeared for mass at St Owen's chapel on Michaelmas, it was the first time in three days she'd ventured outside her rooms, the excuse being that she'd been suffering from a severe case of sniffles. Pale and collected, she was escorted by her youngest son, both of them in garments of various shades of green and blue. The queen's mantle in particular attracted whispered attention, the brilliant green fabric decorated not only with gold-thread embroidery but also with jewels—the same, some said, as those that adorned her crimson mantle on her wedding day.

Kit made but a cursory inspection of the clothes, rather more interested in how wan Isabella looked, her pallor tinged with a grey hue that indicated sleepless nights and restless days. A lady with a burden, and some steps behind her came the progenitor himself, concerned eyes never leaving the queen.

It was something of a contrast to watch the younger queen come gliding up the central aisle, pink cheeks and bright eyes shouting to the world that here was a most blushing and contented bride. Beside her, the king walked proud and erect. Whenever he looked at her, he beamed, and it was clearly with reluctance he released her hand once they reached the altar.

"She's told him," Kit whispered to Mathilde, who rolled her eyes.

"God grant her that she does not miscarry."

"Amen to that." Kit clasped her hands together. An heir, and Philippa could relax.

The little chapel was so full it was impossible to do more than stand and chant. "Like salted herrings in a barrel," Mathilde commented, jabbing her elbow into the woman standing beside her. "The smell is more that of rotting pork, though. At least from some." She raised a sachet of crushed lavender to her nose while glaring at her neighbour.

Kit was glad of her height, which allowed her to see something beyond the back of the women in front of her, with the added benefit of giving her an opportunity to localise her husband, just behind the king's back. These last few days, Adam's mood had been unpredictable, his temper flaring at any suggestion he rest and see to his foot. Instead, he was overdoing things, causing little beads of sweat to spring forth on his upper lip with every painful step he took.

Most irking of all was Adam's refusal to talk about it. At her every attempt to raise the subject, he went blank, mouth setting in so thin a line she knew it was useless to continue the discussion. So lost was she in her contemplation of her husband that only when Mathilde nudged her did she realise it was their turn to kneel and receive Christ's body, the host sticking to the roof of her mouth as she mumbled her responses.

After mass, Adam came to find Kit. They held back to avoid the crush at the door to the hall, and once inside Adam took a firm hold of Kit's hand while making for seats some distance away from the high table. William was already there, waving to them, and soon enough they were on a trestle, facing William over the table.

The servers entered, a procession of plates laden with roasted geese, and up by the high table the king stood to formally carve the first bird, offering his lady wife the choicest meat. Adam was as conscientious, ensuring Kit got her fair share of meat and crispy skin.

Conversation was lively, the din bouncing back and forth between the heavy walls, up to the rafters and down again. At the high table, the king and queen were conducting an amorous little discussion, at least to judge from how he kept on feeding her morsels he speared on his eating knife.

Philippa's dark hair was visible beneath her sheer veil, a simple coronet of braided golden threads keeping it in place. For the day in cream and pink—colours that enhanced her flushed skin and glittering eyes—her radiant presence easily eclipsed every other lady there, including that of Queen Isabella.

"A first, I believe," Adam whispered in Kit's ear. "Little Philippa outshining her mother-in-law."

"Not so hard to do today," Kit replied. Isabella was sitting to the side, drinking steadily from her goblet. As far as Kit could see, she'd not touched any food, this despite Mortimer's cajoling, his laden knife repeatedly hovering before her mouth. But she'd gripped her lover's hand and held on to it as a drowning man to a spar, ignoring the annoyed looks the king threw at their joined hands.

"Aye. Two women in the same condition, and one is overjoyed, the other desperate." He kept his voice at a murmur.

"God have mercy on her," Kit said, shoving her food away.

"You don't want it?"

"No. You have it." She pushed the trencher his way, unable to tear her gaze from the silent effigy that was Queen Isabella.

Adam set down the last of the clean goose bones and grinned at his brother. "I love Michaelmas."

"Because of the food?" William wagged a greasy finger at him. "Our mother would not be pleased."

Adam smiled slightly; he had few memories of his mother, but he did recall just how often his mother had told him of St Michael, the bravest, most ferocious of the angels set to guard God's kingdom.

"Because of St Michael. I wanted to be like him," he said.

"An archangel?" Beside him, Kit laughed. "Lofty ambitions, my dearest husband."

"Brave and ferocious would do." Adam crumbled the last of his bread, wondering how brave and ferocious St Michael would be with only one good foot.

"You are brave." William reached across to punch Adam lightly. "Perhaps not quite as devout as an archangel should be, though."

"Too carnal," Adam agreed, slipping an arm round Kit's waist. "Would angels ever…?"

"No." William scowled. "Not something to jest about. Angels are free of all sin—including lust." He wiped his hands

231

clean and smoothed at his hair, now tamed into a neatly clipped fringe. "That's what separates them from us, weak and fallen creatures that we are."

Adam was about to reply when a messenger pushed by the guards and hurried towards the king.

"That's Kent's arms," he said, studying the soiled tabard. He stood and jostled his way through the crowds, reaching the dais just as the messenger went down on his knees before the king. Edward's hand trembled as it gripped the roll.

"From your dear, traitorous uncle?" Mortimer asked, appearing just behind the king. "I wonder what he might have to say for himself—assuming it is from him."

"Who else?" Edward said, breaking the seal.

"I don't know. His widow? Travelling in foreign lands can be a dangerous business."

"Seeing as you know how dear my uncle is to me, I am sure you've held him in your prayers," the king replied smoothly, eyes on his letter. "Good news! Edmund is on his way back."

"Back? But wasn't he supposed to go to Santiago?" Mortimer made as if to snatch the missive out of Edward's hands, but thought better of it.

"He was? First I hear of it." The king smirked. "Maybe all those ears of yours misheard, Mortimer." He clapped his hands and called for more wine. Mortimer returned to his seat beside Queen Isabella, and from the look in his eyes, several Mortimer men would spend long, uncomfortable hours being interrogated by their disgruntled lord—chief among them Richard of Monmouth, who'd ridden in only yesterday.

"Oh dear," the king said in an undertone. "A cat among the pigeons?" He looked straight at Adam. "Imagine what he'd say if he knew it was you who foiled his little plan. He wouldn't like that, would he?"

A threat? Adam bowed and limped back to his seat.

"Bad news?" Kit asked when Adam slid in beside her.

"No." He grabbed her half-full cup and downed its contents. "But foul play all the same."

"How foul?" William asked, making Adam frown at him.

"Never mind." Adam stood. "Coming?" He held out his hand to Kit.

They were almost at the door when someone yanked at Kit's skirts.

"The queen wishes to see you, my lady," the little page said. "In her chambers."

"Now?" Kit looked at Philippa, laughing at something the king had just said.

"Not that queen." The page shuffled on his feet. "Queen Isabella."

Kit exchanged a quick look with Adam. "Very well."

The page offered to guide her, but Kit assured him she could find her way. Adam accompanied her across the ward to where the royal apartments hugged the curtain wall, and for a little while they lingered in the autumn sun.

"What might she want?" Kit smoothed at her skirts.

"Company?" Adam suggested. He squeezed her hand. "Want me to wait?"

"No need." She leaned against him. "Who knows how long you'll be waiting?" She laughed when he told her he'd gladly wait until hell froze over if so required and sent him on his way with a kiss.

Kit was admitted by yet another page. The queen was alone in her solar, the smell of new paint sharp enough to have Kit look at the walls.

"Beautiful, isn't it?" Queen Isabella touched the detailed depiction of a dragon's claw. "My son loves it."

In red on white, the wall depicted St George vanquishing the dragon, the saint bearing a startling resemblance to their young king, the terrified princess a passable likeness to Philippa.

"No French lilies in here, my lady?" Kit asked, still with her eyes on the larger-than-life saint. The other walls had recently been whitewashed, their only decoration a series of miniature red St George's crosses in a border along the ceiling. Quite austere in comparison to Queen Isabella's normal preferences, even if the large bed, also in white and red, was heaped with pillows and silks.

"Not here. French lilies and warrior saints do not go together." Isabella took off her veil. "How late is she?"

The sudden change in subject confused Kit. "My lady?"

"Don't play the simpleton with me, Kit. My dearest daughter-in-law glows like a jewel in a pile of sheep dung." She raised her brows. "Besides, I make it my business to inform myself about her health, and so I know she's not had her courses this month. At last, I might add."

"Then why ask me?"

"Confirmation, I suppose." The queen seated herself at a small table and picked up an ivory comb. "I am happy for her—and for my son. Very happy." Two of the teeth in the comb snapped. "Very, very happy." She threw the comb away from her. It bounced against one of the painted chests that lined the further wall, and Kit kneeled to retrieve it.

"You know," the queen said to her back.

"Know what, my lady?" Kit attempted to sound confused.

"Don't deny it." Isabella picked at the few pieces of jewellery that lay on the table, a faraway look on her face. "Roger admitted he'd told Adam, and what he knows, you know."

"Yes, I do know." Kit took a hesitant step towards her, the broken comb in her hands.

"A child, fathered by the man I love, but how am I to carry it?" Isabella placed her hands on her belly, the blue silk rustling as she knotted her hands in it. "What will my son say when he finds out?"

"What can he say? The child is there. It cannot be undone."

Two green, unflinching eyes met hers.

"My lady! That is a grievous sin."

"And you think I don't know that?" Isabella hid her face in her hands, and for some moments, all there was were the sounds of her breathing, loud and ragged. Kit moved closer, wanting to offer comfort but uncertain how it would be received.

"I love him," the queen said. "I love this child as well, but to keep it is to risk everything—first and foremost Roger's life."

"What does he say?"

Queen Isabella snorted. "Men are softhearted fools at times. He is so elated he ignores the truth staring him in the face: if this child lives, Roger may well die, and as to me, my son will have every right to demand I enter a convent." Yet again, her elegant hands smoothed over her belly. "I wish…" She choked.

Kit put a tentative hand on the queen's shoulder. "I am so sorry, my lady."

"Sorry?" Isabella surged to her feet. "Do you think I need your pity? Me, a daughter of France?" She lifted her chin, displaying the elegant line of her neck. "I will do what must be done, and you can keep your compassion for those that need it."

"My lady, I—"

"Shut up! Shut up, shut up, shut up." Queen Isabella collapsed to the floor, loud sobs racking her body. "My baby," she moaned. "Our child."

Kit knelt beside her and embraced her, rocking her gently back and forth. "It will pass," she whispered over and over again. "This too will pass, my lady."

By the time the queen quieted, Kit had a cramp in her leg. She did not know quite where to look when Isabella disengaged herself and went to wash her bloated face, so she busied herself with straightening the few items of clothing she found thrown over a chest.

"I don't need to tell you never to tell anyone, do I?" the queen asked once she was composed.

"No, my lady."

"Good. Bring me the wine. All that weeping has left me parched."

Kit lifted the pitcher from the larger table by the hearth and brought it over to where the queen was sitting. The queen held out her goblet, Kit went to pour, but stopped. There was already some liquid in the cup, and Kit did not need to ask to know what it was—she recognised the scent.

"Pour," the queen ordered. "It tastes awful on its own."

Kit did as told, her hand shaking. "Pennyroyal is a dangerous herb, my lady."

"Life is dangerous," Queen Isabella retorted. "Surely, you know that by now."

It took Kit some time to recover from her afternoon with Queen Isabella. In need of silence and solitude, she retreated to the chapel, where she sank down before the carved image of Our Lady and prayed for Isabella, for the poor innocent child, and for Mortimer, a man soon to be robbed of a son or a daughter.

This was where Adam found her, his slow, measured steps adverting her to his presence long before she saw him.

"Sweeting?" He lowered himself to the floor. "What is it?" He caressed her face, his thumb tenderly wiping at her wet cheeks.

"It is all so sad," Kit said, leaning her forehead against his shoulder. His arms came up around her, holding her close and safe.

"Aye, it is. But there is nothing we can do. Nothing at all."

Over the coming days, Philippa bloomed while Isabella withered. Kit's heart broke at the sight of her—and at the constant look of concern on Mortimer's face. Wherever Isabella was, there was Mortimer, offering an arm, a cup of wine, a seat, a freshly picked apple—anything his lady love might desire. But it seemed to Kit she desired little, her smiles wan, her voice listless. And far too often there was a sheen of tears in Isabella's beautiful green eyes, tears that had Kit clasping her hands together and begging God for a miracle, a happy ending.

Chapter 26

Some days after Michaelmas, the court moved to Dunstable, where the king was hoping to cover himself in glory at the upcoming tournament.

It was difficult to listen to the king as he planned for the event and know himself excluded. Edward would never pick Adam to ride with him, not when he'd be no use whatever when fighting on foot. Adam tried not to let it show, but day after day of discussions about the tournament left him with an urge to kick at something—except that he couldn't even do that these days.

"Lame," he muttered to himself, having escaped to the stables to curry Raven—as soothing for him as it was for his stallion—rather than stand about while the king and his friends went at it with blunted swords. "Lame and useless," he told the horse, and in response Raven twitched his ear.

"Feeling sorry for yourself?" Will Montagu sauntered over to pat Raven on his big, shining rump. "I thought I'd find you here, hiding among the horses."

"I'm not hiding."

"No, you're just muttering to yourself like all old men do." Will bumped his fist against Adam's shoulder. "As I hear it, the king's lame knight is high in the royal affection."

"Don't call me that!"

"Everyone does, Adam." Montagu crouched to pick up one of the stable cats, a black-and-white creature that reminded Adam of Flea. "It looks painful," he added casually, having watched Adam shuffle round to the other side of his horse.

"It is." Adam hid his face against Raven's flank. "Pancio says most of the pain will go away with time. How was France?" he asked, not wanting to talk about himself any longer.

"French. Full of overdressed courtiers and clerics. And spies." He laughed. "Not that Bartholomew would appreciate being named as one. He insisted he was in France to forward the king's interests and nothing more."

"And did he?"

"Forward the king's interests? Yes. A capable man, even likeable under that grumpy exterior." Montagu released the cat. "He's hedging his bets, our dear Baron Bughersh. I fear Mortimer will find his report most detailed and utterly uninteresting."

"And was your mission a success?"

Montagu gave him a wary look. "It was. And more than that I will not say."

Adam shrugged. "I'd never ask you to."

"Good." Montagu stroked Raven's neck. "Well, I must be off. I've set my squires to polishing my jousting armour, and I fear I may have to lengthen the straps." He patted his stomach. "Too much food, too much wine."

"Aye, beware they don't name you the fat knight," Adam said, ducking with a yelp when Montagu made as to swipe him over the head.

"I'm not fat!"

They ended up in the hay, laughing as they wrestled.

"Will?" Master Bury stuck his head in through the door. "Are you there? The king and I are waiting for you."

"Oh dear," Will murmured, hastily brushing straw off his clothes. "I'll be right out," he said in a louder voice. "I just—"

"—had to roll in the hay," Master Bury finished for him. "Come on, man! We have important matters to discuss."

Adam picked himself up slowly and limped over to the door. Just outside, he bumped into his brother-in-law, red curls peeking from beneath the outlandish creation that adorned his head.

"A hat?" Adam tweaked at the saffron velvet, decorated with embroidered stripes in red.

"Most certainly a hat. Maud tells me these are the latest rage in Paris."

"Ah."

"Was that Montagu I saw?" Richard asked.

"It was." Adam limped towards the main hall.

"And was his mission successful?"

Adam turned. "Ask him, not me. I am no Mortimer spy."

"I was just asking you a question." Richard sniffed. "And besides, you'd be no use as a spy. The king's lame knight is too conspicuous." He darted out of reach and snickered. "Like baiting a chained bear, Adam."

"Beware," Adam snarled. In response, Richard made a lewd gesture and departed at a trot.

The moment the king's banner was raised at Dunstable, the petitioners came flocking: envoys and messengers, clerks and sheriffs—the line was endless, every free man within ten leagues taking the opportunity to bring whatever grievances they might have before the king.

"A whole morning," Edward groaned. "Hours sitting there listening as they bring their petty little problems before us. What do I care that Robert the smith purportedly cheated Samuel the baker?"

"Hmm," Master Bury offered, making Adam smile.

"Yes, well, I do care; laws are there to be obeyed, but must they burden me with it?" Edward stretched. "I have a joust to prepare for. I'll leave these matters in the capable hands of my mother and Lord Mortimer." His face fell. "Mortimer's hands, mostly. My lady mother was absent today as well."

"Is she ailing?" Master Bury asked.

"She says it's nothing but a persistent headache." The king looked about for his cloak. "I must go. Philippa and I mean to visit the priory." Yet another little grimace. "More hours wasted, this time with the added discomfort of being on our knees."

"My lord!" Master Bury sat up straight. "God must not be trifled with."

Edward looked adequately chastened. "I did not mean it like that. It's just…" He gestured at the patch of pale blue sky visible through the window. "Such a fine day," he said wistfully. "Besides, it's not as if I have pleasant memories of my last visit to the priory."

"Well, this time the Earl of Lancaster is nowhere close," Adam said. It had been a tense situation last year, when Lancaster had surrounded the king and his followers at Dunstable and threatened them with the might of his assembled army.

"And he has submitted to you," Master Bury added.

"So he has." But the king looked less than pleased. "For now."

"For now, my lord?" As far as Adam was aware, Lancaster was in France, there on the king's business.

"Mortimer says he has heard that Lancaster and my uncle of Kent have been spending time together. Too much time, in Mortimer's opinion." He gnawed at his lip. "I don't like it—and even less seeing as Edmund is openly stating my lord father is alive, locked away at Corfe Castle."

For an instant, the king's eyes met Adam's.

"But that is a lie, my lord," Adam said smoothly. "However much Earl Edmund may wish it otherwise, it is a sad fact that your father passed away two years ago." He crossed himself. "May he rest in peace."

"Amen to that," Edward said, winking at Adam behind Master Bury's back. He tossed the cloak over his shoulders. "And now to please my little wife."

Over the coming days, the king focussed on the tourney, and it fell to Mortimer to handle the more tedious aspects of ruling a kingdom. It was rare indeed not to see light spilling from the small room he had made his own at all hours of day or night, and whatever time he had left over he spent at Queen Isabella's side, only rarely appearing to dine in the small, dark-beamed hall.

Isabella herself moved silent and aloof through her days. Other than when she joined the court for mass, she was rarely seen outside her rooms, and then only to spend time with her sons or young daughter.

Kit was dragged back and forth between the queens—mornings preparing nutritious possets for Philippa, late afternoons called to wait on Isabella.

"I don't like it," she said to Adam, sitting down on a stool

240

to unbraid her hair. "Queen Isabella is playing with fire." She looked about for her comb, and Adam reclined on the bed to watch her as she worked her way through her long, lustrous hair. "Tonight, she insisted I bring her wormwood." Kit's hand shook. "It's not right, Adam. She's poisoning the babe in her womb, and should anyone find out…"

"How? She won't tell, and neither will you."

"Of course not!" She flashed him an indignant look. "But I feel guilty. A new life is a precious thing, and surely God will frown on her for what she's doing?"

God must have been frowning for years, Adam reflected, ever since the queen first welcomed Lord Roger to her bed.

"I pray for forgiveness," Kit went on. "But I don't dare confess—not here, not now."

"No, best not." He patted the bed beside him. "Come here, sweeting. Let me take your mind off things."

Kit's mouth curved. "And how will you do that, my lord?"

"That's for me to know and you to find out, wife."

She came to a halt beside the bed, backlit by the burning wood in the brazier. It set her hair on fire, made the shape of her body visible through the sheer linen of her chemise. Adam raised his hand and tweaked her nipple. It hardened, pushing against the fabric, and between his legs his member stirred and thickened.

He rose to his knees on the bed. It swayed and dipped, and he had to grab at her waist for balance. Her hair tickled his skin, releasing a faint fragrance of roses. He dipped his head to her breast and suckled her through her chemise. Kit pushed her chest forward, her hands travelling lightly over his head and down his nape.

They undressed each other. Laces were undone, drawstrings released, each garment sliding slowly over skin that was hot to the touch—or so it felt, his fingertips coasting over her bare belly. She joined him in bed. Under coverlets and sheets they came together, him shaping his body round hers, content for now to lie this close, his lips on the racing pulse beneath her ear, his hand cupping a breast.

She turned, and her hands were all over him. Adam fell over on his back and gave himself up to the sensations her touch woke, curious fingers exploring his cock, his balls, sliding over the planes of his belly and the muscles of his thighs.

He knew what she was going to do even before she set her lips to his clavicle. Soft kisses down his front, that dragging weight of hair spilling over his chest as she moved downwards, inch by excruciating inch. That first flicker of her tongue, the way her lips tightened round his cock, and he exhaled, hands clenching round the bedsheets.

The logs in the brazier sputtered, sending sudden flames to light up the room before dwindling into muted embers. The bed swayed and rocked, the rope frame creaking in time with their movements. He rolled her over, tasted the saltiness of her skin, the faint remnants of honeyed wine in her mouth.

"I love you," he whispered as he came inside of her.

Kit smiled. "I know," she whispered back, lifting her hips to take him deeper. So much deeper, the toes of his good foot finding purchase against one of the posts to drive into her, over and over again.

The next morning, they were all up and about by prime, the king breaking his fast with cheese and ale while examining his men and their horses.

"A true warrior." Lord Roger's sarcastic voice had Adam tearing his gaze away from the king, already astride his caparisoned mount.

"A good fighter, at any rate," Adam replied, eyes narrowed as he studied the various combatants. Young, vigorous men, mounted on horses worth more than a knight's annual income. "Aren't you taking part, my lord?"

"No. Truth be told, I feel too old." Lord Roger leaned back against a wall, face turned to the sun. He closed his eyes, brushed at an unruly lock of dark hair, now liberally sprinkled with grey. Deep grooves bracketed his mouth, and there were permanent lines on his brow, numerous wrinkles radiating from the corners of his eyes. For all that he'd have shaved that same morning, there was already a blueish tinge to his cheeks, spreading to beneath his chin.

"She doesn't want it," Lord Roger said without opening his eyes. "She hasn't said as much, but I can see it in her eyes, hear it in her voice." He exhaled. "My precious lady is afraid; that child which I already love, she sees as a lethal threat." He opened his eyes. "As if we don't have threats enough."

"We do?" Adam looked at the king, surrounded by his chosen companions. The flower of English nobility, loud voices and laughter testifying they had not a care in the world—beyond unhorsing their opponents.

"Need I name them? Kent and now also Lancaster. Plus there's that wily Philippe and," he broke off to spit to the side, "our former king himself."

"He would never be a threat to his son."

"But to his adulterous wife? His rebellious baron?" Mortimer slid a finger across his own throat. He nodded in the direction of the royal party now setting off, accompanied by banners and heralds, cheering squires and men-at-arms. "He plays at war and danger. I live it—every day."

Someone called for Lord Mortimer, and with a sigh he straightened up, shaking himself as a dog does when it comes in from the rain. "Duty calls." His fingers pressed into Adam's shoulder. "Thank you for listening."

"Always, my lord."

"It's not fair!" Prince John stood beside Adam and scowled. "I'm not too young."

In front of them, King Edward's side had crashed full force into the opponents, ridden through, and were now turning in formation, the king standing in his stirrups as he called out to his men. In the stands opposite, Queen Philippa was on her feet, cheering loudly, and as the king rode past her, he lowered his lance in salute, his men following suit.

There were people everywhere, those that could not afford a seat crammed into the area closest to the jousting ground. An old woman trundled by, offering apple fritters from a huge tray she'd balanced on her head; lads wove in and out selling ale or wine by the beaker. From somewhere to Adam's right came the smell of frying tripe and onion, and right in front of him two of the baker's daughters were selling warm pasties from their baskets. Adam called one of them over, gave her a groat, and helped himself to two pasties, offering one to Prince John.

"Your lady mother would never allow it," Adam said through a mouthful of spicy dough and filling. At thirteen, John was tall and strong for his age, but he stood no chance against the fully armoured knights on the field.

"Not fair," John repeated, biting into the pasty.

Adam winced as the king was thrown backwards when a lance hit him full on the shield, held his breath when Edward hung halfway out of his saddle, breathed out in relief when he righted himself. He shared a grin with the prince.

"If he doesn't win—"

"—he'll sulk for days," John filled in, licking his fingers. He straightened up. "One day, I'll knock him off." He craned his head back to look at Adam. "Have you?"

"No, my prince." Adam shifted slightly, taking the weight off his foot. "It would be unwise to do so."

"He hates it when he loses." John chuckled. "Which is why I make sure I always win at chess."

Adam laughed out loud. "Ah, but you see losing at chess is something he does in private. Being knocked off his horse in a joust by his younger brother—or his lame knight—is another thing entirely."

The lad had the most remarkable eyes: as green as his mother's, they were fringed by long, fair lashes and set wide apart, giving him the expression of a wary cat. "So even if I am better than he is, I must let him win?"

"Or not ride against him."

Prince John mulled this over, his gaze on the back and forth of the melee. The king's side regrouped and charged again, and it was evident to all the other team was vanquished, smashed apart by the sheer force of the king's attack.

"Is that how they reason as well?" he asked, gesturing at the knights presently surrendering to the victors. "Do they just let him win?"

"Your brother is a fearsome man in a tourney," Adam sidestepped.

There was a sudden gleam in those wide green eyes. "But not as fearsome as he thinks." The prince grinned. "Surely, a prince may unseat a king? Just once?"

Adam laughed. "It's your neck, my lord. Not mine." He returned his attention to the field, where the king had pulled off his helmet and was calling together his men, loud and generous in his praise of their skill and valour. They milled about him, all these young valiant knights, but at the king's raised hands they fell silent, regrouping at haste. Adam smiled; he might not be the best jouster, but he was undisputedly the leader. That would serve him well as king.

On the day after the tournament, Adam came out from the stables just as King Edward rode in from yet another hawking expedition. Dunstable offered excellent hunting, which was why that ancient Henry, first of that name, had established the royal hunting lodge here. Not that much was left of the original buildings, the present palace owing most of its exterior to Edward Longshanks.

"Beware, or your lady wife may think you prefer your birds to her," Adam said with a laugh as Edward dismounted, his face ruddy after a day of sun and wind.

"Fortunately, she is as fond of hawking as I am," King Edward replied without taking his eyes off his bird.

"That I find most improbable, my lord."

"Mmm?" The king was busy with his tiercel, talking softly to it while the falconer adjusted the hood and inspected the jesses. "Yes, you're probably right. He is, isn't he, my beauty?" he added in a crooning voice, stroking the bird's plumage.

"Have you any idea what is ailing my lady mother?" Edward handed over his bird to the falconer, tucked his glove into his belt, and gestured for Adam to accompany him.

"Your mother?" Aye, he did, but it was neither his place nor his responsibility to say anything. "Why would I know if you don't, my lord? Your lady mother would never take me into her confidence before you."

"No?" The king vaulted a wall, looked sheepish as Adam had to climb over carefully. "Sorry, I forgot. These last few days, Maman has looked as if she's been weeping—all night." He faced Adam. "You don't think Mortimer is hurting her, do you?"

Adam had to laugh, despite his throbbing foot. "Any man who raises his hand to your lady mother had best prepare himself for losing his balls."

The king grinned. "Ha! And painfully at that. Come to think of it, Mortimer is looking none too happy either."

"I wouldn't know, my lord," Adam lied smoothly.

"A lover's quiff?" Edward's voice lightened with hope. "Have they tired of each other?"

"I don't think so, my lord." If nothing else, the fact that he'd seen lord Roger emerging from the queen's rooms very early in the morning indicated this was not the case. Yet another thing Adam had no desire to share with the king.

"No." Edward sighed. "Neither do I. Whatever his other faults, Mortimer loves my mother dearly—much more than my father ever did." He made a face. "He preferred hose and braies to kirtles and garters, I fear."

Adam saw no need to comment.

Chapter 27

"Are we at odds?" Richard de Monmouth asked when he bumped into Adam in the stables.

"I don't know. Are we?" Adam finished examining Raven's girth and nodded to Stephen to lead him out together with Kit's mare.

Richard hemmed and hawed, his shoes scuffing at the straw-strewn floor. "The thing about Tresaints…"

"Yes?" Adam had no intention of making this easy for him, watching with some amusement as his brother-in-law squirmed.

Richard cleared his throat. "I handled it badly."

"Aye, you did. Kit was very hurt."

Richard flushed but nodded. "I know. I'll talk to her." He extended his hand. "Friends?"

"Friends." Adam shook on it.

"Did you hear about Lancaster and Kent?" Richard asked as he followed Adam outside. "Quite a dangerous alliance, those two. It would have been better to have executed that old man back in January." He nodded in greeting to Will Montagu, who fell in step with them.

"He submitted," Adam reminded him. "And to kill Lancaster would have set the north on fire." He shivered as he recalled just how cold that January day of 1329 had been. Not quite ten months ago, and since then the humbled earl had risen like a phoenix from the mud in which he'd kneeled.

"Maybe." Richard sighed. "Those northern lords have still not forgiven Lord Roger for the Scottish treaty."

"Neither has the king," Will Montagu offered. "Mention the Scots and you'll have him gnashing his teeth, even more so now that his youngest sister is being raised among them. A Plantagenet princess, brought up at the uncivilised Scottish court."

"They're no more uncivilised than we are," Adam objected.

"Tell that to the king, not me. Do you truly fear that Lancaster and Kent are planning a rebellion?" Montagu swivelled to face Richard.

"The earl of Kent is up to something, isn't he?"

"Seemingly to proclaim the resurrection of a dead and buried king," Montagu replied. "Guilt, I'd hazard: it's eating him from within, to have had a hand in his brother's deposition."

"Or thwarted ambition," Richard said. "Had it been Kent heading the royal council, he'd not be in France spreading discontent."

Montagu's eyes hardened. "He has a point: our dear Earl of March may cut an imposing figure, but there were others better suited to being regent."

"Such as?" Lord Roger asked from behind him, causing Montagu to jump.

"Norfolk," Montagu replied. "Kent or Lancaster." He met Lord Roger's eyes. "A moot point, seeing as our king will soon be old enough to rule in his own name."

"Some years yet," Mortimer replied. "Until then, speaking out against the regents is tantamount to treason." He set a hand on Montagu's shoulder. "Best keep that in mind, Montagu." His fingers tightened; Montagu's nostrils widened. With a chuckle, Lord Roger left, taking Richard with him.

"Bastard," Montagu muttered.

"Aye, he has strong hands."

"Too strong. Too grasping." Montagu spat to the side, his gaze nailed to Mortimer's fluttering cloak.

An hour or so later, Dunstable had been left behind, the royal household making for distant Kenilworth. Philippa was travelling in a litter, her lord and husband ensuring she had every comfort required to make the long journey bearable. As yet, there'd been no official proclamation of the news that the queen was expecting, but Adam suspected there wasn't a soul within the queen's household who didn't know—if nothing else, Philippa's greenish face in the early morning light would have given things away.

"She'll be over it soon," Kit said. "And other than in the mornings, she's as rosy as a winter apple."

In difference to Queen Isabella, whose features had grown starker over the last few weeks. Today, she reminded Adam of a leek, her pale face enveloped in a white veil and wimple while the rest of her was in a venomous shade of green. But she'd refused a litter and was riding well in front, flanked by Mortimer and Bishop Burghersh.

"She's running out of time," Kit said. "With every week, she comes closer to the day when she must tell her son." She held in her horse, stroking its glossy neck. "Mortimer is begging her to do so, but she just refuses, telling him they don't know for sure." She sighed. "Poor him, poor her."

"A persistent child," Adam said. "Strong, the way it clings to life."

"And would you expect it to be any different, given its parents?" Kit clucked her horse into a walk, guiding it to the grassy verge rather than the rutted road. "It's a miracle it has survived." She shifted in her saddle. "I have stopped taking my infusions."

"You have?" He wasn't sure if this pleased him or not. He regarded her from under his lashes: so vibrant, so full of colour, from the dark brows that arched above her cornflower eyes to the soft red of her lips. The nippy October day left her cheeks flushed, the air damp enough to make her skin glisten in the sunlight. In truth, she looked in the best of health, fully recovered from having carried and birthed their twins.

"God's will, Adam. Who am I to tamper with it?" She inclined her head in the direction of Isabella. "Who is she?"

Adam nodded, no more, tightening his hold on his reins. He cleared his throat and scouted about for another subject.

"Did you see Meg's efforts?" he asked.

Kit laughed. "Well, she is better at forming her letters than embroidering."

Adam smiled, his hand closing round his pouch, in which he carried his daughter's little missive. She was well, Father

Owain was well, Ned was well, Flea was well, Mabel was well, Harry was well—that was the essence of what she'd written, in Adam's opinion in a remarkably well-developed hand for one so young. Pride fizzed through him: he'd learnt to read and write late, courtesy of William, and it pleased him that his children would all be tutored in letters.

They ambled along at some distance from the rest, sharing an apple Adam produced from one of his saddlebags and cut into slices. At some point, he rode close enough to take her hand, and they rode like that for some time, side by side in comfortable silence.

On the third day of their slow journey, some miles north of Deddington, the Earl of Norfolk joined the royal party, and after having greeted his nephew, Thomas rode his horse up beside Raven.

"As hale as ever?" he asked.

"Well enough." Adam smiled at him. "It's good to see you, Thomas."

"And you." Thomas adjusted his heavy cloak. "What news from court?"

That made Adam laugh. "As if you don't keep yourself informed." He studied his friend. There were a few new lines round his eyes, but other than that he was remarkably unchanged. "I gather she died, your wife. I am sorry."

"Hopefully, she's in a better place." There was a sardonic twist to Thomas' smile. "So say the priests, at any rate."

Adam raised his brows but held his tongue. He had moments when he found the notion of an afterlife incomprehensible, and he imagined the loss of a wife would make you less benevolently inclined to God and all His trappings.

"And your children?"

"In good hands." Thomas urged his horse into a trot. "Where is Kit?"

"Over there." Adam pointed at Kit, presently jesting with the king.

"Ned is very fond of her."

"He is." The mare Kit was riding was as fiery as its rider,

chestnut hide matching chestnut locks—mostly hidden from sight by Kit's veil. "Not that it pleases everyone," he added somewhat darkly.

Thomas laughed. "That our Ned is fond of your wife does not bother anyone unduly—least of all his little wife, who adores Kit. That he is so fond of you does."

"Fond of me?" Adam squirmed in the saddle.

"Don't be coy—it doesn't suit a man." Thomas reverted to studying Kit, and for an instant Adam could see naked yearning on his friend's face. "She rides well—like my sainted mother." He shook himself and grinned at Adam. "Nearly birthed me in her saddle, she did."

"Aye." Everyone had heard the story of Queen Margaret, second wife to the mighty Longshanks, and her penchant for following the hounds, even when she should have been in confinement. "But your mother was a queen," Adam said, chuckling despite himself when his Kit set off at a gallop, challenging the king to a race. Now and then, their liege needed to forget his lofty status and revert to being a wild youth on a wild horse, and no one seemed to understand that better than Kit.

"Queens are allowed to flaunt convention," he went on, frowning when Kit's skirts lifted in the wind, displaying far too much of her shapely leg. His wife seemed oblivious, urging her horse on. Her veil came off, fluttering to the ground like an oversized butterfly, and as always that thick braid of hers did little to restrain the exuberance of her hair, chestnut wisps of hair standing every which way. "Hoyden," he muttered, but couldn't suppress the proud smile. His hoyden.

"Not all conventions." Thomas cleared his throat and transferred his gaze to Queen Isabella, riding side by side with Lord Roger. "We may all enjoy hearing the troubadours sing of illicit love, but we rarely condone it." He nodded in the direction of their king, flushed after his ride, triumphant after having won. "He does not condone it, Adam. That is why our Ned is so determined to remain as faithful as possible to his lady wife."

"Either you're faithful or you're not." Adam grinned. "My

Kit would flay me should she find out I'd bedded elsewhere, no matter how much I protested I was being as faithful as possible."

"Yes, I imagine she would." Thomas gave Adam a curious look. "Does that mean you've not bedded anyone else since you wed her?"

Adam's cheeks heated. "Is that any of your concern?"

"No, not really." Thomas leaned towards him. "But if you haven't, there must have been times when your balls have been near on black."

Adam shrugged. There'd been such moments, but so far he had not strayed—had not even wanted to stray.

Their conversation was interrupted when Kit rode over to join them. She'd retrieved her veil, arranged her clothing, and was back to looking as demure as she could, blue eyes flashing with laughter, cheeks flushed after the recent race.

"Thomas!" She treated him to a dazzling smile.

"Kit." Thomas grinned. "Oh dear, you lost."

"Lost? I let him win." She rode close enough that her leg brushed against Adam's. "Are you all right?" she asked Thomas with evident concern. "I've been thinking so much of you."

"You have?" Thomas and Adam said simultaneously. Thomas sounded gratified; Adam couldn't quite keep the censure out of his voice.

"Praying may be a better word," Kit amended, frowning at Adam. "It must be difficult to lose a spouse."

"It is," Thomas said curtly. He bowed and muttered something about wanting to talk to his nephew.

"A sad if handsome man," Kit said, studying Thomas' back.

Sad? Careworn, aye, but sad and handsome? Adam clapped his heels into Raven's sides with such force his horse snorted and set off at a gallop.

Two days later, they reached the Brays, the king slowing his horse to ride beside Mortimer as they discussed the defences to the approach to Kenilworth. An animated discussion, the

252

young king listening and nodding as Lord Roger pointed and explained.

The king and his baron rode together through the first gatehouse and up the long causeway that bordered the huge man-made lake—as Adam recalled, it was King John who'd decided to reinforce the stone wall defences with this expanse of water, making Kenilworth one of the best-protected fortresses in the realm.

On the further end of the causeway, a second gatehouse loomed, an impenetrable combination of heavy gates and portcullis. Today, the gates stood open, the castle garrison drawn up in formation to welcome the king and his court to the Earl of Lancaster's most formidable castle. Built in red sandstone, it was an impressive combination of endless walls and towers, and over it all loomed the ancient keep, like a fat, giant pillar thrust up towards the sky.

Horns blew, banners flapped, and the king waved and smiled, Mortimer being wise enough to hold in his steed, thereby ensuring the king entered first, closely followed by his mother, who'd ridden up to join them.

Kit grimaced as they passed beneath the portcullis. "I have no fond memories of this place."

"Neither do I." Adam cast a look at the huge keep, recalling a January day some years ago when he'd witnessed the former king's enforced abdication.

It bothered him that the king was to be lodged in the self-same rooms his father had once been held captive in. Aye, it made sense, the large rooms on the second floor of the keep having recently been redecorated, the windows fitted with glass, but all the same it woke restless memories, and Adam made a mental note to speak to Nicholas and double the guards—both at the entry to the keep and to the king's rooms.

Once he'd ensured his men had been adequately lodged, Adam took the long walk down to the outer ward. He'd been given a room in the Water Tower, a relatively new addition to the castle's curtain wall, and he walked up the steep stairs to find himself in a narrow and dark passage, a couple of arrow slits at either end the only source of natural light. Two doors, and one of them gave to his and Kit's cramped accommodation, so small the chests would have to be stacked atop each other. But at least there was a bed, and Kit had already found a lad to make it with her own sheets, linen that still smelled faintly of lavender.

There was also a small window, an opaque square of dried pig's bladder serving the function of glass. No view, but some light, he reflected. Best of all, there was a small fireplace, which was probably why Kit was looking so pleased, seated as she was on a small stool, her hands clasped around her knees.

"Clean," she said.

"Small," he replied, sitting down on the bed, which effectively meant she could lean her back against his legs. "The lads?"

"They're with your men, said they preferred sleeping over the kitchen to sharing this room with us."

"They can't share this room," Adam muttered. "Squeeze Gavin and Stephen in here, and none of us will be able as much as to turn in our sleep without waking the others." He threw himself back on the bed. "I wish we were home."

"So do I." She clambered into bed, lying down with her head on his shoulder. "Maybe you could ask the king," she added, hope lightening his voice. "Maybe he'd not mind giving you leave now that—"

"I'm lame and useless?" he interrupted, instinctively flexing his toes. It hurt as much as it always did.

"I did not say that." She sat up. "I would never say that!"

"But maybe think it?"

"No! You're twisting my words." She took a steadying breath. "I was going to say that maybe he'd allow us to go home seeing as they're planning on staying here at Kenilworth over Christmastide."

Adam groaned. "Two months and more? Here, in a room the size of a garderobe?"

"At least we'll not be cold." She picked at a loose thread on his sleeve. "Will you ask him?"

"I'll do it on the morrow." Adam stared up at the ceiling. "But he'll say no."

"How do you know?"

"He may find me lame and useless, but his wife swears by your decoctions, as does his mother." He covered his face with his arm. "It's not me they want to keep here. It is you." He was speaking the truth: Nicholas would leap at the chance of becoming captain of the king's guard, and knowing the man, he was probably already putting himself forward as a replacement for poor, crippled de Guirande. Adam gritted his teeth. A cripple.

"The king—"

"—is fond of me, or so Thomas says. Fond, as if I were some sort of lapdog or jester. The king's lame knight, that's me." He rolled over on his side. She set a hand on his shoulder; he shrugged it off.

"It's not my fault," she objected. Adam didn't reply. With a sigh she got to her feet and left the room. Adam squeezed his eyes together, feeling his lashes grow damp.

Chapter 28

He asked—or so he said—and was refused. Other than that, Adam did not refer to their conversation some days earlier, and Kit chose to not do so either, hurt by his words and by his determined efforts to keep his pain to himself. Did he think she didn't see just how much it cost him to walk up all those stairs to their little room? How he had to stop repeatedly and take the weight off his foot? But to propose they ask for rooms lower down would surely be met by yet another of those scowls every attempted discussion about his foot inspired.

Besides, she had other matters with which to concern herself, primarily that of brewing daily decoctions for the young queen—simple things her mother and Mabel had taught her: chamomile to promote sleep, ginger to alleviate morning sickness, and dried nettles to strengthen the walls of the womb. And then there was the other queen, who demanded other herbs, other infusions, and Kit's hands shook as she brewed yet another pot of wormwood tea in their little room.

Adam complained the room smelled like an apothecary's shop. Thomas had stopped by one evening in search of Adam and wondered if they had problems with moths. And as to Kit, the pungent fragrance of the wormwood infusions left her with a headache—and a conscience in uproar.

It was one thing to avoid becoming with child, another thing entirely to drive an innocent, living creature from the womb, and so Kit spent hours on her knees, praying for forgiveness, when it wasn't her sin to begin with. Or was it? She desperately needed someone to talk to, but Adam was presently occupied with proving himself irreplaceable—despite his foot—and there were no others with whom she could share her concerns.

Kit's daily visits to Queen Isabella did not go unnoticed. One morning, after having swallowed down her morning

256

drink of ginger laced with honey, Philippa sat back in her chair, feet clad only in hose propped on a footstool.

"My ladies tell me you spend almost as much time with the dowager queen as with me," she said.

"They do?" Kit studied the stiff backs of Montagu's wife—a stunningly beautiful woman named Katherine, who had only recently joined the circle of the queen's ladies—of Lady Blanche, Lancaster's daughter, and her substantially younger sister, Joan. She stuck her needle through the heavy material she was presently embroidering. "Is it any of their concern?"

"I prefer it if my ladies are *my* ladies," Philippa said, nibbling carefully at the thin wafer Mathilde handed her.

"I am your lady," Kit replied. "Queen Isabella has merely requested some help from me."

"Help? She has ladies of her own, doesn't she?"

But none of them knew the queen's secret. Kit bent her head over the fabric and concentrated on the shaping of the rosebud, in various shades of pink and white against a background of dark green. She raised her face only to meet Philippa's dark eyes, scrutinising her intently. Kit's cheeks heated.

"Fetch me my shoes," Philippa ordered one of her pages. "I think I need some fresh air."

"Now?" Mathilde looked out at the grey day beyond. "It is raining, my lady."

"And yet I must. I feel…unsettled." Philippa stood. "Lady Kit can accompany me."

Blanche tittered, a sly look at Kit. These highborn ladies did not attempt to hide their resentment of Kit's presence among them—the wife of a mere knight did not belong among these blue-blooded, sharp-nosed harpies.

"Is she ailing?" Philippa asked the moment they were out of earshot from anyone. She peeked at Kit from under the large hood that covered her head.

"She is."

Philippa came to a halt. "She looks hale enough as she moves about her business. Somewhat more sharp-tongued than usual, or so Ned tells me."

257

"She's not ill as such, more fraught," Kit said.

"Fraught?" Philippa darted over to the cover offered by the roof over the open smithy. "How fraught?"

"I can't say, my lady."

"Will it pass?"

"In one way or another, yes, it will." Kit clasped her hands together. "I can't tell you more than that, my lady. Queen Isabella would disapprove."

Philippa pursed her lips. "Very well. I shall not ask—for now." She pulled her cloak closed. "Race you back?" And with that she was off, skirts held high as she sprinted for the inner bailey. Kit came after at a more sedate pace, having to laugh at the childish exuberance of her queen when she splashed through a series of puddles.

That same day, Kit was returning alone to her room after having delivered the daily infusion to Queen Isabella. It was still raining, and the winter dusk was seeping into night, making it difficult to see just where she set her feet. Kit was lost in thoughts as she hastened towards the lower bailey, which was probably why she lost her footing, landing painfully on her hands and knees.

"My lady, are you hurt?" Thomas materialised out of nowhere, took hold of her, and lifted her up. Her hood fell back. "Kit!" His arms slid down her arms to her hands, turning them over to study her palms. His fingers closed over her wrists, warm and strong.

"Scrapes, no more," she told him, disengaging herself. He smelled of wine—he often did these days.

"And your knees?"

Kit laughed. "If you think I have any intention of lifting my skirts up out here, then you will be severely disappointed, my lord."

"Do they hurt?" he asked, looking unamused.

"A bit." She took a careful step, took another. "I dare say I'll survive."

"Aye. Rarely does one die from falling on one's face." He looked up the way she'd come. "Yet another session with my sweet cousin?"

"I think she prefers it when you refer to her as the queen."

"No, she doesn't; she hates it when I call her the dowager queen." Thomas' teeth flashed white. "So I do, of course, whenever I get the opportunity."

They were drawing near to the chapel, its doors still standing open to those in need of prayer. Kit dithered; she'd made it a habit to stop here on her way back from Queen Isabella.

"Shall we go inside?" Thomas ushered her towards the dimly lit interior, two large beeswax candles spreading a soft golden glow on the altar. "I like to come here at this time, when it is mostly empty."

"Do you come here often?"

"Of late, yes." He fumbled with his pouch. "I pray for her," he admitted, and in the candlelight he looked tired and sad. Thomas produced a candle and lit it from one of the others, spilled a few drops of wax on the little ledge upon which a worn statue of the Virgin stood, and carefully affixed the burning candle. "She never liked the dark." He sighed softly. "Is purgatory dark, do you think?"

She had never considered the question before. Her lost babies had been innocents, and so must have gone straight up to their heavenly Father. "Something in between," she said, and it made him nod, a small smile on his lips.

After their prayers, Thomas insisted on following her back to her room, and she was laughing at one of his jests when Adam opened the door from inside.

"There you are," he said, and it sounded like an accusation, his eyes lingering on the shadowy shape of Thomas behind her. "Thomas, what are you doing here?"

"Kit fell, and so I felt it best to see her safe." Thomas bowed slightly. "And now I must be off. My dear nephew has requested my presence in his chambers."

"Are you hurt?" Adam asked once he'd closed the door behind them.

"No." She lifted her skirts, frowning at the bloodied hole in the hose covering her right knee. "Shame on my new hose, though."

Adam grunted, no more. He dipped a rag in the pitcher of water and helped her peel off the hose and wash the shallow scrape.

"Shouldn't you be with the king?" she asked.

"Me?" He threw the rag to land beside the pitcher. "No, my presence has not been requested. Instead, the king suggested I rest my foot after our strenuous day. Strenuous—pah!" He kicked out, cursed loudly when his foot connected with the stool. "How has it been strenuous for me when all I can do is stand and watch while the others do their sword work?"

"Must you stand and watch?"

"Aye. They're my men, most of them." He sounded so angry, so bitter. "It used to be none of them could best me— none, not even Grosmont or the de Bohun twins. Now…" He banged his fist against the wall. "I'd not be able to hold my own against any of them."

"But surely—"

"It will improve?" He scrubbed at his face. "God knows— it's been two months, and I still cannot put my full weight on it."

He threw himself on the bed; she came after, slipping her arms round him to hold him as best she could. She nuzzled his neck, inhaling that distinctive scent of horses and leather, male sweat and steel that always clung to him. Kit moved that much closer.

"Not now." He pushed her aside and rolled over on his side. In silence, she undressed and slipped in under the covers, ensuring he didn't see the tears his rejection had caused.

It felt as if she'd just fallen asleep when someone knocked at their door.

"What?" Adam demanded, stirring into life beside her. He was still fully dressed, still atop the coverlets.

"It's me, Richard."

"At this time of the night?" Adam looked at Kit. "What might your brother want?"

"I don't know. But I don't think it is good news." She retrieved her chemise and pulled it on.

Yet another series of knocks—hard, insistent. "Open up!"

"I'm coming," Adam yelled back. "I just need some light." A taper flared into life, one of the tallow candles was lit, and Adam limped over to the door.

Bare-legged, in only his shirt, Richard was shivering and wet after what must have been a very hasty run across the darkened wards of the castle. "The queen," he gasped. "Now."

No need to ask why. Kit threw on kirtle and cloak, pulling the hood up to cover her hastily braided hair.

"Only her," Richard said when Adam reached for his cloak. He frowned. "God knows what ails her, but Lord Roger sounded desperate."

Kit shared a quick look with Adam. This secret was like a millstone round their necks. "Men are squeamish," was what she said. "I am sure it is just a female complication."

"Which would explain why he asked for you, not her physician." Richard stamped his feet. "God's blood, but it's cold. Hurry up, will you?"

"I'm ready." Kit picked up the pouch that contained her various herbs and followed Richard into the dark passage beyond. The stone floor was uneven and slippery with cold and wet, the stairwell a dark pit with no light whatsoever, and only by gripping the rope hard and shuffling her feet from one tread to the other did she make it down in one piece.

Other than the distant red glow from the braziers at the various gatehouses, the castle was sunk in darkness. Kit cast a look at the sky. No moon, so it was well after midnight, and as yet not a glimmer of dawn to the east.

"Come on!" Richard hissed. "I'm freezing my balls off."

He took her hand to pull her along. They ran over the frosted grass, skirted the chapel, and he hastened her through the gatehouse, curtly telling the sentries all men were entitled to a piece of skirt now and then. They hugged the shadow of the keep and adjoining kitchens—already buzzing with activity, male voices, warmth and light spilling from the small air vents—and followed the stone-flagged path that bordered the hall. Through an arch, down a dark passage, and they

261

were at the back of the building housing the queen. Some distance away, a door stood ajar, and they were almost there when Richard drew them to an abrupt halt, bundling her into a darker patch of shadow.

Two guards walked by. One of them laughed, the sound of their voices growing fainter once they'd turned the corner.

"Now!" Richard had them running the last few yards, relaxing only once they were safely inside.

"No sentries?" Normally, Mortimer had his own men guarding him and his lady—at both entrances.

"They were given the night off by Lord Roger." Richard sounded terse. "What is going on?"

"How should I know? You came for me."

Richard had a lantern lit and showed her up the stairs. "You do not seem surprised, dear sister."

"Stunned," she replied lightly. "And still half-asleep."

Queen Isabella had graciously declined the king's offer to lodge in the queen's apartments, saying an expectant mother required the highest level of comfort possible—this with a warm smile at Queen Philippa. Instead, she'd been given rooms in one of the buildings adjoining the new hall, apartments which had the added benefit of being close to Mortimer's rooms.

As always, within hours of taking up residence, the queen had converted the rooms to her taste, with her furnishings, her textiles, her various personal items marking the space as hers. Kit recognised the tapestries, the elegant pearwood table, the various candlesticks, and the beautiful portable altarpiece, a fixture in Queen Isabella's life since first she came to England.

"In here," Mortimer called, and Kit made for the inner door, halting for an instant at the sight of him.

"She bleeds," he said, gesturing at his bloody hands and splotched shirt. "She won't let me help."

"Let me see." Kit moved towards the bed. The hangings were closed, but from within came the sounds of a distressed animal, a low, constant keening. "My lady?"

"Kit? Is that you?" the voice was weak and broken.

"It is, my lady." She took hold of the hangings.

"No! I don't want him to see me like this, I—"

Mortimer cursed, strode over, and yanked the hangings open. "I don't care how you look as long as you're alive," he said, and then his eyes went to the bloody mess between her thighs, and all of him sagged, hands gripping the closest bedpost. "Dearest Lord!"

"Water." Kit shoved him away. "Hot water, preferably."

"Yes, yes, water." He collected himself. "I'll be right back."

Kit helped the queen to sit against the pillows.

"It's gone," Isabella whispered. "It is gone, isn't it?"

"Yes, my lady." Kit wrapped a linen towel round the collection of blood and tissue and put it to the side. This they would have to dispose of in secret.

"It's gone," the queen repeated, and her mouth fell open to release a low, long howl.

"What?" Mortimer burst through the door and flew to her side. "Isabella, what?" The pitcher crashed, spilling hot water everywhere, and then he was in the bed, cradling his weeping woman to his chest.

"It's gone," she repeated, banging at his chest. "It's not fair! You and I…" She wailed again, the sound muffled by Mortimer's body.

"My lord?" Richard appeared in the doorway.

"Get out!" Mortimer yelled, and Richard ducked out of sight. Kit ran after.

"Richard! Hot water—now!"

He looked up at her, already halfway down the stairs, and nodded. "Is she dying?"

"Of course not." Kit wiped her hand down her skirts. "If you can find it, honey as well."

She returned to the room. In the bed, Isabella had quieted but was still squashed to Mortimer's chest in a manner that had to be uncomfortable to them both. He was speaking softly to her, dark eyes glistening with unshed tears.

"My lady, I have work to do," Kit said, eyes on the spreading stain of blood beneath the queen's bare legs.

"Yes, of course." Isabella lay back down, clutching at Mortimer's hand.

"My lord, I'm not sure—"

"I'm staying." Mortimer interrupted, brushing at the queen's dark hair. "I will not leave her when she needs me the most."

An hour later, the queen was clean, the linen changed, and the queen's nether regions wrapped in yarrow poultices and multiple rags.

"A cup every hour," Kit said, handing Isabella a mug. She'd mixed dried leaves of mallow, raspberry leaves, nettles, and yarrow and poured boiling water over it all. "Add some honey, my lady."

"I'll make sure she follows your instructions," Mortimer said, bending down to kiss his lady's pale cheek. "Find your bed, Kit—and thank you."

Thus dismissed, Kit picked up the towel that contained the sad remains of the queen's babe and slipped out of the room.

Outside, morning had broken. Above flapped a couple of rooks, risen from the trees that stood beyond the eastern wall; in a nearby thicket sparrows chirped. Sun caught the frost that decorated the grass, setting it all a-glitter. The red walls of the keep and the surrounding buildings glowed in the sunlight. A perfect day, Kit reflected as she walked slowly through the inner bailey. In one corner, she spied a recently planted rosebush, and after ensuring no one was in sight, she knelt and dug a shallow hole, ignoring just how cold the earth was.

"Rest in peace, little one," she murmured as she patted the earth back into place. And may God forgive your mother— and me—for procuring your death, she added silently.

Chapter 29

"And my lady mother?" The king looked up as Lord Roger entered the chamber and indicated that Adam should stay.

"She remains unwell." Mortimer shrugged off his cloak and wandered over to the large hearth to warm his hands. He nodded a greeting at Adam, smiled briefly at Bishop Burghersh.

"That's the third day in a row she misses our council." The king frowned. "I cannot remember her ever being ill before."

Adam ensured not to make eye contact with Lord Roger but noted the set jaw and sighed. Kit said a slight fever was not unexpected, but at present Mortimer refused to leave Queen Isabella except for these meetings with the king.

"I shall come and see her later today," the king added, frowning down at the large roll on the table in front of him.

"I'm not sure she wants that," Mortimer replied, the lid of his right eye twitching.

"I'm not asking her opinion—or yours. She is my mother, and I will see her." The king tapped a finger on the roll. "Is all of this true?"

"True?" Mortimer moved closer, reading over the king's shoulder. "Nothing new, is it? Lancaster, supposedly in France on your behalf, and lo and behold, there we have him dining near on every day with dear Uncle Edmund and your beloved Cousin Philippe."

The king scowled. "Remember yourself," he warned. "Edmund of Kent is a royal earl, and Philippe is the king of France."

"Ah yes, the Valois upstart on the throne that rightfully belongs to the Capets." Mortimer helped himself to a fig. "And I am also an earl, my liege, albeit not in France planning God knows what mischief."

Edward shoved the roll away from him. "Or it may all be malicious gossip, an attempt to drive a wedge between me and my uncle." He regarded Mortimer. "And there's a difference between an earl born to the title and one who is created."

"Oh?" Lord Roger threw the stalk of the fig in the fire. "An earl is an earl, my lord. Just because you're born to it doesn't necessarily make you good at it." He smirked. "Your father would be an excellent example of that, wouldn't you agree?"

"Roger," Bishop Burghersh said, shaking his head.

"What? I am but stating a truth, am I not? Had it not been for me and your lady mother, that disaster of a king, your father, might still have sat on the throne you now have claimed." Mortimer crossed himself. "And God help us all had that been the case."

"But it isn't. I am king now."

"So you are. But for how long, eh? Your beloved, true-born earl of an uncle seems determined to reverse events—however impossible, given your father's sad demise. Or maybe he is just using Edward of Caernarvon as a pretext, while instead he intends to crown himself." Mortimer gave Edward a vicious look. Adam took a step or two closer. "How many would join him, do you think? How many would prefer the dazzling image of a full-grown handsome king to that of a royal whelp still wet about the ears?" He gripped the carved armrests of the king's chair, looming over him. "You'd not have survived this long without me. Me, not your blue-blooded peacock of an uncle!"

"Roger!" Bishop Burghersh thundered. "That's enough!"

Edward sat as if frozen, blinking up at Mortimer. Adam took hold of Lord Roger's closest arm. Mortimer's face crumpled. He closed his eyes, dragged in air in loud, harsh gulps.

"My apologies," he said, straightening up. "I…" He turned to Adam, looking utterly helpless.

"He's not been sleeping lately," Adam told the king. "He's been sitting with your lady mother."

"So she is seriously ill!" Edward shot to his feet.

"Ill?" Mortimer began to laugh, then to Adam's consternation he broke into tears, and even the king looked genuinely affected when Adam helped Lord Roger sit. "She'll recover," Mortimer mumbled. "But he will not."

Thankfully, the king did not hear this cryptic comment. Instead, he followed Adam across the room, standing to the side as Adam poured Mortimer some wine.

"I get the impression you know more about this than I do," Edward said. "My mother, what ails her?"

Adam licked his lips. "I don't know." Once, he had promised his lord he would never lie to him, and here he was breaking that promise. The king's brows rose, his lips compressed into a thin line. There was but one thing to do. "Ask Kit. She can explain—I cannot." And please God his wife could come up with a plausible story, Adam thought as the king stormed out of the room.

"What in the world got into you?" Bishop Burghersh asked once they were the only three in the room. He mopped at his brow, fleshy face all a-wobble.

Mortimer shrugged. "About time someone told him the truth. Without me, he is nothing."

"Without you, he is still the king," the bishop said. "Best remember that."

"King?" Lord Roger held out his goblet for more wine, eyes as hard and cold as pebbles. "And who does the ruling, dear Henry? Me. Not him, me. It is I who wields true power; it is my men who hold this realm together." His mouth curled into a smile. "In his name, of course."

The sight of the king coming marching towards her had Kit's mouth drying up. She folded away the latest little missive from Meg—yet another list of all who were well—and stood up, clenching her buttocks to stop her legs from trembling. He'd found out, how else to explain the way his fair brows had knitted themselves into a formidable scowl, the speed at which he was striding? Frantically, she cast about for a valid excuse, something to stop him from punishing her and Adam for not telling him—as they should have done.

And then he was standing in front of her, flushed from his recent exertion. Blue eyes drilled holes in her, and Kit sank into a deep reverence, wetting her lips as she prepared to beg for forgiveness.

"What ails her?" he demanded, and hope fluttered into life in her belly.

"My lord?" She looked up at him, and he gestured for her to rise, taking a step that brought him so close to her she could feel the heat radiating off him.

"I have a right to know. She's my mother! And don't you dare tell me you don't know!" A fine spray of spittle dampened her face, and she took a step backwards. "Well?"

A curious audience had assembled, standing in a loose half circle behind the king.

"Not here," she said, and he looked about, went the colour of a scalded ham, and gripped her arm. She had to trot to keep up with him as he marched her across the bailey.

"Out!" he ordered the few people in the chapel. "Now!" he snarled, and the resident chaplain nearly fell over his feet in his haste, ushering the others before him.

"Well?" the king repeated once they were alone.

"You should ask your mother," Kit tried.

"We both know she'll never tell me the truth." He sat down on one of the few benches but did not invite her to sit. "How serious is it?"

"She's recovering," Kit said, attempting to assess what he knew.

"Recovering from what? And why has no one told me she's been so ill she now has to lie abed and recover?"

"It's not something she wants talked about, my lord."

"No?" He stilled. "Why not?"

She dropped her voice and ducked her head. "It's a female indisposition."

A loud intake of breath had her lifting her head, only to see the king gape at her.

"Is she…No, she can't be!"

"Is she what, my lord?"

"Breeding."

"No, my lord." Not anymore, not since the night that had ended with the hastily buried linen towel and its contents.

"Thank God!" He braced his elbows on his knees and hid his face in his hands. "Imagine having a Mortimer bastard as my half-brother. So then what?"

"A large internal boil," she lied.

"Internal?" He lifted his head and stared at her. "Internal where?"

Kit made a vague movement in the direction of her nether parts, and the king blushed.

"It burst," Kit went on, making him look horrified. "A lot of blood and pus, and…"

"Yes, yes, I don't need the details." He made room on the bench and gestured for her to sit. "And she is truly on the mend?"

"Truly, my lord." Kit gnawed her lip. These last few days, the queen had been uncharacteristically silent, facing the wall as Kit attended to her. "But she needs peace and quiet."

"Hmm. So no visits?"

"Not yet." She looked away. "It still bleeds."

"Oh." He studied his hands. "It is common, for women to be thus afflicted?"

"No. But it happens."

"And you will care for her?" He sounded so young as he said that, a small lad concerned for his beloved mother.

"I will."

After that somewhat harrowing experience, Kit chose to climb up to the wall-walk, thinking some time alone would allow her to regain her composure. Three days and more of icy cold had left the slopes that led to the mere shiny with ice, and at present every child from within the castle seemed to be sliding shrieking down the incline, landing with soft thumps on the frozen surface of the mere.

At times, the ice cracked, and the shrieks grew louder, no doubt due to icy water leaking through the garments, but so far the ice held, and the lads shoved and yelled, the little maids now and then taking their turn to slide, but just as often content to stand to the side and watch.

"Kit!"

She turned at the sound of her name, and there was Adam in the bailey, waving at her. She raised her hand but made no move to go to him—she had kept her hands to herself these last few days, hurt by his recent rejection. So she went back to watching the children, wishing she was home with her own brood.

"Did the king find you?" Adam asked, out of breath when he joined her.

"He did—and I lied." She winced when a small lad was thumped by a larger boy, causing the little one to cry. "I hate having to lie."

"Aye." He rested his arms on the wall. "So do I." They lapsed into silence, and despite the icy bite to the wind, Kit had no desire to return indoors. He shifted closer to her and reached for her hand. Their fingers braided. He drew her close enough to drape his other arm around her shoulders, enveloping her in his cloak. They stood like that for some time, close together and silent.

Queen Isabella made a remarkable recovery. Within a week, she was back to being her normal, poised self, and the king was even heard to grumble he had almost preferred it when she was bedridden. After weeks of blending into the background, she once again dazzled and glittered, a queen bee among the courtly drones.

No wonder, Adam reflected as Queen Isabella entered the hall for dinner. No other lady in the realm could walk with such a seductive combination of swaying hips and regal bearing, the elegant folds of her robes lifting and swirling in time with her steps. One step behind her came Lord Roger, these days seemingly permanently affixed to her, in that nowhere did Isabella go but her loyal earl went with her, conscientious to the extreme.

Ever since she'd lost the child, there was a renewed tenderness between them, but Adam also saw the sadness that lurked in Lord Roger's eyes, the way his eyes would fix on a small child while his mouth turned down. And as demonstrated by his recent outburst in the king's chamber, Mortimer was more irascible than ever, causing one conflict after the other between him and the king.

"It's as if he wants to provoke him," Adam had confided to Kit only last night. "What does it matter that the king has decided on the date for Philippa's coronation without asking the regents? In fact, why should he have to ask them? He's no witless child, he's their king!"

"She's being crowned?" Kit had asked. "That will please my lady greatly."

"And beggar the royal coffers," Adam muttered, "at least to hear Mortimer go on and on about needless expenses."

"Isabella does not want a second crowned queen in England," Kit said. "She prefers it as it is: one crowned king, one crowned queen."

But soon there would be two, and for all that Philippa had none of her mother-in-law's magnificence, she was the soon-to-be mother of kings. The news that the queen was with child had been officially announced today at mass when Bishop Burghersh prayed for her health and that of her unborn child, and so this dinner was a celebration of the young queen, for the day in mild shades of green and yellow, her surcoat generously trimmed with glistening otter fur.

The king entered, accompanied by five or six companions, and all stood. He took his time making his way down the room, stopping frequently to talk to one man or the other, and Adam had the impression he was doing this on purpose, a not so subtle reminder to all those present that it was him, Edward, the third of that name, who was the king.

The trestle tilted as Thomas slid in to sit beside him, followed by Eubulus Le Strange.

"No Kit?" Thomas asked.

"She's with the queen's ladies." Adam preferred it when Kit and he could share a trencher, but it wasn't always possible.

"Ah." Thomas finished washing his hands and nodded his thanks to the lad holding the basin.

"Shouldn't you be up there?" Adam asked, inclining his head in the direction of the high table.

271

"I should. But I prefer this company." Thomas grinned and elbowed Adam. "We can share a trencher, you and I." He batted his eyelashes, making Adam laugh.

"You're not my type, Norfolk." He served himself of the thinly sliced tongue and crispy sausage.

"No?" Thomas pouted prettily. "What a pity." He gulped down his wine, gestured for more.

Beside them, Eubulus snorted with laughter. "Looking to emulate your dear departed brother, Earl Thomas?"

Thomas stiffened. "No." One word, laced with ice, and Eubulus fell over himself apologising. "No matter," Thomas cut him off. "How are things in Lincoln?"

"Well enough." Eubulus scratched at his ragged beard. "De Novo is a good sheriff, keeps things on the straight and narrow. Mortimer's man to begin with," he added with a sly look at Adam, "but these days more committed to the king. The north as a whole has little love for the Welsh Marcher lord, and even less since Lancaster was so humiliated."

"He rebelled," Adam reminded him drily, frowning when Thomas yet again drained his cup.

"True enough. But against whom? The king or the Earl of March?" Eubulus cleared his throat. "The north stands with the king. Only the king."

"Don't be ridiculous." Thomas parted the manchet neatly with his knife. "The north is as cowed as the rest of the realm. Mortimer rules everywhere."

"For now." Eubulus dabbed at his mouth. "But not forever."

No matter that Adam hated admitting it, Eubulus was right. Sooner or later, the king would demand to rule in his own name—as he should—and God alone knew what would happen then. Over the expanse of the hall, Adam looked towards the high table and met Lord Roger's gaze. A nod, the glimmer of a smile, and Adam looked away, confused by all his contradicting emotions. For an instant, he wished he could just leave, set Kit in front of him on Raven and ride home, leaving the king and Mortimer to sort things best they could.

Chapter 30

The closer to Christmas, the more people converged on Kenilworth, invited—or ordered—to celebrate Christmastide with the king and his regents.

"God's blood," Thomas groaned as the Earl of Lancaster rode in some days after St Lucy, "did he have to come with every single one of his retainers?"

An exaggeration, but all the same, the constable of Kenilworth paled significantly as his eyes roved the collected Lancaster household.

"He's making the point it is his castle," Adam said, an interested eye on a troupe of acrobats that were descending from one of the carts. One of the women was most scantily dressed, her braided hair uncovered. Minstrels in colourful robes came by cradling precious vielles and flutes; there were a couple of jesters and their pet pig, a solemn creature named Salome, which everyone found quite hilarious, urging the pig to get up on its back trotters and dance.

"His castle?" Thomas chuckled. "Aye, it is, but in name only. Dear Isabella has made it quite clear she expects Kenilworth to be at her disposal when she so requires."

"Ah." That must be quite the blow to the proud earl's pride.

Once off his horse, Lancaster straightened up to his full height. This last year had stripped him of weight, leaving him as tall as ever, but gaunt. Somehow, this only served to increase his presence, as did his elegant if sober clothes, the cloak thrown back to reveal the fur-lined interior.

One step at a time, he progressed towards the keep, a light hand on his son's forearm the only support he needed on a path he must have walked a thousand times, if not more.

"My lord." Thomas bowed in welcome, and Adam followed suit. Rheumy eyes turned their way, and the earl inclined his head, his long grey hair falling forward.

"Norfolk and de Guirande," Grosmont murmured, and Lancaster nodded.

"The king?" he asked.

"He awaits you in his chamber," Adam said, taking a step forward. "I was to request your presence there."

"Very well." The earl swept up his robes. "Lead on."

Adam escorted Lancaster towards the keep, keeping a respectful distance as the earl negotiated the stairs. One of the guards outside the king's rooms saw them coming and opened the door, bowing deeply.

Their entrance disturbed the trio presently at the large table in front of the hearth. Master Bury, Montagu, and the king broke apart, the quill in the king's hand dripping ink all over the piled documents. With shaking hands, Master Bury sanded the parchment the king must recently have signed, rolled it together, and sealed it, stamping the wax with the king's Privy Seal.

"I'll send this off immediately, my lord," Master Bury said, scurrying like an overweight rat towards the door. The king nodded, met Adam's eyes for an instant, before turning his attention to his guest. Adam was dismissed, as was Montagu.

"No need to tell anyone," Montagu said casually as they made their way down the stairs.

"Tell anyone about what?" Adam concentrated on the treads; his foot was in a bad way today, but he was damned if he intended to let it show.

"The…" Montagu frowned. "You know exactly what I mean."

"And you know just as well I'd never tell anyone about what I see and hear in the king's chambers," Adam bit back.

Montagu held up his hands. "No offence intended."

Outside, they ran into Grosmont and Stafford, and soon enough Montagu was dragging them away, promising them good wine in the privacy of his chambers. Adam excused himself—he wasn't quite sure he'd been included in the invitation—and made for the stables instead.

It was impressive just how much one could find out by asking the odd question here, the other one there. By the time

Adam had finished his daily inspection of his men, he knew that the king had ordered the messenger be given the fleetest horse available and that the missive was destined for France.

"Always bragging about his travels, he is," Nicholas the Hainaulter told him with a snort. "Had us believe he'd just come from Avignon and was expecting to be sent back. Ha! If Jack has been further south than Dover, I'll gladly eat my shoes."

Avignon? Adam stood on the causeway and looked to the south. In Avignon sat His Holiness, and Montagu had returned most secretive after his meeting with the pope. So maybe Jack was telling the truth, and if so, whatever he carried in his pouch was a secret message from the king to the pope.

"That Richard of Monmouth was also asking about the messenger," Nicholas continued. He grinned. "I told him that as far as I'd heard he was riding for Scotland to deliver a letter to the king's sister. To whom the king sends messengers is none of his bloody business, as far as I'm concerned."

"No." Adam fixed his eyes on the royal banner, unfurling lazily in the wind. The English lions rippled and snarled, gold on scarlet.

The king took charge of the planned festivities, insisting that a main component would be a series of fighting contests, a fat purse offered to the winner. Without quite understanding the humiliation he was inflicting—or so Adam hoped—the king made Adam responsible for arranging the sword fighting, saying he himself would supervise the equestrian events.

Adam itched with the need to prove himself as able a fighter now as before his injury, but despite daily sessions in which he worked himself into a sweat, he knew there was no point in even trying. With one foot more or less bolted to the ground, he stood no chance against a skilled opponent, albeit by now he'd regained sufficient mobility to be able to defend himself should he have to. Defending was one thing, attacking to win in a one-on-one fight an entirely different matter.

With every contest, Adam's mood soured further. A year ago, he'd have been a serious contender for the king's best knight; now he had to live with the moniker the king's lame knight, not that anyone dared call him that to his face. Behind his back, they whispered it, those that knew him with a modicum of respect, those who did not as a jeering insult.

"Don't mind them. You have nothing to prove." Thomas shoved an overflowing cup in Adam's direction. This cider was strong stuff, and already Adam was mellowing, a comforting glow in his belly radiating through his limbs.

"What's the point of a knight if he's lame?"

"Loyalty?" Thomas suggested drily. He hiccupped, sloshed some more cider into his cup. "Now forget all that and concentrate on the fair Aeline. I swear she can't have a bone in her body."

Adam grunted but looked all the same, as captivated as all of them by the lithe Aeline, all long limbs and skin the colour of heather honey, dark and golden. In transparent veils that covered not only her head but most of her face, this enchanting creature danced, her bare arms and bare midriff enough to have the men howling and stamping in approbation, even more so when she began her tumbling routine.

"Wouldn't mind having her in my bed," Eubulus plunked down beside them, eyes shiny with too much cider.

Adam gave the girl a bleary look. Neither would he, had he not been married. He sipped at his third—fourth?—mug of cider. A lame and married knight: life was truly over.

"A man needs variation," Eubulus continued, "he needs—" He broke off abruptly. "Isn't that your priest brother?"

With an effort, Adam raised his head sufficiently to squint at the newcomer.

"Adam!" William spread his arms, and Adam rose unsteadily to greet his brother, still in his travelling cloak.

"William," he mumbled, his nose crushed to his brother's shoulder. He smelled of wet wool and mud.

"Are you all right?" William helped him sit down. Adam blinked and waved his hand for more cider.

"Drunk," Thomas informed William. "We all are. All of

us, even Eubulus here." William studied Le Strange closely as he undid his cloak.

"Le Strange? Alice de Lacy's husband?"

"The same." Eubulus gave William a belligerent stare. "And what is that to you?"

"Nothing." William sat down opposite Adam and rubbed his hands briskly. "Any cider for me?"

"Where did you come from this time?" Adam asked.

"Gloucester." His mouth thinned. "And Corfe."

Even in his befuddled state, Adam picked up on William's tension. So did Thomas, a thoughtful expression on his face as he helped himself to some almonds. William, however, said nothing more, complaining instead about the dratted weather.

"I need to talk to you. Now!" No customary my lord, no by your leave, just an angry Mortimer pushing by the guards and entering the king's chambers.

"Good morning to you too, Lord Mortimer," the king said calmly, straightening up from his perusal of the starting order in the upcoming jousting event.

"Ah. More games, I see." Mortimer sneered, looking from the king to Norfolk to Lancaster, who'd already been with the king when Adam and Thomas had arrived some time previously. "And even better, in the company of would-be traitors."

"Watch your mouth, Mortimer," Lancaster said.

"As you should watch yours! I have it on good authority that you've sat and talked for hours with Kent, and we all know his dearest wish is to somehow resuscitate the dead and return the erstwhile king to his throne."

Lancaster's narrow cheeks darkened. "Don't be a fool, Mortimer. And don't take the rest of us for fools either. We know he isn't dead."

"Do you?" Edward said. "Interesting, seeing as I do not."

Lancaster turned his face blindly in the direction of the king. "That's not what I hear, my lord."

"See?" Mortimer said to the king. He swung to face Lancaster. "And is it you who sent that armed band of men to Corfe to free the former king?"

"What armed band?" Edward asked, rising to his feet.

"Twenty or so—masked and well-armed. They bought their way in and went on to wreak quite some havoc before Maltravers brought them down."

"Well, it wasn't me," Lancaster said. "I am not planning a rebellion—how could I? You have me bound over for more money than I make in a year, damn it."

"Ah. Am I to understand it is only the fine that is keeping you loyal?" Mortimer purred.

"I submitted to my king," Lancaster said stiffly. "To him, I owe loyalty and service—him, not you, Mortimer."

"So who sent those men?" Thomas asked.

"God knows." Mortimer looked squarely at Thomas. "But if not Lancaster, my money is on your brother."

"How dare you?" Thomas had his dagger out.

"Stop this." Edward slammed his hand down on the table. "Surely, we can find out who sent them. It's just a matter of making them talk."

"They're dead," Mortimer said. "All of them."

"How convenient," Thomas muttered, and for a moment it seemed as if Mortimer would attack him.

"Enough!" Queen Isabella's voice was no louder than usual, but all present turned her way. She glided over the floor, the soft soles of her shoes a shushing sound, no more. "We'll have no more talk of rebellion or undead kings. It unsettles the court, and what unsettles the court unsettles the country." As she passed him, she set a hand to Mortimer's back, a lingering caress that had his stance softening. She smiled at her son. "I assume none of us want a return to war and unrest, so therefore I propose we throw ourselves wholeheartedly into the upcoming Christmas festivities." Green eyes studied Thomas and Lancaster in turn. "A unified front, my lords. I expect all of you to show that."

Thomas was still seething when he and Adam left the room.

"To accuse Edmund like that! And did you see Ned's face? He believed him, goddamn it."

"But you have to admit Edmund has—"

"—acted like a fool, aye. But he would never do anything to harm Ned. Never. And isn't it convenient how these purported attackers are all dead?" Thomas spat to the side. "One could almost think Mortimer arranged it so as to convince Ned of the threat Edmund poses."

Adam came to an abrupt halt.

"What? You don't think him capable of such?" Thomas asked.

"I-I…" Adam stuttered. God help him, but for the briefest of instances he did. And then his belief in Lord Roger's basic honour reasserted itself. "No."

"Mortimer is fighting for his life!"

"His life?"

Thomas rolled his eyes heavenward. "Look about you, Adam. The king, Montagu, Stafford—even Le Strange—they're all chafing under the Mortimer yoke. As am I, as are Lancaster and Edmund. Do you truly believe Mortimer will willingly slink off into oblivion?"

"No," Adam admitted, and his guts coiled and clenched.

That same evening, the king formally inaugurated the Christmas celebrations, and the thronged hall filled with laughter and song, Lancaster's minstrels having to work hard for their board. After an endless parade of dishes—fish in all its form—the tables were cleared and the king led the way with his wife in a ronde. Soon enough, the floor was filled with dancing, stamping people, but Adam sat to the side and watched, Kit at his side.

She hummed along, her foot tapping in time with the pipes and the drums, and all of her yearned to dance—he could see it in how she threw him covert glances, in how her cheeks flushed. Adam drank some more wine and ignored her subtle hints. Damned if he intended to lumber about like a tame bear, made ungainly by his foot, and if he couldn't dance, then neither could she.

"Kit? What are you doing here, sitting in a corner?" A flushed Thomas appeared before them. "You should be dancing!"

"I'm not sure," Kit mumbled, throwing a longing look at the floor. "Adam says he can't, and—"

"Adam won't mind," Thomas interrupted. "You won't, will you? Just because you're lame doesn't mean Kit here can't enjoy herself."

Adam gritted his teeth.

"No," Kit said quietly. "I'll stay."

"Go." From somewhere, Adam produced a smile. "Go on, I know you want to."

"Truly?"

"Truly." And he meant it, but he didn't, sick with jealousy as his wife danced off with Thomas. One dance, two, and she swept by, as flushed as Thomas, and she was laughing out loud, her head thrown back. And then it was another ronde, and Adam clenched his hands as Thomas lifted his wife—*his* wife—high, Kit's hands clasping his shoulders as Thomas slowly set her down again, his hold on her waist lingering for far longer than necessary.

Over the following days, it seemed to Adam that whenever he looked, chances were he'd find Kit in Thomas' company.

"I am?" Kit washed her hands in the proffered basin and carefully dried her hands. They were sitting side by side in the hall, so full of noise it was impossible to conduct a conversation with anyone but those sitting closest. "To me, it seems I spend most of my time with our expectant queen. Today, she craved cheese and honey; yesterday it was almond paste. At this rate, she'll grow very plump."

"And yet I saw you walking with Thomas this morning, and yesterday you came out of chapel together."

Kit set down her eating knife. "What are you insinuating? I was at prayers; Thomas came in. And we weren't alone in there—your dear brother was with me."

Adam persisted. "I don't like it. First, all that dancing, now all these moments when it's only him and you. It makes people talk."

"Ah." The look she gave him made him twist inside. "People, Adam? Or are you putting words in their mouths?"

She stood, lifting her skirts to climb over the trestle.

"Where are you going?"

"Out. Anywhere. I've lost my appetite." She'd averted her face, but he could hear the tears in her voice.

"Sit down," he hissed. "You're making a spectacle."

"I am?" she hissed back. "You're the one to blame, with your snide comments." She was off, half running for the door.

"What got into her?" William asked, leaning over the table.

"Women," Adam answered cryptically, quelling the little niggle of shame with yet another goblet of wine.

She avoided him after that. In fact, she avoided everyone but Philippa, and the coming days any attempts Adam made at conversation were cut short, with Kit either in a hurry to rejoin the queen or on an errand to find a tonic to soothe Philippa's queasiness.

Come night, she maintained an almost constant silence, responding to his questions as briefly as she could. She wanted an apology, he sensed that, but she *had* been spending too much time with Thomas, and so what should he apologise for? Caring for her reputation?

In bed, she neither rebutted nor accepted his advances. She just lay there, dousing any arousal he might have as effectively as if she'd thrown a pail of ice-cold water over him. So he didn't try, and neither did she, and as the Christmas season progressed, a chasm yawned wider and wider between them.

Chapter 31

"What's the matter with you?" Thomas complained one morning, appearing with the red-rimmed eyes and sour breath that indicated he'd spent yet another night in communion with too much wine.

"Nothing." Adam shoved by him. "Going hawking today?" Not only was he avoiding his wife, he was also keeping his distance from his friend, anger bubbling constantly in his gut.

"No." Thomas made a face. "Too windy, too cold."

"Some of us don't have a choice," Adam muttered. "Where the king goes, so go we."

Thomas gave him a strange look. "If you don't want to go, I'm sure Ned will excuse you."

"Who said I didn't?"

"Adam?" Thomas pulled his brows together. "Why are you acting like this?"

"As if you don't know!" Adam growled before leaping down the narrow stairwell. Too fast, and inevitably his bad foot gave way, causing him to bump down the last steps on his arse. Thomas came after, offering help, but Adam would have none of it. Not from him. He tore himself free and limped off, ignoring Thomas' hurt and confused expression.

As if in tune with Adam's dark mood, the weather had taken a turn for the worse. Days of rain had left the ground soggy and muddy, a far cry from the brittle beauty of those wintry days a week ago. Before the dancing, before he had quarrelled with his wife. Adam slipped in a puddle and cursed.

He inhaled, held his breath, and let the air out slowly. It helped, the cold air cooling his temper. Again, and he could admit that he was being unfair to Kit, taking out on her the constant and gnawing frustration caused by his damned foot.

Maybe he was making too much of things; maybe all the times he saw her with Thomas were coincidental. Maybe.

When he entered the stables, he encountered Prince John, accompanied by his younger sister.

"She wants to come with us." John adopted a long-suffering look. "I keep telling her she's a baby, too young to ride with us." There was a mute entreaty in his eyes that had Adam stifling a smile.

"I'm not too young." Eleanor tossed back her hair. "Maman was not much older when she married our Father."

"Maman is Maman," John replied. "You're just silly Nellie."

Adam cut through the ensuing argument by offering the young lady to ride with him. It was like watching the sun come out of the clouds, a slow smile spreading over Eleanor's face. Her Maman to the day, he thought, albeit she had her father's bright blue eyes.

"Ah, relegated to being a nursemaid?" Montagu teased when Adam rode up with the princess in tow.

"The young lady needs an escort. I am honoured to be of service."

"Well, at least being lame is no impediment," Stafford said. He chuckled at his own joke, stopped when no one else laughed with him. "My apologies," he muttered, wheeling his mount round.

"Do you mind?" Princess Eleanor asked once they were on their way. "Being lame, I mean."

"Aye." He smiled slightly. "But I've had a bad foot for many years, my lady."

"Maman says a foot is of little consequence. What matters is what a man has here…" She touched her head. "And here." She touched her chest, a vivid pink staining her cheeks. Adam shared her embarrassment, wondering just how often the king's lame knight had been the subject of discussion in the royal quarters.

Fortunately, the release of the king's tiercel captured the princess's attention, and no more was mentioned of feet, damaged or otherwise.

The moment Adam left the room for the hawking expedition, Kit rolled out of bed and began her morning ablutions. From under her lashes, she'd watched him do the same, now and then casting a look in her direction, and she'd closed her hands round the need to extend her arm, allow her fingertips to slide down his naked back. But she was too hurt by what he'd said, determined that he owed her an apology, and so she'd pretended to turn in her sleep to stare at the wall instead.

She dressed with less than her normal care, pulled her hair back in a tight braid, and covered it with one of her darker veils, carefully draping the material round her neck in lieu of the wimple she preferred not to wear.

"You look ill," Queen Philippa stated, looking Kit up and down.

"Tired, more like it, my lady." Kit massaged her neck. "Nightmares." Six days of icy silence, of nights lying as far away from him as she could were taking their toll.

"Am I to take it Adam suffers from the same nightmares? Seeing as he walks about with a face so long it's a miracle his chin doesn't scrape the ground."

Despite it all, Kit had to laugh. "He does?"

Philippa shook her head. "Don't pretend you don't notice. So why are you walking about like a doe with an arrow through her neck while Adam acts the desolate huntsman?"

"It's nothing, my lady."

"Best sort it, Kit."

"I cannot do that, my lady. It is him who has to sort matters with me."

"Ah." Philippa moved closer. "So none of this is your fault?"

"No." Kit raised her chin.

"Not even when you danced so many turns with dear Thomas?"

Kit's face prickled and heated. "It was nothing! We were just dancing, and—"

"So it is Thomas," Philippa interrupted.

"It is not Thomas! I would never—" Kit broke off. "If you'll excuse me, my lady, I don't think I feel well."

Philippa nodded. "Hiding won't help," she said as Kit was leaving. "It never does." What would she know, so young and starry-eyed, with an adoring husband and her first child growing in her belly? But Kit nodded to indicate she'd heard and fled.

She wanted to go home. Kit stood on the battlements and looked to the southwest, calculating how many days it would take her to ride home. Seven? If she were to saddle her palfrey, she could be gone within the hour, but even in her present agitated state she recognised the notion as foolish. For a woman on her own to brave the roads was to invite all sorts of calamities, and none of Adam's men would ride with her without first informing him.

Kit shivered in the wind. In the distance, she could see the king's party returning, and as she had no desire to watch them—him—ride in, she descended from the wall and made for the garden that Alice de Lacy had told her she'd planted some years ago 'as a distraction from my husband'. In winter, there was little to see but some bare shrubs and the thorny branches of overgrown briar roses. Yet it served the purpose of distracting Kit from *her* husband, and she crouched as she attempted to identify the few herbal plants from their withered stalks and leaves.

There was a little bench tucked into what would be a glorious rose-covered bower in summer. Now the rattling canes offered some protection against the wind, and Kit pulled her cloak close and sat down, eyes on the worn statue she supposed represented a unicorn.

"Kit?"

Kit stiffened.

"What are you doing here in the cold?" Thomas joined her.

"I could ask you the same."

"Me?" He hiccupped. "I needed the air. Too many hours spent on my own with a pitcher or two of wine."

Kit shifted away from him. "You're drunk."

"Agreeably so." He placed his arm along the back of the bench. "Do you think she was very unhappy?" he blurted.

"Who?"

"My wife." He sighed, belched, and sighed again. "The mother of my children, the maid I wooed and won, too stubborn to listen to the advice of all those who said she was not at all what I needed." He laughed harshly. "Even she said that."

"Did she seem unhappy?"

He turned haunted eyes her way. "I don't know. I never spent enough time with her to be able to tell."

"She had her children, a comfortable life. She may not have been happy, but she was probably not unhappy." Not that Kit knew if that was true, but if Thomas needed to hear that, she was willing to say it.

"So not happy, but not unhappy." He sat back, squinting at the pale blue sky. "And you?" he asked in a voice so low she barely heard him. "Would I have made you unhappy, do you think?"

"Me? I am married elsewhere—as you well know."

"Oh, I do. 'Tis not fair," he mumbled. "Not fair, not fair." He looked at her, and there were tears in his eyes. "Sometimes, I fear I killed her."

"You?" The pain in his voice had her moving closer. "She fell ill, Thomas."

"Or she died of a broken heart." He rubbed at his chest.

"Your wife died of a fever. It wasn't your fault." She cupped his cheek. "Let it go, Thomas."

His hazel eyes widened, and before she fully understood what he was about to do, he had her by the nape, his mouth on hers. Kit spluttered. Thomas moaned her name. She got hold of his hair and pulled, hard enough to have him choke out a curse. Out of the corner of her eye, she saw a flurry of colour, a tall shape limping away as fast as he could.

"Adam!" She surged to her feet.

"Adam! Damn it!" Thomas leapt up. "Kit, my apologies, I—" She punched him, full on the mouth, and then she ran after her husband.

Adam had returned from the hunt in a lighter mood, determined to make the effort required to heal this widening rift between him and his wife. Once off Raven, he asked Stephen if he knew where Kit might be and was told he'd last seen her on the further side of the keep. The garden. Adam smiled to himself, thinking that in this his wife was most predictable. Whenever she needed solace, she retired to whatever patch of garden she could find.

He was rehearsing just what to say to her when the little bower hove into sight, and sitting side by side on the bench were Kit and Thomas. His heart ached when she stroked Thomas' cheek, and when Thomas kissed her…Adam whirled on his toes, limping away as fast as he could.

"Adam!"

He heard her calling, heard her footsteps in the gravel, and it just made him increase his speed so that he reached their little room some instances before her, sufficient time to divest his cloak and stand with his arms crossed when she fell in over the threshold.

"It wasn't…" she began, out of breath and flushed.

"It wasn't what? A kiss? I have eyes to see with!"

"It wasn't like that. He—"

"Kissed you, and you kissed him right back."

"I did not!"

"I saw you!" He slammed his hand down on the table, and she jumped. "My wife, playing harlot to the earl."

Kit visibly reeled. "You misconstrue."

"I do? So why were you kissing him?"

"I wasn't kissing him!" she screeched. "He kissed me, and I—"

"Liked it."

"No." She shook her head. "How can you think that?"

"And how can you think a rich and handsome earl can have any genuine interest for the scarred, bastard-born daughter of a minor lord? Come to think of it, I'd never have looked twice at you had I not been duped into believing you were someone else." He wanted to take it back the moment he'd said it—all of it—because he didn't want her to look at him like that, her eyes transparent windows to a heart he'd just trampled all over.

Kit took a step back, teeth sunk into her wobbling lower lip. She blinked. And blinked. And then she was gone, and Adam sank down on the bed and groaned out loud.

He didn't see her at supper. Or Thomas. His innards coiled and roared in anger as he imagined all sorts of little scenes in which Kit and Thomas partook of a private meal.

"Kit? With Thomas?" William looked at him as if he'd gone insane. "Never. Besides, your friend the earl is drunk—as he seems to be most of the time lately."

"Not my friend," Adam muttered.

"Of course he is," William replied calmly. "Just as she is your faithful and loving wife."

Adam twisted. "They kissed."

"And did you ask her to explain why?" William looked at him. "No, I thought not. So what did you say to her?"

"Nothing I wasn't entitled to say," Adam replied defensively. When William made as if to say something more, Adam stood up. "I don't want to talk about this."

"As you wish." William held up his hands.

Adam returned to their room. No sign of Kit, and he supposed she intended to punish him by staying away. Very well, if that was what she wanted. Besides, it was him in the right, seeing her kiss another man! He pummelled his pillow into shape and tried to sleep. It did not work very well.

Come dawn, he was wide awake and irascible. He kept on seeing her expression as he'd called her scarred and bastard-born, and it made him burn with shame that he, who knew just how insecure she felt due to her illegitimacy, should have shoved it in her face. And as to the scar…He rarely thought about the faded cross that disfigured her cheek, but he knew she did.

He came face-to-face with her at the entrance to the chapel, and everything inside of him shrivelled at the way she'd dressed, an unfamiliar wimple leaving but a narrow stretch of face visible. She came to a halt at the sight of him, and he couldn't help but wonder where she'd spent the night, her eyes tired in purple hollows.

He bowed; she inhaled. When he straightened up, she was gone, and belatedly he realised she'd taken his courteous gesture as yet another snub. Adam scrubbed at his face. Women were at times incomprehensible, and he had a throbbing headache due to lack of sleep, his stomach clamouring for food. Later. He'd find Kit later and put things right.

He broke his fast alone, and then he was called in to arrange mounts and guards for the king and his companions, off on yet another day of hunting despite the wind and clouds heavy with rain. He begged off for himself, but all the same near on half the morning had gone before he found the time to go searching for his wife.

He did not find her. Instead, he ran into the man he most definitely did not want to see.

"Adam." Thomas uncurled himself from the embrasure in which he'd been sitting. "I have to talk to you."

"About what? Your itch to bed my wife? Her responsiveness to your caresses?" Anger clouded his brain, made it difficult to breathe.

"Responsiveness?" Thomas shook his head. "She punched me full in the mouth."

"She did?" Now that he'd mentioned it, Adam could see just how swollen Thomas' mouth was; in places the lip had cracked and scabbed.

"I was drunk," Thomas said. "Heartsick and drunk, and she was sitting in the garden looking lonely, so I joined her." He sat down again. "I never meant to kiss her."

"But you've wanted to do so for a long time."

"Maybe." Thomas sounded pained. "I've said it before, and I realise it may be difficult for you to believe at present, but I would never do anything to hurt you or Kit. You're my friends, and yesterday was a huge mistake, fuelled by too much wine and that damned persistent ghost of my wife." He laughed softly. "I've spent more nights thinking of my dear departed Alice now that she is dead than during all the years we were wed. Some sort of revenge from beyond the grave, maybe?"

"It sounds like fancies to me." Adam sat down beside him. "What happened?"

"Nothing. I was going on about Alice, she comforted me, and I…" Thomas licked his broken lip. "Kissed her without her leave." He gave Adam a perceptive look. "What did you do?"

Adam hid his face under his hair. "I told her no one would want a bastard-born, scarred wench and that I'd never have wed her had I not been duped to do so."

"Ah." Thomas cleared his throat. "That was bad."

Adam nodded. "I was too angry and hurt to think straight."

They sat in silence for a while. "Between the two of us, we've made quite a mess of things haven't we?" Thomas finally said. "The two men she trusted the most, and we both ended up betraying her."

Put like that, it made Adam drown in guilt.

"Where is she now?" Thomas asked.

"With the queen, I suppose. She's been kept busy making possets for the expectant mother."

Thomas stood. "We're going to have to crawl." He held out his hand. "Will you forgive me?"

"Maybe." Adam gripped the extended hand. "Probably."

Drizzle converted into a veritable downpour, so the hunting party returned in time for dinner, the king none too pleased at being soaked through.

"Bloody weather," he complained to Adam. "Why would anyone choose to spend winter here?" He shot a venomous look at Lord Roger—just as wet—and Queen Isabella—remarkably dry, seeing as Lord Roger had wrapped her in his cloak as well.

"It sends a signal to the local lords," Isabella explained in a tone that showed just how often she'd repeated this. "You're not only king over the nice and sunny south."

"Someone else wants this part, they can have it," Edward muttered.

"What did you say?" Queen Isabella's voice dropped into the darker regions while she herself grew, straightening up to look as tall as she possibly could. Despite being close to a head shorter than her son, she managed the feat of looking down her nose at him, green eyes so cold it was a miracle the king did not freeze to death.

"Nothing."

"Good. After all, if you don't want it, why not invite the Scots to hold it? Black Douglas would be more than thrilled to annex whatever part of England you don't want to the Scottish kingdom—all the way through the north to here, in the western midlands.

Edward scowled. "Let him try and take one inch of English soil, and I'll have him eating it."

Isabella softened her stance. "I'd love to see that."

"Oh, you will, Maman. Someday."

The king hurried off to change, as did most of the returning hunters. Adam stood hovering at the door of the hall, impatiently waiting for Queen Philippa and her ladies. From inside came the promising smell of warm pies and roasted meats, and here at last came their little queen, serene and glowing.

"Kit?" Philippa spread her hands over her belly, her lower lip curving slightly. "She came with my posset some hours ago, but since then I haven't seen her." She waved a hand at the sprawling buildings that dotted Kenilworth's large baileys. "She could be anywhere, I suppose. Maybe with your brother? Or with the resident healer? She begs herbs off her for me."

William hadn't seen her, neither had the healer. Somewhere between the chapel and the healer, the skies broke open, yet another icy downpour that chilled him to the bones in moments. Adam was halfway to their room, hoping against hope that she'd be there, curled up before the hearth, when Stephen came running from the direction of the stables.

"My lord," he gasped. "The horse!" He was wet through, his tunic clinging to his narrow frame.

"The horse?" Adam asked, pulling up the hood of his cloak.

"It came back." Stephen drew in a long breath. "The mare."

"What mare?" But he knew, and already he was striding towards the stable, Stephen loping at his side.

"Lady Kit's." Stephen dragged his sleeve under his nose, remembered himself, and mumbled an apology, producing instead a crumpled rag. "She left just after the hunting party, said she was going for a ride."

"And why didn't you tell me?" Adam demanded.

"Tell you, my lord?" Stephen gave him a bewildered look. "Lady Kit said you already knew."

"Where did she go?" Adam yelled, and Stephen backed away so fast he overbalanced and landed on his rump.

"I…I…don't know, my lord. She just said she was going for a ride."

"A ride?" Alone, in this weather. He limped as fast as he could for the stables, and behind him came Thomas and William, yelling for him to wait.

"We need a plan," Thomas said, having grabbed hold of Adam. "Where would she have gone? Down to the abbey?"

Adam shook his head. "Likely the woods. In this wind…" Adam pointed at Kit's mare, standing with her head down and blown sides. She was muddy and wet well over her hocks, froth covering her nose and neck. "Something frightened her." He picked at a twig tangled in the mare's mane.

"So we start in the woods beyond the mere." Thomas called out orders, yelled for Stephen to come along as well. He placed a hand on Adam's arm. "We'll find her."

Chapter 31

His bow had been the equivalent of being knifed in the belly. No apology, no Kit, just the polite greeting he would bestow on anyone crossing his path. It had left her incapable of facing anyone else, and so she'd ordered Stephen to saddle her mare, saying she was in need of fresh air.

"Today?" Stephen had given her an incredulous look. "My lady, the ground is treacherous, all that water has dislodged it in places."

"I've been riding since long before you were born, and no one has died of a little rain." But one could, she believed, die of suffocation caused by the presence of the man who'd so cruelly repudiated her. All night, she'd heard his harsh words echoing in her head, seeing yet again the icy steel in his eyes.

She walked the horse across the causeway, the rising wind buffeting her towards the mere. All the recent rain had caused the pool on the other side of the causeway to expand into a small lake, and one of the sentries warned her from trying to ride to the nearby abbey—the ford was impassable. Once beyond the outer defences, she set the mare to gallop, cantering up a gently sloping knoll that offered a good view of the surroundings. Not today, though, as the wind whipped her cloak and veil, rain driving like nails into her face. The mare turned her rump to the wind, and before them were the woods, naked trees stretching rattling branches towards the sky. Clouds of every shade of grey imaginable scudded across the sky, and a sudden gust of wind had a nearby bramble bending to the ground, its long canes rattling in protest.

Kit turned the horse towards the woods. The closer they got to the trees, the more skittish the mare became.

"It's only the wind," Kit told her, guiding her firmly along a narrow path. Some way in, the howling of the wind abated, and they picked their way along the little path, surrounded by trees that sighed and whispered, boughs bending and creaking in the wind.

The path turned to meander alongside the stream that fed the mere—at present swollen with water. The ground was wet, the mare's hooves making a slapping sound as Kit urged her into a canter. To her right, the stream; to her left, the trees that groaned and swayed, and the mare threw with her head and snorted. A loud snapping sound, and the mare neighed and half reared. A huge alder came crashing down. The horse bucked and screamed. Kit was thrown, most of her landing in the water. God's teeth, but it was cold! Kit found no purchase on the muddy ground and slid further into the water. She kicked, she heaved, and beside her there was a rending sound as the fallen tree tore free of what remained of its trunk. It tipped over, a heavy branch settling like a deadweight over her back.

The mare was gone. She had no notion of how long she'd lain here, trapped half-in, half-out of the frigid water, but her hands were black with mud, her fingernails torn with her efforts to pull herself free of the tree. Water was now lapping at her waist, her legs so cold she had lost all sensation in them. She rested her cheek in the mud and closed her eyes. So tired, so cold.

She woke to the sound of a distant rumble. She was drenched to the skin, her hair plastered to her head, and she kicked feebly in the hope of dislodging the branch. The water was higher, almost up to her breasts. The rumble came closer, and the ground shivered and shook. Water. Kit twisted her head and screamed at the sight of the foaming waves rushing towards her.

"Did you hear that?" Thomas stood in his stirrups. "Over there!"

Adam looked in the direction Thomas pointed but could see nothing but trees, more trees, and rain, this damned infernal rain that made it difficult to see much beyond his horse's head. And then he heard it, a faint cry in the distance, and Raven snorted in protest as Adam drove his spurs into his sides. There was an odd roaring, and at first he thought it was in his head, but then he heard William yell, and before them was a growling river where normally there was only a stream. Further downstream, a huge alder had fallen, blocking the water, and something dark was floating beside it, seemingly trapped beneath it.

Hair. He registered it without really doing so, and now he was riding madly through the frothing water, ignoring his companions' warnings. He fell off the horse, and she was there, almost entirely submerged in water, but her eyes were wide open, and she coughed and gasped, now and then disappearing underneath the surface of the angry, roiling waters.

Thomas landed beside him. "Grab her! We have to get her out before—"

A wall of water hit them, and Adam lurched forward, slamming into the trunk of the alder. The tree shifted, something hit his leg, and he grabbed at the dark bundle of cloth that was being dragged out into the deeper water under the fallen tree. His hands slipped. Dear God, she was floating facedown! Another grab, and this time his fingers tightened on fabric. He pulled her free, and she hung like limp seaweed in his arms, her head falling back so that her hair dragged in the water.

"Dearest God," Thomas groaned. "Is she…?"

"No!" Adam rounded on him with a snarl. "She is not! I won't let her!" But she was still and quiet, and he carried her over to drier ground with his heart in his mouth.

"Kit?" He shook her. She twitched. Not dead.

"Here." Thomas pulled off his gloves. "Hold her facedown." He stuck his fingers in her mouth, and she retched, spewing water and mud. Adam set her down, holding her as she voided her guts. At long last, it was over, and she drew in loud, rasping breaths, shivering so badly she collapsed to the ground.

"We have to get her back," Thomas said. "Stephen, you ride ahead and ensure there's a hot bath waiting for her. William, we're going to need your cloak—ours are drenched."

"Of course." William dismounted and crouched beside

Kit. "Here, Kit, let me help." He undid her drenched cloak and covered her with his own. "It won't help much. She's chilled to the bone."

Adam went to hold her. She looked at him from under a mess of wet and muddy hair and crawled backwards.

"Kit, my love," he said, his voice breaking. She hesitated. He took two long strides and fell to his knees beside her. She turned to him, her hands clutching at his sodden tunic, her face hidden in the crook of his neck.

Somehow, they mounted the horse, she refusing to let go of him.

"Go!" Thomas said, and Adam clapped heels to Raven, racing back towards the red walls of Kenilworth while she clung to him.

The moment they reached the stable, Stephen was there, holding out his arms to take her. Adam shook his head. He wasn't letting her go—in fact, she wouldn't be leaving his sight until he had assured himself she was healing, both inside and out. So he slid off Raven as carefully as he could, couldn't quite suppress a gasp when their combined weights landed on his right foot, but straightened up and limped slowly if steadily in the direction of the small room dominated by a huge, steaming bath.

She looked as pitiful as a drenched kitten. He peeled off layer after layer of sodden garments, knelt to undo the single shoe left to her, and led her over to the bath. He placed her in the water and stood back to shed his wet tunic and shirt, happy for the warmth of the fire on his cold back. Someone had thought to leave dry clothes on a stool, a large, fur-lined cloak hanging off a hook.

No words, at first. He was tongue-tied; she was elsewhere, eyes on a strand of curling steam. She was stiff with cold and streaked with mud, and her hands were held in tight, tight fists, but bit by bit she softened, her head lolling back as she submitted to being washed by him. There was mud everywhere: in her ears, in the crack of her buttocks, in her secret folds. She quivered when he touched her there, and for an instant her eyes met his, dark and wide, before sliding to the side.

"Sweeting," was all he said, sliding his hands up her body to her breasts, as much an examination as a caress. She was whole, thank the Lord, for all that an ugly bruise decorated her lower back, causing her to wince when he gently washed her there as well.

It took several rinses before her hair regained its normal colour. He dipped his finger into the pot of soap and worked up a lather in his hands before he sank his fingers in her hair, strong fingers kneading her scalp until she groaned out loud, slipping even deeper into the now scummy water.

"I'm sorry," he said, gentling his hands as he carefully soaped one, then the other of her ears. "For how I've behaved, but mostly for what I said." He returned to her hair, hoping she'd say something, but she didn't. "I don't care about your birth, I never even see your scar. I only said that to hurt you."

"And you did." As low and dark as always, her voice was hoarser than normal, as if there was gravel in her mouth. Come to think of it, maybe there was, and when she coughed, he hastened to fetch her some spiced wine, inhaling the scents of cinnamon and cloves, black pepper and honey.

"I know." He waited until she'd drunk and then urged her to lean forward, pouring a pitcher of water over her head. All of her tensed, her arms tight round her knees. "Shhh," he crooned. "It's only water, warm, clean water."

She gargled and wiped the wet hair out of her face. "I think I've had enough of water to last me a lifetime." She shuddered. "I thought I was going to die, that God was taunting me by allowing me one last glimpse of you before He took me from you."

It made him smile, this indirect admission that she loved him.

"As if I would ever let Him take you from me," he replied, adding some more wood to the fire. Only when there was a blaze did he allow her to get out of the bath, standing her before the warmth of the fire as he rubbed her dry, every single inch of her. Her skin glowed in the ruddy light of the fire. It set her hair alight, both that between her legs and that on her head, and he couldn't resist brushing his fingers carefully through her pubic curls before ordering her to sit at his feet while he addressed her hair.

"I should have danced with you myself," he said as he combed her hair, strand by strand. "I could see how much you wanted to, but all I could think of was that I'd be ridiculed, laughed at behind my back—again."

"Do they?" She craned her head back to look at him, and the cloak he'd wrapped her in slid off her shoulders.

"Those that don't know me, aye, they do." He frowned down at a particularly large tangle. "Before, it was just a limp. Now it is an impediment. That bastard de Langon pulverised what bones I had left, and I can no longer even crook my toes. It hurts to walk, it hurts to stand, I can only imagine how much it would hurt to dance, but most of all it hurts my pride." He laughed mirthlessly. "And it has not helped to be named the king's lame knight, as if I were some sort of exotic creature, useless but intriguing."

"You are never useless." She leaned back against his legs. "Not to me, not to the king. Thomas says…" She fell silent, and he realised with a flash of irritation that she'd been discussing him with Thomas. "I had to talk to someone," she mumbled. "You closed me out."

He concentrated on his combing.

"So what did Thomas say?" he asked after a while.

"That the king loves you." She looked up at him. "But you already know that."

"I do?" He mulled this over. At times, aye, he did. At others, he'd see the king's eyes dart between him and Mortimer, and there was speculation, not love, in that blue gaze. He finished with the task and set the comb aside, raising her to sit in his lap. The room was warm, but he swept the cloak tighter round her shoulders before gathering her as close as he could. "Will you forgive me?"

"I will." A light finger traced his mouth. "Will you kiss me?"

"Gladly." He swept her damp hair off her face, gripping her gently by the chin as he covered her mouth with his.

Their lips touched, and he was overwhelmed by a vision of her floating upside down in the icy water, her cloak and hair tangled in the fallen tree. A shudder rippled through him. He could have lost her—at this very minute she could have been lying still and cold in the chapel, surrounded by lit candles while her soaking garments dripped tears onto the floor. Adam groaned her name and hid his face against her neck.

"It didn't happen," she said, tugging gently at the hair on his nape. He lifted his head, and she sought his mouth, arms winding themselves tight—so tight—around his neck. No, it hadn't happened, and she was warm and safe in his arms, urgent and demanding.

They broke apart to breathe. Eyes collided with eyes, fingers met and braided. She could have been dead. She was alive, she was hot, and she was damp, and all she seemed to want—to need—was him. Now. She tore at the cloak. Skin against skin, and he just had to set his hand over her heart, feel it beating into his palm.

On the floor, and he hastily ordered their clothes into some semblance of a bed. He kissed, he touched, he wanted. Her. Only her. Beneath him, she made sounds of impatience, a loud hiss escaping her when he took her. And then they were one, moving to the same unsung melody, soul calling to soul. Release, moments of oblivion, of soaring upwards, before slowly whirling back to earth and landing, as softly as a falling leaf, in her welcoming arms.

Adam lifted his head. A tear glistened in her eye, slid down her cheek, and he tenderly licked it off. It made her smile, a wobbly little thing.

"I could have died," she whispered as he rolled them over, inviting her to pillow her head on his chest.

"I know." Without her, he'd be lost, a desperate creature in an endless wilderness. The insight shortened his breath, a painful squeezing round his heart. She could have died. But she hadn't, and Adam resolved to spend some time in the chapel thanking the Holy Virgin for her deliverance—later. At present, he wasn't about to move, not with the comforting weight of his wife on his arm.

A loud knocking on the door had them starting awake.

"Are you still alive, or have you both drowned?" Thomas asked through the heavy door. Kit flinched. Adam tweaked at her hair.

"I know what happened—he told me." In a louder voice, he assured Thomas they were both hale. "He's struggling," Adam confided to Kit. "What he did was wrong, but it was more about his dead wife than you."

Kit looked away. "I hit him."

"As he well deserved." Adam frowned down at his hose points. One of them was broken, torn apart rather than untied.

"Adam!" Thomas banged on the door again.

"Coming!" He pulled on a dry shirt, a dry tunic. No hose, and the boots were so sodden he decided to go barefoot. "Your hair," he said, handing Kit a length of fine linen. She hung back; he took her hand and led her out into the passage where Thomas was pacing.

"Kit!" He rushed forward, she shied, and to Adam's surprise, Thomas knelt before her. "Forgive me. Please."

"Get up," she said. "You're making a fool of yourself, my lord."

"My lord?" Thomas grimaced. "I am truly out in the cold."

Kit rolled her eyes. "Thomas, get up!"

He did. "Forgiven?"

To Adam's satisfaction, she looked at him for guidance. He nodded.

"Forgiven." Kit slipped her hand into Adam's. "But don't ever do it again."

"He does, and he'll be missing his balls," Adam growled. He used his free hand to punch Thomas lightly on the arm. "We need some food. Coming?"

Thomas' face lit up. "With pleasure."

Chapter 32

"It's not fair." Queen Philippa peered at Kit from swollen eyes, her nose an unbecoming bright red. "You nearly drown in all that icy water, and I end up with the cold." She sniffed, produced a linen cloth, and blew her nose.

"Fortunately, very few die of this condition, my lady," Mathilde said, handing the queen an earthenware cup. "Drink up."

The queen lifted her feet in the direction of the hearth and sipped at the heated wine. "We must start preparing for my coronation. The king wants me to look my very best." She spread one hand over her belly. "He told me to spend as much as I like, and so…" She grinned. "This time, it will be me they look at, me they gawk and stare at, not my dearest mother-in-law." Philippa looked at Kit. "Miniver and samite, velvet and gold spinet, and I want green and red, and silk linings, and—"

"Precious Virgin, my lady, we're talking one day, are we not?" Mathilde interrupted.

"Then I will change attire throughout the day. My husband wants me to shine, and shine I will." She beckoned Katherine Montagu over. "Fur hoods, Katherine, I want two or three, and Ned says I must have an ermine mantle." She sighed happily. "Ermine!"

"What else to adorn a crowned queen?" The mild voice had Philippa jerking upright, spilling wine over her chemise.

"My lady," she said, rising gracefully to her feet, as did all others present.

"Your hair is undone," Queen Isabella commented. "That is unacceptable, my sweet. A queen always maintains appearances, even while she sneezes and snivels."

"My lady has not finished with her *toilette* yet," Mathilde said.

"No?" Isabella shook her head slowly from side to side.

"That will not do, Philippa, not at all. As of tomorrow, you will accompany me to prime." She smiled. "I expect to see you perfectly attired."

"Yes, my lady," Philippa said, staring at the carpet on which she was standing.

"Good." Isabella did a little turn, and Philippa's ladies made their reverences. "There's more to being a queen than dressing in precious fabrics and birthing babes. I suppose it is time you learn." She settled herself on a chair and looked Philippa up and down. "You are pleasing and mild, and my son is besotted—a good start, for sure. But in difference to those of us born to wear a crown..." here she stretched, lifting that long neck of hers so that everyone in the room could properly appraise her beautiful features, "you, my child, have much to learn."

"Yes, my lady," Philippa repeated.

"A queen must be decorative and wise; she must be seen to be the most loyal and supportive of her husband's subjects—"

From somewhere came a muffled snort. Isabella's head whipped round, green eyes narrowing.

"I was," she said icily. "For years, I stood by him." Heavy silence followed this remark. Kit studied the patterns on the floor tiles and listened to the sound of eight women breathing. For almost twenty years, the queen had lived in a court dominated by her husband's male favourites. And then she'd rebelled, imprisoned him, and forced him to abdicate in favour of their son. Not the most loyal of behaviours, however understandable.

Isabella no longer seemed inclined to continue her description of a queen's duties. She stood, collected her robes about her, and left, as always seeming to float across the floor.

Mathilde closed the door behind her. Philippa shook herself.

"Prime?" She coughed. "Every morning? God help me."

Mathilde pursed her lips. "It will do you no harm, my lady. A devout queen is a good queen." She crossed herself. "I will gladly go with you."

"But prime," Philippa wailed. "Who in their right mind

302

wants to spend dawn on an ice-cold floor in that draughty old chapel?" She sat down on a stool. "It's different for her. She has sins to do penance for—all sorts of sins."

"Oh, and you are as pure as driven snow, are you?" Mathilde chided, pulling an ivory-backed brush through the queen's dark hair. It was beautiful hair, thick and shiny, that curled slightly at the ends. And once Mathilde was done, all that exuberant glossiness had been constrained to two heavy braids, intricately looped on either side of Philippa's face.

Lancaster's younger daughter came with a clean chemise, her sister Blanche with kirtle and a matching cotehardie, the dark blue wool bursting into colourful life along the hems. A lovely design, miniature suns surrounded by even smaller stars in red and gold.

"There," the queen said once she'd been dressed. "Now that I am *perfectly attired*, may I please sit by the fire and feel sorry for myself?" She sneezed. "Or maybe queens never do. She makes me feel inadequate," she muttered, so low only Kit and Mathilde could hear her. "But I am not."

"Most certainly not," Mathilde agreed. "Your mother knows everything there is to know about being a loyal noble consort, and she has raised you well."

"Ah, but you forget that my dear mother is not a queen, and so she doesn't quite count." Philippa sneezed again. "Although I do not think my husband wants me to model myself on his mother." She giggled. "What husband would?"

Later that morning, the queen chose to walk outside, saying sunshine was so rare these days every beam had to be savoured. The other ladies fell behind as Philippa walked quite briskly along the curtain wall, with only Kit keeping up.

"The pope has pledged support to Edmund," Philippa said all of a sudden. "Mortimer had it from one of his many servants and took great pleasure in informing Ned last night."

"Support for what, my lady?"

"Why, to reinstate Ned's father as king." Philippa worried at her lower lip.

"But the former king is—"

"Alive. We both know that. Of course I know; I'm Ned's wife."

"I was going to say *not here*, my lady." Kit gave the queen a little smile. "I assumed you knew."

"You did?" A flush travelled up Philippa's cheeks.

"Your husband trusts you—and rightly so."

Philippa did not reply, leading them instead past the smithy and up to the northern gatehouse before turning towards the little orchard. They walked among the naked trees, Philippa touching the gnarled trunks as they passed. "This matter with Edmund, how serious is it, do you think?"

"Serious enough." Kit ducked under a trailing branch. The grass was long here, and their hems were wet through, no matter that they both lifted them. "It would have been even more serious had Sir Edward still been in England."

"But how can the pope both support Edmund and offer that self-same support to Ned?" Philippa's hand flew to her mouth. "I shouldn't have said that."

"I won't tell." Kit refrained from saying Adam had already guessed as much. Instead, she halted at the little gate that led to Lady Alice's garden, allowing the queen to precede her. "And I dare say the pope sees merit in both cases."

"He was a bad king!"

"Yes, my lady, he was. But he was an anointed king, and some would argue that once anointed, a king cannot be deposed."

"He wasn't deposed. He abdicated—that's what Ned says."

Kit left it at that. An enforced abdication smelled more of deposition than anything else, but maybe their king needed the lie that his father had willingly surrendered his crown.

"How can Edmund do this?" Philippa dug about in her sleeve and produced a nose rag to wipe at her dripping nose.

"Strictly speaking, he hasn't done anything yet. And the earl of Kent is very fond of his half-brother, always was, as I recall. It caused him heartache to side with Queen Isabella—however much he agreed with the need to rid England of the vile Despensers." She shivered at the unwelcome memory of

Hugh Despenser, his dark eyes far too close, his hands roving over her body at will. "Everyone agreed the Despensers were the canker. Not everyone understood that the king had forfeited the trust of most of his barons, nor did they necessarily agree with the king being imprisoned."

"And now Edmund wants him back," Philippa said, "no matter the risk to my husband."

"It will not happen, my lady."

"No, it won't," Philippa agreed. "Because Mortimer will do whatever it takes to ensure Edward remains on his throne." She patted her belly. "And I want him to. Whatever needs to be done, let it be done to safeguard the future of my husband and my child." Philippa stooped, broke off a drying stalk of lavender, and crumbled it between her fingers. "One thing at a time, I say. First Kent, then Mortimer." She dusted her hands free, releasing a faint fragrance.

Kit was taken aback by the queen's candour. "Mortimer?" She licked her lips. Did she dare to ask? "What about him?"

Philippa laughed. "Mortimer? He carries the seeds of his own destruction within." She pulled her brows together. "So capable, so powerful, and so blind to his own pride." She slipped her arm under Kit's. "Now what do you think I should wear tonight? Ned has promised me love songs and tumblers." Her eyes shone. "I love Twelfth Night."

The giddy girl was back, easy to please, easy to dismiss as unimportant. But there was steel within that slight frame and far more intelligence behind her beautiful almond-shaped eyes than people gave her credit for. Kit listened with half an ear as the queen discussed her wardrobe, wondering if King Edward knew just how fortunate he was in his wife.

At dinner, Adam came to find her, politely requesting the queen's permission to dine with his wife. Philippa waved them off, and they retired to sit some way to the back.

"I've had a message from home," he said, handing over a roll of parchment.

"From Meg again?" Kit asked, smiling as she unrolled it. Her daughter's penmanship had improved, albeit she had as yet not learnt the art of variation, writing yet again that she was well, as were her brothers, the babes, her cat, the priest and… "Tom is ailing?"

"It would seem so, aye."

Kit read on. After the first few lines, Father Owain had taken over, reporting firstly that they'd had problems with thieves stealing sheep, and so had the fools frightened the ewes that some of them had dropped their unformed lambs. Now the flocks had all been brought down closer to home, despite the resulting issues of feeding them, and John had men out looking for the rogues.

As to Tom, Father Owain wrote, the lad had foolishly attempted to stop one of the thieves, and for his trouble he'd been knifed in the shoulder. It was healing as well as it could, and other than most of them walking about with coughs and sniffles due to this very cold and wet winter, the household was doing well.

"Healing as well as it can?" Kit looked up from the letter. "What does that mean?"

"That he's healing." Adam tapped the parchment. "Read on."

Father Owain finished by saying that John had taken it upon himself to threaten little Meg with a thrashing should he ever again find her astride Goliath.

"What?" Kit gasped.

"Aye." He looked grim. "That disobedient sprite of ours and I are going to have a long talk when we get home."

"Home." Kit sighed, going back to the letter. "I wish we could go now, this instant." But she had to smile when Father Owain confided that, in his opinion, Goliath had been too in awe of his little rider to even dare attempt to dislodge her.

"Like mother, like daughter," Adam said with a smile.

"I was never disobedient. Nor do I recall clambering atop a warhorse at the age of four."

He laughed. "Only because there were none around, I imagine."

They turned their attention to the food—simple fare, as the cooks were expending all of their efforts on this evening's supper. But the bean soup was tasty, the bread was warm, and Kit was happy to be sitting beside Adam, which not only allowed her to lean against his warmth, but also gave her the opportunity to study all those present at the high table.

Lancaster and his son were at one end, Thomas was sitting somewhere nearer to the middle, listening gravely to whatever Montagu was saying to him. Montagu? She'd never seen him at the high table before, but he was seated beside the king, who now and then turned to join the conversation with Thomas. Queen Philippa sat side by side with Alice de Lacy, a generous gesture towards a lady who'd lost so much over recent years, and then came Bishop Burghersh, Queen Isabella, and Mortimer, who looked tired—he always did lately.

In a low voice, Kit recounted her recent conversation with the queen.

"A wise lady," Adam commented. "She is right in that Edmund must be handled somehow. Thank the Lord he has no notion of where Sir Edward is."

"Wouldn't Philippe have told him he might be in France?"

"He might. But Edmund seems convinced his brother remains in England, more specifically in Corfe." He leaned closer. "Lord Roger is ensuring it looks that way. The look-alike prisoner was hastily transferred from one dungeon to the other in plain daylight. Most of the garrison got a peek at him, and whoever it is that is feeding Kent information will surely have got word to him by now, describing just how badly his poor brother is being treated."

"How do you know?" Kit asked.

"William told me." Adam finished his food. "And so all we have to do is wait."

"Mortimer is setting a trap." Kit glanced at Thomas. "Does he know?"

"No." He studied his fingernails. "And I can't tell him because to do so might have him riding off to save his brother, and then they'd both be trapped." Adam shifted his shoulders. "Mortimer is having Thomas watched—all the time. Yet another little nugget I got from my brother." He gave her a

307

little smile. "And I am watched as well—not that William told me that; I don't even think he knows."

"You are?" She leaned closer, as if cuddling up to him.

"Mortimer knows I care for Thomas." He turned his cup around. "What I can't make up my mind about is whether he wants me to warn Thomas or not."

Kit sat back. The answer was evident to her—Mortimer and Thomas rarely saw eye to eye—but from the way Adam was looking at her, he was hoping she'd scoff and tell him that Mortimer had no reason to entrap Thomas. His mouth twisted into a parody of a smile, his eyes dark and unreadable.

"Aye, I think as you do. And God help me, I still love him," he said, standing abruptly. He was gone before she had time to react, limping heavily as he made for the door.

Kit pursed her lips. She needed to get him away from this corrosive environment, this constant being torn in two between his loyalties to the king and his precious Lord Roger. There was only one thing to do: talk to the queen.

"Home? Now?" Queen Philippa looked at Kit as if she'd lost her wits.

"We've had word from home," Kit said. "One of the children is ailing." She'd waited until they were sitting somewhat apart from the other ladies, both of them sewing.

Queen Philippa looked less than impressed. "Children are sick all the time."

"True. But then there's Adam. He needs time to heal, my lady."

"Heal? He will never heal," the queen said bluntly. "Surely, you know that by now?"

"I do. He still hopes." Kit stroked the heaped velvet in her lap, intended for a kirtle for the queen. "And while we are here, he exerts himself every day, which does not help."

"Hmm." Philippa finished the rose she was working on, admiring her handiwork in silence. "Yes, I have noticed his limp is worse of late." She set down the embroidery frame. "He should use a cane, methinks."

"So does Pancio, so do William and Earl Thomas. Adam,

however, does not agree." Adam had admitted he felt foolish with a cane, old before his time. "I'm only thirty-three," he'd told her bitterly, "supposedly still in my prime." Kit threaded her needle and began her stitching, not sure whether to push further or wait.

"Very well." Philippa sighed profoundly. "You may go. I will talk to Ned as well. But you must be in London no later than a week after Candlemas—and you can take that velvet with you and finish sewing it."

"Yes, my lady. Thank you, my lady." Kit expelled her held breath and bit her lip to stop herself from smiling.

At first, Adam did not sound happy. Instead, he berated her for having taken it upon herself to decide they should go home. But midway through, he ground to a stop and smiled instead.

"Home!" He gripped her by the waist and lifted her. "We're going home."

That night, the king hosted the last feast of the Christmas celebrations. There was wine, there was meat, there was music and song. And there was dancing, with Adam leading Kit out to join the others in a ronde that took her back to the first dance she'd ever danced with him, the one at their wedding feast.

Chapter 33

It was a relief to be home, to wake in their own bed, to watch his wife move about in the generous space of their solar as naked as the day she was born. Adam propped himself up on an elbow and offered a series of increasingly lewd comments, all of them with the explicit purpose of having her return to bed and him.

She did, finally, and it was a good while later that he yet again had the pleasure of watching her arise from his arms, her naked skin rosy, her hair undone. She hummed as she dressed, thick woollen hose in bright green underneath her old blue kirtle and a padded cotehardie that had seen enough wear to require new cuffs in contrasting green. Then she turned her attention to her hair, braiding it with blue and green ribbons. She left it uncovered—she always did when they were home, unless they had visitors—and came over to sit on the bed.

"My turn to ogle," she said, her hand sliding up his hairy shin. And she did, making so many ribald comments he threatened her with taking her right back to bed unless she held her mouth. That only made her laugh, a carefree sound he rarely heard anywhere but here, at Tresaints.

They'd ridden hard over the last few days, arriving late on the previous day—so late their little manor had been sunk in darkness. But they'd been expected, Stephen having ridden in advance, and so there had been a fire in their solar, clean linen on the bed, and a simple meal of cheese and bread awaiting them. What more could a man want?

The moment they set foot in the hall, they were surrounded by their children. Damp kisses and sticky fingers, warm soft bodies and high voices—Adam had to sit down so as not to fall when their three eldest swarmed all over him.

He produced a little clay horse for Meg, a juggler's ball

for Harry, and for Ned he had a wooden sword. Rattles for the twins, ribbons for Bridget and Mabel, and for John three arrowheads of Saracen design. Meg tugged at his tunic.

"And for Tom?" she asked. Adam threw his wife a desperate look. He had nothing for the foundling.

"Tom gets a silver penny." Kit slipped her fingers into the small pouch she carried on her belt and produced a coin. Meg looked doubtful. "That way he can choose himself." Kit looked about. "Where is he?"

"Out in the pastures," Mabel said. "Where else? The lad has chores to do."

"And his shoulder?" Adam asked.

"Well enough." Mabel slid Meg a look, and Adam decided to ask her again later.

John came in just as Adam was swallowing down the last of the heated wine, and with him came a gust of fresh air and Father Owain.

The conversation turned to work, and Kit excused herself, going over to sit with the women and the children. Adam heard her laugh, arms full of their two youngest, Meg leaning against her side.

"…and the court will hear their case tomorrow, my lord."

"What?" Adam blinked.

"Three of the thieves, my lord," John explained. "They were caught some ten days ago."

The rest of the morning was spent reviewing the accounts, and then John suggested they go out and inspect the sheep.

"Has she stayed away from Goliath?" Adam asked as they walked across the bailey, making for the small postern beyond the chapel.

John chuckled. "Aye, that she has, the little minx."

"And how is Tom? Truly?" Adam considered the stepping stones in the stream, looked down at his feet.

"The lad will be fine." John sounded curt. "He'll not regain full use of his arm."

"Ah." One stone at a time, fully aware of how clumsy he must seem, and Adam was across. "And the sheep?"

John tugged at his grey beard. "Lost half a dozen or so

of the lambs, and they carried off with twenty ewes, the bastards."

"Twenty?" Adam came to a standstill. "But surely you've recovered some of them?"

"No. Apparently, they were sold to a drover bound for Bristol."

Adam cursed. "Twenty? With lamb?" In his head, he calculated the lost income.

"Aye, my lord. I'm sorry, my lord."

"It's not your fault. And the shepherds?"

John scowled. "Two of them were in on it. Poor Tom saw and raised the alarm, but by the time the other louts were up and about, Robbie and Davvy were gone with their comrades—and the sheep." He shook his head. "To stab an unarmed lad like that—what is the world coming to, eh?"

"Happens all the time," Father Owain said. "Being young and innocent has never offered much protection."

Adam nodded, no more, having to concentrate on his footing. Grass tussock after grass tussock made the ground uneven and it did not take long for his foot to protest, a dull, steady throbbing that increased in volume with every step.

The sheep were too crowded—even Adam could see that—and John nodded and said they'd be moving some of them a bit further off now that the damned thieves had been caught. Other than that, the animals seemed healthy enough, most of them bulging with unborn lambs.

"Some weeks, and they'll start dropping," John said, leaning over to rub a nearby ewe between the eyes. "May God give us mild weather." He raised his hand and called for Tom, who came loping over, accompanied by two of the dogs. He had his arm in a sling, but other than that he looked hale enough.

"Settling down to your life as a shepherd?" Adam asked and was rewarded by several enthusiastic nods, words bubbling from the lad as he described his new responsibilities. He scowled when he recounted his encounter with the robbers, going on to say that John had promised him a dagger of his own, so that next time—

"No next time," Adam said firmly. "I'll not have you risk your life."

"Besides, the brigands have been apprehended." Father Owain drew his coarse, homespun mantle tight. "They'll soon be dangling from their necks."

"As they should," John filled in. "Scum."

They returned home, Adam gritting his teeth with every step. He caught Father Owain looking at him and scowled in response. Once back in the bailey, John wanted to show Adam the new filly and the expansion of the stables, and Adam suggested he lead the way, hobbling after him as best as he could.

It seemed to him everyone stared. From the dairy maid to the stable lads, they looked at him with pity, and Adam wished he could sweep his cloak around himself and disappear into invisibility, as did the heroes of the fairy tales his mother used to tell him when he was a child. Instead, he limped, eyes on the stable door.

"A cane would help," Father Owain said.

"So everyone tells me. But I don't want one."

"No? Why not?" The priest scratched at the red curls bordering his tonsure.

Adam turned on him. "Because I'm not old and decrepit!"

"No," Father Owain replied, "you're middling young and crippled." Adam was tempted to strike him, even raised his arm to do so, but the priest stood his ground, regarding him steadily out of eyes the colour of amber. "No use lying to yourself, my lord." He pointed at the foot. "It will never get better, and the only choice you have is whether you will make it tolerable to walk or live through days of endless pain. God does not like needless suffering."

"I don't want a cane." Adam made an effort to keep his voice calm.

"So instead you'll limp and hobble and further destroy your foot." Father Owain nodded. "A wise choice."

"You don't understand," Adam said.

"No, of course I don't—I don't walk in your shoes. But if it were me—"

"It isn't." Adam held up his right hand. "This is my sword hand, Father."

"You have another hand. Besides, think of the cane as a weapon," Father Owain suggested. "A heavy cane, well wielded, can offer quite some protection, and if you were to reinforce it with steel…"

"Oh?" Adam said, interested despite himself. "And what do you know of fighting?"

Father Owain grinned. "I have not always been a priest. Once I was a devil of a fighter. Come to think of it, at times I still am, which causes my confessor much concern."

Adam could well believe that. The man was built like a barrel and was surprisingly light on his feet. "A former man-at-arms?"

"Me?" Father Owain burst into laughter. "Bless you, my lord, no, nothing like that. I merely have a bad head for ale." He grew serious. "It is a foolish man who allows vanity to rule him."

"Vanity? I am a knight, a fighting man."

"Not anymore. Not on foot." The priest stood aside to allow Adam to enter the stables first. "But you already know that, my lord."

Two days later, Adam gave in. All this walking back and forth over the uneven terrain of pastures and fields ready for the ploughing had his foot shrieking in agony, and so he ordered the resident carpenter to make him a stout cane.

"I already have one for you, my lord," Sam said. "Father Owain told me to have it ready as soon as possible." He produced a heavy, polished length of dark wood, the tip shod in iron, its entire length reinforced with ironwork. "Crack someone over the head with that and they'll not move much."

"No." Adam swung the cane back and forth a couple of times before inspecting the intricate design on the knob, thin bands of iron shaped into a sphere.

"Gareth did that," Sam said, referring to blacksmith. "Do you like it, my lord?"

"As much as one can like a cane," Adam replied. Gingerly, he leaned his full weight on it. It would do.

He found Father Owain in the chapel. "You knew I'd give in."

"No. But I supposed you wise enough to understand what was best for you." The priest continued polishing one of the silver candlesticks that normally stood on the altar. The little space was alive with light, the winter sun streaming in through the eastern window to dance over the tiled floor. Adam approached the altar and crossed himself before sitting down beside the priest.

Other than the brisk back and forth of the vinegar-drenched rag Father Owain was using, the chapel was peacefully quiet, as if slumbering in the January sun. From outside came the muted sounds of dogs and pigs, laughing children and talking men, but in here it was just Adam, the fat priest, and his thoughts.

"It's not only the foot, is it, my lord?" Father Owain's soft voice broke the silence. "Something else is bothering you."

Adam crossed his arms over his chest and leaned back against the wall, long legs extended in front of him. Father Owain went back to his polishing, Adam went back to his thoughts.

"I am being torn apart," he said, surprising himself by voicing this out loud. "By loyalties," he explained with a crooked smile. "Those I have sworn and those of the heart."

"Not uncommon these last few years." A final swipe, and Father Owain decided he was done, setting down the candlestick.

"No." Adam found an unravelling thread on his sleeve and rolled it back and forth between his fingers. "I love them both—my present master and my first one."

"And is that a problem?"

"They don't always love each other." He fixed his gaze on the triptych that adorned the altar, and the painted Christ smiled benignly at him. "Sometimes I fear that in doing my duty to one, I will hurt the other."

"It is out of your hands," Father Owain said. "You can

only do your best to help them both." He pointed at Adam's cane. "Maybe it's God's will that you be the prop they need."

"Kings and earls rarely need help from men like me."

"All men need a friend when things are dire." Father Owain gnawed his lip. "Is it Mortimer or the king you fear for?"

Adam looked for the painted angel peeking out from behind one of the pillars. "They say it is dangerous to fly too close to the sun," he replied cryptically. Mortimer would never hurt the king—Queen Isabella would never forgive him if he did. But should the king move against Mortimer, there was nothing Queen Isabella could do to stop him.

"It does help, doesn't it?" Kit clapped a hand to her head to keep her green hood from flying off and turned her back to the wind. Her cheeks were red after their hour out among the sheep, and when she slipped her hand into his, it was like grabbing a trout from an icy stream. They'd seen the first of the lambs into the world earlier that day, and it was Kit's opinion there'd be more the coming night. Adam hoped not. Lambing had his wife out at all hours of the night, and where she went, he felt obliged to go too.

"What helps?" He tugged at her hand, bringing her close enough to envelop her in his thick sheepskin cloak.

"The cane."

"Aye." A week of using it on a daily basis, and he could already feel the difference in his foot. That he also enjoyed using the cane to swipe at shrubs and stab at tussocks was not something he felt inclined to tell her—but he suspected she knew, having caught a glimpse of her some days earlier while he was swinging the cane this way and that, cheered on by Father Owain.

"Have you spoken to Meg?"

"Mmm? Oh, about Goliath. Aye, I have. She'll not ride him again." No need to tell her the bribe had been huge, Meg skipping with joy when he promised her the new filly to be hers—if she behaved. Beside him, Kit chortled.

"I already know," she said. "Did you truly think a child

that young could keep something like that a secret?" She leaned closer. "Or that I don't know that you and Father Owain spend hours perfecting your skills with your cane?" She stood on her toes and kissed his cheek. "Our priest is quite the worthy opponent, isn't he?"

"Aye." And relentless, coming at Adam over and over again with his yew stave. "He quotes Scripture in time with his blows," he told Kit. "Quite intimidating to hear him yell about the riders of the Apocalypse."

Kit crossed herself. "May we be spared such beasts in our lifetime."

"Amen to that."

Chapter 34

Prior to her coronation, Queen Philippa was lodging in the royal apartments at the Tower.

"Whenever I ride in here, I think of…" Kit's voice trailed off. Very few knew of Adam's role in Lord Mortimer's escape, and from the look he threw her, that was how he wanted it to remain. Once within the inner wall, they dismounted, Kit complaining she was frozen stiff.

Adam shrugged and rubbed a gloved hand up and down his leather riding breeches. "You could wear something like this. Under your kirtle."

"And what makes you think I don't?" She shook out her skirts.

An interested gleam appeared in his eyes. "You do?"

"Should my husband want me to, I can show him later."

"Your lord husband is looking forward to it." He leaned closer. "And to divesting you of them."

Their banter was interrupted by one of the queen's pages. Kit squeezed Adam's hand and told the page to lead the way.

The windows in the apartments faced the Thames, the brown waters choppy with the returning tide. Queen Philippa was seated in one of the embrasures, playing with a puppy. Kit greeted her mistress with a deep reverence, was graciously invited to rise, and soon enough she was seated among the other women, making huge eyes at the various half-finished garments. Cloth of gold in red and green, samite and velvet, miniver furs, and a magnificent cloak edged with ermine—a minor fortune was displayed on the large table, further augmented by pearls and jewels, which were to be sewn on at the last moment.

"Here." Queen Philippa handed Kit a heavy girdle, encrusted with pearls and gold thread. She spread her hands over her round belly. "Mathilde says I must emphasise my belly with my garments. I am not convinced it needs emphasising." She frowned down at herself. "Do I look fat?"

"Fat, my lady?" Kit shook her head. "What does your king and husband say?"

"Ned?" Philippa cupped her breasts, so much rounder and heavier than before. "He likes it, I think."

"All men like it," a familiar voice said, and Kit turned to smile at Margaret, Countess of Kent. She'd missed the lady, and had been relieved to hear she'd returned safe and sound to England, the plans to go on a pilgrimage to Santiago abandoned. "Kit, how nice to see you again," Margaret continued, shaking her head when Kit sank into a reverence. "Not between friends, Kit."

Margaret sat down beside Philippa, puffing loudly as she patted at her large belly. "I have yet to meet a man who does not swell with masculine pride at the sight of his equally swelling wife." She winked. "Even their cocks swell."

Mathilde pursed her mouth. "Copulation is forbidden while the woman is with child."

Margaret rolled her eyes. "A lot of things are forbidden, and yet people do them all the time. Had God not meant for women and men to take pleasure in each other, why construct them so that he fits perfectly with her?"

"Hmph!" Mathilde frowned. "Do not listen to them, my little queen. I am sure your mother would not approve of such lewd observations."

"Nothing lewd in a wife and a husband lying with each other," Margaret reprimanded sharply. "It is a gift, to find carnal love within a marriage. Far better than finding it outside of it."

"We must think first and foremost of our souls," Mathilde said primly.

"You do that," Margaret said with a laugh. "I think life is far too short not to live it to the full. Now," she added, turning to the queen, "how are you feeling about the upcoming event? Edmund says he and Thomas are to act your pages on your ride to the abbey."

"The king wished it so." Philippa smiled blandly. "His

two handsome uncles, showing the Londoners just how loyally they stand by the king and his queen."

"Just so." Margaret sat back, a shadow crossing her face.

"Yes," Philippa continued. "Ned says it is important that the royal family present a unified front, especially now that there are all these ridiculous rumours about the former king—may he rest in peace—still being alive."

"Not everyone considers them ridiculous," Margaret said.

"No?" Philippa slid her fingers over a half-assembled sleeve, pausing to inspect an embroidered vine. "Well, those that don't are indirectly fomenting rebellion." She looked directly at Margaret. "And we can't have that, can we?"

Margaret blanched. "No, my lady, of course not."

"Rebels should be hanged, I say," Philippa said. "Don't you agree?"

"Y-y-yes, my lady." Margaret stuttered. Kit pretended great immersion in her embroidery, uncomfortable with how elegantly their little queen was flaying the countess.

Philippa smiled. "I knew you would. After all, how would it look if the Countess of Kent expressed any sympathy for rebels?" She stood. "I need to try this on," she said, picking up the sleeve. "Kit, will you help?"

They retreated behind a screen.

"Ned told me to warn her," she confided to Kit in a whisper. "Do you think she understood?"

Kit couldn't suppress a bubble of nervous laughter. "Oh yes, my lady."

"Let's hope it is not too late," Adam said when Kit told him all this. "As I hear it, Mortimer will soon have proof of Kent's treason."

"Proof? If he had such, would he not act?" It had been a long day, and her fingers were numb after all that sewing. The coming days would be just as long, to judge from the unfinished state of the queen's wardrobe

"Aye." Adam opened one of their chests and dug about, disordering what she had ordered. "Without evidence, he can do nothing unless the earl acts. And if the earl heeds his wife, he will desist." He pulled out new silk hose and the new tunic she'd recently sewed him. "What is this? Even new braies?" he teased, producing a pair.

"The queen wants us all to look our best at her coronation." Kit sighed. "I just wish it was over."

She would be going by barge to Westminster while Adam and his men were riding guard to the procession through London. The king had presented his wife with a new palfrey, a gentle little thing with a tail that nearly swept the ground and a mane to match. Caparisoned in the royal arms, the mare would carry the queen through the city, with Kent and Norfolk riding on either side of her, for the day dressed as the queen's pages.

"Norfolk was none too pleased about that," Adam said with a laugh, replacing the new clothes once he'd found a clean shirt. "Thomas would have preferred to ride in his earl's robes."

"I dare say he can change later." Kit set down her brush. "Philippa is planning a cavalcade of different garments." It fell to the queen's ladies to supervise all this, and Kit had her head full of things to remember: silk hose, garters, new sleeves, cloaks, veils, circlets, jewels, embroidered footwear, fur-trimmed hoods…

"The king will be equally resplendent." Adam pulled off his shirt and limped over to the ewer, proceeding to wash himself thoroughly. He used his discarded linen to dry himself and ran a hand over the bristles on his face. "A waste of gold, all this finery."

"The queen says the people expect a pageant."

"Aye. But they'd prefer lower taxes." He scrubbed at his damp hair. "It still itches," he grumbled, and Kit came over to inspect it.

"Nothing," she told him. "No lice, no fleas."

"Thank the lord for that. I wouldn't want you to threaten me with a spanking." He grinned. "Most fun I've had in months, seeing you chase after our children to scour them clean of vermin."

"They had fleas," Kit reminded him but couldn't quite stop herself from smiling back.

"*A* flea," he corrected. "In Ellie's cradle." He pulled a clean shirt over his head.

"It's the cat," Kit said. "Meg shouldn't be sleeping with him."

Adam burst out laughing. "Now that you've washed him, I'm sure he is as flea-free as she is. But he will never forgive you for doing it—and neither will Meg."

"As I won't forgive him for scratching me."

"What did you expect, sweeting? Flea is no biddable kitty." Adam kissed her brow. "But a very clean kitty."

She looked radiant. Adam bowed deeply as the queen approached. Her unbound hair had been brushed to a shine and was covered by a veil so sheer it added to the lustre rather than hiding it. Heavy folds of green velvet spilled down to the ground, the fabric further enhanced by intricate embroideries in gold and red. One of the ladies approached with a cloak, the afternoon sun setting the red-and-gold cloth on fire.

At last, she was mounted, and her ladies made the final arrangements, draping the heavy cloth of gold to lie just so over the horse's rump. The earls of Norfolk and Kent rode up to take their place. Adam called out orders, his men fell in line, and with a dazzling smile at her husband, Queen Philippa urged her horse into a steady walk.

All along Tower Street, up towards Cheapside, people stood as crammed as herrings in a barrel, waving and cheering as the queen rode by. The streets had been swept, the trollops and beggars banished out of sight, and someone had even gone to the trouble of washing the gutters clean of waste. People shouted blessings, they threw posies of dried herbs tied with ribbons, and Queen Philippa smiled and waved, dipping her head in a slight bow at every church they passed. From the upper storeys, people wished Philippa happy, yelled to tell her they were praying for a prince. Church bells rang, in a corner a group of minstrels broke out in song, and everywhere people drank the queen's health, the wine and ale provided by the king flowing freely.

In some of the narrower portions, the crowd got too close,

hands reaching out to touch the queen. Her two overlarge royal pages placed themselves protectively at either side, Adam had his men on foot trot up to encircle the queen and her horse, and there was jostling and curses. Someone cried out that all of this was a sham—the old king lived and would soon return to claim his throne.

If she heard, Queen Philippa chose to pretend she hadn't, maintaining a smile on her face, but from where Adam was riding just behind her, he saw her hands tighten on the pommel. Thomas, however, turned to look for the speaker and scowl. Once on Cheapside, the pressure eased, and it was back to posies and cheers, to wine-fuelled outbursts of songs lauding their queen.

When they finally rode into the large bailey of Westminster, the king was already there, pacing impatiently from side to side.

"Philippa!" He leapt towards her, the dark blue of his robe billowing behind him. Up went his arms to receive his queen, who slid into his embrace and was gently held in his arms for a heartbeat or two before he set her down on the cobbles beneath. "You are cold," he said, taking her hands in his and rubbing them briskly.

"My face is stiff," she replied. "I had no notion smiling could be such an effort."

"But it was fun, was it not?" The king gave her an indulgent smile.

"It was. I think they liked me."

"Better for them that they do," Edward growled, making her laugh.

Adam handed over Raven's reins to Stephen. "Lady Kit?"

Stephen nodded in the direction of the older parts of the palace. "You have rooms beyond St Stephen's."

"And you?"

"The anteroom, I reckon." Stephen gave Adam a quick smile. Recently promoted to squire now that Gavin had become one of the king's men-at-arms, he was entitled to a pallet in Adam's chamber, but invariably this converted to a pallet just outside the door—Adam preferred it that way.

Adam fell in step with Thomas. "You make an excellent page. Not, perhaps, quite as handsome as your brother, but all the same a passable page."

Thomas snorted. "Dress Edmund up as a monk and he'd still look handsome."

"Aye, the features of an angel, that one." Tall and fair, with a face that would have made the archangel Michael weep with jealousy—assuming angels were ever afflicted by such base human emotions—Edmund commanded attention wherever he went.

"A pretty face can hide all sorts of sins," Thomas replied, looking glum. "My brother is up to something."

"Rebellion?" Adam asked in an undertone.

Thomas scowled. "Dear God, I hope not." He unbuckled his sword belt and called for one of his pages to take it. "If so, he is a bigger fool than I took him for." He shot Adam a piercing look. "Have you heard something?"

Adam inhaled. "Aye. I—" He broke off as Mortimer came strolling towards them.

"Norfolk," he said. "May I have a moment of your time?"

"I must change." Thomas tugged at his tabard. "I'm not about to wear this to the hall."

"No?" Mortimer looked him up and down. "I think it rather suits you—an overt declaration of your loyalty to our king and queen."

"I have no need to declare my loyalty," Thomas said stiffly. "So what is this matter you want to discuss?"

"Beatrice." Mortimer's face softened. "Her mother misses her, and I hoped to convince you to allow her to visit Ludlow for some weeks."

"Ah." Thomas pulled the tabard over his head. "That should not be a problem—once all her dowry lands have been turned over to my stewards." He bowed slightly. "And now, if you'll excuse me, I must rush."

"Bastard," Lord Roger said to his back. "A mother pining for her daughter, and he quibbles about the dowry?" He turned appraising eyes on Adam. "What were you talking about?"

"Angels," Adam replied.

"Angels?" Mortimer burst out laughing. "That is so incredulous I am inclined to believe you."

"I am glad to hear that, my lord," Adam retorted. "I must to my rooms, my lord. I too am expected to change."

Mortimer waved him on his way. He was already attired for the coming festivities in red and black adorned with silver. The cloak alone had to cost what Adam's entire wardrobe was worth, black velvet lined with red silk, embroidered with silver roses and trimmed with marten fur.

Mortimer gave him a little smile. "Being an earl comes with expectations."

"Begging your pardon, my lord, but you have always had a weakness for rich and colourful garments."

"Yes," Mortimer drawled, adjusting his black robe. "How fortunate I can afford being vain." He turned his back on Adam and raised his arm to catch the attention of his two sons, as richly, if somewhat more soberly, dressed.

A day later, and all Kit wanted to do was to retire to the comfort of her bed and the arms of her husband. She'd been up at dawn to help dress the queen in her first set of clothes, and then it seemed to her the day had been a whirlwind of clothing changes, the most striking of all being the grey-and-scarlet samite she'd worn for the short procession to Westminster Abbey, where she'd been crowned by the archbishop. Not that Kit had been there, being far too busy preparing the next set of garments.

"Too much food," she groaned to Adam as they hurried towards the hall for supper. "Too many people, too much incense, too much wine, and far too many garments and girdles and…ugh!"

They bumped into Geoffrey Mortimer at the entrance.

"Back from France, my lord?" Kit asked.

"Yes." Geoffrey stood aside to allow Kit to enter first. "Montagu and I came over on the same ship from Wissant." He shivered. "Awful crossing. Had me thinking of that old story about Henry the first of that name and the drowning of his son."

"My lord?" Kit was perplexed.

"The son was crossing from Normandy to England, but the ship he was on went down," Adam explained. He smiled at Geoffrey. "Close to two centuries ago. These days, ships are more seaworthy than they were then."

"Tell that to Montagu. At one point, he lashed himself to the railing so as to be able to spew up his innards without falling overboard."

Adam laughed. "Not a sailor, our Montagu."

"No," Geoffrey agreed. "More of an emissary—to the pope." He studied Adam intently, as if hoping for some sort of reaction. Kit, standing close enough to her husband to press her thigh against his, felt his muscles tensing, but other than that all he did was look mildly bored.

"How can he know where Montagu has been?" Kit asked Adam as he handed her down the long lines of tables to where they were to sit, far from the centre of things but with a view of the high table. Snow-white tablecloths covered the tables that extended endlessly down the large space; torches in their sconces cast flickering light that did little to dispel the shadows that lurked beneath the dark ceiling so high above.

From the walls, a procession of knights stared down at the revellers, and it took Kit some time to identify the various tapestries as depicting King Arthur and his knights. Tonight, the image of King Arthur and Guinevere hung just behind the king's elaborate chair, his newly crowned queen seated beside him on cushions of red. Candlelight gleamed off goblets of gold and silver, off the crowns that adorned both the king and his lady.

"Nothing happens here without Mortimer finding out." Adam's voice could scarcely be heard above the surrounding din. He held her as she stepped over a trestle, a hand to her back as she sat down, and then he swung his own legs over to join her, propping his cane up between them.

"No?" Kit had her mouth to his ear. "And yet I'd wager Mortimer doesn't know what Montagu went to see the pope about."

Her husband grunted in response, muttering that he'd not even known Montagu had gone to France in the first place.

"You were at Tresaints," Kit reminded him. She shook her head at the page who scurried forward to offer her wine and leaned forward to study the selection of dishes. At the high table, a swan was being presented, lifelike for all that it was dead and cooked. At their end, it was goose and pork with mushrooms, hare stewed in sweetened wine and onions, an assortment of smoked meats and dried fruits, and various pies—most of them no more than middling warm.

A group of troubadours entered to serenade the queen, and she blushed prettily while holding her husband's hand as they sang of roses without imperfections, ladies of honour and virtue, and brave, gallant knights. Kit picked at her food, studying the high table. Thomas was involved in a heated discussion with his brother. As always, Edmund outshone all males present, white-and-red robes adorned with pearls and jewels ensuring everyone looked his way at least once. Beside him, Thomas looked sombre, dark clothes matching the scowl on his face.

"She's not looking well," Kit commented to Adam, discreetly gesturing at Edmund's wife. Margaret wasn't eating, her hands moving up and down over her distended belly.

"A restless child?" Adam asked, showing more interest in the roasted ribs.

"A son, she says." Kit nibbled at a piece of cheese. "Or hopes."

"Aye." He speared a mushroom. "The earl needs a spare." He lowered his brows. "Now what?"

"Hmm?" Kit dislodged a corn of allspice from the piece of pork on her trencher.

"Maltravers," Adam said. "And one of his men."

The two men were making their way to the high table, moving as discreetly as they could along the walls. At their approach, Mortimer rose, leaned over to whisper something to Queen Isabella, and moved to meet them. The three men disappeared into the shadows.

Kit had just bitten into a dried apricot when they

reappeared, Mortimer tucking a document into his sleeve before returning to his seat. Maltravers and his man made for the door, and at the high table Lord Mortimer raised a goblet to his mouth to hide his smile.

Chapter 36

"That man, he looks as content as if his geese were laying golden eggs," King Edward commented to Adam. "It makes me itch, the way he smiles at my uncle."

"Aye, my lord." Ever since that secret delivery, Mortimer went about with a spring to his step and a lurking smile that broadened into a grin whenever he clapped eyes on Kent. If it made the king itch, Mortimer's smile caused Kent to scamper off like a rabbit faced with a lurcher.

"He's up to something," the king said, whistling for Lancelot, who'd disappeared into a nearby copse. "And I'm not convinced I'm going to like it." He looked at Adam. "Do you have any notion what he's planning?"

"No." Adam gave him an affronted look. "I'd have told you if I did, my lord."

The king rolled his eyes. "I'm asking, not accusing." He grinned. "And don't sulk, Adam, it doesn't suit you."

Adam snorted. "I wasn't sulking."

"Yes, you were." Edward gave him a perceptive look. "You don't like it, that I spend so much time with my young barons, and so little with you."

"It is not my place to have an opinion on whom you spend your time with, my lord," Adam replied, not about to admit how excluded he'd felt lately, the king rarely inviting him to join him and his companions. Not like it had been in the past, when Adam was the self-evident choice of confidante.

"No, it isn't. But the fact that I choose to spend my time with Will and Ralph and those two burrs up my arse, the de Bohun twins, does not mean I hold you in less regard."

Adam pretended interest in his gauntlet. "Aye, it does, my lord. Not to wonder, what king would want to spend time with his lame knight?"

The king flushed. "I said that in jest."

"And now everyone calls me that. Besides, the reason you avoid me has nothing to do with my foot. It has everything to do with him, Lord Mortimer."

The king's nostrils widened. "How so?"

"You know I love him. And despite saying that you trust me, you don't always do."

"*I* do," the king said softly. "I trust you with my life, you know that. But others—"

"—don't," Adam filled in flatly.

The king halted his horse. "There will come a time when you won't be able to save us both."

"And you think I don't know that, my lord? That I don't live and breathe that every day?" Adam searched the surrounding horsemen for Mortimer, riding side by side, as always, with his queen. With his hair uncovered, his high cheeks flushed, and those dark eyes sparkling with amusement, Lord Roger looked happy and carefree, and Adam couldn't stop himself from smiling as his former lord raced his roan over to a nearby willow to pick a sprig of catkins for his lady. He turned back to the king. "But I am your man, my lord."

King Edward had his eyes on his mother and Lord Mortimer, at present riding so close together they could hold hands—were holding hands.

"You are," he finally said before urging his horse into a canter. "My trusted knight, mine to command." Adam gave Raven his head and followed him.

When they reached the Itchen, Adam held in his horse. The bridge spanning the river was packed with people on their way out and into Winchester, but at the sight of the royal banners and the men-at-arms, they pressed to the sides so as to allow the king to pass. Someone called out a 'Bless you', and the king stood in his stirrups and waved his hat in response.

"He knows how to handle a crowd," Thomas said, having ridden up to join Adam. He smiled at his nephew. "And look at them, they adore him."

"The wenches do," Adam corrected, watching the king blow a kiss to a blushing maiden. More cheering, more hands extended towards him, and Adam brought Raven up closer, ensuring no one came close enough to harm his lord. They rode up the High Street in tight formation, took a left, and soon enough the gate of the castle stood before them, the English lions snapping in the March breeze.

The Bishop of Winchester was waiting in the bailey, accompanied by the Earl of Lancaster. Mortimer's mouth thinned, and yet again Adam wondered what had gone wrong between him and Bishop Stratford, such an eager supporter of Mortimer and Isabella back in 1326, now more often than not found siding with Lancaster.

The king greeted the bishop affably, stopped Lancaster from bending knee to him, and suggested the three of them repair indoors without waiting for Mortimer or Queen Isabella to dismount.

"That will not go down well," Thomas said with a little chuckle. "Look at them, running in their haste."

Mortimer wasn't running. He was striding. Isabella, however, was trotting, veil billowing behind her.

"What is going on?" Thomas asked casually.

"Going on with what?" Adam threw his reins to one of the stable lads and made for the litters.

"Mortimer." Thomas pulled him to a halt. "If I didn't know better, I'd think he was planning to cook Edmund and eat him whole."

"I don't know." Adam waved at Kit, who returned the gesture listlessly. She hated riding in litters, and from her green face, today had been no exception. "Why don't you ask your brother?"

"Edmund? How would he know why Mortimer looks as content as a rat in a cheese cellar?"

"It has to do with him, doesn't it?" Adam lowered his voice. "He hasn't done anything foolish as regards the former king, I hope."

Thomas paled.

"Thomas?"

"I don't know," Thomas said hoarsely. "But knowing him as well as I do, I don't take it for impossible."

"If he has, Mortimer knows—has known since Philippa's coronation."

"Knowing and proving are two different things. If he had proof, he would have acted."

"Aye," Adam said, more to reassure his friend than because he agreed with him. Mortimer was an excellent chess player and rarely made any moves without having considered the consequences. "Maybe you should suggest to your brother that he leave."

"Leave on the eve of Parliament? And how far do you think he'd get? Better to brazen it out and slip away to France afterwards."

"Maybe you should still suggest it. But if he is to leave, it must be soon." The sun had already slipped down beneath the castle walls. At most an hour to sunset, and come compline, the gates would close, making it impossible to leave Winchester without a royal writ.

Thomas' mouth quirked into a little grimace. "It is already too late. Look." He pointed to where Isabella was beckoning for Edmund to join her. Thomas inhaled and cleared his throat. "It will come to nothing. Look at how she smiles at him."

As a spider to a fly, Adam thought, but was saved from saying anything by Kit.

"Never again. No matter how much the queen insists, never again." She held a hand to her mouth. "I need some mint to chew on."

"I must say you do look green." Thomas peered at her. "But maybe that's due to the kirtle." She was in the same green she'd worn when they were wed close to nine years ago. It still fit her, although it strained over a fuller bosom now than then, something Adam found an improvement. He met her eyes and smiled, setting a hand over his heart. She flushed, and Thomas groaned loudly before excusing himself.

"He looked fraught," Kit said.

"Everyone is fraught—everyone but Lord Roger." He tucked her hand into the crook of his arm. "Food?"

Kit made a face but accompanied him to the hall.

Next morning began with early mass. The king, his wife, and mother attended, but of Mortimer there was no sign—or of Kent. Had his brother warned him? Adam frowned, attempting to remember if he'd seen the earl at last night's supper, but he couldn't quite place him there either. So maybe Kent was away, and Lord Mortimer was at this instant gnashing his teeth. Adam squirmed at this mental disloyalty towards his former lord and was so caught up in his own thoughts it was a surprise to realise mass was over, people queueing at the door to exit the little chapel.

Once outside, Adam hurried as best as he could for the main door to the hall. He had men positioned at various places throughout the bailey, others at the door to ensure no one entered with arms.

"Adam!" Thomas grabbed hold of him and yanked him to a stop. "He's been arrested!" he gasped. "My brother, Mortimer had him arrested last night." His mouth trembled, his hazel eyes shiny with tears. "I just found out—I went to look for him when he wasn't at mass, and," he coughed, "I wasn't allowed in to see him."

Adam pulled him to the side. "Have you spoken to the king?"

"Ned?" Thomas' brow cleared. "Ned! Of course, I must talk to him."

"Not now," Adam said. "He's already in the hall. Talk to him at one of the recesses."

Thomas nodded but remained standing where he was.

"Thomas?" Adam shoved him gently. "Go on, you must go inside."

He followed Thomas into the hall. Despite it already being March, a fire blazed in the huge hearth opposite the main doors, spreading little warmth in the chilly space. Light fell in through the arched stained-glass windows that gave onto the bailey, decorating the stone floor with splashes of vibrant red, yellow, green, and blue.

Men were standing in little groups, some huddled round the pillars that formed an impressive aisle leading to the dais, others by the windows. There were whispers and muttered comments, and it seemed to Adam everyone already knew: Kent had been arrested, and Mortimer intended to act the prosecutor himself.

There were calls to order, and the various representatives took their places. The king nodded for Mortimer to begin, and it struck Adam that he, of all the people in the hall, had as yet not heard the news.

"Sire," Mortimer began, and that in itself had Edward straightening up, a little wrinkle between his brows. "I have the most grievous news." He bowed deeply to the king. "A traitor, my lord. A man you trusted and loved. Your uncle—"

The king paled, half rising from his seat. "Edmund?"

"No!" Thomas said. "This is a farce!" He shoved at one of the men standing in his way. "Let me through, you oaf!"

Mortimer held up his hand. "My Lord Norfolk had best respect this assembly, or else—"

"Don't believe anything he says, Ned," Thomas yelled, and the king flinched at the far too familiar address. "Mortimer is—"

"Silence!" Mortimer thundered. "Hold your tongue, Norfolk, or I'll have you dragged out."

Adam had hold of Thomas, arms tight round his waist. "There's nothing you can do," he whispered urgently. "Mortimer will have you thrown in a room somewhere if you don't behave."

"Behave?" Thomas hissed. "It's my brother, Adam."

"I know." Adam hugged his friend. "I know, but for now you must listen."

"Listen as he spews out lies?" Thomas half sobbed. "As he presents concocted evidence?"

Adam held him even harder. "He'd never concoct evidence, Thomas."

"No," Thomas moaned, collapsing against Adam. "No."

Adam staggered under his weight but managed to remain standing. At Mortimer's command, Kent was led in—in chains—and the king stood.

"Chains, Lord Mortimer?" His mouth twitched, and

he avoided looking at his uncle, a pitiful sight, far from his normal, elegant self. There was a tear in his hose, blood stained his tunic, and one eye was swollen shut.

"A precaution, sire," Mortimer said smoothly. He waited until the king had sat down and turned to address Parliament. "I have here a letter; allow me to read it out loud." He cleared his throat, and at that moment Adam could have punched him in the face. Mortimer was enjoying this, all the way from how Kent was quaking in front of him to the king's stony silence.

"*To my worshipful and dear brother, I pray heartily that you are of good comfort, for I shall soon ensure that you are freed of your prison and delivered from the ordeals you have suffered. You should know, my dearest liege and brother, that I have pledges from almost all your barons and promises of men and gold sufficient to ensure you will once again be king and that those who ousted you will lie defeated at your feet.*" Mortimer paused, taking the time to look at the king, Kent, and the assembled lords. "Signed by Edmund, Earl of Kent, and with his seal affixed."

Thomas sagged but said nothing. The silence was such one could have heard a pin drop. No one looked at anything but the earl, standing very alone in the midst of the hall, but it was evident the notion of the former king being alive came as no surprise to anyone. Not a man in the hall had not heard that rumour before, and Adam would hazard quite a few held it to be true.

At long last, the king cleared his throat. His hands gripped the decorated armrests of the chair set beneath the large, gaily decorated round table that adorned the wall.

"What nonsense is this?" His voice shook. "Am I being accused of having imprisoned my father? Holding him like a common felon in a dungeon?"

"Ned," Edmund began but was silenced by the king's hand.

"King Edward, the second of that name, is dead," the king said coldly. "You should know; you were at his funeral."

"Ned, listen to me! God knows what Mortimer has told you, but I swear he's alive. Alive, Ned!" Kent gave the king a wobbly smile, unaware of just how big a hole he was digging for himself. "He'll never blame you, Ned. He knows it's Mortimer and his false French whore—"

"Enough!" King Edward snarled, and on the other side of the room, Thomas of Norfolk hid his face in his hands. "Take this traitor away." Edward's voice was thick with tears.

"Ned! Please—" Kent held up his chained hands in supplication.

"No." The king stood, wiping at his sleeves. "Take him."

"Don't touch me!" Kent snapped when one of Mortimer's men made as if to take hold of him. "I can walk on my own. Ned, don't do this!" Two beefy men had hold of him and were propelling him towards the little door that led from the hall to the private apartments. "You have to listen to me, damn it. Ned!" He clung to the stonework that adorned the doorframe. "Edward, please! Thomas, help me. Thomas!" Kent yelled, and Thomas jerked as if he'd been whipped in the face. One more man, and Kent was jostled out of the room, the door muffling his continued but fading protests.

Edward shook out his robes, adjusted the weighty mantle and gold collar. He lifted his head, looking for a long time at the assembled men before him.

"This kingdom has one king," he said. "One. There is no former king, there is nothing but the king you see standing before you. And by God, anyone says differently and I'll have them disembowelled."

Slowly, he walked down the length of the hall, head held high. As he passed, the assembled men fell to their knees. Only as he paused in the doorway did his mask collapse, the frightened lad within visible for an instant before the royal face was back in place. Adam fell in behind him, and at their backs the hall erupted with noise.

"The queen," Edward said. "I must see my queen." And he was off, running for the queen's apartments.

Kit was helping the queen out of her bath when the king barged into the queen's chamber.

"Treason," he gasped, out of breath and with a wild look

to his eyes. "Damn it, Philippa, Mortimer was right. Kent, he…he…Oh God." He slumped on the bed.

"What has happened?" Philippa wound the bath sheet around her. "Leave us," she commanded the few women in the room, but a hand on Kit's arm indicated she should stay—as should Mathilde, sitting by the hearth.

"A letter. The damned fool wrote a letter." The king kicked at one of the queen's dogs and was sharply reprimanded by his wife. "Sorry," he muttered. "I need something to drink."

Kit poured him some mulled wine and handed a cup to him. The king gripped it with two trembling hands. His mouth quivered, corners drooping, and he averted his face, dashing at his eyes.

"So?" The queen asked, turning her back on the king when she began dressing. His eyes lingered on her round buttocks, on her rounder belly.

"Somehow Mortimer got hold of a letter addressed to my father—and written by Edmund. Well, by his wife, I assume: Edmund has never been much for letters and the like. How could he be so foolish?" he demanded, his voice rising. "To send a letter like that to the constable of a royal castle and expect him to deliver it unread?"

"And what does this letter say?" Philippa asked, lifting her hair to the side while Kit did up her lacings.

"Everything." King Edward drained his cup. "He aimed to free my father and reinstate him on my throne. *My* throne." He fell back on the bed and covered his face with his arm. "And now what? Damn him to hell and back! There's nothing I can do for him," he said in an anguished voice. "Now that the accusations have been made in Parliament, there is no way I can stop the proceedings."

"Which Mortimer well knew," Philippa commented, thanking Kit as she helped her with the robe.

"Of course he did—as did my mother." He laughed humourlessly. "They've tied my hands in this matter. I must have Edmund tried. I must insist he is speaking treasonous nonsense. To do otherwise would be to admit there's a kernel

337

of truth in what he's saying, and that would leave me open to accusations of having broken my coronation oaths."

"I don't understand," Philippa said simply, coming over to sit beside him.

"A king may not hold a man imprisoned unless he's been tried and convicted by his peers," Edward explained, tracing the shell of her ear. "So if we were to assume my father was alive," he smiled crookedly at Kit, eyes sliding over in the direction of Mathilde, "which is preposterous, of course, then I'd be breaking the law by holding him a prisoner."

"Why would the earl believe your father is alive, my lord?" Mathilde asked, coming over with combs and ribbons for the queen's hair.

"I do not know," the king replied, giving her an innocent look out of bright blue eyes.

"Hmm. Might it not be in Mortimer's interests to make him believe it?"

The king gave her a long look. "Edmund wrote that letter on his own. What does it matter how he came to believe my father was being held at Corfe?" He scrubbed his hands through his hair. "He betrayed me." His eyes filled with tears. "Dear God, Philippa, what do I do?"

She opened her arms to him, and he clutched at her, hiding his face against her breasts. Kit gestured for Mathilde to leave them alone.

Chapter 37

One of Norfolk's young squires came to Adam after compline. "I can't find him," he blurted. "Not anywhere."

Adam rested his face in his hands. God's blood, but would this day never end? He felt Kit's hands on his head, her fingers tugging through his thick, unkempt hair. He knew for a fact it stood on end, a consequence of repeatedly dragging his hands through it.

"You have to find him," Kit said.

"Aye, my lord," the squire said. "Mortimer has men out looking for him, and if they find him…"

Adam nodded. An enraged Thomas would attack, and if sufficiently provoked, there'd be a murder or two, with Thomas locked up in a dungeon as well. He stood, ignoring the protesting twinges in his foot. Even with a cane, today had been too long.

At the gatehouse, he found Nicholas.

"They're out to arrest Norfolk," he said, nodding at the backs of the departing Mortimer men.

"On what grounds?" Adam asked.

"I don't know. Curfew violation?" Nicholas stroked his beard. "Does not generally have you thrown in a dungeon, but it seems in this case it will. I don't like it. Mortimer is only doing it to stop Norfolk from defending his brother."

"So we'd best find him first," Adam said, tugging on a tabard that identified him as one of the king's men. "Will you come?"

"Do cows eat and shit?" The Hainaulter grinned. "Of course I'll come, Sir Adam."

"I can come too," a young guard said. "Might help, seeing as I'm Winchester born and bred." He stepped forward, lantern in hand. "I know every tavern, every bawdy house."

"Let's hope we don't find him in one of those," Nicholas

muttered. "Imagine being apprehended with your braies at your ankles and your cock in a whore."

They moved out, lanterns shedding weak light on the cobbles underfoot. Adam said little to his companions, limping a few feet behind them. Winchester at night was different from the bustling, heaving place it was in daylight. The shutters on the ground-floor shops were firmly bolted, weak light framed doors, spilled from the odd glazed window, but other than that the streets were dark, requiring a man to mind his step unless he wanted to trip. Now and then an upper-storey window opened, and Adam had to step aside to avoid the contents of the emptied chamber pot.

The sludge in the gutters gleamed in the light of the lantern, an odorous combination of shit and urine, rotting food, and other garbage. A dead rat, a broken earthenware mug, patches of solidified grease—Adam used the tip of his cane to shove a gnawed bone aside.

It was tedious business, one tavern after the other. At one, they found Mortimer's men sharing a pitcher of wine, and they slipped back out unseen.

"How many more?" Adam asked Matt, their guide and lantern-bearer.

"Five?" Matt shrugged. "Once we reach St Swithun's gate, we'll turn back—no taverns to inspect within the close."

They reached the second to last tavern, and Adam turned to Matt.

"Here?" Adam had to laugh. "He's an earl, not a villein."

"Serves its purpose if you want to drink alone." Matt wrinkled his nose. "Stinks, doesn't it?"

"Aye, and that's on the outside," Adam said, shoving the door open. Not, he decided immediately, an establishment he'd ever frequent again, taking a step back at the pungent smell of wet wool, piss-drenched straw, and warm ale.

It was relatively empty, the keep glancing up to look at Adam.

"What do you want?"

"I fancied an ale." He peered into the smoky interior.

"Here?" The keep spat to the side. "Well, to each his own."

"Not your place?"

The keep gave him a horrified look. "Mine? This dump?" He poured Adam an ale, and after passing over a groat, Adam moved further into the room.

Sitting at a table just in front of the hearth was Thomas. More correctly, he had his head in his arms, snoring loudly.

"Thomas." Adam shook him hard.

"Eh?" Thomas lifted his head, hair and beard sticky with spilled wine.

"We have to get you out of here," Adam said. "Mortimer has men looking for you."

"Damn Mortimer," Thomas mumbled. He banged his fist on the table. "Damn Mortimer!"

"Shh!" Adam said. "Mortimer has spies everywhere." He scowled at the bawd who came prancing towards them. In a kirtle striped in yellow and green, she shouted her profession to the world, breasts near on spilling out of the generous neckline. Uncovered dark hair had been arranged in artful curls, but there was no hiding the sagging dugs, the lined face. A man would have to be desperate indeed to avail himself of her services.

"What do I care?" Thomas gave Adam a bleary look. "I'm an earl. An earl," he repeated, wagging his finger in Adam's face. "An earl, an earl, and look how much that helps." He stood, grabbing at an upright for support. "I'll kill him for this." He nodded. "Kill him."

Adam shushed him and gestured for Nicholas to come over. "We have to get back," he said. "And you have to sleep. You're no help to your brother drunk as a flea in a goblet of cider."

Thomas just looked at him, swaying on his feet. "Help? No one can help him now."

No, Adam sighed, that was probably true. "Come on. Kit will kill me if I don't get you back safe and sound."

"Kit." Thomas smiled dreamily. "Kit."

Nicholas threw Thomas a curious look.

"Just help him out of here," Adam barked.

An hour later, and Thomas was sleeping in his bed, more or less cleaned up. Adam thanked Nicholas and Matt for their help and spent some moments outside. No moon, only a scattering of stars visible in the few patches of uncovered sky. Adam leaned back against the wall, allowing himself to feel just how tired he was.

"Ah, Adam."

Adam stiffened but had no option but to bow when Mortimer appeared beside him.

"Home from your errand of mercy?" Mortimer said with a chuckle.

"My lord?"

"Oh, I have eyes and ears everywhere," Mortimer said, sounding smug. "Everywhere." He beckoned for Adam to follow him, leading the way into a little closet. A fire burned in the grate, a candle spilled light over the desk piled with documents. Somewhere among those deeds lay that damning letter, and Adam toyed with the idea of setting the whole pile on fire.

"As transparent as ever," Mortimer said drily, sitting down in the single chair. "Now please explain to me why you took it upon yourself to find Norfolk when I'd already sent men looking for him."

"Thomas is my friend." Adam shrugged. "Not that I owe you an explanation, my lord. I am the king's man, not yours."

"Is there a difference?" Mortimer enquired.

"After today, aye, there is."

Mortimer sat back and regarded Adam out of eyes as hard as flints. "And what is that supposed to mean?"

"You know well enough, my lord. You blew life into the rumour that our former king was detained at Corfe, and you made sure Kent's informants heard and saw enough to convince them—and their master—that Sir Edward was there."

"So what if I did?" Mortimer studied his nails. "A loyal man would not have acted on such information."

Adam erupted. "It was a trap! You baited it, waited, and left the fool enough rope to hang himself."

"And?" Mortimer cut himself a wedge of cheese. "He was a disaster waiting to happen—proud and vain and with the constancy of a bitch in heat."

"That is an unjust assessment."

"Does it matter? He is in chains." Mortimer smiled slightly. "It will teach Lancaster to toe the line."

"Or it will drive him over it." Adam shook his head. "You've made an enemy of Thomas for life. Will you do the same to him?"

"No." Mortimer shrugged. "Norfolk is far too cautious to fall for such a ruse."

"So then what?"

"He will get over it. Norfolk is a pragmatic man." Mortimer sounded bored.

Adam dragged a hand through his hair. "There is no honour in what you did here."

"He threatened the crown!"

"It isn't your crown."

"No?" Mortimer laughed. "I think you will find that it is. Your lordling would streak his braies with shit if he had to manage it all by himself."

"You're underestimating him, my lord."

"I think not. Our Edward wants glory and love. He wants the people to hail him with joy, bend knee at his passing. I'll make sure he gets that." Mortimer braced his hands on the table and heaved himself upright. "And if you ever dare question my honour again, I swear I will crush you as well."

Adam met his eyes. "God help you," he said softly. "No one else can."

Adam had hoped that late night conversation would have brought Mortimer to his senses, or at least appealed to his mercy. Instead, on the morrow, Mortimer was adamant: the earl had to die. The jurors huddled together, a long whispered conference that ended just as Mortimer wanted it to: the earl was condemned to die, his heirs disinherited, save by the mercy of the king.

"No!" Edmund of Kent collapsed to his knees. "No, Ned, don't…" His eyes went to his brother, back to his king. "I am your uncle! you know I never meant you any harm, never you!"

King Edward sat immobile, staring straight ahead.

"Damn it, Ned, look at me! At me!" The earl began to weep. "I don't want to die. Please, not for the sin of wanting to free my brother. I'll do anything, I'll…" He snivelled, dragging his sleeve under his nose, and Adam's heart cracked at the sight of the proud nobleman reduced to weeping like a child. "I'll walk barefoot to London and back, I'll beg forgiveness for my sins, I'll retire from court, I'll…I'll…anything," he added, "anything but death."

"Edmund," Thomas said, making as if to go to his brother, but the massive arm of a man-at arms blocked his way. "Ned, look at him," Thomas pleaded. "Please, Ned."

"There is no reprieve from the crime of treason," Mortimer said. "The king cannot pardon someone who has so threatened his crown."

For an instant, the king looked at Mortimer, and there was hatred in those eyes. He swallowed and went back to staring straight ahead.

"Ned!" Edmund flung himself forward, grovelling at the king's feet. "Dearest lord and master, forgive me. I beseech you, don't…" He hiccupped and snivelled, and all the king did was pull his robes out of reach. Kent sat back on his heels, head bowed as he wept, loudly. "My wife. My children, my unborn babe—what of them?"

Mortimer looked at him with distaste. "You should have thought of them before you rose in rebellion."

"I didn't rise! I wrote a letter. That's all I did, Ned. A letter. And you will kill me for it?"

All through the hall, men shifted, heavy fabric rustling.

The earl fell forward, gripping the king's foot. "Mercy, my liege. Mercy."

King Edward rose and left, and on the stone floor the earl of Kent curled together and wept.

Adam had to hop to keep up with the king as he rushed away from the hall. When Thomas caught up with them, the king wheeled.

"Not now!" he snarled. "And don't ask me to reconsider. I can't reconsider, damn it, I can't!" He shoved Thomas aside, tears streaking his face.

"Ned, you have to! He's my brother—your uncle."

"I have no choice!" the king roared, spittle flying every which way. Thomas made as if to grab him, the king shied away, and Adam stepped in between.

"My lord, now is not the time," he said formally.

"So when is the time?" Thomas asked bitterly. "When, Ned? After Edmund is dead? Executed as a traitor on your orders?"

The king flinched.

"Just go, Thomas," Adam said.

"My brother," Thomas' voice broke. "My fool of a brother." He whirled, pulled his hood up, and left, shoulders so bowed Adam wanted to run to him and comfort him.

"Christ and all his saints," the king whispered. "Dear God." He cleared his throat. "Make sure someone keeps an eye on him—and keep him away from Mortimer."

"Already done, my lord."

The king nodded, no more, before leading the way to his chambers.

"Have Mortimer and my lady mother escorted to my rooms," he ordered one of his squires before barking at the servant presently lighting the fire to get out. Adam inched towards the door.

"Dismiss the other guards, but you stay," Edward said, throwing mantle and robes to land in an untidy heap on the floor.

"Yes, my lord." Adam had words with the sentries posted outside and directed them to step away. He had someone fetch his sword and was buckling it into place when Queen Isabella and Mortimer were ushered inside.

Queen Isabella's brows rose at the sight of Adam's sword. "Is that truly necessary?"

"One never knows who's a traitor these days," her son replied, his back to them. He drained a third goblet of wine and turned to face them. As he remained standing, they had no choice to but do so as well.

"By what right?" he said coldly. "A royal earl, goddamn it, and the two of you took it upon yourselves to arrange that sham of a trial without informing me beforehand. You forced my hand, damn it!" He picked up a wrinkled apple. "That letter should have been handed over to me immediately. I—not you—should have decided what I wanted to do."

"These matters are better handled by adults," Queen Isabella said. Moments later, she threw herself to the side when the king hurled his apple at her. It hit the wall with a loud splat.

"These matters are best decided by the king! By me, Maman, not you!" He picked up another apple. "Instead, what can I do but order his execution no matter how much he weeps and begs." His voice shook. "All he wants is his life. His life, and I can't give it to him, not now when you've read his letter out loud, the one that proclaims my father is still alive."

"He's a traitor," Mortimer pointed out, his voice low and clipped.

"To me? I think not. My uncle would never have harmed me."

"His intention was to reinstate your father!"

A wolfish smile flashed across Edward's face. "Difficult to do as he is dead." His smile widened. "After all, you made sure of that, did you not?"

Mortimer froze. Blood drained so fast out of his face Adam feared he would keel over. Isabella hastened to his side, her eyes shooting green fire at her son.

"You know that is not true," she said. "Your father remains alive."

"Unfortunately. How much more convenient if he were truly dead." Edward bit into the apple and chewed industriously, raising his hand when his mother made as if to speak. "What matters is that we've told the world my sire is dead—I've repeated it before Parliament on several occasions, and as we all know, initially even I believed him dead." He looked from Mortimer to Isabella and smirked. "So one could argue that you did have a hand in killing him—the king rather than the man."

Isabella's hand came down like a clamp on Mortimer's arm.

"We had no choice, son," she said in a mild voice that did little to mitigate the fire in her eyes. "It was force him to abdicate or—"

"Murder him," Edward filled in calmly, taking a seat. "So, in truth, there was not much difference between what you did and having him killed, was there?"

"I would never…" Mortimer spluttered.

"No, of course not." Edward inclined his head in the direction of Mortimer. "Baron Mortimer's honour does not allow for assassinations, however convenient they may be." His face tightened. "But you have no scruples when it comes to using the law to do your dirty work. You forced my hand on this, Mortimer, and now my uncle will die."

"He threatened your crown."

"My crown or your power?"

Mortimer's eyes glittered dangerously. "I can assure you there is little difference. Without me to administer your realm, there'd be precious little gold for new armour and new horses. I work while you play at war, my liege."

"Play?" the king said through his teeth.

"What else to call your jousting?" Mortimer leaned closer. "Make no mistake, without me, you would not be at liberty to live the life you so enjoy, prancing about in all your fancy garments, all your new weaponry, while your lady mother and I keep the realm safe."

"How dare you?" Edward shot to his feet. Mortimer responded by increasing his volume.

"You are the young and golden king, the hope of your people. No need to sully your fine hands with the darker side of kingship. After all, you have me to do it for you, don't you?" His fist crashed down on the table. "Edmund overreached. Such behaviour must be punished—brutally—to ensure others don't try the same."

"And what will you do when I overreach?" Edward asked quietly. From Queen Isabella came a soft gasp. "Because one day I will, Mortimer. One day, I will reclaim my authority from you. Will you punish me too?"

"I…" Mortimer licked his lips, shared a look with Queen Isabella. His face sagged, the furrows that bracketed his mouth deepening. "I live to serve your pleasure, my liege."

"No," King Edward said. "You live to serve my lady mother's pleasure. We both know that."

Chapter 38

"No, my lady, I will not." Kit crossed her arms over her chest. "While this matter with Earl Edmund remains unresolved, I stay with my husband."

Philippa flounced onto the bed. "Unresolved? There is nothing to resolve. Ned cannot reprieve him, and so all there's left is to count down the days until his execution." She pulled a face. "How callous I sound," she muttered. "A man to die, and my husband distraught…" She looked at Kit. "They've placed Margaret in custody at Salisbury Castle—she and her children."

"They, my lady? Is it not the king who decides such?"

"You and I both know the answer to that." The queen studied her nails. "For now." She rose, elegant despite her belly, and moved over to the window. "I leave for Woodstock in the morning. I expect you to accompany me."

"I stay." Kit gave the queen a mulish look. "The king, in his wisdom, has appointed Adam as responsible for the earl's safety and well-being these his last days on earth. It is not a pleasant task, my lady, and he needs me."

Adam had gone mute. He spent more time staring at the wall than doing anything else. Come night, he lay stiff like a board in their bed, and she knew he was holding back tears—not on behalf of the earl, but on behalf of Thomas and Mortimer. So far, her attempts to have him talk about it had been spurned, but she knew her husband, and when he finally reached the breaking point, she wanted to be there, to hold him and comfort him.

"Very well," Philippa gave her a sour look. "I suppose your loyalty to your husband must be commended." She sighed. "Men need us more than they think, don't they?"

"More than they like to admit, rather," Kit corrected. She offered the queen her daily infusion, thinking few expectant mothers looked as healthy as their queen. Philippa wrinkled her nose—she always did—but drank obediently.

"It's bad for Ned as well," the queen said. "Very bad. And he hasn't exchanged a cordial word with his mother or Mortimer since the trial." She set down the cup. "I think he is afraid."

"The king?"

"He has a younger brother," Philippa said cryptically, covering her belly with her hands.

"No." Kit was adamant. "His mother loves him."

"He is no longer a child she can control." Philippa lifted one shoulder. "Once Edward comes into his own, Mortimer is gone—as is fair Maman."

"Gone?" Kit crouched to help the queen with her shoes.

"As far away as possible, preferably forever." She gave Kit a mischievous grin. "Maybe I should suggest to my dear mother-in-law that she go on pilgrimage to Jerusalem with her lover to do penance for her sins."

Kit laughed. "Taking him with her would require even more penance."

"She'll never go without him. And he would go through the fires of hell for her." Philippa pursed her lips. "I'm not quite sure Ned would do the same for me."

Kit hid a little smile: she, on the other hand, knew Adam would do anything for her.

The king and his queen left the day before Kent's planned execution, accompanied by Queen Isabella and all the ladies except one. No matter that Adam had told her—ordered her, even—to go, Kit refused, saying her place was with him. When she slipped her hand into his, he squeezed, grateful for her presence even if he had no words to tell her so.

Why the king had chosen him for this unpalatable task was at first incomprehensible until Kit quietly suggested it was because he trusted him. And so Adam had made the condemned man's last days as bearable as possible, ensuring the earl had access to good wine and good food, priests, and clerks to write his last letters. He also took care of the sealed letters himself, ignoring a scowling Maltravers.

"Mortimer will want to see those," Maltravers said.

"None of them are addressed to him," Adam replied, stuffing them inside his shirt. "A man's last words to his wife are none of Mortimer's business."

The March day dawned cold and clear. Adam had his men drawn up in good order round the scaffold, nodding at two of them to fetch the earl.

"Where's the executioner?" Nicholas asked.

Adam did a slow turn. The axe was neatly propped against the scaffold, but of the man himself, there was no sight.

"De Guirande!" Mortimer called, and Adam cursed under his breath. Of late, it was never Adam, always de Guirande.

"My lord?" he replied politely.

"The executioner has fled."

"Fled?" Adam repeated, just as the earl, in only his shirt, was led onto the scaffold. The man was trembling, whether due to cold or fear, Adam had no idea. His fair hair was dirty and lank, dark pouches under his eyes indicated he hadn't slept, and he was breathing in loud, short gasps.

"You'll have to do it," Mortimer said.

"Me?" Adam shook his head. "No, my lord, I will not do it, and neither will any of my men."

"I'm giving you a direct order," Mortimer snapped. "The man is a condemned traitor, and by order of the king he is to die—today."

"Not by my hand." Adam drew himself up straight. "It is wrong to execute him—and you know why, my lord."

"Who are you to say such? Are you perhaps a man of law? A baron of this land? You're nothing but an upstart knight, de Guirande, and I am ordering you to do as you've been ordered and sever Kent's head from his shoulders."

Adam pointed at the axe. "You do it, my lord. I will not."

Mortimer stepped up to him, close enough that his breath tickled Adam's face. "You'll pay for this. I'll make sure you do."

"I cannot do it." Adam met his eyes. "I cannot. Just as I would never have been able to sever your head when it was you who was a condemned rebel."

Mortimer blinked, took a step back. "That was different."

"Aye. You *were* a rebel—however worthy your cause. He is a misled fool, a brother drowning in guilt. And I will not kill him."

Mortimer sneered. "Always so upright, aren't you? Or is it his brother who has begged you to do this, hoping thereby to save his brother?"

"No. Thomas has shunned me these last few days." Incapable of looking his brother's appointed guard in the eye, Adam presumed.

Mortimer swivelled to look at the earl, his bound hands clasped in front of him. "I'll just have to find someone else then. Someone who is willing to respect the law."

"You do that, my lord. Or you could show clemency."

"To him? And ever after have a rabid dog snapping at my heels? I don't think so." Mortimer waved Richard over.

"You wanted something, my lord?"

"Find me an executioner," Mortimer told him. "Do it soon—before the damned earl expires of cold."

Richard looked at Adam. "Can't you just do it?"

"Or you?" Adam retorted, and Richard reared back.

"Just do it!" Mortimer growled. "Surely, you can find a wretch among the prisoners who'll wield an axe in exchange for his sorry life?" He stalked off.

"Adam?" Earl Edmund said in a high and breathless voice. "What's…" He coughed. "No executioner? Does that mean I…"

"Dear God," Richard muttered. "Poor sod."

"Aye," Adam sighed. "Poor bastard."

"Two hours!" Adam took yet another turn. "Two hours, and him in his shirt, weeping and begging for his life." He went to pour himself some ale, but his hand shook so hard he couldn't hold the pitcher. Kit moved him aside.

"Here," she said, holding the cup to his mouth as he drank. "It isn't your fault."

"I know." He gulped. "But to see him like that, reduced to a shivering wreck of a man, hoping that somehow there'd be a reprieve… Thank God the man they finally found did a clean job of it."

"It is over."

"Is it?" He quivered under her touch. "I feel soiled."

"Shhh." Her hands slid up his chest, round his neck, her fingers knotted themselves in his hair, tugging him downwards. Her lips brushed his. "Sit down."

He perched on a stool, and she knelt before him, worked off his boots, one by one. Her hands slid up his legs, under the folds of his tunic, and soon enough she was rolling down his hose. She helped him out of his tunic and shirt, crouched to feed more wood into the fire, and poured some water into the small pot she had propped against the grate.

He just sat there, drinking yet another cup of ale. Kit smiled at him over her shoulder and rooted about in one of their chests. She sprinkled crushed lavender into the ewer, carefully poured the warm water over it, and set it down on the floor beside him. She dipped a rag and began washing him.

She started with his face, gently wiping at the tears he was unaware of shedding. The warm rag, the fragrant water, the sounds she made when wringing the cloth out—Adam rested his head against the wall and wept: for the fool of a man who'd lost his life in such an undignified manner; for his king, who'd been obliged to order the death of his kinsman; for Thomas, who'd just lost a brother; and for Mortimer, his beloved Lord Roger, who had somehow lost his way.

Kit just kept on washing, her movements firm, and at some point he stopped weeping, glancing down instead at her. She was kneeling between his legs, the rag sliding carefully over his damaged foot, up his hairy shin. The firelight danced over her uncovered hair, bringing out the red in it, and when he set a finger to her cheek, she raised her face to look at him.

Kit rested her chin on his thigh, her hands slowing as they progressed up his legs. He stroked her hair, undoing her braids as he went, and at some point she shook it out, a dark cloud that spilled down her back.

Adam urged her to stand. The heavy wool of her kirtle

sighed as it fell to the floor, her chemise landing on top. She was cold, her skin breaking out in goose pimples. He rubbed his fingers gently up the skin of her belly, and she shivered. Adam stood, slid his hands down her arms to clasp hers. Kit exhaled, stepped close enough to place her head against his shoulder.

A log in the grate crackled and spat sparks over the floor. The bed creaked when he placed her ever so gently on top; it creaked again when he joined her, his mouth seeking hers. She tasted of ale, smelled of lavender and roses. Her hair tickled his skin, and her lips were so warm, so soft. Her tongue darted out to meet his, and Adam groaned, cradling her face as he kissed her until there was no air in his lungs.

They broke apart to breathe. Adam leaned his forehead against hers. She clutched at his hair and brought his mouth down to hers, ravenous, it seemed, for him. Her legs widened. He slid a hand under her buttocks and came inside—hard. She said his name. He whispered hers. They did not move. Kit brushed a strand of hair off his face.

"Love me," she whispered. "Take me, carry me with you."

"Always, my love," he replied. "Always."

Kit woke the next morning to a crick in her neck, her man a heavy weight in her arms. They had made love repeatedly, at long last falling asleep midway through a tender touching session, and she was sticky and sore—but reluctant to move. Adam slept the sleep of the dead, his exhalations warm and moist against her skin. She tugged gently at his hair and shifted to her side, causing him to grunt when his pillow disappeared.

Kit traced his thick, fair brows, the line of his stubbled jaw with her finger. A digit on his lips, and his mouth twitched, those long, straight lashes of his fluttering against his cheeks. Even in repose, he looked drawn, the mouth downturned, his brow furrowed. She leaned forward to kiss his eyelids. One corner of his mouth curled upwards.

"Sweeting," he rasped, hands reaching out to draw her closer. He was aroused, that morning cockstand of his prodding at her thigh. They rolled over, she astride, he below, already joined at the groin. No mad gallop for the finishing line, this was more an unhurried canter, a collection of sinuous movements, his eyes never leaving hers while his hands tightened their hold on her waist.

She lay spent in his arms, head on his chest. His heart hammered under her ear, and when she scraped her nails over his skin, he twitched and dug his chin into her head, telling her to lie still. He pulled the bedclothes over them, and the warmth, the familiar scent of his skin had a lulling effect. She yawned, on the verge of sleep.

"How could he do it?" he asked.

"Who? Kent or Mortimer?"

He sat up, spilling her to the side. "Mortimer, of course! He's the one who's in the wrong here."

"Is he?" Kit sat up as well. "Has it never struck you that, more than anything, your Lord Roger is afraid?"

"Afraid? No one dare touch him!"

"And yet very many want to." When he made as if to speak, she set a finger to his lips. "What would have happened to Mortimer and the queen had Kent succeeded? Do you see Kent sending them off into exile together?"

"No," Adam said after a while.

"Her they'd lock away, and him they'd kill—in a far more painful fashion than what was done to Kent." She shivered and drew up her legs to her chest. "He'd have suffered the same death Despenser did."

Adam crossed himself. "Heaven spare him that." He rolled out of bed, busied himself at the shutter to open it wide. She reluctantly left the bed and hunted about for her chemise. She should wash, but she liked smelling of him, and under all her clothes only she would know his essence and scent lingered.

Adam turned the contents of their chest upside down in search of clean braies and hose. "Mortimer and the queen duped him."

"Kent had not been discreet in his opposition to Isabella and Mortimer, had he? And besides, duped or not duped, it was Kent who wrote the letter. A letter in which he promised

355

to reinstate his brother and cast our king aside. That is treason, Adam."

"Aye." He sighed. "It just sticks in my craw, the way Mortimer went about it."

"Of course it does. Despite everything that has happened, you still hold Mortimer to be some sort of paragon of honour, but he isn't. He's a man who sits atop a very narrow pinnacle and contemplates just how hard he'll hit the ground when he finally topples."

Adam paled.

"It's inevitable," she said gently. "Even he knows that. But let us hope it happens without bloodshed. If Mortimer is wise enough to retire from court before the king comes of age, then maybe…" She laughed. "Perhaps Philippa is right: maybe the solution is for Isabella and Mortimer to depart on pilgrimage together."

The comment made him smile, albeit wryly. "Lord Roger has never expressed a desire to go on pilgrimage."

"No," she agreed, noting with an inward smile that he used Lord Roger, not Mortimer. "But maybe he can be convinced to do so—by the queen."

Adam sat down to pull on his boots. "Do you truly believe that? If Lord Roger thrives on power, she is addicted to it."

"I don't know." She poured some ale and handed him a cup. "But one can always hope."

He nodded, no more. "What I don't understand is why Kent had to be executed. Why not lock him up somewhere?"

Kit just looked at him. "If there is one person on this earth who knows just how dangerous it is to keep your enemies alive, that is Roger Mortimer. After all, he is the living example of what imprisoned men can do to those who imprison them."

There was a strangled sound from Adam, and then he spat lukewarm ale all over the floor. "Kent is no Mortimer," he said once he'd recovered.

"Kent is dead because Mortimer is Mortimer." She leaned forward to dab at the ale that was dribbling down his cheek. "And, I might add, King Edward could have reprieved him. But he chose not to."

Adam laughed. "Next you'll tell me Mortimer and the king have more in common than one might think."

"I don't need to tell you what you already know. The difference is that Edward is born to be king. Mortimer just wishes he was."

"King? Lord Roger? He's never aspired to be more than one of the king's barons."

"Until he bedded a queen and found he liked it. Until he and his lady managed to depose a king and set an untried lad in his place. Until, for a brief few weeks, he could dream of a child of his own becoming the king." Kit fiddled with the embroidery that adorned the neckline of his tunic. She'd made it herself, a recurring pattern of St George crosses and stars, red and blue against the soft grey of the worsted, a colour that matched his eyes. She lifted her face to meet his eyes. "Mortimer is not the only one who is afraid. The king is too."

Chapter 39

They rode north from Winchester. On the second day they came within sight of Stratfield Mortimer, Lord Roger's magnificent fortified manor, and Adam shared a quick look with Kit, recalling with surprising clarity that day in September of 1321 when he'd first seen her.

"You wore green," he said softly, "and your hair hung loose down your back."

She smiled at him. "I'm glad you remember. I don't." Drunk on wine laced with poppy, she'd swayed towards the little chapel, accompanied by that dragon of a woman, Lady Cecily, who played the role of the bride's mother.

"But you remember what came afterwards, don't you?" He took her hand, kissed every finger before placing one last kiss on her palm.

She laughed and nestled back against him, making him reflect that sharing a horse with her was something he should do more often. At present, this was due to necessity, her chestnut mare offered as a mount to William, who'd shown up at Winchester just as they were setting off.

For the first few miles, they'd been accompanied by Thomas, a silent and grim shadow of himself, who'd said at most half a dozen words. He'd been that way since the funeral of his brother, a hasty affair conducted at Greyfriars with only Thomas and Adam present.

When they parted, Thomas to ride east to his family and lands, he'd reached across and taken hold of Adam's forearm.

"Thank you."

With that he'd been gone, a dust cloud rising behind him and his men.

"Difficult to lose a brother," William commented.

"Aye. Especially like that." Adam did not want to discuss this with William—he could see too much of his own disgust at the recent events mirrored in William's eyes. So instead they talked about those hazy, golden days in which Baron Mortimer had brought the king to his knees and obliged him to exile the hated Despensers—days in which it seemed Edward II would hold to his promises and oaths, days in which Kit and Adam had been married as part of Mortimer's victorious celebrations.

"Did not last long," William said with a sigh. "All of two months and our former king was back to plotting the return of his favourites."

Adam slid a hand round Kit's waist to hold her closer. In the aftermath of the king's broken promises, Mortimer rebelled, and Adam had feared he'd never live long enough to see his wife again. She covered his hand with hers and pressed it harder to her belly. Or any child of his, he reflected with a little smile, splaying his fingers wide over her stomach.

"Another one?" he murmured in her ear.

In response, she just tightened her hold on his hand.

"Will it be a son, you think?" William asked, and for an instant Adam thought he was referring to the little life that had just started to grow in Kit's womb, but then he collected himself and assumed he was referring to the king's long-awaited child.

"Philippa says she's certain," Kit said with a laugh.

"One must pray and hope," William said, "as does Joan of France. She is to be brought to bed of a child by midsummer if things go as planned. Philippe is hoping for a son—the little heir is a sweet boy, but not in the best of health, and it is always best to have a spare." He went on to tell them more about his recent travels to France, eyes aglow as he described long nights discussing the finer points of theology with the learned men of the university. "They're a wild lot, those students," he said with a laugh. He grinned at Adam. "I should know after my years at Oxford."

"Were you wild?" Kit teased.

William did not reply at first, battling his cloak when a sudden gust of wind lifted it. "No," he said. "I was too poor, too intimidated, too anxious to make my lord proud. So I, in difference to most, applied myself wholeheartedly to my studies." He set his hands together as if in prayer and rolled his eyes towards the skies. "I probably deserve a sainthood for that."

Adam enjoyed riding through the forests that surrounded Woodstock. Rich in game, the huge royal park was one of the king's favourite hunting areas, having the further benefit of creating a rustling, living barrier between the palace and the outside world. Once inside the outer walls, yet more woodland followed until at last the walls of the palace itself rose before them. Old like the hills, this palace was, built by one of the Conqueror's sons and since then substantially expanded and refurbished.

They rode into the bailey and were met by a cacophony of sounds, well over two dozen hounds straining at their leashes. The king was inspecting the pack, walking among them with Lancelot padding beside him. If anything, the silent presence of the king's half-wolf increased the frenzied barking. Lancelot remained aloof, ignoring all but his master.

"They're riding out now?" Adam asked one of the guards, casting a look at the sun, already dropping to the west.

"Aye." The guard shook his head. "Don't ask me why. Either he's hawking or hunting—or just riding with the hounds."

Horses were being led forward, men in hunting gear converging on the king. He recognised Montagu and Stafford, the de Bohun twins, and Ufford among them, and was surprised when Eubulus Le Strange joined them. At the king's command, they sat up, and off they went, riding by Adam without as much as a greeting. It hurt.

"He might not have seen you," Kit offered.

In response, Adam looked at Raven. It would take a blind man not to see his coal-black stallion.

He was in the stables, talking to that devil of a horse, Boreas, when the hunting party returned some hours later. He remained in the stall, large hands gentling the horse that remained as skittish as ever, listening to the men dismount, some of them calling for wine, others for ale.

The voices grew faint, the stable lads returned one by one with horses that had to be rubbed down and watered, and Adam fed Boreas the last of the parsnip he'd brought with him, rubbing his nose.

"Three mares in foal," the king said from behind him. Adam turned to bow, arrested by the king's hand. "No need, Adam." He came to stand beside him. "I heard you refused to do as Mortimer commanded you to."

"Aye, my lord." Adam gave Boreas one last pat and slid out of the stall.

"Did he die well?"

Well? Was it to die well to kneel in your shirt while a reprieved prisoner prepared to lop off your head? "It was quick, my lord."

"Quick? He was kept waiting for hours!"

Adam gave him a guarded look. "Aye, he was. The executioner ran off."

"Damned man! I find him, I'll have him taste his own axe."

Adam didn't reply.

"I'll never forgive them for this," Edward said, casting a look over his shoulder to ensure they were alone. "Never."

"And yourself, my lord?" Adam asked, causing Edward to jerk. For an instant, he feared he'd gone too far, but then the king's features relaxed into a wry smile.

"Like being pierced through the heart," he said. "One can never fault your honesty." He stooped, picked up a discarded scrap of leather, and twisted it round his hand. "No," he said at long last, "I cannot forgive myself either. Edmund was a fool—and he did write that letter—but he did not deserve to die. Some years in the Tower would have mellowed him." He inhaled. "When it truly mattered, I was not as brave as I should have been."

They emerged into the yard, golden in the evening sun. On the far side was Queen Isabella, laughing at something her daughter was saying while resting a hand on Prince John's arm. Edward's gaze locked on his brother.

"He's almost fourteen," he said. "The same age I was when my father was deposed."

"He's your brother. He loves you." Elegant where Edward was powerful, Prince John had more of his mother than his father in him—and was as vain as his entire family, the robes he was wearing in an emerald green that complemented his eyes and matched the rings on his fingers.

"I thought Edmund did as well." The king turned hollow eyes on Adam. "I never know who to truly trust."

"Being king is being lonely," Adam said with a nod. "But you have your wife, my lord. You have your brother and your friends—Montagu, Stafford, and those de Bohun pests would die for you. You have Master Bury. And you have me."

"Yes, I do, don't I?" Edward's lips curved ever so slightly. "Not bad, all in all."

It was evident the king had not made peace with his regents. While unfailingly courteous, he maintained a careful distance from both his mother and Mortimer, mostly through the simple expediency of riding out at dawn to hawk or hunt, return for dinner, and then spend most of the afternoon with his companions in the tiltyard. Not once did he participate in a council meeting; only rarely would he join in the discussions at the high table—unless they pertained to his jousting and hunting.

With one week following on another, some sort of order reinstated itself: the king was left to his youthful pastimes, and Queen Isabella and Mortimer returned to the matter of ruling the realm as they saw fit. Except, of course, that they did not know how the king spent his evenings—in seclusion with Master Bury who, as holder of the Privy Seal, more than once had to be included in Mortimer's and the queen's discussions.

"It would appear every single royal officer has been branded with the Mortimer arms," the king commented one morning, stamping his feet in the unseasonal chill of the April dawn. They were standing slightly apart, the king, Montagu, Stafford and Le Strange, with Adam not quite part of the little circle.

"Not me, my lord," Le Strange was quick to reply. "Would you want proof?" He fumbled with his clothes, and the others burst out in laughter.

"Then you must be the exception to the rule," the king said, still grinning.

Le Strange sidled closer and lowered his voice. "Being branded a Mortimer man does not exclude serving the king first."

Edward's gaze went to Adam. "No, I dare say it doesn't."

Adam wasn't sure whether to be insulted or pleased. So he concentrated his attention on Lancelot instead, one ear to the continued conversation, now conducted in hushed tones that were barely audible.

"…time is running out…" Montagu murmured.

"…once the babe is here, then…can't risk anything…" Edward said in reply.

"…plan. Now. And then…" Le Strange lowered his voice to a whisper.

Adam regarded him from under the fall of his hair. He was in two minds about Le Strange, so openly a Mortimer detractor when the man himself was nowhere close, so quick to bow and scrape whenever his path crossed that of Mortimer. A dangerous adversary—Eubulus Le Strange might be old but was as solid as an oak, built like a sumpter, for plodding perseverance rather than for the light gait of a palfrey.

The discussion ended when Adam straightened up. None of them met his eyes. With a little bow, he begged to be excused, was even more hurt when the king waved him off.

After that, Adam assumed that unless specifically ordered to, he was not expected to accompany the king on his hunts. Instead, he organised men to ride with him and spent his mornings in the deserted tiltyard, doing whatever sword work he could with only one good foot or bettering his sword skills with his left hand. It was with quite some satisfaction he then challenged some of the men-at-arms and found he could easily hold his own, sword in one hand, iron-banded cane in the other.

All the same, time weighed at times, and Kit was kept busy by the great-bellied queen, who, now in the last weeks prior to her confinement, was suffering from a constant rash.

So Adam took to walking along the Glyme, returning to the spot where Kit and he had bathed many years ago, when Tom was still in smocks and very much alive.

He was sitting in the shade, throwing pebbles in the water, when he sensed someone come walking out of the dappled forest behind him. He knew who it was without turning around. For days, he'd felt the weight of Mortimer's gaze on him, was more than aware that at times Mortimer had stood to the side and watched him in the tiltyard. But he was damned if he was going to rise and bend knee, so he pretended not to hear anything beyond the steady plops the pebbles made as they hit the water.

"I know you know I'm right behind you." Mortimer sounded amused, the soles of his leather shoes near on noiseless as he picked his way down the grassy slope.

"My lord." Adam began to rise.

"Sit, sit." Mortimer came to stand beside him. "May I join you?"

In response, Adam swept out his arm and moved his cane out of the way.

"Am I still unforgiven?" Mortimer asked as he sat down.

"What am I expected to reply, my lord? You are the power that is, I am but a lowly knight—does it even matter what I think?"

"It does to me," Mortimer said. "I will not excuse what I did. For months, Kent had been spreading lies about how his poor brother was being mistreated and abused at my behest, snide, vicious rumours painting me as a monster."

"Not only him," Adam objected.

"No." Mortimer reclined on his elbows and crossed his feet. "But Kent was building a following—his word carried weight, what with him being a royal earl. And whether or not he believed his own rumours, he was becoming a threat— to me, but also to our king." He found a straw of grass and nibbled at the soft, pale green end. "Surely you see that?" he asked in view of Adam's silence.

"Aye." Adam exhaled heavily. "I do. But—"

"I know. And no, I am not entirely proud of what I did."

Mortimer scrubbed at his jaw, uncharacteristically covered by stubble. Grey bristles, Adam noted, just as the hair at his temples was grey. "But I am human too, and Kent threatened me. Had he rallied the barons to his banner, things may well have ended cordially with the king, but me…" He shrugged. "I live in fear. There are days when it is as if I can feel the noose tightening round my neck."

It was a statement delivered in an emotionless voice, but Adam recognised the twitching in Mortimer's right eye, the way he clenched and unclenched his hands.

"So why don't you leave, my lord?" Adam kept his eyes on the water and the speeding circles his last pebble had caused.

"How can I? I can't leave her to the wolves, and she won't leave her son—she says he needs her. He doesn't." Mortimer laughed hollowly. "I know that, but she doesn't. Besides, she likes running things—as do I."

Adam turned to look at him.

"Yes," Mortimer admitted with a wry smile. "I enjoy the power. That cannot come as a surprise to you."

"No, my lord." Adam nodded in the direction of the west. "But you could wield power there, as the greatest among the Marcher lords."

"Settle for Wales when I can run it all?" Mortimer shook his head. "I was destined for this. I was made to rule, to lead. If only it had been mine…" He studied his fist. "If only he had been mine."

"My lord?"

"Edward. A son like that, what father would not be proud?" The thick gold ring round his middle finger went round and round. "The child she carried, it could have been a son. Our son." He sighed. "She says it was for the best. Me, I wish…" He cleared his throat. "No matter."

They lapsed into a comfortable silence. Adam threw yet another pebble, Mortimer chewed on his stalk of grass.

"I still think you should step aside, my lord," Adam said. "Make way for others."

"You do? And what would happen to me and mine,

do you think? They'd come after me, all of them: Lancaster and Norfolk, Surrey, and every other greedy bastard in the country."

"The king would protect you."

"The king?" Mortimer tilted his head to the side. "You don't really know him all that well, do you? Edward would not lift a finger to save me."

"I disagree," Adam said, stung by his comment about Adam not knowing the king. Perhaps more than he should be, seeing as lately he was rarely privy to the king's thoughts.

"You would," Mortimer said drily. "You have a tendency to imbue the men you serve with virtues they don't always have." He leaned over and ruffled Adam's hair. "He's no paragon. I'm no paragon. And we are both equally ruthless when so required."

Adam jerked away from his touch. "I am no mindless lad, my lord."

"No. You're the most loyal man I know and burdened with far too much integrity. In this the king agrees with me, why else is our dear Edward ensuring you are not involved when he meets to plot with his friends?" A shadow flashed over his face. "They mean to bring me down."

There was no point in denying it—Adam had heard too many bits and pieces to disagree. "What will you do, my lord?"

"Me?" Mortimer stood and brushed his long robes free of grass. "I aim to crush them."

"Crush the king? I can't let—"

Mortimer held up his hand. "The king is sacrosanct. Always. And hopefully his breeding wife will present the kingdom with an heir." He chuckled. "Any chances he will consider naming him Roger, you think?"

"None," Adam replied flatly.

"No, of course not," Mortimer murmured. "Who would want to name a babe after me?"

"My lord, I didn't mean it like that. I—"

"Of course you did." Mortimer stood looking down at him, dark eyes inscrutable in his lined face. "Do you despise me a little less now?" he asked, a hesitant tone to his voice.

"Despise you?" Adam surged to his feet. "God's truth, my lord, how can you say such? I can never despise you, however disgusted I am by your actions. I—" He bit off, cheeks scalding. "I love you," he finished.

"Yes, you do, don't you?" Mortimer's features softened. For an instant, his hand brushed Adam's cheek. "You do me proud, Adam. You always have." In a whirlwind of velvets smelling faintly of wormwood and cloves, he left.

Chapter 40

The confinement chambers were ready. The bed had been re-hung in the mildest of yellows, the walls adorned with tapestries depicting flowers and gentle creatures such as unicorns. A sanctuary for the expectant mother, the rooms were furnished with cushions and expensive carpets, a brightly coloured wooden statue of the Virgin and her child adorning the altar in the adjoining little chapel.

A new chair set before the hearth, a basket of embroidering silks with which to pass the time, ells of fine linen to convert into smocks and gowns for the eagerly awaited babe. Yes, all in all, the chambers were ready—and as asphyxiating as a prison, Kit thought, supervising the two men who were finalising the hanging of the heavy drapes that were to cover the windows. Once Philippa retired within these walls, she would not be seen until after the birth of her child.

"Never," Kit told Adam when she was given leave to accompany him on a walk. "Promise me you'll never demand that I retire to my chambers for my laying in." They were well into the cooling shade of the woods, the river running silent and dark beside them.

"You've been brought to bed of seven babes without being thus confined. Why would things change now?" He drew her close and kissed her brow. "Besides, I dislike being deprived of your company and proximity, no matter that Mabel maintains it is most inappropriate that we share a bed all the way to the birthing." There was a twinkle in his eyes. "Sharing in every sense, sweeting."

She laughed softly. "Philippa is of a like mind, but for her there is no escaping the conventions. Isabella is adamant: the queen goes into confinement after Sunday mass." She pressed her bosom against his arm in a provocative gesture. "Five more days in which she can share her nights with her husband."

"Best make the most of it, then. God alone knows how the king will manage without her."

"Oh, I am sure time will pass quickly for him. He seems most adept at amusing himself." Always with his boon companions, rarely with Adam. It made her seethe on her husband's behalf, that he be so excluded.

"Aye, he is good at that." He looked down at her, eyes dark in the shadow of the trees. "And you don't have to be indignant on my behalf, sweeting. I prefer not knowing what they might be plotting."

"Plotting or just complaining?" she asked.

"Both. But in my experience, complaining often leads to plotting." He took her hand. "What I don't understand is why Le Strange is such a welcome addition to their little group."

She heard the jealousy in his voice: he had been replaced— or so he felt—by Le Strange, who this time round had joined the court unaccompanied by his wife.

"Maybe he has knowledge of some sort?"

"Oh, aye, he knows the north like the back of his hand— every castle, every hillock. Goes on and on about it as well."

"Sounds boring."

Adam laughed. "He's none too bad, actually. And he strikes me as a man who will stand by what he says."

He led her down towards the river and a shallow indention in the ground just above the bank. They helped each other out of hose and footwear. His hands lingered for longer than required on her inner thighs as he undid her garters and rolled down her hose.

Adam took her hand and they waded out into the shallows. The water was cold, and despite the warmth of the May day, Kit had no inclination to swim. Neither, it seemed did Adam, who instead invited her to join him in the warmth of the sunny hollow.

He spread his cloak and they settled down in the grass, his hand resting on her belly, already visibly rounded. He splayed his fingers, and five distinct points of pressure travelled up her stomach, over her bosom to rest on the patch of exposed skin just below her neck. A finger slid tantalisingly along her neckline. She turned towards him, hands extended to cradle his face. He smiled under her gentle kiss, eyes closing for an instant.

His hand moved under her skirts, travelling up her legs. The sun warmed her face and her bared shins; it haloed his head. When a sudden wind soughed through the trees, it filled the air with the fragrance of linden blossoms and cool water, but when Adam kissed her, it was his scent that invaded her nostrils, that combination of leather and horse, warm, salty skin, and wool that she could recognise in the dark.

Deft fingers stroked her, sliding through her wet warmth so that she arched her hips towards his touch, desiring more than this teasing, this gentle stimulation. She could feel his arousal—hot and hard, it pressed against her thigh. And then she couldn't quite feel anything beyond his lips covering hers, his fingers causing her to climax, thighs clamping round his hand as all of her shook.

Finally, he was there, inside of her, and his voice was close to her ear as he told her just how much he loved her and needed her, how every time he saw her he wanted her, and may God be praised for having brought her into his life. It made her cry, tears leaking out of the corners of her eyes while yet again her insides clenched, arms and legs coming up to hold him close—impossibly close—as he poured his release into her.

Kit was in a mellow mood after her afternoon with Adam. Her head was full of images of her man, the afterglow of their lovemaking causing her to smile as she walked through the herbal garden, snipping mints for the queen's evening tonic. Mixed with powdered rose hips and new raspberry leaves, the end result was a pleasant enough drink that would ensure an easy labour.

Kit snorted to herself at the ridiculous thought of any labour being easy. Children were brought into the world through their mothers' pain, eternal punishment for Eve's sin in the Garden of Eden. But it was worth it—both the birthing and most certainly the begetting, at least with a man like her Adam.

She came to a halt, overwhelmed by a rush of longing for her own babies. It seemed a lifetime ago since she'd seen them last, and for all that Father Owain was meticulous in keeping them appraised of their children, it was one thing to read they were all well, another thing entirely to hold them to her heart, inhale their scent, and feel their warm weight in her arms. Once the royal infant was born, she hoped to be allowed to return home—assuming, of course, the babe was hale. Kit crossed herself, sending off a quick prayer to St Margaret and the Holy Mother that they see the queen and her child safely through the travails awaiting them.

Kit skirted a stand of black currants, turned the corner beyond the elder, and tripped over an extended leg.

"Ouff!" She landed on her hands and knees.

"Who goes there?" the owner of the leg demanded. "Who?" The Earl of Lancaster groped for his dagger.

"My lord, it is only me, Kit de Guirande."

"Kit?" Lancaster's lined face relaxed. "Ah yes. Just what any garden needs—a fair lady."

"You flatter me, my lord." She sat down beside him and brushed vigorously at her skirts.

"Truth be told, I wouldn't know. These days, I must rely on memories, and if I am to be honest, I cannot recall much of you beyond your height and willowy shape. But you have an intriguing voice, low and dark, and so I conjure up a series of pleasant images to match it."

Kit stooped to pick up her spilled herbs. "It must be difficult to lose your sight.

"Yes." A gnarled hand gripped the cane he had beside him. "A slow sinking into permanent darkness."

"Can you see nothing?"

He turned rheumy eyes her way, a whitish layer covering what had once been blue eyes. "I can still discern light and shadow."

Kit's cheeks heated. "My apologies, I should not have asked."

"It makes for a refreshing change." The old man barked out a laugh. "No one else asks. They think if they pretend

371

they do not notice I am blind, I may well believe I still can see. Fools!" His free hand fidgeted with his belt, long fingers rearranging the pleats of the tunic beneath. No matter the man was blind, he was still impeccably dressed, rich fabrics of various hues of green adorning his tall frame.

"Does it hurt?" Kit asked, studying his encrusted lashes.

"No." He gave her a little smile. "And it has the benefit of making me quite invisible to some. A blind earl is an inconsequential earl."

"But you're not, my lord."

Lancaster pressed his lips together. "I hope not."

Kit made her excuses and went on her way. In the furthest corner of the garden, two huge rosebushes were covered with buds, some of them already open into flower. White roses always made Kit think of her mother, which was why she drifted off in the direction of the bushes. The queen would like a bloom or two, so Kit stood on her toes to pick one just as the king came barging through the thorny brambles.

"Damnation," he muttered.

"My lord," Kit said politely from behind him, wondering why on earth he'd chosen to enter the garden through the rose brambles rather than through one of the gates.

The king whirled. "Kit!" He flushed. "I…" He looked at the flower in her hand. "I was going to pick some roses for Philippa."

A lie, as demonstrated by how his face went an even darker shade of red.

"Here, my lord." She handed him the one she'd picked. "She will be most pleased."

"Truly?" He laughed. "These days, my lady wife is difficult to please."

"Is she?" From what Kit had gathered, the king and queen enjoyed their nights together, Edward ignoring his mother's displeased frown when he announced he was planning on spending yet another night with his wife.

"In some ways yes, in some ways no." He winked. "Is it common that breeding women become so eager and welcoming in bed?"

"Really, my lord!" Kit arranged her face in an expression of censure, biting her cheek not to grin. "It is a sin to bed with your breeding wife. Besides, such things should not be discussed with others than your wife—or your chaplain."

"And what would a chaplain know about breeding women?" the king asked. "Maybe I should ask Adam instead," he added with a grin.

"Quite the novelty, for you to talk to him about anything." Kit endeavoured to keep her tone light.

King Edward scuffed at the ground with his boot and avoided her eyes. "Who I talk to or not is my concern, Lady Kit."

She made him a reverence, and for the third time his face flooded with colour. "Of course, my liege. But best not come to Adam for marital advice when you do not as much as give him a good day."

"That is an exaggeration."

"Is it?" She collected her herbs and the rose she'd picked for herself. "I think not. And while Adam will not tell you as much, I can assure you he's hurting."

"Some matters do not concern a lowly knight," the king said frigidly.

Kit took a step back from him. "I beg you excuse me, my liege. Your wife needs me." She turned and half ran down the path lest she do something truly stupid like slap the inconsiderate lout.

At the gate, she threw a look over her shoulder. The king was no longer by the roses. Instead, he was sitting side by side with Lancaster.

After mass on a beautiful May Sunday, the king and queen presided over a splendid feast before the king escorted his lady wife to the rooms in which she would await the arrival of her babe. Adam had the guards turn their backs on the king and the queen, their bodies forming a screen of sorts, behind which Edward bid his teary-eyed wife a tender farewell and God speed.

Someone coughed, and the king and his queen broke apart.

"Take care of our son," he said, setting his mouth in a final kiss on Philippa's brow. "Take care of yourself, my precious lady."

The doors to the chambers stood wide open, the dusk within standing in stark contrast to the bright sunshine outside. With one last whispered endearment, the queen released her hold on Edward's hand and stepped inside, accompanied by her ladies. The doors closed, and sentries moved into place in front of them.

Other than the ladies who attended on the queen, no one would have access to her until after she was safely brought to bed of a child—or died. Adam crossed himself and whispered a heartfelt prayer that their little queen come through the ordeals of childbirth safe and sound.

"Like being entombed," Kit told him later with something of a shudder. "In the greatest of comforts, to be sure, but all the same. Queen Isabella says all well-born women take to their chambers before the birth so as to ensure the mother spends the last few weeks in peace and quiet." She grinned. "Philippa is not all that fond of her mother-in-law's version of peace and quiet, and I dare say there will be one or two excursions out into the woods at dawn."

Adam frowned. "That could be dangerous."

"With the king and his guards accompanying her?" Kit laughed. "Those two have no intention of spending an entire month apart, and it gladdens my heart that it is like that between them."

"Aye," Adam said, making a mental note to talk to Nicholas and ensure he had more guards than usual in the woods closest to the queen's chambers. "Let us hope she stays out of the trees." They shared a little smile. In her present condition, Philippa was a far cry from the lithe urchin who scrambled up and down trees with the ease of a squirrel.

"Let us hope Queen Isabella doesn't find out," Kit said. "She sets a high price on decorous behaviour."

"Thou shalt not cast the first stone…" Adam muttered, and they shared yet another little smile. A somewhat sadder smile, he reflected, braiding his fingers with hers.

Chapter 41

"A son!" the king bounded out into the bailey. "I have a son!"

Loud cheers erupted from the assembled men. Montagu and Stafford came forward to embrace him, tagged by the rest of the king's chosen companions. Le Strange stood to the side, grinning broadly, and Adam took a step back into the shadow offered by the stable, not wanting to stand too obviously left out when his lord went from one jubilant friend to another.

In the event, the king surprised him. "Adam!" He came running across the bailey, and for an instant he looked as young as he'd been when Adam had met him, an eager boy with mesmerising blue eyes. "A son, Adam!"

"I am so happy for you, my liege."

The king threw his arms around him, and Adam could do little but hug him back. Edward clung to him for an instant before releasing him.

"An heir," he said. "My Philippa has given me an heir."

"The first of many, I trust, my lord," Adam said, bending down to retrieve his cane.

"Amen to that." Montagu appeared beside the king. "We need wine, my lord. Wine and ale and song and music."

"Wine!" Stafford yelled. "A son, a prince! We need wine to drink his health."

And just like that, Edward was gone, carried towards the hall by his friends.

In the hall, the king was approached by his mother. She held out her arms, and for the first time since Winchester, Edward and his mother embraced. A hush fell over the hall, even more so when Mortimer approached and bowed low, congratulating the king with tears in his eyes. Someone called for a toast; the king raised his brimming goblet and leapt atop a table.

"I give you Edward of Woodstock," he yelled. "Your prince, my son."

People stamped, banged fists on the tables, the hall ringing with huzzahs. In all that hubbub, the queen mother and Mortimer slipped away, accompanied by the older members of court—all but Lancaster, who sat in his corner grinning like a fool while beside him sat the ever dutiful Grosmont.

What followed was one long feast. At some point, Adam slipped outside, needing fresh air and relief from the echoing noise in the hall. He had not seen Kit since yesterday morning when the queen had gone into labour, and on the off chance he made his way over to their little room.

He hit his head on one of the rafters in the passage—he always did. He had to shove the door open, the edge scraping against the heavy oak-boards of the floor. From the bed came a grunt, a tousled mop of dark red hair all that he could see. She had washed, three empty pitchers standing on the small table, and she'd left her clothes in a neatly folded pile on the floor. He sniffed, capturing a faint smell of blood and other fluids. Closer to the bed, and it was more lavender and roses, her hair still damp. He wound a tress round his finger; come morning, she'd be battling knots and tangles.

"Adam?" She turned in his direction, all naked, rosy skin and drowsy eyes.

"Sleep, sweeting." He bent over to kiss her cheek. "I just needed to see you."

She smiled through a yawn and closed her eyes. "Adam," she murmured, dropping back into her dreams.

Adam returned to the hall, to loud voices raised in hoarse song, to trestles stained with spilled wine, floors sticky with ale. Inebriated men sat in little huddles or sprawled on the benches, cradling cups to their chests. At the high table, the king was calling for more wine, and he and his companions were as loud as anyone else in the hall, but their movements were still distinct, and as Adam got closer he heard low, intense voices. To judge from his face, Le Strange was stone sober, and neither Montagu nor Stafford seemed as drunk as they sounded.

"…Castle." Le Strange said, as yet unaware of Adam's presence. "As good a place as any."

"That's months from now!" the king hissed, sounding just as sober as Le Strange.

"Things take time." Montagu shifted closer to Edward and lowered his voice. "Trapping a rabid dog requires patience lest it kill you."

An ice-cold fist closed round Adam's throat. He took a step backwards, another, and then coughed to announce himself.

The tight group fell apart. Le Strange laughed loudly and slapped Montagu on the back, saying such jests should not be repeated with ladies present. Stafford sloshed wine into their goblets, belched, and stood, swaying on his feet. A good performance, truth be told, but there was no disguising the acuity of his gaze.

"Adam!" Edward gave him a bright smile. "Been here long?"

"No, my lord. I've been with Kit."

Four pairs of shoulders collectively slumped. Le Strange handed Adam a goblet and urged him to drink the prince's health with them. The king regaled them all yet again with a description of his son—essentially, all he'd seen was a swaddled infant, carried out by Mathilde for a moment before being whisked back inside to his mother.

"He's so small," Edward said, making an approximation with his hands.

"I dare say your lady wife may not be of the same opinion," Adam put in, and Montagu and Stafford laughed.

"Woman is born to it," Le Strange put in, earning himself dark looks from both Montagu and Adam. "All female creatures are."

"Best not liken my wife to a mare," Adam warned him. "And whether born to it or not, it requires fortitude to birth one child after the other. It is not without its perils."

"I wouldn't know," Le Strange said bitterly. "My lady wife has never been thus blessed."

"Which," Montagu commented to Adam as they left the hall together, "would have been a right miracle if it had happened, given Alice de Lacy is as old as the hills."

"Not that old," Adam protested with a laugh.

Outside, the June night was at its darkest, the horizon to the west still rimmed with lingering light. Woodbine perfumed the air, and over by the herbal garden the large rosebushes snowed petals on the ground beneath. Adam set both hands on his cane and inhaled, considering whether to ask Montagu what he had meant about his comment about a rabid dog. It did not take a man of much common sense to understand he'd been referring to Mortimer, and it rankled to hear Lord Roger described as an insane beast, but it would have been interesting to hear Montagu's attempts at explaining himself. Yet caution had him holding his tongue, craning his head back to look at the faint stars instead.

"Will you be riding out with us tomorrow?" Montagu asked.

"Me?" Adam turned to face him. "Why would I? Lately, the king rarely requires my presence."

"It's not like that," Montagu protested. "It has nothing to do with you, but—"

"—everything to do with my past with Lord Mortimer." Adam nodded a greeting to one of the sentries and continued on his way to the gatehouse. With a newborn prince in residence, it was more important than ever to ensure the palace was secure.

"He is concerned for you," Montagu said.

"Is he?" Adam shrugged. "Why should he be? I am but the captain of his guard, no more, no less."

"You know that isn't true. Ned—the king—considers you as much more than that."

"Of late, I find that hard to believe." Adam prodded at the legs that protruded from beneath a bush. Their owner groaned in protest. "Get yourself to bed, Simon," Adam ordered. "Now, or I'll dunk you in the trough." The man scrambled to his feet, weaving his way towards the stables and the hayloft above.

Montagu chuckled. "He took you at your word."

"Aye." Adam slid him a look. "I stand by my word. All my men know that."

Even in the dark, he could see Montagu's flustered expression. "The whole world knows that," Montagu replied in a testy tone. "Honourable to the point of intractability, that's you."

Adam stopped abruptly. "And what does that mean?"

Montagu exhaled loudly. "Some things you will never compromise on, will you?"

"Some things one cannot compromise about."

"Not even if your king asks it of you?"

"An honourable king would not ask me to do something that stands in conflict with my integrity."

"Which is why he hunts without you," Montagu muttered. "God's blood, Adam. Life is not so simple as to be black and white!"

"What do you take me for? Some callow lad?" Adam gouged at the ground with the tip of his stake. "I am no fool, Montagu. Nor am I a total innocent, and I am fully aware we are fast approaching a point in time when the king will claim his right to rule in his own name, as he should." He broke off, swiping his cane through the nearby shrubs. "I just wish—"

"That his gain would not be Mortimer's loss," Montagu finished for him. "Unfortunately, very few are of that opinion. Mortimer has made his bed, and he must lie in it."

"He didn't make it on his own."

"No. And whatever else one can say about our dear Earl of March, he has made a good job of restoring order to this land of ours. I am sure it will count in his favour."

The knot of ice in Adam's belly thawed somewhat. Relegation, diminishment even, but not death. Thank the Lord, they were merely planning to depose Mortimer as regent, not kill him. He closed his eyes, grateful for the darkness that hid the sudden wetness in his eyes.

Some weeks later, the king's son and heir was christened and his wife churched. In celebration, the king organised the most exotic of feasts, converting Woodstock into a Saracen city of tents. Courtiers were ordered to dress as infidels, and the king presented both his mother and Mortimer with gifts of Saracen dress, exquisite garments in sheer silks that lifted and billowed in the summer breeze.

"Do Saracens drink wine?" Kit murmured to Adam from where she was sitting beside him on a cushion.

"These Saracens do," he replied with a little smile, eyes wandering over his wife's costume. Her hair was loose, visible through the fine fabric of her veil. Other than her eyes, the rest of her face was veiled, making her complain it was right difficult to be a Saracen woman and hope to eat or drink. She too was in silks—the queen had generously gifted her some ells of saffron silk, and a wide sash of green hugged her hips—but that was as far as her participation in these Moorish fancies went. Kit had her heart set on going home, had spent all day carefully packing together their belongings.

Adam put a finger on his pouch, containing the last little missive from Tresaints, penned so carefully by Meg. This particular letter had been longer than most, expressing just how much she missed them—as did Flea.

They were riding off at dawn tomorrow, Kit feeling relieved, him feeling dismissed. After his conversation with Montagu, Adam's fears for Mortimer had abated, but his sense of exclusion had not. Not that there weren't benefits: these days, Adam de Guirande did his duty as captain of the guard and could then retire to other pastimes, such as noting just how often the king would spend time with Lancaster and Grosmont, or with Montagu and Stafford.

Since the birth of the prince, the king had also resumed his daily attendance at the councils, and it warmed Adam's heart to see Edward laughing with his mother or talking confidentially with Mortimer, his fair head close to Lord Roger's grizzled hair. For the first time since Winchester, Mortimer was seen smiling—even laughing—in the king's company, and it had hope unfurling in Adam's innards.

"How long before you must return?" Kit asked, nibbling daintily at the skewer of lamb's meat on their trencher.

"Not until Michaelmas." He smiled at how she stopped eating, a surprised look on her face. "Now that he is a father himself, the king understands my desire to spend ample time with my own brood—or so he says." More than two months away from court—he couldn't quite recall when last he had been allowed to be away for so long. "Nicholas is to take over my duties."

Kit dabbed at her mouth and drank some wine, two parallel furrows between her brows. "And how does this make you feel?"

"I'm not sure. Redundant? Old?"

"Old?" She moved closer to him. "You've just turned thirty-four. That's not old."

"Compared to the king, it is."

"Wet behind his ears, he is," Kit replied, making Adam laugh. "Would you mind if he were to release you from his service?" she continued, blue eyes studying him intently.

Adam sipped his wine while mulling this over. "No," he finally said, surprising himself. "Do you think he will?"

Kit shrugged. "Not yet. But once he rules in his own name, he may want to be rid of all reminders of his mother and Mortimer."

"Out with the old, in with the new," Adam muttered, eyes on Montagu and Stafford, sitting so close to the king. "Well, at least he will not lack loyal companions." On the other side of the king was Prince John, of late a constant shadow to his older brother.

"They are close," Kit commented, nodding in the direction of the prince. "As brothers should be."

"Unless John unwittingly defeats his brother in the tiltyard." The gangly John took every opportunity to test his strength and prowess against his elder brother. Now and then it happened he emerged victorious, which would result in a scowling king and a crowing prince.

Of late, the brothers did more than joust. More than once Adam had found them in deep discussion in the king's chambers, surrounded by deeds and rolls from which dangled seals. Now and then Master Bury was in attendance, occasionally Montagu would be lounging in a corner, but more often than not it was just the brothers, their conversation hushed but intense.

"Who better to trust than his own brother?" Kit asked when he shared this with her. "His brother and his wife—the two people he knows he can share everything with."

"And now he has a son too."

Kit gurgled with laughter. "Not much sage advice from that quarter, I fear. Not for many years to come."

"Laughing at me, wife?" he murmured, moving close enough to set a big hand on her thigh. He squeezed down, causing her to gasp and laugh some more. "I do believe we need to do something about your lack of respect, woman. Now."

"Now?" The look she gave him caused a most pleasant tightening of his balls.

"Now. Unless you have other matters you prefer attending to."

She took his offered hand and got to her feet. "Never, my lord."

Chapter 42

Midway through September, a message reached Tresaints ordering Kit to return to the queen's service immediately.

"How immediately?" Kit asked the messenger, a young man who threw repeated and hungry looks in the direction of the hall.

"Now, m'lady." He held out the sealed message, yet again glancing at the hall. Kit carefully wiped her hands—elderberries made for messy picking, but the cordial was a valuable ingredient when treating winter coughs—and took it from him.

She hesitated before breaking the seal. More than six weeks at home, and Kit had hoped to stay there, surrounded by her children and her household. Instead, here she was, ordered to attend the queen as if she were a dog recalled by its master. It irked her, but her irritation quickly became tinged with concern: the message was brief, and that in itself conjured images of an ailing queen.

Kit sent the messenger off to find some food while she went in search of her husband. He was in the chapel, sitting side by side with Father Owain, and at first Kit feared she'd intruded upon his confession, but then the priest laughed out loud and said "Lord Mortimer", and she recalled here was a man as enamoured of Lord Mortimer as was her husband—albeit Father Owain's first love was Lady Joan.

"Am I intruding?" she asked, halting for a moment to greet the three saints.

"No. I was just telling Father Owain it is our young queen's suggestion that Queen Isabella and Lord Roger go on a pilgrimage."

Father Owain chuckled. "Lord Mortimer has never shown such inclinations."

"But the queen has," Kit said. "Queen Isabella is most devout."

Father Owain's normally so benign expression was replaced by one of extreme disapproval. "A pious lady does not tempt a married man into her bed."

Kit raised her brows. "Surely, Lord Mortimer is capable of saying no?"

Father Owain snorted. "Women are carnal, seductive creatures. What man stands a chance against a determined temptress?"

Kit felt a flare of anger. "So what you are saying is that a man thinks not with his head, but with his cock," she retorted, and Adam made a strangled sound she took for laughter.

"My lady, I am merely stating the known facts. The learned fathers of the Church have long since made it quite clear that woman is weak in the flesh. She does not have the spiritual resilience of a man."

"Not all women," Kit told him.

"Father Owain isn't talking about you, sweeting." Adam looked at the priest. "If he were, I'd be obliged to rearrange his face. What is that?" he asked, pointing at the piece of parchment in her hand.

"I am recalled to court." Kit sighed. "Immediately."

"The queen?" Adam asked, getting to his feet. Kit nodded, no more, leading the way back to the door.

"I had hoped..." she began but fell silent. No point in weeping over spilled milk, but the sight of her children playing in the orchard made her wish there was no queen, no message recalling her to distant Westminster.

Meg had Ellie by the hand, with Flea padding behind them. Ned and Harry marched before them, sticks brandished as swords, and right at the end came Peter, dragging his stick. Kit sighed. They were growing up so fast, Meg now all of five and Ned closer to four than three.

"They will be fine," Adam said, slipping his arms round Kit's waist and resting his chin on her shoulder. "Well, as long as our lads do as their sister tells them to."

Kit reclined against him. "They wouldn't dare not to." She laughed softly. "When the time comes to find her a husband, you'll have to find a man who enjoys a challenge."

"Or one who loves her." He nuzzled her neck. "Or maybe both." He released her. "I shall see to the horses for tomorrow. Raven needs a new shoe."

Kit watched him cross the bailey, his cane tapping over the cobbles. These last few weeks had left him with sun-bleached hair, his face and forearms tanned after days out in the fields. Today, he was bare-legged under his old grey tunic, so faded the embroidery she'd decorated it with several years ago was no longer visible. The fabric fell to his knees, allowing a glimpse of hairy shins above the supple leather of his favourite boots.

This Adam was a man who laughed often, who was content to spend his evenings with her and their little household. This Adam slept soundly through the nights, did not spend his days in the exhausting endeavour of navigating the constant undercurrents at court. Kit sighed and placed a gentle hand on her swelling belly. She had no desire to return to serve the queen. All she wanted was to be allowed to remain here, at home, with her man.

"I'm coming with you, m'lady," Mabel announced when Kit told her they had to pack.

"You?" Kit frowned. "But I need you here, with the children."

"They have Bridget, bless her heart. And Father Owain— and John, old and useless though he may be."

"Old?" Kit teased. "John is younger than you are."

"True enough—but I carry my age so much better."

Kit pretended great interest in the content of her chest. Mabel was surprisingly light on her feet for a woman as broad as she was tall, but other than that, there was no disguising she was close to three score ten. Her face was a collection of wrinkles, her hands were spotted and gnarled, and what had once been a most generous bosom had melted downwards to recline comfortably on her round belly. In comparison, John was lean and spry, his face baked into the consistency of well-cured leather after an entire lifetime spent outdoors.

"Why should you come with us?" Kit asked.

"Why?" Mabel snorted. "Because this time round you are

not finding it quite as easy to carry the child. And because—"
She broke off.

"Yes?" Kit straightened up, rubbing her hands in small circles over her lower back. Mabel was right: this babe had a tendency to cause her discomfort.

"Because I dare say I will not be doing much more jaunting about after this."

The way she said it had Kit turning to properly look at her. "How so? Are you ailing?"

"No. But I am old, m'lady. And I'd like to ride abroad one more time before I die." Mabel fiddled with her wimple.

"Very well," Kit said. "But I take you along on one condition."

"My lady?"

"That you promise you will not die on me. Not yet, not for many years yet."

Mabel smiled broadly, revealing a gap or two among her teeth. "I shall do my best, m'lady."

They left Tresaints the next morning, on one of those magical September days when the light was golden and hazy with light mists, the ripening rowanberries bursts of red against foliage already shifting to yellow.

In view of her condition, Adam had insisted she ride before him on Raven. Kit hid a little smile: she'd not protested, not because she was in any way incapable of managing her own mount, but because she enjoyed the proximity offered by sharing a horse, and after all these weeks with unrestricted access to her husband—and him to her—she was not looking forward to days without him.

Mabel was astride one of their sturdy packhorses, walking sedately along behind Raven on a leading rein. "She needs both hands to grip the pommel," Adam had told Kit, overruling both women. "It's years since she was astride a horse."

"Years?" Mabel scoffed. "I'll have you know I've ridden for more years than you've been on this earth, m'lord."

"But not recently." With that, Adam had considered the subject closed.

386

"Will it always be like this?" Kit asked as they rode up the lane, trailed not only by Mabel but two men-at-arms and Stephen. "Will we always be at the beck and call of the king and the queen?"

"Every one of their subjects is, sweeting." He covered her hand with his. "I owe him service for my lands—will always owe him such service."

"That's different. In case of war, of course you must ride as the king commands, but this…" She shook her head.

"She needs you. She's a young woman, just recently a mother. Surely, you won't begrudge her?"

What could she say?

They arrived at Westminster with a nasty wind at their backs. It was gone vespers, and the lengthening shadows submerged the interior of the large bailey in a collection of dark and light. Adam swung off Raven, nodded a greeting to the stable lad who came running to take the horse, and carefully lifted Kit off the horse. They were all wet after riding the past few hours in rain, and at present all Adam could think of was a bowl of hot soup and preferably a steaming bath as well.

Nicholas came loping over and greeted Adam enthusiastically before informing them Kit was expected to attend on the queen immediately on arrival.

"I shall change my clothes first," Kit said, sneezing into her sleeve.

"Best hurry," Nicholas said, eyeing Mabel with some admiration as she slid off her horse—rather daintily for one so stout. "The queen," he lowered his voice, " is distressed."

"Our rooms?" Adam asked, and Nicholas waved over a page and told him to show Sir Adam and his lady their chambers. Adam ordered Stephen to arrange for their belongings to be taken to their rooms, had Nicholas send for hot water, and strode off with Kit, Mabel trotting after them.

Yet again, they'd been given rooms in the older parts of the palace: low ceilings, dark walls, small windows—at present tightly shuttered against the rising wind—and, thank the Lord, a small hearth. One room for them all, two pallets and a bed, and Adam wished he was home, lounging in his chair by the large fire in his hall, or better yet, lying in his bed while watching Kit go through her evening ablutions.

Mabel shook out a dry kirtle and shift; Kit poured water into a basin and washed her face and hands before shedding the wet garments that clung to her like a second skin. Adam barked for Stephen to wait outside while his wife dressed and then proceeded to undress himself, dropping wet and muddied clothing on the floor before washing.

"Ready?" Adam looked about for his belt and pouch, scooped up the dagger from the chest, and turned to look at Kit, already dressed but busy with her veil, ensuring she arranged it so as to cover neck and chest. "We must make haste."

He escorted Kit to the queen's chambers and stood for a while considering what to do next. The king had not requested his presence, but after some vacillation Adam decided it was best he present himself to his master before attending to his grumbling stomach.

The sentries at the entrance to the king's chambers nodded in greeting and let him through.

"Nice to see you back, Sir Adam," one of them said, and Adam recognised Matt, the lad from Winchester. The lad grinned. "Come seeking Norfolk this time as well?"

"Is he here?" Adam brightened at the thought of seeing Thomas.

"With the king," Matt said. "He rode in some days ago."

Adam took the broad stairs one tread at a time, emerging in the well-lit antechamber, where two more sentries were standing.

He entered the king's large chamber, and it was full of men and heated voices, the king and Thomas very much in the midst of things.

"I agree," Thomas was saying. "No choice, Ned. None at all."

A heavy silence greeted this remark.

"So be it," the king said with a sigh. He stood and caught sight of Adam. "De Guirande! I did not hear you come in."

If anything, the silence deepened, six pairs of eyes turning on Adam.

"I just did, my lord," Adam replied evenly. "Takes time to mount those stairs for me."

"Ah yes." King Edward beckoned him forward. "From the look of you, you've been working side by side with your villeins these last few weeks."

Stafford snickered, a sound quickly quelled at Thomas' displeased look.

"When the weather is good and the crops stand ready, all hands are needed," Adam said with a shrug.

"Good harvest?" Thomas asked, and Adam wondered why on earth the king and his uncle would have any interest in his crops.

"Aye, my lord." He scratched Lancelot behind his ear when the huge hound lumbered over to greet him. "I did not mean to interrupt, my liege," he continued, addressing himself to Edward. "I just wished you to know I am here."

"And I am glad that you are." The king frowned. "Lady Kit, is she with my lady wife?"

"As we speak, my lord."

"Good, good. Philippa has asked repeatedly for her." He approached Adam and lowered his voice. "She lost a babe and is most distraught. I dare say she feels it more than I do—I never knew she was with child until she lost it." He gnawed his lip. "She will recuperate, won't she?"

"Most women miscarry once or twice," Adam said in a soothing voice. "And to hear it, she was not long gone." Behind the king, his companions had resumed their conversation, but now in hushed tones. Only Thomas distanced himself from the group, light eyes never leaving Adam.

"Yes, that's what Maman says as well." Edward relaxed. "Well, I shall see you tomorrow. I must rejoin my friends."

"My lord." Adam bowed, hiding the stinging heat in his cheeks at being so casually dismissed—and put in his place. The king had friends, and he had men who served him: Adam de Guirande did not belong among the former.

He was halfway across the darkened courtyard when Thomas caught up with him.

"Rather you than them," he said, making Adam feel less unwanted. "Wine?"

"Food," Adam countered, making Thomas laugh.

Kit entered the dimly lit chamber of the queen and was immediately accosted by Mathilde, who drew her aside and told her the queen had miscarried—not in itself unusual or alarming—but had bled profusely.

"She's still not herself," Mathilde continued. "It is a right relief she has her baby son to gladden her heart."

"And he thrives?"

"Thrives?" Mathilde beamed. "A true prince, mark my words, as beautiful as he is patient and mild."

Kit held it unlikely that any infant was patient but made an agreeing sound, amused by Mathilde's monologue lauding the babe as the future saviour of England, France, and potentially the entire world.

"Kit? Is that you?" A hand appeared from among the coverlets on the bed.

"My lady," Kit replied.

"You took your time," Philippa said, levering herself up to sit. "I sent the messenger well over a week ago."

"I came as soon as I could, my lady."

"Not soon enough! I should never have given you leave to retire to your manor, then you'd have been on hand to save my child."

"God's will," Kit said, suppressing the burst of anger she felt at the queen's words. "What can any of us do against it?"

"Easy for you to say. It would seem you conceive and whelp with the ease of a bitch."

"Philippa!" Mathilde exclaimed. "Where are your manners, child?"

Philippa's mouth drooped. "I'm sorry," she whispered, tears forming in her eyes. "I didn't mean it, Kit, it just came out." She fiddled with the sheets, a wan look on her pale and pinched face. "It has been too much at present," she added in an undertone. "And losing the babe…" She sobbed. "I had hoped to surprise him with a second son."

"The second son will come, my lady," Kit assured her. "As will the daughters."

Philippa gave her a teary smile. "Thank you for saying that. It's just…Ned needs a distraction at present." Her lashes swept down. "God knows all of us do. It will be such a relief when it is over and done with."

"When what is over, my lady?"

Philippa shook her head. "Nothing. I'm just rambling—it's all that wine Mathilde has me drinking."

For the next half hour or so, it was all about babies and invigorating tonics. By the time Kit was allowed to leave, she had almost forgotten the queen's odd comment. Almost.

Chapter 43

A week after Michaelmas, William rode into Westminster, his mount muddy to well above its forelocks.

"I stink," William said in lieu of greeting when Adam went to enfold him in an embrace. "Too many weeks since I properly washed."

There was a grey tinge to his brother's skin that corroborated this statement, as did the sight of his tonsure and cheeks, at present sporting far more hair than they should.

"Not every hovel has a barber," William commented with a slight smile. "God alone knows how many hovels I've seen lately."

"Oh?" Adam studied William's bulging leather pouch.

"Matters of the realm," William replied, averting his eyes. "I have reports to give Mortimer."

"From hovels?" Adam teased.

"From everywhere," William bit back. "It is not easy to keep an eye on everything that happens in this kingdom of ours."

"Why anyone would try is beyond me," Adam said.

"Mortimer does more than try," William told him. "How else is he to maintain control? There are always outlaws and would-be rebels out there, easily tempted to follow fools like Kent—God keep his soul."

"Always?" Adam asked.

"Always. Of late, there is a lot of rumbling and discontent, little flames eagerly fanned by such as Lancaster and our king's closest friends." William pinched the bridge of his nose. "I must go. Lord Roger awaits me." He patted Adam on the arm and swept off, his heavy sandals clacking over the cobbles. Halfway to the hall, he almost bumped into Thomas. William apologised and hastened on, while Thomas sauntered over to Adam.

"A most unusual priest, your brother," Thomas commented, sharp gaze on William's receding back. "And as loyal to Mortimer now as when first I met him."

"William is nothing if not constant," Adam said, moving in the general direction of the stables.

"And you?" Thomas asked lightly. "Do you still have bonds with Mortimer?"

Adam came to a halt. "You know I do. He took me in when I had nothing; he made it possible for me to become who I am. That is a debt impossible to forget—or repay. But that doesn't mean I'd betray my king, if that is what you're wondering." He strode off.

"Adam, wait!"

"Leave me alone," Adam growled. "Do like all the others—including the king—and keep me at a distance. After all, why should years of devoted service count in my favour?" It bubbled out of him, all that carefully contained anger and hurt at being excluded, and by the time he was done they had reached the stables, Thomas a silent but determined shadow. "I don't want this anymore," Adam finished. "I just want to go home and be left in peace." He laughed humourlessly. "Tend to my fields with my villeins while my so-called betters fawn on the king."

"They are your betters," Thomas said calmly.

"But that does not necessarily make them better men." Adam disappeared into Raven's stall, presenting his friend with his back. "They're planning something," he said to Raven's rump. "It does not take a wise man to understand it has something to do with Mortimer."

Thomas didn't reply. When Adam glanced at him, he was leaning over the wall of the stall, a faraway look in his eyes. Adam went back to his grooming. When next he looked, Thomas was gone.

For all that he limped, Adam could move with the stealth of a cat when he chose to. Over the coming days, he took to doing just that, flitting about silently and mostly unnoticed on the periphery of the company surrounding the king. He rarely heard anything beyond the odd venomous comment about Mortimer and the queen, but now and then things were said that had him adding two and two together. Whatever it was the king was contemplating, it would happen sometime in the coming weeks, evidenced by the increased tension among the king's closest companions.

"Do you truly want to know?" Kit asked him one night, resting her head on his shoulder. "What can you do if you find out what they're planning? After all, you can't betray the king to Mortimer."

No, Adam agreed. There was nothing he could do, and so he heeded her advice, and instead of attempting to overhear things, he distanced himself—even from Thomas—concentrating on his tasks and nothing more.

One morning, he was in the kennels seeing to a new litter of pups when he heard Montagu calling for him. He was just about to rise from behind the low wall that shielded the bitch and her litter from the draught when he heard Montagu curse. Adam peeked out from behind the wall.

"Ah, Montagu," Mortimer said. "Just the man I want to see."

"Here? In the kennels? Why not approach me in the hall?" Montagu crossed his arms over his chest.

"Why not here?" Mortimer lifted his hand, and Richard de Monmouth came into view, closing the door and leaning back against it.

"What? You aim to strike me down in cold blood?" Montagu demanded, a quaver to his voice.

Mortimer tut-tutted. "Really, Montagu, what do you think of me? I am no assassin."

"No, you have others do the killing for you," Montagu muttered. Moments later, he was crowded back against the wall, Mortimer gripping him by the throat. Adam licked his lips and gripped his cane. He couldn't let Mortimer harm Montagu; the king would never forgive him if he did.

"Proof," Mortimer hissed. "You give me one example of where I have had a man killed. One."

In response, Montagu gargled.

Mortimer released his hold, and Montagu slid down the wall, cradling his neck.

"It is not me, but you who dabbles in unlawful conspiracies," Mortimer said. "A little bird tells me you're conspiring against the powers that rule this realm."

"Little birds are rarely known for their veracity," Montagu replied, sounding remarkably unruffled. "I can assure you I am loyal unto death—I would never betray our king."

Quite the elegant evasion.

"Most commendable," Mortimer said. "We all live to serve our king."

"Oh yes. And sometimes we must die for him," Montagu replied in a tone that had the hair along Adam's nape bristling.

Mortimer laughed. "Is that some sort of threat, Montagu?"

"Threat, my lord?" Montagu took a step towards the door. "I was merely stating a fact. Now have your man move out of the way, will you?"

Richard scowled, but at Mortimer's curt command he stepped aside. With one last bow, Montagu left.

"I want him followed," Mortimer said. "I want to know who he meets, what he eats, where he shits. And then we'll bring him in for some more questioning—preferably while Edward is busy elsewhere." He was already at the door.

"Yes, my lord," Richard replied, following Mortimer out into the sun.

Adam took his time exiting the kennels, all the while considering what to do. The decision was taken from him by the simple fact that the first person he ran into when he entered the hall was Will Montagu.

"No king?" Adam asked.

"Out somewhere," Montagu croaked. There was a discolouration on the side of his neck.

"He's having you watched," Adam said, incapable of taking his eyes from Montagu's bruise.

Montagu's brows shot up, his hand coming up to rub absently at his neck. "And you think I don't know?" He poured some wine, his hand shaking so much he spilled wine all over the table. "I've been beset by spies ever since I went to see the Holy Father, but now and then I fear there is an assassin or two among them." He looked Adam up and down. "You don't know what leg to stand on in this matter, do you?"

"I only have one leg to stand on," Adam retorted.

"Ah. Well, let's hope it's the right leg, then." Montagu drained his mug, setting it down with a bang. "And now if you'll excuse me, I must see the king."

Adam chose to accompany him, ignoring Montagu's less than welcoming scowl. They entered the king's chambers just as Stafford stood up and loudly declared he'd be more than happy once this matter at Nottingham was concluded.

"What business?" Adam asked innocently, and Stafford whirled.

"Parliament," Montagu drawled. "God's blood, but those are boring days!"

"Not so boring last time," Adam muttered.

"An exception to the rule," Will de Bohun offered. "Well, at least I hope it was," he added with a grin. "Imagine if at every parliament an earl was executed—we'd soon run out of earls."

"Run out of earls?" King Edward asked as he entered from the inner room.

"Nothing, my liege," Montagu said. "We were discussing the upcoming parliament."

"Oh." Edward's gaze leapt from one to the other, rested for an instant on Adam before returning to Montagu. "Bloody boring business." He turned to Adam. "Have you seen the pups?"

"I have, my lord. Lancelot breeds true—they look like wolf cubs."

"They do, don't they?" Edward snatched an apple from the large bowl on the table. "The dam is half-wolf too—or so they tell me." On and on he prattled about his dogs, and Adam nodded and pretended enthusiasm, while all the while he had his attention riveted on the other four men in the room. Stafford, Ufford, de Bohun, and Montagu were all as brittle as a cracking sheet of ice come spring.

"I just wanted to see if I still remembered how," was Philippa's response when Mathilde scolded her for climbing the single tree of any size in the palace gardens.

"And you did, my lady," Kit said, still smiling after finding their queen swinging in a most unladylike fashion from one of the stout branches before dropping lightly to the ground.

Philippa grinned. "I did." There were smudges on her hands and on the fine wool of her kirtle, but more than that she looked happy for the first time in weeks, as if the extended stay outdoors had at last cleansed her of the sadness brought on by her miscarriage. "See, my little prince?" she crooned, leaning over to peer at her son, carried safely by his nurse. "Your mama climbs trees with the ease of a squirrel."

"Best she remember she isn't a squirrel," Mathilde said with an exasperated snort. "You're the queen, my lady. Queens do not clamber about in trees."

"And here was I thinking that a queen can make such decisions on her own." Philippa stretched out her arms and tilted her head up to the sun. "It's a lovely day, isn't it?"

"It is," Kit agreed, coming to stand just behind her. "A day to treasure when winter envelops us in dark and cold." By then, she'd have birthed the child presently tumbling about in her belly, and hopefully the mauling pain to her lower back would be gone.

Philippa slipped an arm under Kit's. "You look tired."

"I am tired." Their little room was cramped, the bed sagged, and on top of all this, Mabel snored. Not that Mabel admitted to doing so, insisting it was Stephen who sounded as if he were milling gravel through the night.

"Maybe I should make *you* a posset for once," the queen said, a mischievous look on her face.

"No, thank you, my lady. It suffices with Mabel's concoctions." Having Mabel with her had been a godsend. Other than the possets and the various infusions, Mabel had hands that knew just how to work up and down her spine and buttocks so as to relieve the tension.

"It's a long ride to Nottingham," the queen said. "Maybe you should consider a litter."

They were leaving tomorrow, and if Kit had had her wish,

she'd have returned to Tresaints instead of accompanying the king and queen up north, but the queen had insisted she required Kit's services some more weeks.

"After Nottingham, you can go home," she promised. "And I'll talk to the king and convince him to allow Adam to go with you—and stay home over Christmastide." Like dangling a sausage in front of a starving dog, that was, so Kit had agreed—not that she had any choice—and now she was fearing the long ride but was determined not to travel by litter.

"Of course not," Adam had told her when she shared this with him. "You ride with me. I still don't understand why she insists on having you come along," he grumbled. "Surely, that old nurse of hers can see to her health?"

"One would think so." Kit sucked in her lip, trying to put her finger on what it was precisely that had her suspecting there were other things at work here. With an effort, she rid herself of such thoughts: some more weeks, and she and Adam would be on their way home.

Travelling with the court was like marching with ants. Tediously slow, the long line of riders and litters, carts and men-at-arms, snaked its way due north through a countryside draped in fogs, the ground carpeted in leaves. The king travelled in a colourful group close to the head of the column, his banner snapping overhead, a troop of mounted knights riding in protective formation. Some distance behind the king came Mortimer, Queen Isabella, and their following, a collection of darker robes and garments—well, with the exception of Geoffrey Mortimer, who had joined them some miles north of Peterborough and was as gaudy as any of the king's men.

The queen spent most of her time in her litter but would now and then emerge to ride side by side with her husband, conspicuously so whenever they approached a village or town. The young king and his wife were welcomed enthusiastically, and Edward smiled and waved, now and then throwing a handful of silver groats to fall like glittering rain at the feet of his subjects.

Seven days after setting out, Nottingham rose before them. The closer they got to their destination, the more thronged the road, men from all over England converging on Nottingham for the upcoming parliament. At times, all this traffic slowed progress to no more than a walk, and when the town of Nottingham finally rose before them, Kit released a little sigh of relief.

Other than a brief night while on the road to York some years ago, Kit had never been to Nottingham. That time, they had arrived just after sunset, had been on their way at dawn, and she'd been left with little but a jumbled impression of city walls and gallows situated high above the rest of the town. This time, they approached at leisure, the meadows to the south of the town allowing an unimpeded view of the town and the adjoining castle, by many considered the finest in the land.

"Impregnable." Adam used his hand to shade his face, eyes on the castle walls that adorned the sheer cliff on the opposite side of the river. "Except, of course, that there are rumours about old tunnels."

"There are? Maybe we should go looking."

"No." He sounded curt, and belatedly she remembered he hated confined spaces.

They slowed to a walk across the Leen bridge. The king's guards shoved people and carts aside to make way for the king and queen, held the throngs back as the king's party clattered over the bridge. Adam and Kit were among the last to cross, and by then the guards had left, leaving them to jostle their way through as best they could. Mabel squawked and clung to her saddle when her mount shied, and Adam's arm shot out to hold her steady.

Before them, steep streets rose upwards, a sheer cliff to the right, while to their left extended a flat stretch of land, leading all the way to the distant castle.

"Old like the hills," an unknown man said, nodding in the direction of the town. "Well, the hill is anyway." He grinned. "They say it's been a town for hundreds of years."

"He's right." Adam indicated they should take a left,

a long street bordered by houses, some of them small and squashed, others impressive timbered things. "Long before the Conqueror came over, this was a thriving place."

They passed a friary, monks in grey robes coming and going through the main gate, rode by a church adorned by a most impressive tower, and there before them was the gatehouse to the castle itself.

One gatehouse later, and they were in the middle ward. Kit dismounted, rubbing discreetly at her back. To her left, the upper ward clung to the uppermost part of the old cliff, the huge keep looming over them. Impregnable, and even more so with all the men-at-arms thronging the lower and middle bailey, most of them sporting the Mortimer colours.

"I wish we were back home," Adam muttered. So did Kit, feeling small and insignificant among all the people around her. Servants ran back and forth, a group of ladies minced by, laughing softly among themselves, and to the right three men were arguing, angry voices accompanied by sweeping gestures.

"A fortnight, then we can go home," she told him, waving at William, who was making his way towards them.

"A fortnight," Adam echoed. "Thank the Lord."

Chapter 44

"A secret tunnel?" Montagu choked on his ale, and Adam had to slap him on his back. "Where have you heard such nonsense?" he croaked once he'd got his breath back.

"From one of my men-at-arms," Adam replied. "If it exists, it is a threat to the king's safety. They say it links to the caves at the base of the cliff."

Eubulus snickered. "Tunnels? The cliff is riddled with caves and passages, one of them an ancient sally port. But I can assure you the king need not worry. The constable keeps those tunnels under lock and key—all six gates of them. So if you were hoping for a secret route for the damsel in distress to flee her ogre of a gaoler and be reunited with her stalwart knight, you'll be disappointed." He fluttered his eyelashes and simpered.

"If the damsel looks anything like you, it would be the ogre fleeing," Adam commented drily, and they all laughed before turning their attention to the food.

Three days here, and Adam had as yet not had the pleasure of his lady wife's company at any meal, the queen having spent most of her days in a darkened room, complaining of headaches. Not so Queen Isabella, for the evening the only woman at the high table—and clearly enjoying it.

She was in saffron and scarlet silk tonight, colours that added warmth to her skin while the fabric clung to her limbs in a most alluring fashion. No veil despite the displeased looks not only from the king but also from some of the bishops. Instead, Queen Isabella had dressed her hair in various intricate braids that had been coiled into a dark weight at her nape, a net of gold holding it all in place. Jewels decorated the braids, glinted off her fingers and round her neck, and beside her Mortimer looked surprisingly stark, having opted for grey and black, silver embroideries the only decoration.

A group of minstrel lads were regaling the high table with one quavering love song after the other, and a veritable army of pages ensured goblets were kept replenished. In all this hubbub, the king sat slouched, now and then sharing a word with his uncle, at other times leaning over to listen to whatever his mother had to say. But mostly he stared straight ahead, drinking steadily from the goblet he held in trembling hands.

"Is he ailing?" Adam asked Montagu.

"Mmm?" Montagu covered his goblet with his hand when a page offered him a refill. "Our Ned?" He glanced at the king. "Of boredom, I'd hazard."

"Aye, two full days locked up with his council has not left him in the best of moods," Eubulus put in. "More ale?" he asked Adam, beckoning for a page.

Adam shook his head, his gaze on Queen Isabella—or rather on how her hand was lifted to Lord Roger's cheek, a tender if brief caress before Mortimer returned to his conversation with Bishop Burghersh. Kit appeared in one of the doorways, standing on her toes as she scanned the thronged room. Adam rose and waved; she smiled and threaded through the crowd, one hand resting on her belly.

The men made room for her, Eubulus gallantly relinquishing his seat to allow Kit to sit beside Adam. She sipped from his goblet, shook her head at the offered roasted pork, seemingly content to just sit beside him, resting her head on his shoulder.

At the high table, Queen Isabella rose. Mortimer and the bishop followed suit. After bidding her son a good night, Isabella excused herself, waiting while Mortimer and the bishop bowed to the king before leading the way through the hall. They collected people as they went: Richard de Monmouth wiped his mouth and downed the last of his ale before hurrying after them, while Geoffrey Mortimer rose out of the shadows closest to the hearth and strolled after his father, William at his side.

"Work," William said with a sigh when he passed Adam. "God's truth, but this master of mine never rests."

"Feathering your own nest is a wearisome business," Eubulus muttered to their backs, and Adam was tempted to reach across and slap him. Kit tightened her hold on his arm.

Stafford strolled over, accompanied by the de Bohun twins.

"Let's see what Nottingham has to offer in the way of wine," he suggested.

"It's gone curfew," Adam reminded him drily, but Stafford waved his objection away, saying a royal writ would sort that little matter.

"I'll come," Robert Ufford said, tugging at his dark beard. "Very little else to do to pass the time." Close to Adam in years, Ufford rarely gave him as much as the time of the day, preferring the company of Stafford.

"Us too," Will de Bohun answered for him and his brother, and Montagu stood and said he'd come along as well. He nudged at Eubulus. "And you, old man?"

"Oh, I'll come. Young lads like you would never find your way to the better hidden secrets of Nottingham." He winked. Ufford and Stafford scowled, and Montagu went quite still. Will de Bohun laughed loudly and pulled Eubulus to his feet. "Lead the way, granddad!"

"We'd ask you to come along, Adam," Montagu said. "Except we know you prefer the company of your wife to ours."

"A grudging invitation if I ever heard one," Kit commented as the boisterous group made for the high table, where the king and Thomas were still sitting, deep in conversation. "Would those secret places be brothels?"

"God knows. And as I'm not going with them, we will never find out."

At the high table, the king shook his head and made a shooing gesture with his hands. Accompanied by laughs and loud voices, the knot of men made for the door, Eubulus in the lead. Their departure brought silence, and with some surprise Adam noted that the hall was virtually deserted. Other than the king and his uncle, only some dozen men remained.

"He looks drawn," Kit commented, nodding discreetly in the direction of the king.

"Aye." Adam studied his lord over the rim of his goblet. Edward fidgeted, his face cast in shadow. "He's been prickly all day." He looked at her. "So do you."

"Hmm?"

"Look drawn." He traced the contours of her eyes. "Tired?"

"Always these days," she said.

"To bed, then."

They had been given lodgings on the same floor as Mortimer and Queen Isabella in the upper bailey.

"Not so much an honour as needing to find use for even the smallest of rooms," Adam had commented, less than enthused by the little closet that had a window no wider than his foot. But the room had a bed and came with the benefit of being so small Mabel's pallet had been placed in the antechamber, thereby according him some privacy with his wife.

Once out of the hall, they walked along the inner curtain wall, took a right, and followed the old wall round the upper ward to yet another gatehouse. All the guards were Mortimer men, both those set at regular intervals along the wall and those manning the gatehouse—all the gatehouses.

"Is that so strange?" Kit asked when Adam said as much, having wished the last set of sentries a good night.

"I'd prefer it if the king's safety was left in the hands of me and my men," Adam told her. "And all these men in Mortimer colours—an unnecessary provocation to all the other barons of the land."

"Is Mortimer afraid?"

"Not afraid, more cautious. And if he weren't, he'd be a fool."

The passage was lit by several lanterns, and from Mortimer's rooms came the muted sound of voices. Adam smiled when he heard Lord Roger laugh, recalling the tender gesture he'd witnessed earlier. It made him tighten his hold on his wife.

Mabel was fast asleep and didn't wake as they stepped over her to enter their own room. Inside, it was warm, the embers in the hearth glowing a dull red. Adam lit a candle and had Kit stand before him, kneeling clumsily to help her out of shoes and hose before relieving her of veil, cotehardie, and kirtle. He undid her hair and sank his fingers into it, strong fingers working over her scalp until she groaned, resting heavily against him.

She nestled into him, her large belly keeping them further apart than he wanted. He slid his hands down her back and rested his cheek against the top of her head. Kit swayed slightly. Adam walked her the few steps backwards required to reach the bed and eased her down before pulling off his clothes. In only his shirt, he joined her. She turned on her side, he curved round her, one hand resting on her belly. The child within kicked vigorously.

"A lad," he said, kissing her nape.

"A mule," she replied, making him laugh. But he could hear how tired she was, so he held her close, rocking her gently.

He was halfway to sleep when something resembling the sound of marching soldiers had him sitting upright.

"What?" Kit scrubbed at her eyes.

"I don't know."

Wood splintered. Voices raised in command and a loud yell. Lord Roger. Adam was out of the bed, groping for his sword.

"What is happening?" Kit asked, clutching the coverlet to her chest.

From beyond their door came an agonised howl.

"Stay here," he ordered Kit as he wrenched the door open. "Inside," he told Mabel, an apparition in messy, thinning grey hair. "Stay with Kit."

He limped towards Mortimer's rooms. At the far end of the passage, a door gaped open, flaring torches illuminating what appeared to be a narrow passage hewn through the rock. Dearest Lord, the ancient sally tunnel—and not at all under lock and key! Adam swallowed in a futile attempt to lubricate a mouth gone as dry as day-old ashes.

A scream—several screams—and the entrance to

405

Mortimer's room was thronged with men in armour. Ufford and the de Bohun twins. Eubulus—the accursed guide to the hidden secrets of Nottingham. Adam shoved through, sending Eubulus sprawling.

In the midst of the room was Mortimer, an enraged, desperate Mortimer, fighting Montagu and Stafford and an unknown third man. On the floor was a body. In the dim light, all he could make out was the bright hair—and the dark pool of blood beneath. Richard de Monmouth was bleeding out before his eyes. Mortimer roared, tore free, and sent Stafford crashing into the wall. Adam tensed.

"Back off, de Guirande," Ufford warned, lifting his bloodied sword.

"Get out of my way." Adam gripped the sword hilt just as someone grabbed hold of his arm.

"There's nothing you can do," Thomas said. Thomas? Where did he come from? Was he in on this too? Of course he was, and Adam screamed inside at this betrayal. He tried to shake him off, Thomas tightened his hold, saying this was all for the best, and then he grunted when Adam elbowed him—but he didn't let go.

Mortimer lunged, trying to reach his sword. Montagu had him by the waist, and Queen Isabella screamed, struggling to free herself from Bishop Burghersh's hold.

"Geoffrey!" Mortimer yelled, and Adam saw Ufford bearing down on Lord Roger's son, still holding his sword. The swishing sound of a blade, Geoffrey stumbled, and a dark shape leapt in front of Geoffrey, arms spread wide.

"Don't—" the man began, and then he folded over before crumpling to the floor.

"Let me go!" Adam hissed, struggling in Thomas' hold. "Damn it, man, I must help him…" An uneven fight, Mortimer buckling under the weight of Montagu and Stafford.

"There's nothing you can do," Thomas replied, and Adam crashed them both into the wall.

Amidst loud yells, Mortimer was forced to his knees. Someone brought rope; his arms were wrenched behind his back and tied.

"Roger!" Queen Isabella fought free of the bishop and ran towards Mortimer. She had her hands on him when someone got hold of her and tore her away. "For pity's sake, don't hurt him," she screamed when Mortimer was hit over the head. "Edward, where are you? Edward, stop them!" Yet again she pulled free. "Roger!" She clawed at Montagu, spat him in the face when he gripped her wrists.

"Isabella!" Mortimer's voice was ragged. "My love, I—" Stafford shoved a gag in his mouth. With a low growl, Adam backhanded Thomas, was free at last.

"No!" Isabella got past Montagu and threw herself over Lord Roger. She clung like a barnacle, impossible to dislodge for men who dared not use too much force with the king's mother. Adam shoved Ufford aside and lifted his sword. To do what? He faltered.

"Enough!" The king stood in the doorway. "What is this? A madhouse? I told you to handle this quietly, you fools."

Adam's chest constricted. He lowered his sword.

"Edward," Isabella said through tears. "At last. Tell them to stop this, son. Tell them—"

"Take her away," the king interrupted.

"What?" The queen's voice rose shrilly. "No, Edward, no!" She prostrated herself before him, clutching at his robe. "Don't do this. Don't harm my precious Roger, don't—"

The king shook her off and nodded at two of the men. His mother was dragged from the room.

"Roger!" she screamed, and her voice was so full of anguish Adam had to control the urge to clap his hands over his ears. "Roger! I love you, my hawk. Only you. Always you."

There was a muffled sound from Mortimer. For an instant, it seemed he would tear free from the men holding him, all of his straining towards the voice of his lover. A clap to his head, and he was manhandled towards the wall, his son dragged with him.

Over and over, the queen screamed her lover's name. She loved him, she yelled, would always love him, and cursed be that hellspawn of a son who—A door slammed shut and the queen's voice was abruptly silenced.

"God's blood," Thomas said, his voice shaking. "What a mess."

A mess? Adam dared not glance at Lord Roger, but he couldn't help but see Richard, dead on the floor. From further inside the room came the hushed voice of the bishop, whispering reassuring nothings, and suddenly Adam remembered who else had been with Mortimer tonight, recalled the anonymous shape who'd leapt to the defence of Geoffrey. No. Not that.

Slowly, he turned. The bishop was on his knees, and in his arms was William.

He was aware of Thomas saying something, of his arm round his waist, but Adam pushed him away and fell to his knees on the bloodied floor. William's chest looked oddly squashed, the dark cloth of his old robe wet with blood.

The bishop relinquished his hold. "William?" Adam cradled his brother, causing William to gasp, fingers closing with surprising strength round Adam's wrist.

"Brother." William licked his lips, staining them a deep red. "My brother." There was an odd rattling sound to William's breathing, and when he coughed, blood trickled from his mouth.

"William," Adam whispered. "God, William. What am I to do without you?"

"Live." William's hold on Adam's wrist slackened. "Tell Kit I—" Yet again, he coughed, spraying Adam with blood. A loud hissing inhalation, eyes that widened with pain, and then he was gone, slumping lifeless in Adam's arms.

With shaking fingers, Adam closed William's eyes and crushed him to his chest.

"We'll never get Mortimer out through the bailey—his men will kill you. So take them out through the secret passage," he heard the king say. "You ride to London immediately. De Guirande, get dressed. You're to escort the prisoners."

Adam released his hold on William. "Me?" He looked at Lord Roger, at Geoffrey, back at the king. "Me?"

"Ned, no," Thomas said. "You can't expect Adam to—"

"I expect him to do as I order him to," the king interrupted.

"Adam de Guirande is *my* man, not Mortimer's." The king turned to Adam. "Get dressed. Now."

Slowly, Adam got to his feet. Anger burned through his guts, scorched his throat. At this precise moment, he would gladly have flayed the man standing in front of him, king or no king.

"Find someone else, my lord. My brother lies dead, as does my brother-in-law," he said and had the pleasure of seeing the king flinch. "And I have a wife to see to."

"You will do as ordered. Kit will come to no harm. She will be escorted back to Tresaints once you have done your duty."

Thomas inhaled loudly. "What are you saying, Ned?"

"I am saying de Guirande best remember where his duty lies," the king said coldly.

Adam looked at him. He looked at Montagu, at Stafford. Neither man could hold his gaze. For a long time, he met Lord Roger's eyes. "As you wish, my liege," he said, stepping round Richard's corpse to get to the door.

"Adam." Thomas was at his side. "I am so sorry—"

"You knew," Adam cut him off. "How in God's name could you not warn me? I would have done it for you."

"I didn't know until this evening," Thomas said. "I swear, I didn't."

"Using Kit as a hostage, my king?" Adam swallowed down on the need to scream out a curse. He reached the door to his room. Without as much as a look at Thomas, he entered, slamming the door in his friend's face.

For what felt like an eternity, he stood leaning against the door, trying to collect his wits.

"Adam?" Kit opened the inner door and recoiled at the sight of him. "Are you hurt?" she asked, hurrying over to him. Belatedly, he noticed his shirt was sticky with blood, as were his thighs and hands.

"William. He's…" He opened and shut his bloody hand. "He's dead."

"Dead?" She whispered. "Our William?"

Adam just nodded, having to steady himself against the wall to avoid collapsing in a weeping heap. His brother. Dead.

"No," Kit moaned, "not William!" She reached out to him, and he fell into her arms, spilling silent tears. She wept, her face pressed to his shirt.

"And Lord Mortimer?" she asked after a while.

"Bound and gagged. And I am to escort him to London."

She straightened up. Her nostrils widened, the hand on her stomach clenching. "You?"

"Me. God's blood, how am I to do this? How can he ask it of me, that I escort Lord Roger to the Tower?" He slumped, his legs giving way. His throat hurt; his head throbbed. "I can't…Dear God, but I must." He saw her through a blur of tears. "He has you as a surety."

"Me?" Kit clumsily knelt beside him, gentle fingers brushing at his face. "You need not worry about me, Adam." Soft lips brushed his. "And you must do this. Not for the king, but for Lord Roger. He deserves to have at least one friend riding with him, one man he can count on to ensure he isn't stabbed in the back on the way." Somehow, she steadied him back to his feet. "First you must wash, then you must dress."

An hour later, Adam sat up on Raven after first having inspected both Lord Roger's and Geoffrey's mounts and ropes. He took off the gags, and when Stafford protested, he wheeled, sword drawn.

"*I* have been charged with transporting the Earl of March and his son to London. Not you. I decide how it is to be done." He took a limping step towards Stafford. "Anyone as much as touches either of them, and I will disembowel them. Right now, I wouldn't mind sticking my sword into someone—preferably whatever coward it was who ran my brother through with his blade." He fixed Ufford with his gaze. "Murderer," he said, and Ufford blanched. "Two unarmed men. How brave of you, Sir Robert."

With that, he limped over to Raven and sat up. They rode out under cover of dark. No one said a word to Adam. He had no words for anyone. But at some point he rode up to Lord Roger, riding with his hands tied to the saddle. He reached across and covered his lord's hands with his. Lord Roger's fingers curled around his.

The sweetish scent of blood had her gagging. Kit held on to Mabel and entered the room that until so recently had housed Mortimer and his queen and now only contained the cooling bodies of two men. Two? Kit staggered back. Dear God, not only William but Richard as well. Her brother, killed while defending his lord. Two men, brutally hacked down by the king's men. Kit's stomach roiled.

The table had been overturned, spilling deeds and rolls every which way. She spied Mortimer's seal beside the bed, there were inkblots on the carpet, on the white silk coverlet that adorned the bed. By the hearth was one of Queen Isabella's embroidered slippers, and on the floor…Kit swallowed and swallowed.

Mabel knelt clumsily by Richard, smoothing back his hair. Kit couldn't tear her eyes away from William, in so many ways so similar to her man, and here he was, dead and cold. A tremor flew through her, a sudden tightening round her belly. Icy sweat broke out along her back, and she had to brace herself against the wall, breathe deeply a couple of times before lowering herself to kneel beside William. Bile burned her throat; the child kicked and turned.

"Oh, William," she whispered, fingers brushing over skin already cool to the touch.

"I'm sorry," the king said from behind her. "I had hoped to avoid bloodshed."

"More fool you, my liege," she replied, lurching to her feet to give him a deep reverence.

"That's not necessary between us, Lady Kit," the king said, squirming.

"Oh, I think it is, my lord. I am your hostage, am I not?" His face reddened. "I—"

She knelt down again, turning her back on him. "Your wife promised me I was free to return home if I accompanied her to Nottingham. She also promised me Adam would be free to ride with me. Promises I now understand were nothing but a ruse." She closed William's mouth, wound a linen band around his head to keep it closed. "Falsehoods—from two people I thought more honourable than most."

"You presume to judge us?" the king asked.

"No. That I leave to God." Kit stood up. "But I will leave for Tresaints as soon as I have buried my kin—both my brothers. And you will not stop me."

"He will not," Thomas said from the door. "If he does, I will personally belt him." He crossed his arms over his chest and eyed the king. Without a word, the king left.

Thomas stepped over Richard. "I am here for you, Kit. Anything you need—"

"A bath," Mabel interrupted. "My lady is shivering."

Distractedly, Kit noted that she was, in fact, shaking like an aspen leave. She wanted Adam, needed his arms round her. Dearest God, what would all of this cost him, her honourable man? The room spun. She would have fallen had Thomas not caught her.

Much later, Kit was warm and tucked into bed.

"What will happen to Lord Mortimer?" Mabel asked, breaking the silence between them.

"This time, I fear his luck has run out. God help him," Kit said. And Adam, she added silently.

The next morning, Queen Philippa demanded Kit's presence.

"My lady." Kit did not smile nor enter beyond the threshold.

"Are you well?" the queen asked.

"Do you care?" Kit bit back, and the young woman before her went a vivid pink.

"I do, even if I understand you may not believe it."

"I want to go home. Today. And I request that you never recall me to your service, my lady."

"That is not your decision, Lady Kit." Queen Philippa drew herself up to her full, rather inconsiderable height. Her beautiful light brown eyes flashed with anger. Kit didn't care.

"Has Queen Isabella also been taken prisoner?" she asked instead, causing most of the ladies in the room to gasp.

"No." Philippa gave her an annoyed look. "The dowager queen has been taken to Berkhamsted, there to reflect on her behaviour these last few years. I am sure mother and son will be reconciled, assuming she returns all those lands and benefices she has so rapaciously granted herself during the last few years." She moved closer. "A new world order. No more Mortimer and Queen Isabella; now dawns the age of Edward, third of that name, and his faithful consort, Philippa." Her mouth curved into a little smile. "I had no choice. Edward wanted Adam here, and what better way than insist I required your services?"

"Why Adam? What has he ever done to be so cruelly punished?"

"Punished?" Queen Philippa's brow furrowed. "Adam serves the king's pleasure, and if it rubs further salt into Mortimer's wounds to have his precious foster son ride guard, why not? Besides, who else to ensure Mortimer arrives alive and whole in London? Ned could entrust no one else with this task. No one." Yet another little smile. "Mortimer must stand trial."

"But the outcome is given," Kit said bitterly.

"Of course it is. Mortimer must die. For the safety of my son, of my husband, and of the realm."

"Without Lord Mortimer, there would have been no realm, no husband, no son," Kit retorted.

"Lady de Guirande had best remember who she is talking to," Queen Philippa said coldly.

"Lady de Guirande begs to be excused. She has men to bury."

For a long time, Queen Philippa said nothing, teeth sunk in her lower lip. "Go," she finally said. Timidly, she reached out and took hold of Kit's hand. "And I am truly sorry. For everything."

Kit disengaged herself. "So am I, my lady. I thought you a better person than this."

Chapter 45

"Here?" Adam halted his men, surprised.

"Yes." Montagu opened the door to the room. It was dark, the shutters closed and nailed shut.

Adam ordered the prisoners untied, not knowing where to look as first Geoffrey, then Lord Roger were shoved into the room. He lifted his head to look at his former lord, and he didn't even try to hide the tears that filled his eyes. Lord Roger reached for him, for an instant their hands touched, and then Lord Roger was pushed inside.

The door was pulled closed, and four men hurried over with stones and mortar.

"What are you doing?" Adam whirled to stare at Montagu. "You're going to wall him up, shut him out of the light?"

"The king's orders," Montagu said, a faint blush crawling up above his bearded cheeks. "He wants no repeat on his last escape. The windows have already been bricked up."

God. Adam staggered over to a wall, braced his hands against it, and vomited. Without a word, he stumbled off, his throat burning with bile and tears.

"Adam!"

The king's voice forced him to stop, but he would not turn, could not look him in the eyes.

"I'm sorry you had to see that," the king added, sounding out of breath. "You must understand I have to take every precaution, and—"

"Stop." Adam's head whirled, his stomach heaved. "If you'd not wanted me to see it, you'd have made sure I didn't, my lord."

Silence greeted this remark. Adam lumbered on, a hand on the wall to steady himself. The floor tilted, the walls shrank, and he had this pounding pain in his chest that made it so difficult to breathe when all he wanted to do was scream.

"I did not give you leave to go, Sir Adam," the king said coldly. Adam came to a halt. Damned if he was going to say anything. He kept his eyes on the floor, said nothing, did nothing.

"Let him go, Ned," Montagu said. "These last few days, it has been like watching a man with a bleeding hole gouged through his chest."

The king inhaled. "Damn," he said. "I didn't mean to—"

But you did, Adam thought, still with his face to the wall. This was the king punishing him for loving Lord Roger.

Montagu set a light hand on Adam's shoulder. "Go. Find your bed. God knows you deserve it."

Adam set his teeth. He didn't want their pity. He wanted to see them bleed—all of them, Ufford and Stafford, Montagu and that accursed Le Strange, even the king. But he nodded and limped off, leaning heavily on his cane.

He slept for two days straight—or so he judged it, when on the third morning he woke to the insight he was in the Tower, and that some distance away Lord Roger had been walled in together with his son.

He was alone in the room, empty of anything but the pallet he was sleeping on and a stool. An emptied pitcher of wine, a half-eaten round of bread—he had no recollection of either drinking or eating. He scratched at his cheeks. He needed to shave, to wash, to change his garments, but could not quite find the energy to do so. Instead, he remained on the pallet, watching the dust motes dancing in the thin beams of sunlight that fell in through the shutter. No such light for Lord Roger, entombed like the living dead.

Adam sighed and rolled over on his back, face covered by his arm. It had been a nightmarish journey from Nottingham to London. The king had caught up with them some miles south of Nottingham and had ridden at some distance from Mortimer, with his friends and Lancaster, a surprising addition to their party, given the haste at which the king ordered them to travel.

In Leicester, the king had wanted to hang Mortimer there

and then, but Lancaster had insisted he had to be tried by his peers at Westminster, and they'd argued for hours, while in a corner sat Mortimer, bound and gagged. It sickened Adam, even more so when Lancaster had come over to gloat, sneering as he told Lord Roger that soon enough he'd dangle from a noose.

There was nothing Adam could do to help his former lord, no way he could make things easier for him, except that he insisted on riding beside him, a bulwark of sorts between Mortimer and the rest. And now they were here, in the Tower, and the king had appointed six men to guard Mortimer's cell, day and night.

Someone knocked on his door. He closed his eyes when it creaked open.

"Sir Adam?" Gavin's voice had him opening one eye. His former squire hesitated by the door. "I brought you food, m'lord. And hot water." His nose wrinkled. "You smell, m'lord. Lady Kit would be most upset."

Adam gestured for him to come in, and soon enough two pages had set down steaming pitchers, a platter heaped with food, and a large jug of ale.

"The trial is set for a month from now," Gavin said, throwing Adam a cautious look.

"Aye." He already knew. It took that long to assemble the peers. He shed his clothes. Gavin was right: he did smell. Adam used his dirty shirt to wash himself, unconcerned by the presence of Gavin. In his leather bag, he found braies and a clean shirt, and attired only in this he sat down to eat, surprised to discover he was ravenous.

He was swallowing back the last of the ale when Thomas entered, not bothering to knock.

"Christ in heaven! What is that stench?" He scowled at the brimming chamber pot, stuck his head out through the door, and yelled for a scullion. Thomas greeted Gavin distractedly, scrutinising Adam from head to toes. "How are you?"

Adam shrugged. He couldn't quite put words to it. Numb went a long way in describing the odd sensation of not being quite here. Frozen would be a good word for the anger that lay in the pit of his stomach, a black, snarling thing that he feared would erupt with disastrous consequences unless he kept it layered in ice. But none of this he said to Thomas. There was no need, his friend searching his face intently before sitting down on the bed with a loud exhalation.

Gavin excused himself. The scullion came and went, bringing firewood and a clean chamber pot, and still they sat silent.

"I told Ned to send you home," Thomas finally said, reclining against the wall. "He should have spared you this."

"So why didn't he?" Adam finished the last of the food and sat back, replete.

"However petty this may sound, I think he's jealous. He doesn't like it that you still love Mortimer."

"Just because I love Lord Roger does not mean I didn't love him." He smiled crookedly at his intentional use of tense. "The heart is not a loaf, a finite quantity of love to be redistributed as our relationships change."

"He's too young to realise that." Thomas scraped at a patch of mud on his hose. "That insight generally comes with the birth of your second child."

The thought of children and births had Adam looking at the west-facing window.

"Kit's on her way to Tresaints with my men as escorts. I even obliged her to go by litter." Thomas rolled his eyes. "She's as stubborn as a mule, your Kit, but this time neither Mabel nor I would allow her on a horse."

Adam sat up straight. "Is she poorly?"

"No. Tired, aye, and distraught. But Mabel says the babe is one of those impatient sorts that knock too early on the gateway of the womb." He laughed. "Mabel assured me only lads would be so discourteous."

Despite it all, Adam smiled, imagining an irate Kit attempting to argue with both Mabel and Thomas.

"Thank you," he said.

"It was the least I could do, seeing as I failed you otherwise." Thomas paused. "William and Richard were buried at the friary."

Adam nodded. His brother…He closed his eyes, willing back the tears.

"You could ride home as well," Thomas suggested. "Ned would not—"

Adam interrupted him with a violent shake of his head. "I stay until it is over. I owe Lord Roger as much."

The following weeks dragged. Adam kept to himself, having no desire to join in the various festivities. The king was celebrating his newfound freedom, declaring to any who cared to listen that from now on it was him and him alone who acted on behalf of the king. As it should be, Adam conceded—but it rankled that the king should drink and cheer while some distance away Lord Roger sat in the dark and awaited his death.

Parliament convened at Westminster. The royal household took up residence in the palace, and Adam went with them, still formally in charge of the king's guard, even if he had not exchanged as much as a word with the king since they'd walled up Mortimer.

Once he'd seen to Raven and found his allotted lodgings, he went to the abbey, thinking to light a candle for William. He bumped shoulders with the pilgrims come to pray at the Confessor's shrine, stopped for an instant to cross himself before the high altar, recalling with a little smile how often he'd seen Kit here, entranced by the magnificent retable beyond.

The air reeked of incense, humming with the sound of endless, repetitive prayers. Monks swished up and down the nave, and Adam retired to the chapel of St John the Baptist, remembering how he'd sat here with William many years ago when Mortimer had been in exile and Despenser ruled the roost.

He prayed for his brother, hoping he'd find grace despite having died unshriven. He prayed for Richard and for Richard's wife, alone in the world with four children and a substantially reduced income now that the king had reclaimed Richard's lands. Fortunately, Maud had lands of her own, so she and the children would not starve. Mostly, he prayed for Kit, soon to be birthed of yet another child.

At least she'd reached Tresaints safely, and from the missive he'd received from Meg, Mama was well but as fat as a bloated cow. Father Owain had added that the mistress was tired and heartsore, but other than that, Lady Kit was in good health, and Sir Adam need not fear for her. Not fear for her? Adam sighed and clasped his hands tighter. It was more a matter of needing her, wishing she'd been here to help him through this.

On one of the later days in November, Lord Roger was conveyed by barge to stand trial in Westminster Hall. Adam ensured he was at the quay to receive him, shocked by the change in a man he'd rarely seen other than neat and clean. A month in the dark had left Mortimer with an ashen tone to his face, his thick hair had seemingly greyed overnight, and to judge from the way his tunic hung off him, he'd not been fed more than enough to sustain him.

He saw Adam, and something gleamed in his eyes. His guards lifted him out of the boat. His arms were yanked behind him and tied together, Lord Roger wincing when the rough hemp was pulled tight.

"No need for that," Adam objected when the rope was wound tight round Mortimer's middle.

"We answer only to the king," one of the guards responded. But he was unable to look Adam in the eye when he produced a gag.

"It's a trial!" Adam growled, attempting to snatch the gag. "How is he to defend himself if he cannot speak?"

"I think that's the entire point," Lord Roger said. "I am not to be allowed to plead for my life or for those of the people I love."

"That's against the law," Adam said, taking a menacing step towards the guard. His two companions pulled their swords.

"We are only doing as ordered, de Guirande," one of them muttered. "Doesn't mean we like it."

"Leave it be, Adam," Lord Roger said wearily. "This is all a farce anyway. The only thing remaining to be decided is whether I am to be merely hanged or if our liege will insist on disembowelment as well."

Adam staggered back. Lord Roger gave him a wry smile, but his throat worked repeatedly, jaws clenched so tight Adam imagined his teeth were cracking.

Once gagged, Lord Roger was led off. Adam stood by the quay until he had his face back under control.

When the trial was concluded, Lord Roger was carried back to the Tower. The verdict had been unanimous—guilty on each and every one of the fourteen accusations.

"Fourteen?" Adam asked Will de Bohun.

In reply, de Bohun recited them, one by one.

"And finally, he was accused of murdering our former king. Most foul, eh?" de Bohun said.

"He did not murder Sir Edward," Adam hissed. "Whoever says that lies."

"The king says so."

With precision, Adam spat. "If so, he perjures himself. I swear on my immortal soul, on the soul of my wife and children, that Mortimer did not murder him."

De Bohun gave him a surprised look. "But Edward said—"

"The king lies! Damn it, he lies!" He inhaled, on the verge of shouting to the world that Sir Edward lived, but at the last moment he regained some element of self-preservation. With a curse, he turned away and marched towards the king's apartments.

The sentries stood aside, and Adam took the stairs two treads at a time. Two more sentries in the antechamber, and from within came the sound of laughter. Adam did not knock—he just entered. It was the equivalent of pouring ice-cold water on a rutting dog. Montagu straightened out of his slouch, Stafford sat up straight, Thomas looked at anything but Adam, and the king stilled, goblet halfway to his mouth.

"Adam." The king cleared his throat. "I did not expect to see you here. I have not requested your presence."

"No, it would be difficult to celebrate with me here," Adam retorted. "Especially when we all know some of the accusations are falsehoods."

"Falsehoods?" Stafford asked.

"This may not be the right time," Montagu began.

"No? So when is the right time, Sir William? When a man hangs, his reputation forever tarnished with crimes he did not commit?"

"Adam," Thomas said, coming towards him. "Let's—" He reached for him.

"Don't touch me," Adam warned, hefting his cane. "I wish to talk to the king alone." He bowed slightly. "If it pleases you, my lord."

King Edward considered this in silence. "Very well." He nodded at his companions. "Leave us."

"Really, Ned, I'm not sure we should—" Stafford said.

"Go," the king ordered. "For all that Sir Adam is in a foul mood, I do not think him a danger to me." He gave Adam a tentative smile. Adam did not respond in kind, standing with his hands braced on his cane while the others left the room.

"Well?" the king asked, settling in his chair.

"You gagged him," Adam said.

"What of it?" the king replied. "Having him speak out would only have delayed the process."

Adam retreated to stand against the wall. "Four years ago, you swore you would never have a man condemned to death without allowing him to speak in his defence. And yet you just did."

The king shrugged. "Expediency."

"Unlawful, my lord. And dishonourable."

The goblet came flying. Adam ducked. "Are you saying Mortimer is innocent? Are you?" The king was on his toes, eyes burning into Adam's.

"Of killing your father? You know he is! And now you've forever tainted his name. No one will remember who Lord Mortimer truly was—all they will remember is that he murdered his king. A lie, my lord, a foul, foul lie, and you would not even allow him to speak in his defence!"

"What was I to do? Have him tell parliament that my father was alive?"

"He'd never have told them that—for your sake, for the sake of your mother."

"No? It was a risk I couldn't take."

"Then why accuse him of a deed he didn't do to begin with? Why, my lord? Why did you—" Adam's voice broke.

"I had no choice!" The king banged his hand down on the table repeatedly. "My father must once and for all be declared dead. And now he is, murdered in his dungeon." He inhaled deeply. "Sometimes, a king has no choice."

"Like when Lord Mortimer had Despenser executed—except that at the time I recall you were revolted. Even worse, Mortimer is not guilty of the heinous deed you've just laid at his door." Adam scrubbed at his face. "God knows how you will live with that."

"How dare you?" The king's voice shook. "You know as well as I do that Mortimer is guilty as sin."

"Of what exactly?"

"He stole my crown."

"He set it on your head! Without him, there would have been no kingdom for you to inherit. Your father and his sodomite of a favourite were tearing this country of yours apart."

"He abused his power! He enriched himself at my expense, tricked my uncle into treason."

"Aye, he did," Adam agreed. "But so did your mother."

"My mother—"

"—is as guilty as he is," Adam interrupted. "Lord Mortimer overreached. But to put him through that travesty of a trial, to sentence him to death, attaint his sons... What exactly are you punishing him for, my liege? Not, I think, for Kent's death. Not for a murder you know he didn't commit. No, this goes deeper, doesn't it? You've never forgiven him for putting horns on your father."

"Quiet!" King Edward yelled. "I will not listen to this, you hear?"

Adam ignored him. "You've just condemned a man to die

422

for having the temerity of loving your mother. In all fairness, shouldn't she be punished too?"

"And who says she won't be?" The king sat down with a thud. "I have to claim my kingdom. It is I, not the queen mother and her lover, who rule this realm."

"And what a great start you have made of it, my lord." For a long time, the king looked at him. Adam just looked back. He was done with this, wanted no more than go home. King Edward pinched his nose and closed his eyes.

"Adam de Guirande," he said in a hoarse voice, "you have served me well for several years. But today I think our ways must part, lest I be tempted to throw you into a dungeon to rot."

"As you wish, my liege." With a deep bow, he made for the door. Dear God, but he was tired, each step an effort of will.

"Adam?" The king's voice arrested him halfway there.

"My liege?"

"Do not think too badly of me."

"It is not my place to think either ill or good of you, my lord." Adam turned to face him.

"You loved me once," the king said, sounding like the young lad he still was.

"I did." No longer, though. "But I have loved him since I was a lad not yet twelve, a lad covered in vermin and welts he took in and cared for. Lord Roger is more of a father to me than my real father ever was—and you know just how entangled those bonds are."

King Edward nodded a couple of times. He frowned down at the floor. Adam remained where he was, uncertain if he dare leave without the king's permission. After an eternity, the king lifted his face. "Go to him, then. Be the son he deserves." A hand raised in dismissal, and Adam left.

Slowly, Adam made his way through the darkened passages of the palace. Here and there, a torch still burned in the sconces, but this late at night most had burned out, leaving him to light his way with a candle.

"Adam?"

"My lord." Adam bowed slightly, injecting his voice with ice.

"What did you expect me to do?" Thomas asked, stepping out of the dark. He must have been waiting for him, standing for God knew how long in the chilly passage.

"Speak up for him?" Adam suggested. "Insist he be ungagged?"

"He killed my brother!"

"Your brother rose in rebellion against his king."

"A trap, damn it—we both know that."

"A trap that worked because your brother was a fool," Adam said. "Besides, no one gagged your brother, did they?"

"No, but I hold Mortimer responsible for his death."

"Aye, I suppose you do. But we both know he did not kill Edward of Caernarvon. And yet you did not speak up for Mortimer today."

"And say what? That our former king lives?"

"No." Adam looked away. "Even I, simple knight that I am—"

"—no one has ever called you a simple knight!"

"—realises we cannot tell the world that the former king is alive. But you—or someone—could have stepped forward and insisted the king had died of natural causes. And yet you didn't."

"The king did not want it so."

"And you lacked the courage to disobey him." Adam tried to sneer but couldn't find the energy. He pushed by Thomas and made for the stairs.

"Adam," Thomas said, "wait."

"Good night, Earl Thomas," Adam said, taking some satisfaction at how the earl flinched at the formal address.

"Earl Thomas? No more friend Thomas?"

Adam shook his head. No more friend Thomas.

This day was turning out to be a day of losses, he reflected as he undressed. Lord Roger to die, the king no longer his master, and now the earl, no longer his friend. He sighed as he settled in the bed. It was many years since he had felt this alone. To be exact, it was twenty-two years almost to the day, on an equally cold and wet night, when his father had beat him to an inch of his life and thrown him out to die on the icy cobbles of Ludlow Castle.

Adam turned on his side, staring out at the darkness. If only Kit had been here. He smiled to himself as he stroked the pillow. Not entirely alone—not as long as he had Kit.

The next day, a page delivered a royal writ granting Adam de Guirande the right to visit the condemned traitor, Sir Roger Mortimer. There was also a formal wording releasing him from his role as captain of the king's guard. He was free to go, ordered, in fact, to retire to his lands.

Chapter 46

The guards at the Tower stood aside. Adam made his way up the Bell Tower to the room in which Roger Mortimer was to spend his last night on this earth. At least he was no longer held in the dark, and from what Adam could make out, Geoffrey had also been moved to a new cell. The Mortimer son faced no charges, and it was assumed he'd be released— once his father was safely dead.

Dead. Adam scrubbed at his face. He was here to offer comfort. After straightening his tunic and arranging his features, he climbed the last flight and stood waiting as the guard turned the key in the heavy lock.

The room bathed in light. Lord Roger stood by the narrow window, hands braced on the wall either side. His hair had been cut short, he'd been washed and shaved, dressed in a clean shirt and an open robe. On the table stood the remains of a meal, to the side was a pitcher of the sweetened wine he so liked, perfuming the little space with the faint scents of honey and spices.

"Now what?" Lord Roger asked without turning around.

"It is me, my lord."

"Adam?" Lord Roger wheeled on his toes. Bloodshot eyes in bruised hollows—Mortimer had not been sleeping much lately.

Adam gave him a tentative smile. "I thought you might need company, my lord."

"Company?" Mortimer dashed a sleeve over his face. "God's truth, but I am happy to see you!" He enfolded Adam in a hug, and Adam wrapped his arms around him, hiding his face against the shorter man's shoulder. No weeping, he admonished himself. Weep you can do later—he doesn't need to see your tears.

Lord Roger released him first. "What did this cost you?"

426

"Nothing I wasn't willing to pay, my lord." He knelt before Mortimer and raised his clasped hands. "Will you take me back into your service?"

"Now?" Lord Roger's voice shook. "Don't be ridiculous, I'll be dead before noon tomorrow."

"And it would be my greatest honour to be your man for the hours that remain." Adam coughed to clear his throat.

"What did it cost you?" Lord Roger repeated. He ruffled Adam's hair, his hand sliding down to cup his cheek.

"I have been released from my service, ordered to retire to my lands."

Lord Roger chuckled. "Not much of a penance, is it?"

"No, my lord. I've lost my taste for life at court." To live out the rest of his life at Tresaints seemed paradise at present. He gestured with his hands. "Will you receive my oath?"

In response, Lord Roger knelt before him and covered Adam's hands with his own. "No, I will not. There is no need for such between us, Adam de Guirande." He smiled. "And I could think of no one I would rather have with me tonight. Unless it was Isabella, of course." He got to his feet. "Does she know that I am to die tomorrow?"

"I don't know, my lord." Adam followed suit, rising clumsily. "She is a virtual prisoner—as is Lady Joan."

"Oh, they've made sure I know that." Lord Roger laughed hollowly. "My Joanie must curse me to hell and back. To yet again find herself imprisoned when she has done nothing." He glanced at Adam. "Will you do what you can for her?"

"Not much I can do, my lord. But aye, what I can do, I will do." If nothing else, Lady Joan would have need of the gold still hidden at Tresaints.

"Good." Mortimer's chest lifted on a deep breath, face to the window. "I don't want to die. Not yet, not like that." He rubbed at his neck, strong fingers sliding down to fret at the neckline of his shirt. "I want…" He exhaled. "I want so much—too much, one could say." A tremulous smile came and went. "None of which I will ever get. Not now." His hands clenched round the thin fabric of his shirt. "Instead, I will…" He cleared his throat, turning his back on Adam.

It took some time before Lord Roger had recovered sufficiently to suggest they share what food he had. Some time later, they were both seated on the bed, Adam leaning against one of the posts, Lord Roger reclining against the pillows. They had wine at hand, the shutters still stood wide open, despite the chilly draught—a man about to leave this earth had need of whatever fresh air he could get, Mortimer had said when Adam had gone to close the shutters.

The night passed in vigil, a sharing of memories of all the years they'd spent together. There were messages Lord Roger wanted Adam to give to his sons and his wife, and Adam promised he would somehow get word to them, taking possession of the rings Lord Roger stripped off his fingers—one for Lady Joan, another for Edmund, and the third... Mortimer's voice broke, his eyes on the simple gold band that was unadorned except for the engraving of a hawk in flight.

"Isabella," he said quietly, dropping it into Adam's hand. "Tell her the hawk flies free and awaits her on the other side."

And then the night was almost done, the paling stars heralding the approaching dawn. It was bitterly cold in the little room, frost crackling in the air. A cold day to die on, the unforgiving light of the new day revealing just how tense Lord Roger was. Deep furrows bracketed his mouth, a sheen of cold sweat on his face.

He jumped when the door was wrenched open. A servant entered with more wine and a chaplain in tow. Adam stepped outside to allow Lord Roger to make his peace with God in privacy, and he was standing in the passage when a page came skipping up the stairs, carrying a fine tunic in black velvet.

"For the traitor," the lad piped, and Adam was tempted to slap him.

"Lord Mortimer to you," he snarled, and the page shrank against the wall.

Adam lifted the garment out of the page's hands. He recognised it, and he wanted to tear it in two. Last time he'd seen Lord Roger wearing it had been at Edward of Caernarvon's official funeral.

When they came for Lord Roger, Adam had to steady him, a hand beneath his elbow ensuring Mortimer managed to walk straight and tall towards the waiting horses. There was some halfhearted jeering, but it sufficed that Adam look at the fools for them to fall silent. It was cold outside, and Lord Roger shivered in his tunic, looking surprisingly vulnerable with his bare legs and feet.

At the last moment, it seemed Lord Roger would baulk, his breathing loud in the silence that surrounded them. His fingers sank into Adam's forearm and he leaned back, away from the horses.

Adam stopped, allowing him some time to regain his composure. One of the horses stamped its hoof, harness jangling as it dipped its head up and down. Behind the horses was the hide on which the prisoner was to lie, his arms firmly tied to the horses.

By the horses, they embraced. A long, silent farewell, and Adam stepped back. Lord Roger waved aside the guards and lay down on his own on the oxhide, lifting his arms as instructed. His hands were lashed to the horses.

"Lord give me strength," he whispered, staring up at the sky. The groom flicked his whip, and the horses began to move. Sir Roger Mortimer's last journey had begun.

All the way from the Tower to Tyburn, Adam walked beside Lord Roger. As his former lord was dragged over uneven cobbles, over stretches of gravel, as his beloved master was screamed at and pelted with everything from stones to rotten eggs, Adam limped by his side. Lord Roger locked eyes with him, two dark pools of tightly controlled fear, of pain and humiliation. Adam's breath came in painful gasps, mirroring Mortimer's heaving chest.

Just beside the gallows, they untied Lord Roger from the horses. He couldn't stand on his own, was so bruised and battered his knees buckled beneath him, his fine black tunic reduced to ragged, dirty cloth, flapping round his bare legs. Adam started forward to support him but was stopped by one of the guards. There was a rending sound when the tunic was torn off, leaving Lord Roger naked before the jeering mob.

Lord Roger met his eyes; Adam inclined his head ever so slightly. Go with God, he thought, may He make your passing quick and easy.

Up the ladder to the scaffold. The noose around his neck, and Adam held Lord Roger's eyes. All through the priest's few words and Lord Roger's little speech, Adam kept his gaze firm and steady. Lord Roger smiled, and Adam's heart cracked. The rope was slung over the gallows. The executioner heaved, and Lord Roger rose, the noose tightening round his neck. The ancient wood in the gallows groaned, Lord Roger's eyes bulged, and still Adam held his gaze, didn't as much as blink despite his tears. Lord Roger jerked. Froth formed at his mouth, the air filled with the scent of piss and shit.

Only when the last flicker of light went out in those dark eyes did Adam bow his head, hands clenched as he sucked in air. Lord Roger was gone, and around him the world was spinning. At a distance he heard the people cheering. He was gone: dearest God, it was over.

"Peace on your soul, my dearest lord," he whispered. "May the Good Lord receive you in heaven."

Somehow, he managed to move some feet away, turning his back on the spectacle of the naked body swinging slightly in its rope. He didn't want that image of the man he had loved as a father engraved uppermost in his memory. Adam planted a hand against a nearby tree, leaned his forehead against the gnarled bark. His heart was torn asunder, and the pain left him short of breath, his windpipe clogged with tears.

An arm came round his shoulders, clasping him hard. "Come," Thomas said. "There is nothing more you can do for him now."

Adam shook his head. He did not think he could walk.

"I'm here. Lean on me if you must." He wiped at Adam's tears with his gloved hand. "That's what friends are for."

"Friends," Adam managed to say.

"Always."

Three days after Lord Roger's execution, Adam set off for home together with his Tresaints men. At the last moment, Gavin informed him he was coming too, and Adam was more glad of the company than he wanted to admit, so he asked no questions, even if he couldn't help but notice that Gavin sported bruises. Likely, his erstwhile squire had been taunted into defending both Adam and Lord Roger.

He rode out of Westminster Palace, making for the bridge and Southwark beyond. Not once did he look back, having said his farewells of Thomas just before prime. His friend—it made him smile to think the word: Thomas of Brotherton was indeed the best of friends—was returning to his lands in Norfolk, there to handle the complicated issue of comforting his young daughter-in-law, Beatrice Mortimer.

Bad weather and a lame horse slowed them considerably, so it was after six days on the road that Adam and his men saw the familiar contours of the manor before them. Adam rode down the long lane, nodding to the few men out in the bare fields. The sturdy gate stood open, and beyond he could see his bailey, hear the sounds of his people. He drew Raven to a halt a short distance from the gate.

"I just want to sit here for a while," he said to Gavin, who nodded, no more, and rode by him, trotting through the gate with the men in his wake.

The winter sun was low enough to be dipping down behind the closest hills, and from the nearby pastures came the sound of bleating sheep. Home. He raised his face to the sky. To the east, the evening star had twinkled into life, while to the west the sky retained a band of golden light. Adam stroked Raven over his powerful neck and drew in breath in preparation for meeting his household.

A flurry of skirts and there she came, the only person who could somehow pull the ragged edges of his heart together and stitch them closed. Kit came alone, and Adam slid off his horse, grasping the stirrup for support. The hood of her mantle fell back, and those tendrils of her hair that had escaped her braid lifted in the wind. His Kit. She came towards him, and now he noticed she was clutching something to her chest.

"Here," she said when she was close enough to touch him. Carefully, she handed over the little bundle that she cradled. "Meet your new son, Roger de Guirande. All of ten days old today."

"Roger," he repeated hoarsely, lifting his son so that he could properly see him. He kissed the little nose that peeked from all those folds of cloth. "A good name."

Kit slipped her arm through his and stood on her toes to kiss his cheek. "You are home."

"Aye." He shifted his son and wrapped his right arm round his wife. He needed to tell her everything, but it would keep until later. For now, it was enough to have her beside him, to nuzzle her and inhale the fragrance of her—lavender and rosemary, warm milk, and clean linen. The moment was interrupted by their children, Ned leading the charge as the de Guirande siblings came rushing towards their father.

Baby Roger was returned to his mother, and then Adam had his arms full of wriggling little bodies, wet mouths showering him with kisses, high voices regaling him with the truly important matters of life, such as the fact that Flea had caught a rat and that Ned was big enough to have his own dog, and Harry tugged at Adam's sleeve and told him he'd found a toad. Ellie pursed her lips and demanded a kiss, Peter had a firm hold of Adam's leg, and Meg slipped her arms round his neck and whispered she loved him very, very much and she hoped he'd not be sad now that he was home again.

They entered the bailey, and there were more people to greet, but here he encountered far too many faces wet with tears. Mabel looked as if she'd been weeping for a fortnight, and several of the older men who'd fought for Mortimer in their younger days looked just as harried.

"Food," Kit said from behind him.

"Leek pottage and sausage." Mall looked Adam up and down. "Begging your pardon, master, but you need feeding back into shape."

"Aye." He caught Kit's eyes. "I've not been hungry of late."

"…and now Lord Roger rests with the friars," Adam finished much later. He slipped deeper into the wooden tub, eyes closing. His face sagged, the corners of his mouth drooping, his long, fair lashes fluttering against the bruised skin beneath his eyes. When she soaped him, she found ridges of tension along his shoulders, the muscles down his back and arms corded and taut.

She ran the washrag along his jawline, carefully washed his face, and under her touch she felt him relax, one heavy limb at a time. This too would heal; this too would pass.

"He came early," Adam said, startling her. He opened one dark grey eye. "Our…Roger."

She could hear it, how he hesitated over the name, and for an instant she wondered if she'd been unwise to name him after Lord Mortimer. She'd intended it as a gift, not a constant gnawing reminder.

"He did. All that jolting on the way from Nottingham—" She broke off, reluctant to relive a journey plagued not so much by the ruts in the road but by her constant fear for him, so alone among the men gloating at having brought down Mortimer.

"And now?" His wet hand caressed her face. "Are you recovered, my lady?"

"Not fully." She leaned forward to give him a lingering kiss. "Lovemaking will have to wait some weeks yet."

"There's lovemaking and lovemaking," he said beneath her mouth. "But for now, all I want is to hold you, sweeting."

Once dry, Adam heaped more logs onto the fire and they retreated to bed, both of them as naked as the day they'd been born. The bedclothes were cold at first, but soon enough she was encased in his warmth, her cheek atop his beating heart. She tugged at the golden fuzz that covered his chest, slid a hand up and down his flat belly, fingers halting to caress the odd scar tissue along the way.

On the further side of the bed, the cradle squeaked when the babe shifted, and moments later a demanding wail cut through the peaceful silence. Adam padded over to fetch him, returning with a red-faced, squirming little package. Presented with the teat, the babe clamped down, causing Kit to inhale and hold her breath for some moments. The infant snuffled and swallowed, and Adam slid down to rest his head against her shoulder, brushing their son over his coifed head with the back of his finger.

"So hungry," he said. "Pray God that he doesn't grow up like his namesake, never fully content."

Kit pressed her lips to her husband's still-damp hair. "It is over, Adam. All these years of unrest, of being torn asunder between the king and Lord Mortimer—over."

"Aye." He shifted closer, his breath tickling her neck. "I just wish it had ended differently."

Kit used her free arm to cradle his big, heavy body as well as she could. "So do I, my love."

It was midway to dawn when she woke to an empty bed. Adam was standing by the window, a hand on the glass panes that he was so proud of.

"No moon," he said without turning around when she joined him, embracing him from behind. He covered her hands with his. "It struck me that had it not been for Lord Roger, I would never have wed you."

"If we're going to be correct, that was due to Lady Cecily." Kit shivered. "Imagine being grateful to that witch for anything."

"Are you?" He turned in her arms. "Grateful, I mean."

Kit snorted. "However unintentional, I do believe it was the single good deed of her lifetime."

Adam laughed. "Uncharitable, sweeting." He tilted her face up. "No regrets?"

"Regrets?" Kit shook her head slowly from side to side. "Never."

Strong fingers combed through her hair, locking her head into place as he first kissed her eyes, then her nose, and finally her mouth. It ignited her, leaving her wanting for more, a soft sound of regret escaping her when he released her lips.

"As I said before, there's lovemaking and lovemaking, sweeting. Will my lady wife do me the honour of accompanying me to bed and sleep in my arms?"

"Always," she breathed. "Always, my dearest lord and husband."

Is this it?

My original intention was to leave Adam and Kit to face their future without me after this book, but being a curious sort I do want to know if Adam is reconciled with the king, and I also have this hunch that the adventures aren't quite over. So I suspect I may well return to my favourite medieval knight in the future—after all, as Adam is wont to point out, he is still relatively young.

Historical Note
The Cold Light of Dawn

Roger Mortimer died on the 29th of November, 1330, more or less as depicted in the final chapters of this book. Opinions about him remain divided: some have a tendency to paint Isabella as a victim and Roger as an ogre, others believe Roger and Isabella were in it together, all the way. I lean towards this latter version. Was Mortimer grasping and power-hungry? Undoubtedly. But he was also capable and hardworking, appointing equally capable and hardworking men to various offices. Testament to this is that Edward III made very few changes to the administration after Mortimer's death.

Obviously, I have taken some liberties. Edward did homage to Philippe in Amiens, not Paris, but as I wanted to mastermind a meeting between Edward and his father, I felt Paris would allow more room for manoeuvring. As far as I know, Edward never threatened someone with tongs—but I believe all successful medieval kings had a streak of ruthlessness in them.

Was Isabella ever pregnant by Mortimer? We don't know. In fact, some argue that they weren't even lovers, but I think a lot of things point to them being intimate, starting with the rooms assigned to Mortimer in Westminster. Assuming that they did share a bed, I find it likely that there might have been a pregnancy—both Mortimer and Isabella had several children with their respective spouses. Ian Mortimer puts forward in his excellent book The Greatest Traitor, that in 1329-30 Mortimer arranged for prayers to be said for the king, the queen, himself, his wife, his children, Isabella, and an unknown Earl of Lincoln. Maybe this was his and Isabella's child. Or maybe not. Whatever the case, even if there was a child, it does not seem to have survived long enough to be mentioned anywhere else.

Likewise, in the matter of Edmund, Earl of Kent, he had been quietly arrested before parliament, subjected to questioning and brought before a specially convened court. His confession was then read out loud to the assembled parliament, at which point Edmund did throw himself on his nephew's mercy, begging piteously for his life. It didn't help, and on a cold March day the poor man was kept waiting for hours because the executioner had fled. The handling of the Earl of Kent is a major blot on Mortimer's character. He baited a trap and fooled the impetuous earl into believing his brother was being held prisoner. When Edmund decided to act, Mortimer's trap slammed shut and Edward III had no choice but to condemn his uncle to die. On the other hand, Edmund did write that letter…

When it comes to Edward II's fate, I belong to those who believe it isn't one hundred percent certain he died in 1327. This has allowed me to give him an extended lease on life, and I imagine he and Egard have a lot of adventures before them.

I have also given Thomas of Brotherton a lot of space in this book—far more than he has in recorded history. For a man born to power and wealth in times of great upheaval, this Earl of Norfolk is a surprisingly invisible character, an unremarkable character living well below the radar. I have chosen to make something more out of him, finding it difficult to believe that any child born to Edward I and his rather impressive second wife, Princess Marguerite of France, would be so…so…beige.

As always, I must remind my readers that Adam de Guirande is an invented character (unfortunately) as are his wife, his family, the people who serve him. However, his brother-in-law, Richard de Monmouth, did exist and was, in fact, killed that night in Nottingham when Roger was arrested. William de Guirande didn't, seeing as he never existed. But if he had existed, I am convinced he would not have hesitated to sacrifice himself to save Geoffrey. That's the kind of man William was.

Lady Joan was destined to spend several months as the king's prisoner. But Edward knew she was innocent of any crimes—as were Mortimer's sons—and a year or so later, Lady Joan was free and some of the attainted lands had been returned to Edmund Mortimer. Lady Joan went on to relentlessly demand the return of her dower lands, and in 1336 Edward III acquiesced. He also reversed the sentence of Roger Mortimer. In 1354, Mortimer's grandson—another Roger—was reinstated as Earl of March and "our" Roger was cleared of the accusation of being a traitor.

Isabella spent a year in house arrest before being allowed to move freely again. Most of the lands and riches she'd awarded herself were returned to the king, but Edward was ever the dutiful son, ensuring dear Maman had the means to live a comfortable life. I dare say there were days when Isabella missed her hawk and the heady sensation of being in charge, but she was pragmatic enough to adapt to her new life.

About the Author

Anna always wanted to be a professional time traveller, but as such a job does not exist she makes do by reading a lot of history books—and writing some as well.

Anna has always had a soft spot for the medieval period, which is why Adam and Kit just had to see the light of the day. She is presently working on a new medieval series, but when she's not stuck in that era, chances are she'll be visiting in the 17th century, more specifically with Alex and Matthew Graham, the protagonists of the best-selling, multiple award winning, series The Graham Saga. This series is the story of two people who should never have met – not when she was born three centuries after him. A fast-paced blend of love, drama and adventure, The Graham Saga will carry you from Scotland to the New World and back again.

For more information about Anna and her books, please visit www.annabelfrage.com or pop by her blog https://annabelfrage.wordpress.com

CPSIA information can be obtained
at www.ICGtesting.com
Printed in the USA
BVHW071446240519
549230BV00002B/156/P

9 781789 010015